Mendel's Dwarf

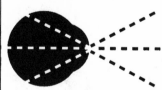 This Large Print Book carries the
Seal of Approval of N.A.V.H.

Mendel's Dwarf

Simon Mawer

Thorndike Press • Thorndike, Maine

Published in 1998 by arrangement with Harmony Books, a division of Crown Publishers, Inc.

Thorndike Large Print ® Basic Series.

The tree indicium is a trademark of Thorndike Press.

The text of this Large Print edition is unabridged.
Other aspects of the book may vary from the original edition.

Set in 16 pt. Plantin.

Printed in the United States on permanent paper.

Library of Congress Cataloging in Publication Data

Mawer, Simon.
    Mendel's dwarf / by Simon Mawer.
      p. (large print) cm.
    ISBN 0-7862-1519-4 (lg. print : hc : alk. paper)
    1. Large type books. I. Title.
[PR9120.9.M38M46   1998b]
823'.914—dc21   98-23615

To the memory of my father
*who gave me half my genes
and much else besides*

Acknowledgments

I would like to acknowledge the help of Dr. Josef Jiricny of Zurich University and Patricia Novelli of the London School of Hygiene and Tropical Medicine. They both gave much assistance with technical aspects of molecular biology. Any errors are, of course, the fault of Benedict Lambert.

[Genome]

Doctor Benedict Lambert, the celebrated Benedict Lambert, the diminutive Benedict Lambert, the courageous Benedict Lambert (adjectives skating carefully around the essence of it all) stands to address the members of the Mendel Symposium. Applause has died away. The silence — eyes watching, breath held, hands stilled above notebooks supplied by courtesy of Hewison Pharmaceuticals — is complete. There before the good doctor, ranged in rows like sample tubes in a rack, are all the phenotypes one could wish to see: male and female, ectomorphic and endomorphic, dolichocephalic and brachycephalic, Nordic, Mediterranean, Slav, Mongoloid (three), Negroid (one). There are chins cleft[1] and normal, hair curly[2] and straight, eyes blue[3] and brown and green, skins white, brown, yellow, and black,[4]

1. autosomal dominant
2. autosomal dominant
3. autosomal recessive, probably controlled by genes at two different loci
4. polygenic control

crania bald[5] and hirsute. It is almost as though the organizers (the Mendelian Association of America in conjunction with Hewison Pharmaceuticals and the Masaryk University of Brno) have trawled through the whole gamut of human variation in order to come up with a representative genetic mix. And yet . . .

. . . and yet there is a constancy that is obvious to all, but consciously perceived only by the truncated figure up on the podium: each and every one of the earnest watchers is subsumed under the epithet *phenotypically normal.*

Doctor Lambert undoes his wristwatch and places it conspicuously on the lecture bench, a practiced gesture of no chronometric significance. Then he smiles, glances at a page of notes (of equally little mnemonic moment), clears his throat, and begins: "We have all of us visited the monastery." They have. Some nod in agreement, wanting to agree with him, wanting to please him, wanting in some way to compensate. "To do so we have all of us passed, with little attention, through the great square outside, which the city fathers have renamed Mendlovo náměstí in his honor. In the days of Gregor Mendel

5. sex-limited autosomal dominant

8

himself and for many years after, this square was simply known as the Klosterplatz, Monastery Square. Right into this century it lay on the edge of the town, between the Spielberg Hill and the water meadows along the banks of the River Svratka."

History lesson? they wonder. Urban planning? Museum policy within the context of a developing tourist trade? Heads nod. Eyes glaze. The entertainment is, perhaps, over. It is a warm day.

"The Klosterplatz was the place where fairs were held. There were booths where fire-eaters blew flames from their mouths and bears danced and pickpockets filched their living. It was also the place of freak shows, the kind of place where monsters were put on display, the kind of place where people with deformities were exhibited for all the world to gaze at in horror and revulsion and amusement. People like me . . ."

And they are lying in the palm of his hand like peas newly shelled from the pod.

"Conjoined twins, as well. Bearded ladies, certainly. Acromegalic giants, wart men, elephant men, children with scaly skin and flippers for arms, in fact the whole gamut of human deformity and disaster. And you, ladies and gentlemen, would have gone to stare. At people like me."

9

Silence. Is anyone so careless as to allow a pin to drop? Guilt is a palpable substance in the atmosphere, a vapor that irritates the air passages and stings the eyes. Although the squat figure on the podium watches them through phenotypically normal eyes (brown), nothing else about him is normal. His body is not normal, his face is not normal, his limbs are not normal. He possesses a massive forehead and blunt, puglike features. His nose is stove in at the bridge, his mouth and jaw protrude. His limbs are squat and bowed, his fingers are mere squabs. He is one meter, twenty-seven centimeters tall.

"It was Gregor Mendel who enabled us to understand all this, and, by understanding, bring acceptance of a kind. It was he who, contemplating his peas, saw within them those units of inheritable potency that, for better or for worse, we all of us possess. He was the Galileo of biology, seeing these moons for the first time, seeing them as clearly as we do today, although he had no instrument to aid him and nothing material on which to project his vision."

A sip of water, for the effect rather than for the thirst. His gestures are practiced, almost rehearsed. He is used to all this, aware of every movement in the hall, every cough, every whisper, every glance of every eye.

"Mendel spent eight years on his experiments with garden peas alone. By the end he had bred a grand total of about thirty-three thousand plants. He developed a rigorous, mathematical interpretation of his results, in the course of which, by implication, he predicted the haploid nature of gametes and the diploid nature of body cells, as well as the need for a reduction division in the production of gametes; and no one saw the significance. He was as great an experimenter as Louis Pasteur, an exact contemporary, and no one recognized the fact. He had a more acute, more focused mind than Charles Darwin, another exact contemporary, and no one listened. He was one of those men whose vision goes beyond what we can perceive with our eyes and touch with our hands, and no one shared his insight. The word *insight* is exact. Mendel had the same perception of nature as Pasteur, who could conceive of a virus without ever being able to see it, or Mendeleyev, who could conceive of elements that had not yet been discovered, or Thomson who could imagine particles yet smaller than the atom. Like them, Mendel looked through the surface of things deep into the fabric of nature, and he saw the atoms of inheritance as clearly as any Dalton or Rutherford saw the atoms of matter; and no

11

one took any notice. He was a true visionary, where a man like Darwin was a mere workaday naturalist putting common sense observations into a hotchpotch, tautological theory that lacked rigor and precision, and bore, deep within itself, a fatal flaw. And no one took any notice. Mendel handed us our origins and our fate for the examining, and no one took any notice . . ."

They applauded after the address, great tides of applause sweeping through the lecture theater; but you will forgive me if I say that I'm used to that. Inured to it, in fact. They would applaud anything that I did, you see — it's a way of assuaging that insidious sensation of guilt that they all feel.

Guilt? How can that be? It is no one's *fault*, is it? No one is to *blame* that I possess this stunted, contorted body, this hideous prison of flesh and flab and gristle. You can blame only the malign hand of chance . . .

Theirs is the guilt of the survivor.

The chairman rose to his feet, beaming like a circus ringmaster, and called them to silence. "I am sure all of us appreciate Ben's coming here and sharing his insights with us." He smiled down at me. People craned to see. "I hope he won't mind my saying that he is not only a great Mendelian but . . ."

Did he really look to me for agreement? I fear that he did. ". . . also a very *brave* man. Ladies and gentlemen, I give you Doctor Ben Lambert!"

A crescendo of applause, like the roar of rain on a tin roof. Photo flashes flickered like lightning in the storm. The ocean of people swayed and roared. They even lined up to shake my hand, as pilgrims might queue to kiss a statue of a martyr. Perhaps they were hoping that by such contact they might acquire something of my grace, that courage of which the chairman had spoken. The secretary of the association, Gravenstein by name, leaned over to endorse the chairman's praise. She was large[6] and quivering, a mountain of concerned flesh shrouded in paisley cotton. "Gee, Ben, that's wonderful. So brave, so brave . . ."

Brave. That was the word of the moment. But I'd told Jean often enough. In order to be brave, you've got to have a choice.

There was an organized dinner in the restaurant of the hotel that evening, a ghastly affair with Moravian folk dancers and gypsy

6. Obesity (OBS gene), probably a dominant located on the long arm of chromosome 7 (Friedman et al., *Genomics* 11, 1991).

violins. A journalist from a local newspaper asked me questions — "What is the general thrust of your researches?" "Is it true that you express your ancestry in the pursuit of your inquiries?" — while Gravenstein and the chairman cosseted and protected me like a child. I was rescued by a call over the public address system: "Phone call for Doctor Lambert. There is a phone call for Doctor Lambert."

I escaped into the lobby. The hotel had been built before the curtain came down on the Czech People's Republic, and the lobby was as brash and shoddy as a station concourse. You expected to see train departure times on the bulletin board. It was almost a surprise to find instead the forthcoming events of the Mendel Symposium: a seminar at the university molecular biology department, a lecture on "The New Eugenics" by Doctor Benedict Lambert, a visit to the monastery library. Bookings were open for a trip to the Mendel birthplace, near Olomouc. Doctor Daniel Hartl of the George Washington University School of Medicine would be wondering "What Did Gregor Mendel Think He Discovered?"

I reached up to tap on the reception desk. "There's a call for me. Telephone."

The receptionist peered over the edge. She

14

had a widow's peak and attached earlobes.[7] You notice such things. Your mind grows attuned to them. Brown eyes. Brown hair. Phenotypically normal. I saw the familiar expressions cross her face at the sight of me: surprise, revulsion, concern, one blending clumsily with the other and all pinned together with disbelief. "There is a call for a Doctor Lambert," she said.

"I am Doctor Lambert."

"You are Doctor Lambert?"

"I am Doctor Lambert."

Disbelief almost won. She almost denied the fact. Then she shrugged and pointed to a row of booths beyond the fountain — "You take it over there" — and went back to filing her nails.

The telephone booth was stuffy and tobacco-stained, with a worse, nameless smell lurking in the corners. I had to stand on tiptoe to lift the receiver down. "Hello?"

A fragile voice, attenuated by distance, by the electrical connections, by anxiety, whispered in my ear. "Is that you, Ben?"

"Jean. Where are you?"

"At the hospital."

"The baby . . . ?"

"They wanted me in early. My age or some-

7. Both possible autosomal dominant

15

thing. Everyone's being so nice . . ."

"Is it okay?"

"They say it's fine."

"How did you get my number?"

A murmur and a twittering somewhere on the line. "I rang the Institute. Aren't you going to wish me luck?"

I told her that she didn't need it. I told her that luck didn't come into it. But I wished it just the same. Then I returned to the dinner, to the loud and various sounds of Gravenstein, to the fussing of the chairman and the cavorting of the folk dancers and the mindless questions of the reporter.

[Mutation]

Next morning I detached myself from the congress. I left the hotel and I walked alone down Husova, the wide boulevard that cuts between the center of the city and the wooded Špilberk Hill. People stared at me. At the end I turned at the junction with Pekařská, where the trams queue up against the traffic lights, and people stared. I went on down the hill, down to Altbrünn, Staré Brno, Old Brno (old in little more than name), past rotting, grimy buildings dating from the last century; and the good people of the town stared. You get used to it. It isn't the straightforward, what-have-we-got-here? kind of stare. They know in an instant what they have got here. It is, perhaps, a there-but-for-the-grace-of-God-go-I sort of stare, a sly and sideways stare, the face ostensibly and deliberately pointed tangential to the line of vision. One woman crossed herself. Another, as I paused to glance into some tawdry shop window, discreetly touched me. They do that, you know. It brings good luck.

And what was I looking for? Good luck as

well? I was thinking of Jean, of course. I was thinking of Jean and I was thinking of luck, which is merely chance masquerading under an alias — the tyranny of chance.

At the bottom of the hill I reached Mendlovo náměstí. The smell of roasting hops from a nearby brewery was heavy on the air. Trams rumbled along the street, surging in and out of the square like air filling and emptying the lungs of the city. Passengers waited in dull lines. I crossed the road at the traffic lights (drivers stared) and approached the monastery. The buildings were red-roofed and white-walled, amiable and placid against the dark brick buttresses and gothic pinnacles of the church: the rational growing out of the irrational, if you like. You look for signs like that, don't you? — the artifacts of Man imbued with something of the spirit in which they were created. Just as you look at Man himself and wonder about the forces that created him.

I walked around the long south wall of the convent, toward the gate. Above everything — lift your eyes for a moment above the pavements, above the red roofs, above the clock tower of the library and the spire of the church, above the grimy flats, above that whole quarter of the city — stood the Spielberg Fortress, where the Austrian Emperors used to keep their political prisoners. It is interesting to reflect that while the secrets of genetics were being revealed for the first time down there in the back garden of the monastery, the secrets of democracy and subversion were being revealed for the thousandth time in the dungeons on the hill above: nature, both human and plant, under torture. Did he know about it? Of course he did. And what did he *think* about it, eh? In 1858 the Habsburgs abandoned the Spielberg as a political prison, but you can't take the stain away from a place like that. Within a century the Gestapo was putting it back to use.

I looked in through the garden gate. *Klášter*, cloister. White buildings bordered the expanse of grass and lent the place something of the atmosphere of a university college — the fellows' garden, perhaps. One almost expected figures in gowns.

I am as suspicious as anyone of appeals to the emotions, but I am honest. I admit I felt a curious excitement as I stood there, a sense that everything had somehow focused down to this: this space, these solemn buildings with their red roofs and dormer windows, this quiet place beneath a summer sky with a woman wandering along the path with her dog (dachshund), and a gardener weeding, and two men strolling toward the archway on the far side, and a sign saying MENDELIANUM. Oh yes, I felt something as I stood looking across the lawns: something stirring in the bowels as well as in the brain, something that evades the grasp of words. The beds beneath the windows were where he first grew his plants. That long rectangle of gravel running across the grass was where his greenhouse had stood, where he'd puttered among the peas, muttering to himself, counting and numbering, dabbing with his camel-hair brush, planting seeds, counting again, always counting . . . This acre of space was where it all started, where the stubborn friar lit a fuse that burned unnoticed for thirty-five years until they discovered his work in 1900 and the bomb finally exploded. The explosion is going on still. It engulfed me from the moment of my conception. Perhaps it will engulf us all eventually.

In the shrubbery at the far side of the garden there was a statue. At a distance it looked like an angel holding out its arms over souls in purgatory. Close to, it was no angel, of course, but an anemic, conventional figure in priestly robes stretching out its hands over a stand of carved garden peas:

P. GREGOR MENDEL
1822–1884

At the foot of the statue, someone had planted a row of garden peas, and on the plinth of the statue itself lay a small bunch of wildflowers. It was almost as though he had become the subject of some secret cult since his death, as though pious geneticists crept along in the night and surreptitiously left offerings to their saint.

"Where did I come from?" I once asked my mother. I was no more than four at the time, but even at that age I recognized the pain in her expression while she tried to answer — a blend of helplessness and guilt — and I never asked again. I wonder now when they first told her about me, how they broke the news. An obstetrician can recognize it immediately, of course. The diagnosis is straightforward. But to a doting mother lying in bed in the aftermath of birth, one crumpled newborn child is much like another — the bones have not yet developed and the malign hand of the mutation has had little time to work its distortions. I wonder how they told her. I wonder when . . .

My father never looked straight at me, can you imagine that? Never, throughout the whole of my life, can I remember his looking directly at me. Always his glance was aslant, tangential, as though that way he might not notice.

I know the way your mind is working. You are trying to picture them, trying to give them shape and substance. You are trying to see if they are normal.

They are normal.

I don't even look like them. Oh sure, I share certain features with them — the dark hair, the brown eyes, my father's cleft chin, that kind of thing — but there is no structural resemblance, no facial resemblance. I don't *look like* my father or my mother or my sister. I don't have my mother's nose or my father's jawline or my grandfather's cast of brow. I am on my own. "You're special," my mother would insist as she dragged me off to one or another of those specialists — pediatricians, orthopedists, neurologists, orthodontists — who could never do anything at all. "You're special, that's why you have all these people looking after you."

For a while I was fooled by her assertions. I even used to imagine that I had been planted on my parents by extraterrestrial beings, a Midwich Cuckoo; but soon enough I learned the truth: I am exactly what I seem — an aberration, a mutant, the product of pure, malign chance.

★ ★ ★

I offer you this image: a desert in the early morning, stretching away toward the sunrise, stretching away toward the perfect hairline of the horizon. In the middle distance over to the left there is an outcrop of rock; in the foreground there is a cluster of military vehicles and a group of soldiers. The men are nervous. They talk in muted voices. There is the sensation that something is about to happen, something momentous, an execution perhaps. The men scratch and kick at the stones on the ground and glance often at their watches, as though time might suddenly have sped up and caught them unawares.

Despite all this anticipation, the disembodied voice that crackles out into the still, chill morning air from one of the vehicles startles them. "Five minutes," it announces. "All personnel are to put on eye protection. Repeat, all personnel are . . ."

There is a little flurry of activity as the men take goggles from their knapsacks and pull them on. Someone cracks a joke about looking like fucking frogs, but no one laughs. When all is ready, they turn and stare out across the desert as though searching for something through the thick, tinted lenses.

A siren begins to wail. That is the only desert sound as the minutes tick away: the wailing of a siren just like those that used to wail across the city during the blitz, Rachel wailing for her children and would not be comforted. Then the siren stops and the men wait and the morning breeze soughs across the land, a soft and mournful sound.

"One minute to go."

And the minute passes like a century.

"Thirty seconds."

There is no muttering now. The men stand still, their figures etched against the pale peach of dawn.

"Five, four, three, two, one . . ."

And dawn breaks suddenly, with a flash, in silence. Like aboriginals, the men stand there watching a new sun rising, bringing in the new age.

Was it then? The men wore welders' goggles against the glare, but at exactly the same instant that the flash of silent light reached them, so too did the other rays, the gamma rays; and while the light was filtered by the dark glass of the goggles, the gamma rays, subtle and unseen, wafted freely through cloth and flesh and bone. In the course of their passage, did they touch with malign and featherlike hands the dividing cells buried deep within my father's testes? Was that the moment when I was conceived?

We have a photograph of him from those

days in Australia. It shows him in the uniform of the Royal Engineers. Sergeant Eric Lambert. He has a bright and hopeful smile, largely stemming from the fact that he had managed to avoid service in Malaya. They sent him to Australia instead, on weapons research; and when he came back he fathered me.

Was that how I came to be?

Who knows? Who will ever know? Certainly it was a single mutation somewhere along the line, for I am, in good Mendelian fashion, a simple dominant. I might have fifty percent of my genes in common with each of my parents, but I don't share that particular one with either of them. I couldn't have come from them without a mutation . . .

Unless my mother had sexual congress with a dwarf . . .

All things must be considered.

[Pedigree]

There is something more in the bizarre genetic equation that adds up to Benedict Lambert. There is Uncle Harry — Great-uncle Harry Wise.

Rawboned and dark-eyed, Uncle Harry sits firmly in my childhood memory in a shabby wing-back chair in the front room of his bungalow on the south coast, with his neck in a brace and his mottled hands clutching the arms of his chair as though thereby clinging to life itself. Uncle Harry was the only person who appeared indifferent to my condition, the only person who never looked at me with affected cheerfulness, the only person who never made ill-disguised asides to my mother about how brave the little chap was. Maybe it was simply that in the clouded world of old age he didn't realize.

"*Kom* here and see, boy," he used to call, and his finger would beckon me onto his knee (the faint smell of damp and mold) to look at family photographs. One in particular showed — shows still, for I have it on my desk in the laboratory — a group of three adults posing beside a plaster column amid a small jungle of artificial plants. They are staring fixedly at the camera as though at the firing squad of history — a squat man in a black soutane; a younger man beside him wearing a frock coat and a rather foppish cravat; and a young woman seated between them. On the woman's knee is a little child.

"My poor *Mutti*," Uncle Harry would say in sorrowful tones. "With me in her arms." The child — four, five — has no expression, no real existence, barely even the distinguishing feature of a specific sex. A blot, a thing decked out in frills and sporting some kind of ridiculous bonnet, it is merely there on its mother's lap like a family heirloom. Long ago, longer ago than it was possible for a child to understand, Harry Wise had been born Heinrich Weiss in Vienna; this photograph was the only relic he possessed of those dead days.

"And that man is your grandfather, boy," Uncle Harry would continue.

"*Great*-grandfather," my mother would correct him.

"*Urgrossvater Gottlieb,*" Harry would admit solemnly, as though the discovery of a further intervening generation had somehow depressed him. "With" — his bony finger would prod at the figure in the soutane, as though trying to prod it into life — "Uncle Hans. That is how he was known to the family. Uncle Hans. He was a famous man, boy, a famous man."

The picture is, in a sense, pivotal. It marks the last moments of the Austrian existence of the family Weiss. A few years later and the mother, that fragile, hopeful thing with the child on her lap, will have been abandoned, dead or alive — family history is uncertain on the point — in distant Vienna, and Gottlieb Weiss will have brought his only son to England. Once in England, Gottlieb found himself a second wife — English, Anglican, etiolated, stern — and, when name-changing became expedient in 1914, a second name: Godley Wise. He might have toyed with the etymologically accurate Theophilus White, but apparently that striking combination did not quite suit one who was a freethinker and agnostic, and a wayward disciple of Freud. So Gottlieb Weiss became Godley Wise — *Doctor* Godley Wise — and young Heinrich became Harry. Later a daughter was born, a half-sister to Harry but nothing like him, so my mother claims. Miscegenation had diluted that Austrian blood beyond recognition. Quite English, my grandmother was.

I will run time backwards, the generations

backwards, back toward that portrait taken in some Viennese photographic studio, and beyond that into the realms of myth and legend: Uncle Harry's mother, Gottlieb Weiss's first wife, was Rosine Schindler. Rosine Schindler was the granddaughter of one Anton Mendel of Heinzendorf in Silesia. Anton Mendel was the father of Gregor Mendel. Gregor Mendel is the priest in the family photograph. Thus Benedict Lambert and Gregor Mendel are related. That is what Uncle Harry used to tell me in his thick and monotonous accent. By some quirk of history, caprice of fate, whim of genetics and inheritance, Gregor Mendel and I are related. We have genes in common: to be precise, three percent. I am Gregor Mendel's great-great-great-nephew.

At the age of eleven I sat an entrance exam for the local grammar school. My exam was called the eleven-plus, and was designed with good Mendelian principles in mind. Sir Cyril Burt of Oxford, Liverpool, Cambridge, and, finally, London universities was the principal advocate of the test, and I have a great deal to thank him for. Sir Cyril was a disciple of Galton. It was he whose work on twin and familial studies claimed to prove what Galton had only surmised, that intelligence is largely inherited, and that if you can measure a child's intelligence, then you can measure its suitability for a decent education: the successful child goes to the grammar school; the failure goes to the secondary modern.

I recall one of the questions, just one: If it takes three minutes to boil an egg, how long does it take to boil one hundred eggs?

The answer, gentle reader, is *three minutes*. Anything else is wrong. At the time, sitting in an anonymous classroom of the local grammar school, stared at by the dozen or so children who, like me, were sitting the exam, I wanted to write, *It all depends . . .* But I was too intelligent to do anything stupid like that. *Three minutes.*

"At least he's got something going for him, poor little chap," one of my mother's friends said. I overheard them talking shortly after news of my success had come through. "At least he's got a brain in his head. Where did he get that from, I wonder? Was it his father? I expect it was. Although you can't tell, can you?" My mother was at the sewing machine, frowning with concentration as she made some kind of shirt that would fit me, accommodate my all-but-normal trunk and my shrunken arms. Whenever she was at home, whenever she wasn't cooking or doing the dishes, she seemed to be sewing clothes for me. It is impossible to buy clothes, you see. The industry doesn't take into account people of my proportions.

At least he's got a brain in his head. Even then I wasn't so sure that was much of a consolation. But I passed the examination and was admitted to the grammar school.

At my grammar school, biology was taught in a classroom like all the others. There was a blackboard and a raised podium at one end, and rows of sloping desks facing it in dutiful attention. Mendel himself would have recognized the kind of place. Elsewhere in the school there were proper laboratories for physics and chemistry, but biology was an afterthought, consigned to a room that was fit for dictation, for sitting and listening and taking notes. There was an atmosphere of lassitude about the place, a sensation that nothing much would ever happen there. A poster on the wall showed the internal organs of the human body in lurid and unlikely color. It was a prudish, sexless picture, and someone had tried to scribble in genitals where none had previously existed. The attempt had been rubbed out, but the crude lines were still visible like the scars from some dreadful operation. Below the poster was a bench with a row of dusty test tubes containing *Tradescantia* cuttings, the debris of some halfhearted demonstration that had been set up weeks before and then forgotten. There were microscopes, but they were locked away in some cupboard and marked for senior pupils only.

I clambered with difficulty onto a chair. The class watched and whispered. The biology teacher, a Mr. Perkins, coughed impatiently as though it were my fault that I was late, my fault that I was an object of curiosity, that I was what I was and am. "Gregor Mendel was an Austrian monk," he informed us once quiet had fallen. He paid scant attention to matters of fact. "The monastery was miles away from anywhere. No one knew about him and his work, and he knew nothing about what was going on in the scientific world of his time, but despite all these disadvantages, he started the whole science of genetics. There's a lesson for you. You don't need expensive laboratories and all the equipment. You just need determination and concentration. Stop talking, Dawkins. You never stop talking, boy, and you never have anything worth saying. You will find a photograph of Mendel on page one hundred and forty-five of your textbook. Look at it carefully and reflect on the fact that it is the likeness of a man with more brains in his little finger than you have in the whole of your cranium. But photographs won't help you pass your exams, will they, Jones? Not if you don't pay attention and don't learn anything and spend all your time fiddling."

I turned the pages. From page 145 a face looked out of the nineteenth century into the twentieth with a faint and enigmatic smile, as though he knew what was in store. I held my secret to my chest, like a cardplayer with a magnificent hand.

"Below the picture you may see one of his crosses," Mr. Perkins said. "Study it with care, Jones."

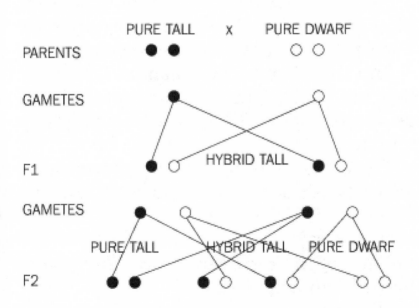

"This is the most famous of his experiments. Mendel took two strains of garden pea —"

"Please, sir, how do you strain a pea, sir?"

"Shut up, boy."

"Dawkins strains while having a pee. Is that anything to do with it, sir?"

"Detention, boy! You are in detention. One of the strains was tall and the other was dwarf . . ."

"Is a dwarf like Lambert, sir?"

The racket of laughter stopped. Mr. Perkins reddened. "That's enough of that, boy."

"But is it, sir?"

"Enough, I said. Now I want to explain what Mendel discovered. You will open your notebooks and take down this dictation . . ."

And then I played my hand. "Please sir, he's my uncle. I mean great-uncle. Great-great-great-uncle. That's what Uncle Harry told me."

There was a terrible silence. Someone giggled. "Don't be foolish, child," Mr. Perkins said.

"He is, sir."

The giggling spread, grew, metamorphosed into laughter.

"But he *is*, sir. Uncle Hans. Great-great-great-uncle Hans Gregor."

The laughter rocked and swayed around the room, around the small focus of my body and around the wreckage of my absurd boast. Great-great-great-uncle. "Great-great-great," they called. "Great-great-great! Great-great-great!"

"Shut up! *There will be silence!*"

The laughter died away to mere contempt. "You will open your notebooks," Mr. Perkins repeated in menacing tones, "and take down this dictation . . ."

After the lesson they confronted me in the playground and taunted me with Uncle Gregor. "He's one of them," they shouted. "He's one of Mendel's dwarfs!"

I'm not, of course. Mendel's dwarfs were recessive. I am dominant. But at that time I didn't know anything very much, except evasive glances and a brisk smile on my mother's face and a cheerful but unconvincing assertion that what matters is what you are like inside. It's easy to say that. All's for the best in the best of all possible worlds. At home I had small chairs and a small bed and low bookshelves. The books were the normal size.

"Mendel's dwarf," they cried after me in the playground. "Mendel, Mendel." The name became a taunt, a chant of loathing. I retreated to the bike sheds, but they confronted me there, their knees hovering in my line of sight, their feet stamping at me as though I were something to be trodden into the dirt, a cockroach perhaps. "Mendel, Mendel, Mendel's dwarf!" they called, and the feet came through the bike racks at me until a couple of older girls came in. "Leave off him," they said carelessly. "What's he done to you, poor sod?"

"He's Mendel's dwarf."

"Oh, piss off."

The boys went, chastened by age and sex. The girls eyed me with distaste through the bike racks. One of them seemed about to say something. Then she shrugged as though the effort didn't seem worthwhile. "Come on," she said to the other. "Give us a fag."

I left them lighting up their Woodbines and scratching themselves.

"It's a problem you have to live with," the headmaster advised me. I told him I'd not realized that before, and thanked him very much for sharing his insight with me. He answered that being insolent wouldn't help. Or being arrogant. I asked him whether being submissive might. Or being recessive. He told me to get out of his study.

A problem you have to live with. That's a good one, isn't it? It isn't something I *live with,* as I might live with a birthmark or a stammer, or flat feet. It is not an *addition,* like a mole on my face, nor a *subtraction,* like premature baldness: it *is me.* There is no other.

The curious thing is that I am doubly cursed. I am like I am, and yet I want to live. That's another character, a more subtle one than dwarfism, but an animal character nevertheless, possessed by almost every human being. The Blessed Sigmund Fraud was wrong. There is no death wish, no *Todes*wunch. If there were, no animal species would survive, and certainly not our own damned one. But if there were a death wish, things would have been a lot easier for me: head in the oven, overdose of pills, fourth-floor window, the possibilities are endless. In the underground I've often stood on the edge of the platform as the train came in, and thought about it. But no, you've got to live with it. You aren't actually given the choice. No one is. I use the second person to include the whole of the human race. No one is exempt. You are all victims of whatever selection of genes is doled out at that absurd and apparently insignificant moment when a wriggling sperm shoulders aside its rivals and penetrates an egg. "What have we got here?" Mother Nature wonders. "What combination have we thrown up this time?" It's like checking over the results of some lottery, the numbers drawn every day, every minute of every day; and every time someone a winner and someone a loser. No need to say which I was.

Two genealogies from dwarf studies, discovered in a book of medical genetics that I found one day in the public library. The diagrams have a pleasing sense of design about them, don't they? There is a balance, a rhythm, a subtle asymmetry that halts the eye. The whole has something of the composition of a Mondrian painting, or perhaps a doodle by Miró:

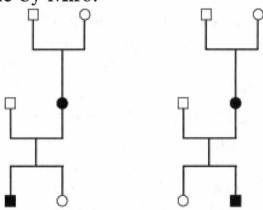

■   ●   □   ○
Affected male   Affected female   Normal male   Normal female

All four of the children of the two achondroplastic mothers were born by Caesarean section. If either of the two affected boys has children, the risk for each of these children being affected is a half.

That was the kind of thing I used to do in my free time, run to the public library. It was a refuge, you see, a place of quiet, a place of sympathy. One of the assistant librarians in particular befriended me. She used to put aside books she thought I might like; she used to talk to me almost as though I were normal. She was not a bad-looking woman. Woman, girl, she was on the borderline between the two, one or two acne spots still lingering on her chin, a blush still coming readily to her cheeks whenever the chief librarian addressed her. Mousy, of course. I feel that all librarians ought to be mousy. It should be a necessary (but not sufficient) qualification for the job. Mousy? Agouti? What, I wonder, is its genetic control? Perhaps it is tightly linked to the gene for tidiness. She was about eighteen, this mousy librarian: eighteen, tidy, and frightened of the chief librarian (also mousy, but fortyish and balding), and her name was Miss Piercey.

"It's Benedict," she used to say as I waddled in. Her tone was almost one of contentment, almost as though she were *pleased* to see me. "How are we today?"

We.

Usually she would be sitting on a stool behind the main desk. Often enough, just often enough for it to be a distinct possibility, not too often for it to be anything more than chance, her skirt would be drawn rather too high up her thighs for modesty. I used to gain an interesting perspective on her when she sat like that. It was the only occasion in the whole of my life when I have been at an advantage over normal people, eyeing Miss Piercey's legs, longing to be able to pierce Miss Piercey. "Are we looking for anything in particular today?" she would ask. "Or are we just browsing?"

We. For those moments we shared my paltry existence. "Browsing," I would reply, my eyes browsing up and over the angle of her knees and into the shadows above. "Just browsing." Sometimes things would become quite difficult. On occasion — when, for example, turning on her stool to deal with another reader, she had to uncross her legs — I would have to excuse myself hastily and rush not to the bookshelves but to the bathroom, there to find solace and comfort at my own hands.

You are surprised? Oh yes, I'm quite *normal* that way. It's only my bones that are deformed . . .

Well, you might *call* it a bone, but it isn't one. The *os penis* or baculum, a heterotopic bone found in many insectivores and rodents and in most primates, is absent in man. It isn't a bone, and I am anything but dwarf in that respect. Because of my shortened arms I have to bend to reach it, but it's quite normal when I get there. Seven inches erect. I measured it on one occasion when it was thinking of Miss Piercey.

A test question: Who praised masturbation as the perfect sexual relationship, because it is the only one in which pleasure given is exactly equal to pleasure received? Answer: Jean Genet.

Once I saw Miss Piercey's underpants. I was standing chatting with her when an old lady called her to get a book down from a high shelf. "Won't be a mo, dear," Miss Piercey replied. "Just coming." And, as she slid down from her stool, her skirt, snagging some splinter in the wood, rode upward over her thighs. "Whoops!" she cried, tugging the skirt down. "You keep your eyes to yourself, young man."

Miss Piercey hurried to the old lady's aid; I hurried toward the bathroom. The incident was trivial and normality was soon reestablished (my desire spent into the lavatory bowl; the old lady equipped with book from upper shelf; Miss Piercey settled once more on her stool with her skirt pulled demurely down to her knees), but the memory lived on. White cotton with pink flowers, Miss Piercey's knickers. They were etched into my mind. I saw the same design at the British Home Stores shortly afterwards, and I rushed in to spend my pocket money. "For my sister," I explained. The assistant looked skeptical; yet surely, if it had been for any other purpose, I would have been rooting around among the black lace, the suspender belts and diaphanous French knickers, not the plain floral underpants. One must look at the matter realistically.

Back in the safety of my bedroom, hugging the scrap of cotton to my face, I dreamt of Miss Piercey lying as white as a mouse beneath my gaze, wearing only those underpants. Sexual dimorphism is under the control of a pair of chromosomes, the X and the Y, but what is it that controls *desire?* That is a question that has defied the greatest geneticists of our time. There are those who claim that a rogue portion of the long arm of the X chromosome (section Xq28, to be exact[1]) may be responsible for homosexual desires; but what was it that drove my body into paroxysms of lust for mouselike Miss Piercey?

I haven't mentioned her eyes, have I? I

1. Hammer et al., *Science*, 1993.

have mentioned, by implication, other parts of her anatomy, and, specifically, her hair; but I haven't mentioned her eyes. They were of differing color. One was blue, the other green. How do you explain that by the mathematical dance of genes . . . ?

Miss J. Piercey. The name card on the librarians' desk said so (I could catch a glimpse of it only if I stood far back). I didn't even know her first name. J? I imagined "June" — June, moon, swoon; it would have been perfect. She was doing some kind of training in librarianship at the polytechnic, combined with work experience in the library. I was sixteen and was studying biology and chemistry and math, all those things that she had failed. The gulf between us was vast, being constructed of things material and things emotional, things structural and things spiritual. I suppose that had she known my feelings she'd have uttered a squeal of revulsion and accused me of being filthy-minded. But it was something approaching love.

I did very well in biology, of course; particularly well in the questions on genetics. The words *segregation, dominance, recessive, mutation* flowed from my pen. My Punnet squares were punctilious. My ratios were rational.

Mice of the strain known as waltzers suffer from a defect in the cerebellum that makes them move around in an uncoordinated way described as waltzing. When waltzers are crossed with normal mice all the offspring are normal . . .

Aren't they lucky?

Humans of the type known as achondroplastic dwarfs suffer from a lack of cartilage cells, so that bones that depend on cartilage models for development cannot grow. When dwarfs of this type are crossed with normal humans fifty percent of the offspring are normal and fifty percent are dwarf.

Aren't they unlucky?

Toss a coin. It is all a matter of probability and chance. Try it. Go on, take a coin out of your pocket or your purse. Toss it, call heads or tails, and there you are. Cursed or not?

The biology laboratory at school possessed five microscopes. They were gleaming, ancient things with more than a hint of brass about them, but their optics were good. Only the seniors were allowed to use them, and then only under the supervision of the dull Mr. Perkins, but there are ways and means, always. I obtained a key to the room (the cleaning lady reported the loss, but everyone just assumed she had mislaid it) and stayed behind one afternoon. The impoverished school library was available for late study on Tuesdays and Thursdays, so I spent some time reading there to establish an alibi before making my way along the corridor and up the back stairs to where the biology laboratory lay at the rear of the building, overlooking a car park and a supermarket warehouse. It was but the work of an instant to let myself in and lock the door behind me.

The microscopes were in a locked cupboard, but I knew all about that. The key lived in Mr. Perkins's desk. In a few moments (dangerous moments, for the cupboard was within view of the glass panel in the door) the best of the microscopes (Czech optics, I remember) was in my grasp. I set the thing up in a corner, away from the door. I got a box of slides and another of cover slips. I found a beaker and a teat pipette.

I was — am — a born research worker. Single-minded, patient, prepared, determined; like Great-great-great-uncle Gregor himself. I had chosen the photograph, a particular favorite, with care. In a boudoir suffused with rose light, a honeyed girl, bedewed and as soft as angora, bent over and presented her backside to the camera and, by proxy, to my hungry eyes. She glanced behind, as though at her behind, while one hand reached back to part her buttocks and reveal the magic of golden pubescence and the mystery of moist, rubescent, pleated flesh. I told you I am a born researcher. No inhibition stands in my way. I propped the picture on a desk and fumbled with my clothing. In a few moments I felt the familiar spasm of delight and had a cupped palmful of nacreous liquid.

> *A million million spermatozoa*
> *All of them alive:*
> *Out of their cataclysm but one poor Noah*
> *Dare hope to survive.*

Author? Aldous Huxley: grandson of Thomas Huxley, the champion of Darwin against the clergy, and brother of Julian Huxley, *Sir* Julian Huxley, sometime professor of zoology at King's College, London, sometime director-general of UNESCO, sometime leading eugenicist . . .

I pipetted a drop of glutinous fluid onto a slide and lowered the cover slip with consummate care; then I arranged the light and slid the slide onto the stage. Low power . . . medium power. I peered, adjusted the diaphragm, turned the nosepiece to the big lens.

46

It locked into place.

One million million spermatozoa, all of them alive. Small exclamations of blind and culpable intent! Interrogation marks asking what absurd question? A thousand periods, each bearing its potent, muddled message . . . They shimmered and shook, nosing toward God knows what dimly perceived ovum, and I knew, oh, I knew that of every thousand that I saw within that brilliant circle of light, five hundred carried the command for height, for normality, for happiness and contentment; and five hundred bore the curse.

But which?

Was that an epiphany? Was that the moment when something, someone — the bleak and austere muse of science — spoke to me? Was my future research determined then, just as my future life had been determined seventeen years before, when a sperm such as one of these had nosed its way up my mother's fallopian tube and encountered a wandering, wondering ovum with its delicate cumulus of follicular cells? Forget about copulation. The moment of true penetration is when the lucky sperm, the poor Noah, nudges against the ovum and explodes its capsule of digestive enzymes. The tail is shed and the head enters. For a moment two sets of chromosomes, one from the egg, one from the sperm, lie alongside each other in uneasy juxtaposition. And one of them carries my curse. The chromosomes, intricate spools of nucleic acid and protein, move together into a single, fateful conjunction; and Benedict Lambert has begun. Chromosomes that were once my mother's and my father's are now mine. I have begun. And I am cursed.

And Gregor Mendel, was he cursed too? A moment of coupling in the massive bed in the peasant cottage at number 58, Heinzendorf, a village at the foot of the Sudety Mountains in Austrian Silesia, not far from the Polish border. It is October 22, 1821, more or less. There is a square tiled stove against one wall, around which the family sleeps during the deep winter nights; but now it is merely autumn, a chill autumn with the larch and the silver birch and the poplars turning to gold and rust, and Anton and Rosine use the great bed. The daughter Veronika sleeps on one side, while the parents couple quietly and methodically on the other side. They get warmth from each other's body, and, for a convulsive moment, something else — a fleeting abstraction from the pains of peasant life. Then they lie quietly in each other's arms while a shimmering galaxy of spermatozoa begins its blind and determined journey up Rosine's genital tract.

Did the particular sets of chromosomes that came together then bring with them Gregor Mendel's particular future? Was that written in the genes? Can you possess genes for genius?

[Restriction]

Francis Galton, cousin of Charles Darwin, looked for evidence that intelligence runs in families — and found it, naturally enough, among his own august relatives. One wonders what he would have made of his exact contemporary, Gregor Mendel. One wonders what he would have made of the meanness of the world from which Mendel came, of the dull stupidity, of the grim labor in the fields, of the poverty and squalor. Mendel's father was no more than a serf. He might have owned his small-holding, but he was still subject to the *Robot*. That was the world from which Mendel came.

Robot is an emblematic word. Of course it was intended to be so from the moment that the playwright Karel Čapek took it from the lumber room of the Czech language and coined its modern sense.[1] In Mendel's day, *Robot* was man, not machine: three days' forced labor out of every week of a peasant's

1. In the play *R.U.R.* (*Rossum's Universal Robots*), 1920.

life. Following the revolution of 1848, in which the peasants were emancipated, the *Robot* was abolished; but not before it had destroyed Anton Mendel. That was the family endowment that Gregor stood to inherit.

Galton, on the other hand, inherited a personal fortune and invented the science of eugenics in order to prove that the superior classes were, in fact, superior (in his particular case they were also sterile, but let that pass). In my thesaurus, "Galton's law" comes immediately next to "Mendelian ratio." There's an irony.

The village is still there, of course, tucked away among the hills of northern Moravia — the very navel of Europe, as far from Madrid as from Moscow, as far from the Baltic as from the Mediterranean. It's a pretty enough place. A rural idyll, you might think. The fields and woods lie quietly beneath the fragile summer sky now just as they did in Mendel's day. The same stream still runs beside the same road (merely tarmacked now) down toward the Odra valley. The same trees — alder and willow and aspen — grow along the stream-bank, while across the fields to the north rise the foothills of the same mountains, still black with spruce. You can almost imagine the family still there in the cottage, Rosine stout and jolly, Anton sallow and saturnine, the two daughters, Veronika and Theresia, and the son Johann. You might imagine all that, but you would be far from the truth.

The fact is that although the geography may be the same and most of the buildings may be the same, the place itself has changed beyond reckoning. The name has changed, the language has changed, the people have changed, the whole world has changed. Nothing is the same. Heinzendorf is a vanished world — it is Hynčice now, a straggle of orchards and cottages and barns along a single street, merging into the neighboring village of Vražné that was once Grosspetersdorf. The mountains that rise to the north are part of the Sudety range.

This is the Sudetenland.

At the crossroads in the center of this idyllic village is a curious building. It looks like a hybrid between a bus shelter and a chapel. Raised above the roof of the hut is a black stone plaque inscribed in gothic lettering:

It is not difficult to imagine a detachment of soldiers in *feldgrau* halting at that crossroads and looking up at that plaque. It would be a fine autumnal day of 1938. They would have a halftrack perhaps; maybe a motorcycle and sidecar. They would look up at the inscription with the satisfaction of the liberator, while villagers — women in floral aprons with flour on their arms, and men in overalls and muddied boots — would come out of the houses and barns to welcome them.

"Hier wurde Mendel geboren," the villagers would explain.

"Mendel? Ein Jude?"

"Nein, nein." Laughter. *"Prälat Mendel. Entdecker der Genetik."*

A grinning, embarrassed relative would be produced as evidence. Conscious of race and blood, of the purity of their genes and the inferior nature of the Slavs, the soldiers would be delighted to learn that they had fetched up in Mendel's home village. It would appear to them an omen. There would be laughter. Perhaps there would even be a photograph taken with a sharp, neat, futuristic Leica to send back to the family in Rostock.

Oświęcim/Auschwitz is a two-hour drive away, just over the Polish border.

The Mendel house itself still stands, a stout cottage set back from the road up an overgrown path, surrounded by cherry and apple trees. There is a metal sign painted in the crude lettering of the onetime People's Republic — *Památka G. Mendela*, the G. Mendel Memorial — and you get the key from the woman who runs the village shop. She is Czech, of course. She understands little German.

There are just two rooms open to the public, both whitewashed, both tainted with damp. On the walls are the usual photographs — Gärtner, Nägeli, Darwin, the Augustinian friars — and the usual facsimiles of Mendel's papers. There are diagrams of some of the pea crossings and a quotation from T. H. Morgan, and a stylized and inaccurate model of part of a DNA molecule. There is little else. Only in the inner room is there something that Mendel himself might have recognized: a tiled stove standing in one corner as mute witness to the long, hard winters.

In the visitors' book someone has put the epithet *SudetenDeutscher* beneath his name.

What was it like, that distant, Sudeten German life one hundred and fifty years ago? Frugal, fearful of God, attentive to duty, I suppose. The future would have been no more than a continuation of the past, not subject to change. You accepted your lot, and visited the family graves regularly just to see what acceptance meant. You prayed and you worked. You didn't question.

Johann Mendel escaped through the only door that stood half-open — education. In 1834, encouraged by the local schoolmaster, he sat the entrance examination to the Imperial Royal Gymnasium at Troppau (Opava) and won a place.

Imagine his mother's pride when she heard the news: picture her in the kitchen, wiping her ruddy hands on a cloth and turning to embrace her young son in a powerful, maternal clasp. She had plans, we imagine: her uncle had once been a teacher, and she had similar plans for her son. And picture old Anton, swallowing bitterness and envy while slapping his son on the shoulder. "In my day you didn't get opportunities like this, my boy. In my day you had to work to better yourself . . ."

"But the lad *has* worked. He's worked with his *brain*." The reproach would have been there just below the surface, the hint that Johann was destined for better things, the suggestion that by using your brains you could escape the clutches of serfdom and the *Robot;* and the implication that by marrying Anton Mendel, Rosine Schwirtlich had somehow stepped down a rung.

Johann was admitted to the grammar school on half-commons — the equivalent, I suppose, of free dinners. He worked hard and did well at his studies — *prima classis cum eminentia* — but escape wasn't that easy, for in the winter of 1838 his father was badly injured while logging in the forests above Ostrau — while working under the *Robot.* A trunk broke loose and rolled onto him, and they brought him home on a cart with his chest half crushed.

Heinzendorf must have been rife with speculation. What would Johann Mendel do? The father survived more or less, but manual work was beyond him. What was the son, the only son, going to do? Grim and implacable, the *Robot* stood waiting in the shadows to claim Johann Mendel for his own.

Can there be a gene for stubbornness? Johann was a stubborn man, sure enough. He was stubborn in his work with the garden pea (eight years, eight generations, more than thirty thousand plants); he was stubborn in his battle with the taxman when he was abbot of the monastery; and he was stubborn then, when he was a mere boy of sixteen and his father was a near invalid and the farm was going to wrack and ruin. It isn't hard to imagine the rural drama that reigned in that cottage in the village of Heinzendorf when he came home. It isn't difficult to picture the internecine quarrel that threatened to split the family apart — the jealousies, the accusations, the false appeals to duty and the dishonest appeals to affection, the whole caustic solution of a family dispute.

"The boy must be allowed to continue his studies," Rosine would insist.

And old Anton, sitting in a chair by the stove, would cough and hack and bring up mucus and blood like evidence. "I've worked myself to the bone for this place. And I get it thrown back at me without so much as a thank-you."

"It's not like that, Father," the son would try to explain, with little success.

"Oh, it's exactly like that. Farm work's beneath you, that's the trouble. You think it's beneath you. You think that you can become grand just by reading a few books . . ." Old Anton, hacking and spitting and pointing his finger at his son, with the daughters hovering in the background, pleading for him to stop. "You'll do yourself an injury, Father."

"You keep out of it. This isn't the business of women."

But it was. It was precisely the business of the women, for it was the daughters who held the key — the elder Veronika with her shining new husband and the young Theresia, Uncle Harry's great-grandmother, then a mere child of eleven. I imagine they plotted the whole thing together with their mother and presented it as a fait accompli to the father. Veronika's husband, Alois Sturm, had some money put away. He could buy the farm and so keep it in the family. The sale would raise enough money for Anton and Rosine to retire — he wasn't in any fit state to carry on, was he? — and there would be something left over to support Johann at the university. And Theresia — stout, sensible Theresia — would surrender her own share of the inheritance, her dowry in fact, to help her beloved brother with his studies.

So he stayed at his studies, living from hand to mouth, doing some private teaching, scratching out a living, battling with poverty and guilt.

The church of Vražné/Hynčice lies up the

hill on the far side of the stream, half-hidden among the lanes and gardens, couched among silver birch. There is a memorial from the First World War with a Mendel (Ferdinand) listed among the dead. The interior of the church is as plain as a Protestant chapel. Here the Mendel family would have walked each Sunday, stumping along the lane in their clumsy Sunday best, stolid in their Germanicism. Little more than serfs, on Sunday they would have looked like free men and women. They would have sung *"Ein feste Burg"* and *"Gott erhalte Franz den Kaiser"* along with all the other good folk of the villages.

A middle-aged couple were cleaning around the altar when I peered in through the open doorway. They stopped and stared at me in surprise. They seemed startled, as though I were a confirmation of what they had always feared, a manifestation of folktale and legend, a dwarf from the Sudety Mountains, where, no doubt, dwarfs had mined for gold from time immemorial. *"Dobry den,"* I greeted them.

The woman recovered her composure and returned my greeting. *"Trpaslík,"* the man muttered. The other words I didn't understand, but I knew that one well enough. I know that word in every language. Dwarf. We stared at each other for a moment, as though across a barbed-wire fence, before I turned and left them to their work.

Farther up the hill I found the cemetery. The center of the field was taken up with the modern graves, the Czech ones, the Markovas and the Chudys, black and gleaming in the sunshine. Prominent at the front was a memorial to Russian soldiers, still gleaming, still with a lamp burning, still with fresh flowers:

NA VECNOU PAMET SOVETSKYM HRDINUM

In eternal memory of the Soviet Heroes, something like that.

I love the ironies of history. This has the taste of one of the sourest, most acerbic of them. Here in Moravia, precisely in this village where the founder of genetics was born and where the Nazis came in pursuit of racial purity and *Lebensraum*, the Soviets came as liberators. They brought freedom from the tyranny of genetics and replaced it with the tyranny of social theory. Mankind is good at tyrannies.

Among the nettles over to one side I found the German headstones. A few faded ones were still standing:

> # FRANZ MENDEL
> ## 1878–1930
>
> # FRANZ MENDEL
> ## 1906–1940
>
> ### OBETRUPPFÜHRER
> ### IM RAD

There was a calvary buried beneath dog rose and brambles. The thorns tore at my hands as I reached up and pulled the branches aside to discover:

> ### THE RESTING PLACE OF
>
> # ALOIS STURM
> ## DIED 1892, AGED 42
>
> ### AND
>
> # ROSINA STURM
> ## DIED 1927, AGED 72

This was Gregor Mendel's nephew, the son of his elder sister, Veronika. Mendel himself married them in 1873, on his last visit to Heinzendorf. But where were the others? Where was Veronika, or Alois's father? Where was Theresia? And where were Anton Mendel and Rosine Schwirtlich?

There is an evolution in the life of a cemetery, as in life itself. There are lines of development, changes with time, adaptations, extinctions. Most of the Mendel tombstones, most of the Sturms, all of the Schwirtlichs, are extinct — dinosaurs and dodos in the exiguous world of Hynčice necrology. Perhaps their fossils lie there in the rubble of broken stones cast aside into the hedge.

Nothing but moss-grown fragments shall remain of the epoch in which the genius appeared.

Gregor Mendel himself wrote those words. Perceptive? Prophetic? He wrote them before he ever became a friar, when he was still young Johann and still living in Heinzendorf. The line is part of a poem, a paean to the art of printing, probably a task set by some forgotten and forgettable teacher, preserved among childhood memorabilia by his second sister, Theresia. Date unknown. Shall we say, 1838 — ten years before the revolution throughout the Empire that led to the emancipation of the peasants; sixty years before

Heinrich Weiss left Vienna with his father Gottlieb; one hundred years before the Munich betrayal?

Yes, his laurels shall never fade,
Though time shall suck down
  by its vortex
Whole generations into the abyss . . .

Abyss. I suppose that's good enough. I stood among the debris of the graveyard of Hynčice and strained to catch a glimpse of Mendel and his family across the abyss. But the Mendels and the Sturms and the Schindlers and the Weisses had vanished, along with all else that was German, in 1945. Heinzendorf to Hynčice. In that year Edvard Beneš returned from exile in London and the brief, fragile democratic government of Czechoslovakia was installed in the wake of the Red Army. In that year the expulsion of the Germans began. *Odsun,* the transfer, the Czechs called it. Nowadays it'd be known as ethnic cleansing. While the Red Army looked on and the western Allies kept quiet (it had all been agreed to at the Potsdam Conference), three million Germans were driven out of the Czech lands to fare as best they could in Germany and Austria; and the Sudeten problem vanished. Heinzendorf and

Mendel lie somewhere on the far side of that event.

I stood beside Alois and Rosina Sturm and thought of ancestry and descent. And of Jean.

[Segregation]

Education is an escape. I took it, Mendel took it. Indebted and beholden, he moved on from the grammar school to the university at Olmütz, giving private lessons to earn his keep. He tried to pay his little sister back, and at the same time he tried to become what he was not: one of the educated middle class. It was not easy. A peasant's son had little chance in those days, and it is hardly a surprise to find that in 1843 he approached the Augustinian Friars at Saint Thomas in Brünn. The Church has always dealt kindly with those of its children who have brains and are willing to pay the price, which is to vow that you will not pass any genes that you may possess, for intelligence or anything else, on to the next generation. It is the very antithesis of eugenics.

He took the name Gregor at his induction. Brother Gregor Mendel. In his first year at Theological College in Brünn he studied ecclesiastical history, ecclesiastical archaeology, and Hebrew; in his second year canon law, scriptural exegesis, and Greek; in his third year, dogmatics and moral theology; in the fourth year, pastoral divinity, catechetics, and the methodology of primary-school education. In his reports he is described as *prima classis cum eminentia* once more, and applauded for his diligence and good behavior, but that hardly makes him one of the geniuses of the nineteenth century. During his last year, with unseemly haste (there is a shortage of priests), he is ordained subdeacon, deacon, and finally priest, all within the space of a fortnight. The ordination to the priesthood took place on his birthday.

LETTER FROM ABBOT CYRILL NAPP TO PRIOR BAPTIST VORTHEY:

It has come to my knowledge that Father Gregor is attending lectures without wearing a college cap. Father Gregor, although he is now a priest, is still only a student . . . I must ask the Very Reverend Prior to inform him that when he attends lectures he must wear a college cap just like the other students.

A little glimmer of pride? Perhaps. But we look in vain for anything else. There is not a trace, not a glimmer, of anything that might be genius. The problem is, we can't come to terms with genius. We don't know where it lies. Is it in the heart or is it in the head? Is it mechanistic or mystical, fortuitous or inevitable? Is it in the genes or in the upbringing? If it's the one, then it is nothing more than pure mechanics; if it's the other, then it is nothing more than pure chance. Either way, no merit attaches. The apple falling on Newton's head may be a fiction, but it is emblematic — the fact that the image exists, I mean; not the fact that it isn't a fact, that the image is no more than a myth. It is the myth that interests me. We don't understand the man, so we create an event, a moment, something we can grasp. But a million other windfalls have dropped at a million other feet and all to no effect, so what are we left with by way of explanation?

I have two photographs of him. I copied them from a book in the Institute library, and had them developed and printed by one of the technicians in the electron microscope department — a group picture of the whole community and a studio portrait of the man alone. You look for clues, don't you? You try to read behind a face. Father Gregor possesses a high forehead, a strong jaw, and a determined mouth; but the expression is that of a gentle man and a dreamer. He gazes out of the portrait with visionary eyes. He seems to be staring into the unknown, into the dim world of discovery, into the future.

Visionary eyes? Be suspicious of everything I have just written. He was merely short-sighted. Physiognomy is a pseudoscience, and crime has been committed in the name of phrenology. You can tell nothing from a man's appearance, nothing except the depths of your own prejudice. And anyway, according to his biographer, that photograph has been doctored, touched up, smoothed out, and generally made what it is not.

And yet . . .

In the group photograph there is something to grasp at, some kind of movement, some hint of the mood of a distant day. The picture seems to cast a shadow forward into the bright light of the twentieth century, a shadow from the occasion when the photographer came, with his panoply of tent and chemicals and glass plates, his self-importance and impatience, to preserve the images of the Augustinian community of Altbrünn for posterity.

"Please, gentlemen, please be still!" The anguish of an artist not being taken seriously. "Fathers, *please!*"

You can almost hear the chatter and the laughter, the protests of Father Thomas, the ironical amusement of Father Baptista, and the insistence of Father Anselm that this new manifestation of scientific progress be taken seriously. Anselm poses with his left finger resting against chin, and gazes into the lens of the camera as though to make clear that *he* understands the importance of this experiment. Father Pavel has brought a book along and appears to be writing in it — choirmaster and organist, perhaps he is working on an arrangement for mass on the next major feast day. Prälat Cyrill, the abbot, has a Bible on his lap. He looks faintly impatient with all the goings-on.

And Father Gregor? Father Gregor holds a fuchsia flower. He holds it up almost for the camera to see, and he squints at it pointedly, with a quizzical expression, as though asking it a question and getting no answer . . .

This is a photograph taken when photography was in its infancy. The arrival of a photographer from the new town would have been an event, heralded with much excitement, much anticipation. You did not pose casually as the photographer vanished beneath the black hood. You thought about what you were doing. And Father Gregor holds a fuchsia flower and asks it a question . . .

Do photographs tell anything?

They took the official photograph of the Institute the other day, out on the lawn at the back of the main building. Jean wasn't there, of course. I stayed away as well.

Do photographs tell anything? Does appearance tell anything?

Father Gregor has a high forehead, a strong jaw, and a determined mouth. But he failed the examination for his teacher's certificate twice because of nerves, and thereafter was never able to work as anything but a substitute teacher. I have a massive forehead and blunt, puglike features. My nose is stove in at the bridge, my mouth and jaw protrude. My limbs are squat and bowed, my fingers are mere squabs. I am one meter, twenty-seven centimeters tall.

Do appearances tell anything? Who knows, whoever knows what goes on beneath?

The school careers officer looked me up and down (mainly down) and hummed a bit. "University," he suggested. "With your exam forecasts, you should be able to get a place. What subjects interest you? I see . . . er, biology."

"Genetics, really. Mainly genetics."

"Right." He appeared to be searching for

escape. "Quite the coming thing."

"And if not?"

"If not?"

"If I don't go to university. If I want a job."

"Ah." The man scratched himself and thought a bit.

"Do you mind if I sit down?" I asked. "My back is hurting. It hurts after a while. Lordosis."

He seemed flustered. "Lordosis?"

"Inward curvature of the spine."

"Oh, of course, of course. Please . . ." He got up and fussed around to get a chair. "I thought . . . Yes, please do sit down . . . yes, do . . ." *I thought you already were . . .*

I clambered up onto the chair and sat there looking at him. He was balding (sex-limited autosomal recessive), brown-eyed (autosomal dominant), and embarrassed (environmental/social character). "You were going to suggest what job I could do," I prompted him.

"Ah, yes. Well . . ." His embarrassment deepened. "Perhaps . . . er, it's a bit tricky, this one."

"I might not get my grades."

"Quite, quite . . ."

"And then what would I do?"

He scratched himself. "Perhaps . . ." He coughed and flicked vainly through a pamphlet on his desk. Then he looked up with the light of inspiration in his eyes. "Perhaps the circus?"

Cretin. Congenital thyroid deficiency in which ossification of the bones is delayed. There is retarded growth of the brain and overgrowth of the anterior pituitary. In an untreated case the child becomes a physical and mental dwarf.

Not me, is that quite clear? Not me. People seem amazed when they discover not only that I am not mentally retarded, but that I am actually more intelligent than they are. Of course I went to university. Not dreaming spires, not towery and branchy between towers, not cuckoo-echoing, bell-swarmèd, lark-charmèd, rook-racked, or river-rounded; but not a bloody polytechnic either. Plate glass and sloping lawns and halls of residence named after worthy and forgotten philanthropists, where things were always a little too high, and the door in the nearest bathroom had to be adjusted because some fathead of an architect had placed the handle right out of my reach. He'd probably won some prize or other, too. The stairs were pitched so that I had to pause on each landing to get my breath back, and in the lift I couldn't reach any button above the second floor; but at least the authorities had the decency to give me a ground-floor room. I began to find some sort of place in life, like an animal discovering its niche in a complex ecosystem.

After Mendel's ordination there was a short period as assistant parish priest in Altbrünn. He found the experience unpleasant. The city hospital was just up the road and came within the ambit of the friary: a *Krankenhaus* like any other *Krankenhaus* of the time. In those days the principal requirement for hospital work was a strong stomach, and the principal qualification for surgery was speed. The song of the bone saw was oft heard, and the shriek of pain. Anesthesia was at the experimental stage in Britain and the United States; Lister's discoveries on antisepsis had not yet been made; Pasteur had only just completed his training. Blood and lymph, feces and urine, the stench of gangrene and the sound of pain — pure, irremediable pain — these were the features of hospital life. There was the powerful sensation that mankind was mere flesh, mere mechanics at the mercy of random and chaotic nature. Mendel found it too much.

"He is very diligent in the study of the sciences, but he is much less fitted for work as a parish priest, the reason being that he is seized by an uncontrollable timidity when he has to visit a sickbed or see anyone ill and in pain." Thus Abbot Napp to the bishop. It was with relief that the young friar found himself packed off to a nearby town as a substitute teacher, while an application to sit the examination for a teaching certificate was forwarded to the authorities in Vienna.

I suppose they were beginning to wonder what they could do with him. People who can, do; people who can't, teach. Shaw, of course. They pushed Mendel into teaching science, but he seemed to enjoy the work, and in the summer of 1850 it was decided that he should sit the examination. His examiners included the Minister for Public Works, von Baumgartner, and the newly appointed Professor for Experimental Physics at Vienna University, Christian Doppler, so don't think we're talking about provincial nonentities. A minister of the government of the Austria-Hungarian Empire, and Doppler of THE EFFECT: he of the ambulance siren that drops in pitch as it passes by; he of the *the eeeee—yowwww* as the ra*cing car* screams past you down the straight; he of the Red Shift that tells us all, poor creatures, that the galaxies are racing away from one another at a few hundred kilometers every second. Maybe they are all trying to get away from *us*.

Thus, in the late summer of 1850, Mendel found himself seated in a bare room in the Ministry of Finance in Vienna, being interrogated about physics. He failed. His answers confirmed the opinion that the examiners had already formed from his written papers:

Still we hope that if he is given opportunity for more exhaustive study, together with access to better sources of information, he will soon be able to fit himself, at least for work as a teacher in the lower schools.

What is the expression? Damning with faint praise? Sketchily educated, ordained in haste and possibly repenting at leisure, Mendel failed at the one thing he apparently wanted to do.

Let me tell you a joke. He who has sides to split, prepare to split them now. When I was still an undergraduate, I thought a girl had fallen in love with me. A normal girl, I mean. The thing is, I don't fancy my own kind. Like attracts like, you say? But it isn't true, is it? There's the attraction of opposites, the lure of the positive for the negative, surely far more powerful than any mutual recognition and understanding; and there couldn't have been anything more opposite than Dinah. The very name conjures her up. She was — still is, for all I know — tall and slender, ectomorphic and dolichocephalic (whereas I am merely phallic). She was blond of hair and cream of skin, entirely perfect and loved by one and all. And she made friends with me. We sat next to each other during lectures, and I was able to explain the odd point to her, matters of recombination and linkage; and we had the occasional coffee together afterwards.

"Come out for a drink with us," she suggested. "Why not? I've got a car, d'you know that?" Carelessly, flicking away the perfection of pale hair, bending her mouth into a carefully constructed careless smile. "Why not come for a drink with us?"

I became something of a curiosity among her friends. They were creatures of that peculiar breed which inhabits a world of certainties. Certain that there is a God, they were certain that he didn't impinge upon their own existence except to emerge once every four or five years and vote Tory. Certain that there is an inalienable right to wealth and material contentment, they were certain that only certain people were entitled to it. Certain that beautiful is good, they were profoundly disturbed by my presence. "It's Ben!" they'd cry doubtfully as I waddled into the inn beside the creamy, callipygian Dinah.

"Good fellow, Ben. Jolly good chap." They said it in such a tone that made you realize they were trying to convince themselves. "Climb up on a stool. Come on, up you come! Have a pint."

"A half," I would insist.

"A half! Only a half?"

"A halfling," one of them exclaimed, the one who had read *The Lord of the Rings* and fancied himself a medievalist.

"Oh, piss off," they answered him.

Those evenings were full of beer and raucous laughter and darts competitions and silly games in which you sat around in a circle and did things that usually involved speed of reflex and mild humiliation of the loser. Banging your hands on the table in the correct sequence and drinking a pint of beer if you got it wrong, for example. To their collective surprise, I could play that one as well as they could.

"Good fellow, Ben! Spot on!"

"What reflexes!"

Once we played some kind of quiz game, but only once. I knew all the answers.

"Quite a phenomenon, our Ben. Quite a brain."

"Big enough head to hold it all."

"Oh, piss off."

"You know he's some kind of relative of

Mendel's," Dinah told them. "That's right, isn't it, Ben?"

"Who's Mendel?"

"What's that make him? Mendel-son?"

"Wasn't Mendel that doctor fellow at Auschwitz?"

"That's Mengele, you berk."

No, the evenings alone with Dinah were more to my taste.

Oh yes: evenings alone with Dinah. "Ben, for God's sake help me" was her plea. "I don't understand a bloody thing." Her eyes were azure (autosomal recessive, with a high incidence among people of Nordic origin) pools of anguish and helplessness. "I'll cook supper for you if you help me with this bloody essay." So, long into many a night, I helped her with the rII section of T4 phage and the cis-trans test and countless other little matters. She was having problems with the microbial genetics course, you see.

"Oh Ben, you are a darling."

I suppose she thought I was safe. I provided not only academic assistance, but a shoulder to cry on (metaphorically, for God's sake: she couldn't be expected to lean down that far) without the concomitant risk normally associated with opening your heart to someone of the opposite sex. Because after the lessons we talked, or at least she talked while, more or less, I listened. Mainly she talked about herself, about her family, about her ambitions. What she was doing reading for a degree in Anthropology and Biology, I couldn't imagine. She wanted to get into television, into journalism, into something creative, so she said, so said whole generations of benighted youth. So it should have been something like English and Drama, something pleasingly adaptable to late-night talk shows and clever dinner parties, but instead it was Anth. and Bio. "Actually it was meant to be medicine, but my grades just weren't good enough. My people were awfully fed up with me."

My people. You can tell, can't you? When she asked about me, it was *your family;* but she had *people.* I imagined them on horseback, the men in the vanguard with spears and swords, the women and children taking up the rear with the kerns and gallowglasses in attendance. They'd possess some peculiar blood group so you could tell them apart from the common mass of humanity, the Kell blood factor or something. Of course, I never met them. I saw her mother once in the distance: she was a tall and equine woman who doubtless neighed and bucked as she straddled the *paterfamilias* during the monthly ritual rutting; but I was never introduced. It wouldn't have been appropriate, I suppose. What's in a distant relationship to an obscure Austrian friar beside the kind of familial connections they were used to?

Anyway, having done badly in her exams and having thus failed to get into medical school, dear Dinah wasn't very good at her biology either. Gene mapping and cistrons just weren't her thing. But she tried very hard. And she learned. And she kissed me.

Ah! You were wondering what would happen, weren't you?

We had just achieved understanding of some particularly difficult matter to do with recombination in *Neurospora;* and she kissed me. We were at the same level — she seated at her desk, me standing beside her — so the maneuver was technically possible. "Oh, you are a *darling,* Benjamin," she cried. Benjamin was, is, not my correct name, of course. It was her name for me. "You are Benjamin," she used to say. "Benjamin Bunny. I am the only one allowed to call you Benjamin. All the others may make do with Ben."

She called me Benjamin and she kissed me.

You are vulnerable. You have little practice, you see. Practice is what is needed, practice in interpreting the signs. Dinah kissed me and I kissed her back and for a moment, just a moment (difficult to measure without a chronometer as sensitive as mine — say about one nanosecond), our lips touched. Then she snatched her head away. "It's late," she said. "I'd better take you back."

A nanosecond is defined as the maximum length of time in normal company during which a dwarf may forget his condition.

Dinah and I were silent in the car, leaving things carefully unsaid. Words have an awful finality about them. You can't *unsay* them, can you? Better choose your words with care, if you decide to use them at all. Better to say nothing at all most of the time. As she drew the car to a halt outside my hall of residence, she turned to me and broke that equivocal silence. "I'm very fond of you, Benjamin, you know that, don't you?" *Fond.* It's an evasion. I remember my father saying that of my mother. In his case it meant he didn't love her. "You know that?" she repeated.

I nodded. You should see my nods. They are big, absurd things, my head being about the same size as my body. You can't miss them. They are the gestural equivalent of screaming. Then she touched me very gently on the cheek. "Now you'd better go or you'll be late. Don't they lock the place up at midnight?"

"I've got a key."

"Still."

She watched me from the car as I waddled my way up to the main door of the hall. As I reached up to turn the key, I heard her start the engine and drive away.

She'd kissed me.

Darling Dinah, I must apologize for my clumsiness in kissing you. You see, I've had no practice and therefore I find it difficult to judge the niceties of the technique, whether and for how long to insert the tongue, whether the tongue should be involved from the start or only after a decent interval, whether to oppose the inner surface of my mucous membrane against the outer surface of yours (a wet one) or whether to keep to the strict lip-to-lip variety (a dry one and therefore possibly more acceptable). I suppose that I might have acquired some information in this regard from my parents, but, you see, I never once saw them exchange a kiss of that nature. And let's face it, trying to imitate what they do in the films is hardly the way. So I write both in a spirit of apology and in the hope that, in return for all the help that I have given you with the work of Seymour Benzer, you may pay me back in kind and instruct me in the details of this particular matter. Personally (you may be at odds with me over this) I favor the wet kiss . . .

No, of course I didn't write it . . . but I found *her* letter the next day in my post box in the entrance hall.

Dear Benjamin, I really must thank you for all the help you have given me. I reckon I know just about everything I wanted to know now, so I won't bother you anymore. Thanks everso. Dinah.

Thanks everso. Not the summit of the epistolary art.

Two days later I saw her in a lecture and I plucked up enough courage to go over to her. She was talking earnestly with one of the lecturers, perhaps rather too earnestly, perhaps with rather too much interest in ignoring the diminutive figure making its way through the dissolving crowd toward her. I tugged her skirt. "I want a word," I said. "About linkage and recombination." She came away without a fuss, almost obediently, really; following me out of the building and around one of those concrete corners that are the main architectural features of such university campuses. There was a kind of flying buttress overhead and the words *Support the Minors* spray-painted on the wall. I couldn't tell whether the slogan referred to little dark men who labored underground or to some obscure campaign for children's rights.

"I'm in love with you," I told her. I was looking at her knees. I know a great deal about knees, the peculiar form of them, the awkwardness, the plain ungainliness of them. But these knees were slender and elegant, the delicate contour of each patella like a nacreous burial mound of all my hopes.

"I knew you'd do this," she said quietly.

"What do you mean?"

She was almost in tears. "Can't you see it's impossible?"

"Of course it's impossible," I retorted. "It's the impossible that attracts me. When you're like I am, who gives a toss about the possible? You are the most beautiful girl I've ever known — correction: the most beautiful woman I've ever *seen,* which includes every edition of *Penthouse* over the last ten years — and I want you to be in love with me too."

"But I *can't* be."

"I'll say it for you: you can't love me because I'm hideous and deformed, a freak of nature, and people would stare. Very well, love me in private. I won't push it. I don't get many moments like this and I'm playing it off the cuff, but I'll offer you this: nothing at all. No obligations, no commitments, nothing. I just want to hear you admit it. You love me."

"This is bloody ridiculous."

"Don't use that kind of language. It doesn't go with the English-rose look. I'll make one concession. You can say this: 'I *would* love you if you weren't a shrunken monster.' "

It is something to make a girl weep. When you are like I am, even that is something. I left her weeping gently and I walked away.

Benjamin is a Jewish name. *Binyamin.* It means "son of the right hand." The right hand is the lucky one, so Benjamin means "lucky." You might consider it rather a misnomer. The extent to which there is a genetic control of left- and right-handedness is not clear. It has been postulated[1] that it is an example of incomplete dominance, dominant homozygotes being right-handed, recessive homozygotes left-handed, and heterozygotes being ambidextrous, but the prejudice of societies toward those who use the sinister hand is totally transparent. The prejudices toward those who have been as unlucky as this particular son of the right hand are something else altogether . . .

1. M. Annett, "A model of the inheritance of handedness and cerebral dominance," *Nature*, 1964.

85

[Promoter]

I got a first class degree. You expected that, didn't you? I got a first, and I got a Medical Research Council grant, and I slid with ease into what I was destined for. No circuses for me. No schoolteaching, either. The true, abstract poverty of scientific research.

"I am certain there will be no problem that we can't overcome together," the Professor of Molecular Biology said at interview. "None whatever." He was referring to physical problems. Scientific ones were another thing altogether. I began my doctorate at Oxford in October of the year that Uncle Harry died.

Harry Wise died of a cerebral hemorrhage at the age of ninety-something, while taking a shower. Longevity has a genetic element to it,[1] as well as a good slice of luck: obviously Great-uncle Harry had a lot of luck. Equally obviously, he didn't inherit his great-

1. Abbot et al., *Johns Hopkins Medical Journal* 134, 1974.

uncle Gregor's corpulence or his failing heart . . . but then neither have I inherited Harry's bony frame or his longevity: achondroplastics do not survive well beyond their fourth or fifth decade. I am awaiting the outcome with curiosity.

The name on both Uncle Harry's death certificate and his will was still Heinrich Weiss. Phenotype may be modified but it doesn't change.

The residue of my said moneys shall stand possessed in trust in equal shares (if more than one) for such of them my niece the said Emily Lambert and my great-niece the said Beatrice Lambert and my great-nephew the said Benedict Lambert as shall be living at my death provided . . .

"He's left the loot to us," my sister Beatrice exclaimed. The final codicil had a romantic flavor to it:

I desire that I be cremated and my ashes scattered to the wind from the seashore when the wind is blowing in a southeasterly direction.

So it was that on a meteorologically apposite afternoon Beatrice, my mother, and I stood on the esplanade at Eastbourne, Beatrice holding aloft an urn supplied by the Eastbourne Crematorium and looking positively pre-Raphaelite in flowing dress and loose hair. Gulls hung in the wind at about the same height as us, eyeing us in case we had sandwiches. Mother held her hat on against the wind. "I think it's morbid," she kept saying. "That Wise family always was a bit touched. Why couldn't he be put in the ground like anyone else?"

But it all appealed to Beatrice. "It's rather endearing. How far do you think he'll get?" She had assumed that he wanted to be blown back toward Austria.

"Pevensey?" I suggested.

"That's not even out to sea. Surely he'll make Calais with this wind."

"Calais is miles away. Dieppe, more like."

"I once went to Dieppe with your father," Mother said. "On a day return. I never dreamt we'd send Uncle Harry there."

The gulls screamed with laughter and derision at the whole absurd performance. Beatrice removed the top of the urn and peered in at him. She showed me a pile of grayish powder.

"I don't want to see," warned Mother. "It's not right, somehow. Like seeing him without any clothes on. Come on, get on with it. I'm dying a death, it's that cold."

So Beatrice raised her arm. She called "Ready, steady . . . go!" as though someone were taking part in a race. Then she shook the urn, and Harry Wise sprayed out into the air like a little puff of washing powder. The gulls swooped expectantly, but even they didn't read the wind correctly, for at that very moment there was a gust and a swirl, and the cloud of powder swept around and blew back in our faces.

"Oh, how awful!" Mother protested, coughing and flapping. "I really think that's the end!"

We were back in his bungalow in time for tea. Mother fiddled in the kitchen while Beatrice and I conducted a rapid search through his desk for unpaid bills and the like. Beatrice opened drawers with relish. "It's horrible going through the old boy's stuff," she complained unconvincingly. "I hope we don't find dirty pictures or anything. I feel he might be watching." It seemed better not to tell her that in a sense Uncle Harry *was* still present, ancestral dandruff in her hair and on her shoulders.

While she went through the contents of the desk, I, partly in hope of those dirty pictures, partly with a sense of continuity with my distant Mendelian past, concentrated on the lower drawers. Perhaps there would be something, a scrap of a letter maybe, from Great-great-great-uncle Gregor. Among the papers — envelopes of dusty photographs, bundles of dusty letters all sequestered away in cardboard boxes — I came across the portrait photograph of Gottlieb Weiss with his first wife and the stout priest, the one taken in Vienna. Somehow it lacked the vividness I recalled from seeing it as a child. The figures appeared wooden and inert, the face of the cleric a patch of white, barely recognizable as the famous friar.

Finally I opened the last box of all. Inside it, on the top of a pile of papers, discolored and crisp with age, was a pamphlet of a dozen pages. It might have been a theater program, but it wasn't. Across the cover was written

GOTTLIEB WEISS'S ANATOMICAL CURIOSITIES

"Oh dear," Beatrice said as I showed it to her. Gottlieb and Heinrich Weiss, it transpired, had once run a freak show.

At that moment Mother came in with the tea. "Didn't you know?" she asked carelessly when she saw what Beatrice had found. "I thought Harry would have mentioned it. He was always going on about the past, the old bore."

Her offhanded manner did not deceive me. Gottlieb Weiss had run a circus of the deformed and the dispossessed, and with strange, Teutonic tact, Uncle Harry had kept the whole episode secret from me. I turned the pages. They were all there in the program, all illustrated and described in precise detail — the conjoined twins, "straight from Siam"; the bearded lady; the human gorilla; the giant; the family of midgets; the wart man, whose face (a blurred photograph bore witness) was peppered with a thousand papillae; the man-mountain (forty-three stone); the three-legged boy. There was even the cat-child, "half human, half feline, with the plaintive cry of a kitten," although that particular act did not survive Manchester. It was expunged from the show and the parents were duly paid off, the fact recorded along with everything else in the leatherbound tome that I found in the bottom of the box. The records were precise. So too was the timetable, from London to Nottingham, to Manchester, to Liverpool, to Birmingham, and back to London for a grand display at the Hammersmith Palladium. Everything relating to the show was preserved there among Uncle Harry's things: copies of contracts (. . . *that the aforementioned Joseph, having the appearance of a chimpanzee, shall agree to display himself, naked but for a covering for the loins, for a fee of* . . .), copies of flyers, a folder of press cuttings ("A remarkable if somewhat gruesome experience," in the view of the *Liverpool Daily Post*), even a photograph (sepia, blurred) of the entrance to the show itself, with the name displayed in a curve of lights above the ticket booth:

GOTTLIEB WEISS'S
ANATOMICAL CURIOS

And in the foreground the owner and son, Gottlieb, now with a large beard, and his son Heinrich sporting a fine, curly mustache.

The last tour was dated 1914. Perhaps the war and the changing of names put an end to it; whatever the reason, Gottlieb had metamorphosed into Godley by the time the next enterprise surfaced among Uncle Harry's papers:

About what did Great-grandfather Godley lecture? I opened a pamphlet and discovered that he lectured about the "Science of Human Genetics, founded on the new Mendelian Principles, being a Full Exposition of the Danger faced by the British Race through a Deterioration of its Genetic Stock."

Former freak-show manager Godley Wise had become a eugenicist. There was a list of initial subscribers to his society. Did they, I wonder, ever see a satisfactory intellectual return on their investment? They included Mr. H. G. Wells, Mr. G. B. Shaw, Mr. H. Belloc. Strange bedfellows, indeed.

Great-great-great-uncle Gregor was sent to the University of Vienna in October 1851, to prepare for another attempt at the teaching examination. Nowadays Vienna is the overblown capital of a small, smug province, but then it was Imperial Vienna, the Vienna of the Habsburgs: Vienna, Wien, Viden, Bécs, a crucible, a melting pot of nations, a fusion of genes — German, Slav, Magyar, Gypsy, Jew, half a million souls, all the nations of *Mitteleuropa* bubbling, arguing, creating, protesting, seething together. The revolution of 1848 was a recent memory. The city was a place of intellectual turmoil and vitality, with the rationalists and democrats in conflict with the church and state. Sigmund Freud was on the way. So too was Vienna's guilty secret, Adolf Hitler. It was to this city that the callow young priest from Heinzendorf set off on the night train from Brünn on October 27, 1851. He carried with him a letter from Abbot Napp to the minister Andreas von Baumgartner. What else did he bring from provincial Brünn to cosmopolitan Vienna? A fine-honed and perceptive mind? An incisive brilliance? An inspired imagination? Genius?

He never even took a degree. He attended Doppler's lectures on experimental physics, and Franz Unger's on botany, as well as a course in higher mathematical physics given by von Ettinghausen; but he never took a degree. Thus is genius educated. But the influence of Unger — an avowed and controversial evolutionist who earned the enmity of the Church — was decisive, as was the mathematics learned at the feet of the physicists. For a while the young friar acted as a demonstrator in Doppler's Physical Institute. He also joined the Zoological and Botanical Society of Vienna. He listened and he thought. He acquired ideas, but little in the way of self-confidence; he acquired intellectual ambition, but little self-assurance.

In 1853 he returned to Brünn, and in the spring of the next year he began work as an unqualified substitute teacher at the Brünn Modern School. He was thirty-one years old, the product of an approximate and inconsistent education; yet somewhere within him an ember glowed. He began to breed plants, fuchsias and others, in the back garden of the monastery.

And peas . . .

Pisum sativum, the garden pea, is a member of the Papilionaceae family, a workaday group with blossoms that dance like butterflies among the foliage. These papilionaceous flowers possess five petals: the large, vivid, and vivacious standard; the two wings; and two others that form the keel or *carina,* a sweet, sleek, and secretive sheath. Within, moist and fragile, lie the reproductive organs.

No chance choice. You select your material with care. Being food plants, they come in a number of distinct varieties, and others have already crossed them artificially with success.[2] The keel ensures self-pollination under normal conditions, so different strains are certain to be pure, and the flowers are large and therefore easily manipulated. Mendel watched and examined and thought. He had the mind of a chessplayer (he *was* a chessplayer) and he watched nature's moves patiently.

Is it possible to draw him out of the past, out of the shadows of the few photographs that remain, out of the vague stories of Uncle Harry, out of fusty recollection and textbook repetition? Can the man live in any sense? "Watch," he said.

Bratranek watched. Scrawny and self-satisfied, Bratranek smiled at the sight of the younger man down on his knees among the vegetables.

"You must get down to see properly," Mendel muttered. "It's no use just standing around like a damned priest. Kneel before Mother Nature."

Complaining, Bratranek hitched up his skirts and knelt, while Mendel rooted among

2. E.g., T. A. Knight and J. Goss in England.

the chaos of stems and tendrils for a suitable flower to show. His fingers were grimy. Just like a peasant's. Blood will out. "These here are the dwarfs. Obviously. Obviously they're the dwarfs. Now what we do is . . ." He bit his lower lip and frowned with concentration, pulling open one of the immature flowers, peering at it through his gold-rimmed glasses, muttering almost as though addressing the plants themselves rather than the thin priest at his side. "There's my little child. Remove the stamens" — scissors snipped — "and there we are. Gone. When she is ripe, that flower will become the female parent. Bag." He snapped his fingers behind him. Bratranek handed over one of the paper bags that he had been given to carry. Mendel slipped it over the selected flower. "Now you may watch the transfer of pollen. The useful thing is that you get flowers at all stages of maturity. Fruit down at the bottom, mature flowers halfway up, unopened buds at the top. Couldn't be better."

The friar clambered to his feet and led the way over to the line of tall plants, huffing and puffing and stumbling over the uneven soil of the bed, muttering as he went. "What did Bacon say? 'Nature reveals her secrets when put to the torture,' was that it? But it is not torture. It is a caress." He grinned at

Bratranek, a camel-hair paintbrush in his hand. "Nature reveals her secrets when she is *stroked*," he said. He opened a mature flower and dabbed at it and held up the brush to show a tiny speck of golden pollen on the tip. "There. This" — returning to the dwarfs, kneeling down among the ragged stems once more — "goes here." Another bagged flower was unveiled for a moment to reveal the sequestered flower. The paintbrush slipped in among the delicate petals like a tongue. Mendel scribbled something on the paper bag and put it back in place. "Female pure tall, crossed with male pure dwarf."

Bratranek look pained. "This is disgusting."

"It may be disgusting, but it's natural. Wasn't your Goethe an admirer of nature?"

"The higher flights of the human spirit, not mere sex. Anyway, what is natural about this . . . *manipulation?*" Bratranek pronounced the word with distaste, as though the modifier *genital* were implied.

"What on earth do you imagine plant breeders *do*, man? Cast spells?"

"And once you've performed this . . . unnatural act?"

"I will harvest the hybrid peas and plant them out. They will all be tall. The tall dominates the dwarf, you understand?"

"If you know the result already, what's the point?"

"But when they self-pollinate and we get the hybrid generation,[3] then we shall see. I have a theory, you see? The dwarfs that have vanished in the first generation will reappear in the second, one dwarf for every three tall plants on average. It is all a question of probability. Just like the lottery. I used to play the lottery in Vienna. What is the chance of a winning ticket, eh? Pretty small. Here the probability of getting a dwarf factor or a tall factor from a hybrid parent is one-half. One-half multiplied by one-half gives one-quarter. The probability of being dwarf is one-quarter. It is no more than a matter of logic."

Bratranek seemed unimpressed. "Mathematics in botany? What on earth is it all about? And *when* do you expect all this?"

"The first pods in a week's time . . . and the hybrids planted out next year. Then I get the first hybrid generation the year after that. Oh, believe me, I would like some way of creating two crops per year, but . . ." Mendel shrugged. "That's not the way with the pea."

3. In Mendel's own terminology this would be the *first* hybrid generation, although standard practice in Mendelian genetics is to call it the *second* filial or hybrid generation.

A bell rang from beyond the monastery building. *"Naturae enim non imperatur, nisi parendo,"* said Bratranek.

Mendel gathered up his things and followed his companion across the court. " 'Truly nature may not be commanded, except by obeying her.' Have I got it right?"

"More or less. Also Bacon; but Francis, not Roger."

"But the thing I don't yet understand . . . one of the things, anyway . . . is where all these different varieties *come* from. Nobody thinks about this. They are just ordinary seeds available from any supplier in the town. They breed true, so they are stable; but do they *arise* in some manner? Sports, they call them. How do they arise? This surely has some bearing on the question of speciation. How do they arise?"

Bratranek shrugged. "I really don't see that it matters much. Would all this apply to animals? That's the main point. Man, even. Would it apply to man? I mean, in man you have *gradations* of height, don't you?" Bratranek opened the door into the building.

Mendel muttered and fussed outside, kicking mud off against a stone. "You don't, you know," he said.

"Don't what?"

"In man. You don't have gradations of

height. Not in this sense."

"What are you talking about? I'm taller than you by . . ." Bratranek drew himself up as though to measure the matter. "A few inches at any rate. And Pavel . . ."

"Dwarfs, you fool, not you and me. Circus dwarfs." Mendel pushed past him through the door. "Come. I'll show you."

"You're keeping circus dwarfs in your room?"

"Don't be an idiot."

They went up the back stairs, Mendel in his socks, Bratranek clumping up behind in muddy shoes. "You've got a hole in your heel," Bratranek said, but Mendel ignored him. He was standing in front of the door to his room, searching for his key among the folds of his soutane. When he discovered it, he gave a small grunt of satisfaction, as though finding it were not always the case. As the door opened, a smell assaulted Bratranek, the warm and fusty smell of acetamide. "Those mice. No wonder the abbot complained."

"They don't smell as bad as he does."

The room was spacious but full, full of desk and papers, a trunk, two upright chairs, a table with a brass microscope on it and a box of microscope slides, a wardrobe, a row of old and battered boots against the skirting board, some seedlings in a tray, and, beneath the window, a row of five wooden cages. Sawdust was strewn on the floor in front of them. The mice scrabbled at the wire grilles with tiny, exact claws. Behind the noise of their scrabbling, there was another sound, a small crying like the sound of nestling birds. Mendel crouched down in front of the cages.

"It's exactly the same," he said, poking his finger at one of the small noses. "I've just completed the first generation from the hybrids. It's exactly the same. I crossed an albino mouse with a dark brown one, and all the offspring were dark brown. Three males and four females. From them I made three pairs of brother with sister." He looked around. "That was six weeks ago. These three cages." He pointed. Mice scrabbled. Bratranek bent down to look. In the backs of the cages the mothers could been seen on their nests. Beneath two of them, small, pinkish blots writhed and squealed. "A total of nineteen pups," Mendel explained. "Their hair is just appearing, so you can tell already. The hybrid parents were all brown, but some of the young are albino. Just as with the peas. The albino disappears in the hybrids, but comes out in the next generation, just as with the peas. There are five albinos and fourteen brown. Of course it isn't a large enough sample yet. Not like the peas. But the ratio is two and four-fifths to one. Just the same as the peas, the same three-to-one ratio. It really is the most basic mathematics."

"But what does all this mean?"

"It means just what you asked. It means mice are no different. It means animals are no different. It means man is no different."

My doctorate took me the statutory three years and created something of a sensation. Not much, but something. "The Effect of Induced Point Mutations in the Homeobox Gene *HOX7* in the Mouse, *Mus musculus*." I published a number of subsidiary papers in the course of the work, and I had one semester at Johns Hopkins University in Baltimore as a graduate student. I heard Nirenberg lecture on the genetic code, and visited the Salk Institute, where Holley had first isolated transfer RNA (1 milligram from 90 kilograms of yeast, can you imagine that?), and argued with Watson at Cold Spring Harbor over the moral implications of recombinant DNA techniques. "Hey, this little guy's something else," I heard someone say of me. With my doctorate came the offer of a post at the Royal Institute for Genetics in London. A job. A salary. Lecturer in Molecular Genetics.

103

[Probe]

The Royal Institute for Genetics was opened as the Galton Institute for Plant and Animal Breeding. It is housed in one of those red-brick piles in Kensington that serve indifferently as museums, hospitals, Anglo-Catholic churches, or university colleges — buildings reeking with that nineteenth-century neo-gothic conviction that almost everything has been done and proved, and anything missing is just around the corner and will be pretty straightforward when you come to it.

The Institute is strung out uneasily between the old and the new, between tradition and innovation, between the imperial past and an empirical present. On the one hand there is the old building with its ogive windows and gothic vaulting and statues of long-dead scientists in niches like sex maniacs skulking in the shadows; on the other hand, very much on the other hand, accessible through the kind of elevated plastic walkway that you find in airports, gleaming and humming like a machine, are the Gordon Hewison Laboratories, a cathedral of the new age where priests and scribes decipher and transcribe the texts, and find damnation written there just as clearly as they ever did in medieval times.

I followed the director, James Histone, into this other world. The lighting was even and pitiless. The air had the smooth texture of dust-filtering and sterility. "Relax, relax," he kept saying to people. He wore a shiny gray suit and a spotted bow tie, and he beamed on everything with the eternal optimism of a television talk-show host. "Just an informal visit. Take no notice." But of course people did take notice. They looked up from their benches as we passed by, and they stared for that fraction of a second that I can time so exactly. Some smiled nervously. One or two nodded as though in recognition. You notice everything, that's the trouble: every wince, every grimace, every dilation of every pupil. You see them looking when your back is turned; you hear them talking when you are out of earshot; you know what they are thinking. In the street it is the fascination of the freak show, of the monster, of the walking gargoyle; in the laboratories, within the temple of molecular biology, it is the thrill of seeing a manifestation of the texts that they read with such minute attention, as though a beast from the Apocalypse were to walk through the scriptorium of a medieval monastery and by his existence confirm the truth of everything that the monks had just transcribed.

In the common room, future colleagues stooped to shake hands. The women looked motherly and uneasy; the men exuded a dreadful, forced bonhomie. "Good to see you, Ben. Good to have you with us." Patricia Primer (red hair, freckles) explained her work on supercoiling and overwinding, demonstrating the processes with twists of her supple fingers that evoked a frisson of delight in poor old Benedict the diminutive goat; Ochre Codon (loose, voluptuous) gazed earnestly down at me and talked about overlapping genes in adenovirus; Vincent Vector (extinct acne craters and oily hair) explained a system for winning the football pools using the linkage analysis computer program. "I'm sure you'll all get on fine, just fine," the director said. His conversation was loaded with random repeats. "You'll have a fine team," he assured me when we were back in his office. "A fine, dedicated team. I predict great things, great things . . ."

His desk bore a shiny silver model of one turn of DNA, a shining spiral staircase that led upward like Jacob's ladder toward an equivocal paradise. A silver plaque at the foot announced that he had received the Biological Institute of Georgia Annual Recognition for Scientific Endeavor or some such. On the walls there were framed photographs of the man himself with Crick, with Nirenberg, with Sanger. His main topic of conversation was money. He talked about supply and demand, production utilities and patents. "We're in the marketplace now," he kept saying. "There are no free meals."

I interrupted him: "There is just one thing. I'm rather keen on my own research project. I'm confident I can get the funding for it . . ."

"Your *own* project?"

"The identification of the gene for achondroplasia."

There was a silence. The director watched me through the intricate latticework of the DNA molecule. "Achondroplasia," he repeated. "Of course. It's a dominant, isn't it?"

"Certainly."

"One hundred percent penetrance."

"Regrettably."

His smile, at first larded with sympathy, metamorphosed. It became a careful, complex thing — a look of disappointment, a subtle blend of understanding and regret, a mute acknowledgment that the world is a bitter place and there is no alternative but to plow one's furrow as best one can. "There's no money in dominants," he said sorrowfully. "Not unless they're late-onset. No money, no future."

"But I can get funding. That's the one advantage being . . . like I am. There are lots of organizations interested. The Little People of America, groups like that. When they see me coming they reach for their covenant forms . . ."

He looked skeptical. "Recessives, that's the name of the game. Recessives play on people's anxieties. They can spend a whole lifetime worrying whether they're carriers, and then we come along and offer them a test. Recessives and X-linked. Look what they're doing with fragile-X nowadays. And cystic fibrosis. Just imagine the commercial possibilities if you can design and patent a probe for something like Gaucher's disease . . ."

Gaucher's disease has a high incidence among Ashkenazi Jews — Ashkenazi Jews control the world's banking and commercial system (vide *Mein Kampf*) — ergo a test for Gaucher's disease will earn lots of money.

"You still can't *treat* any of them," I pointed out.

He opened his hands as though to display the obvious. "You give the parents the right to decide whether to terminate." And then his gesture metamorphosed into one of helplessness. "But with achondroplasia . . . ninety percent of cases are sporadic, aren't they? New mutations. I mean, your own parents . . . ?"

"Both normal."

"There you are." He spread plausible hands once more. "What's the point? Who'll buy a thing like that?"

"People want to *know*. We" — I hated the collective pronoun — "*we* want to know our enemy."

He nodded. "I understand your interest, Ben. Don't think I don't. But the world has moved on from those days when you could find something out for its own sake. Nowadays it has to have a commercial function." Then he brightened up. "Is it true what I've heard? You're some kind of descendant of Mendel? Is that true?"

"A family story."

He pursed his lips and looked at me with his head cocked sideways, like a tailor considering me for a suit. "We could make something of it, you know. A bit of publicity never does anyone any harm. How about if I get in touch with the head of programming at the BBC? Good friend of mine. There's mileage in that, all right. Might even get them to do a documentary. Would you be prepared? We must discuss it . . ."

I smiled back at him. "Only if I can have support for my project. I'll only play the circus clown if you'll come along with me."

"Bartering, eh?"

"The marketplace," I reminded him.

After our interview, I wandered the temple precincts on my own. More by chance than design I found myself outside the library — the Bateson Library, named after the first director of the Institute. A bronze bust of the man stood at the entrance like the image of a titular saint at the door of a chapel. Bateson was one of those who had come second, one of the great losers, a blunt Yorkshireman who worked on inheritance in the last years of the nineteenth century, and found himself trumped by the discovery of Mendel's paper. All that was left to Bateson was to travel to Brünn in the hope of finding out something about the man who had anticipated his own discoveries by twenty-five years. Bateson it was who coined a name for the new science: *genetics*. His etymological originality doesn't even merit a mention in the *OED*.

I waddled disconsolately through the doors of the library, in search of the *Journal of Molecular Biology* or something. Picture me there, standing just inside the doorway, looking down the carpeted length of the main reading room. Traffic in the Cromwell Road is dulled to insensibility by double glazing. The place is warm and hushed, scented with the dry dust of books and a hint of reverence. There are chandeliers hanging from a florid ceiling. A notice warns that anyone wanting to use photocopying facilities will have to pay in advance.

Then, as I watch, someone coughs, and at the sound the woman behind the librarian's desk looks around with a frown of impatience. Her expression barely registers surprise as she notices me standing there. "It *is* you," she exclaims.

How do you describe one of those moments in your life when the past leans forward to tap you on the shoulder? Turning point? Crisis? Epiphany? No such thing in fact. At the time, in time, it was a moment of complete inconsequence: two graduate students were sitting together in one of the bays, holding hands and consulting the same book; another reader was seated at one of the computer terminals, staring morosely at a screenful of luminous green text; the librarian was watching me. With those eyes.

"I thought it'd be you," she went on.

"That'll be that fellow I used to know, I said to myself. That'll be that Benedict. *Doctor* Lambert now. I knew he'd go places."

"Shh," said the man at the computer. The graduate students looked up. Surprise, amusement, curiosity, plain revulsion, you could have read all those emotions on their several faces. It was all rather embarrassing.

"Maybe we'd better go outside," the librarian suggested. So we went out and hovered around the bust of Bateson and didn't know quite what to say. At least, *I* didn't know what to say. She never seemed to have that kind of problem. "You could have knocked me over with a feather, I was that excited when I heard." That was the kind of vocabulary Miss Piercey employed, a farrago of oohs and aahs and fancy-thats.

"Heard what?"

"That the new Doctor Lambert was" — she hesitated and looked embarrassed — "of diminutive stature. Not that I expected him to remember me, of course."

Those eyes, like an ill-matched pair of costume jewels. They brought to mind a teddy bear I had owned as a child. One eye had come unsewn and my mother came to the rescue with a transplant. But she wasn't able to match the startling blue of the original, and so the replacement had been a lucid

112

ochre, like a barley sugar. One cornflower blue, one amber, a strange mutation. "Naturally I remember you, Miss Piercey."

"Mrs., now."

"Mrs. Piercey?"

"Don't be silly. Miller. Mrs. Miller." She made a face. "Not that it's a grand success, but you do what you can, don't you?"

I agreed that you did, and wondered how I was going to get out of this one. There was something faintly embarrassing about being confronted with my adolescent lusts in this unexpected manner.

"Anyway, you'll have your own work to do, won't you?" she said. "Won't want to be bothered with me and my life. If there's anything you want, just you ask." She smiled down on me for a moment and then turned and clipped her way back into the library. I watched the gray sheen of her legs as she went, the slender curve of ankle and calf — a kind of perfection.

Miss Piercey. Miss J. Piercey. Mrs. J. Miller. I laughed when I discovered what the *J* stood for. I had imagined June. June, moon, tune, it would have fitted well enough. Do names fit their owners, or do the owners grow to fit their names? It is true, isn't it? The name seems as much a part of the person's phenotype as his nose or ears or eyes. Even I *feel* Benedict.

Miss J. Piercey.

Jean.

Don't laugh.

Mendel was a celibate like me, although our reasons were perhaps different. What did he do for sex, I wonder? Was he a hand-reared man? Did he lust after choirboys, or after respectable widows? We expect something, don't we? True absolute celibacy is impossible, surely. There must be something, even if it is only a discreet retreat to the bathroom and a thrilling auto-caress — and while that is going on, something must pass through the mind, some image of thigh or buttock or muscled torso, some cerebral picture of silken hair or buttoned boot or tight corset. What was it that stirred Great-great-great-uncle Gregor, I wonder?

There were opportunities, of course — during those three years in Vienna, for example. Who is to say that he didn't succumb to temptation then? Imperial Vienna, the Vienna of the Habsburgs, the Vienna of the operetta and the waltz, the Vienna of encounter and assignation in the Volksgarten. Opportunity knocks on the mind and the imagination. Heart palpitating, did he go for solitary walks around the central markets near his lodgings, where you could buy flesh or fowl for a few kreuzer? Did he look and merely wonder, or did he summon up the blood and once or twice take a girl back to the cramped lodging house just beyond the junction with Invalidenstrasse, where people came and went at all hours of the day, and blind eyes were always turned in this city that knew so much and saw so much? A young priest on his own, struggling with his books, distant from all that he knew. Lonely. Easy enough to doff the dog-collar. Easy enough to stir the sympathy of some young Slovak girl up from the country to earn an easy kreuzer in the city.

Holding strictly to his vows, he shunned all relationships with women. Thus Hugo Iltis in the biography. The late-twentieth-century mind nudges and winks, and doesn't really believe nonsense like that, does it? There is, for example, the conundrum of Frau Rotwang. How curious that even in the modest 1920s, Iltis should follow his disclaimer with this gentle and malicious insinuation: *Niessl, indeed, used to speak of a certain Frau Rotwang whom Mendel called upon frequently in the early years.*

Rotwang. Red-cheek. Cheeks flushed faintly with embarrassment or enthusiasm. Frau Rotwang, wife of the proprietor of one of the cotton mills that had sprung up recently along the banks of the river Zwittawa. Herr Rotwang owns a large town house near the Capuchin church and a modest but productive estate out in the country. He is frequently away on business, in Prague, in Vienna, occasionally in Munich; and Frau Rotwang — pretty, younger than her husband, modest, devout — is often on her own. She is an amateur gardener. It is a respectable pastime, and Frau Rotwang is a most respectable young lady, the kind who might be expected to receive calls from a friar of the Augustinian monastery, a man who can offer her advice both spiritual and botanical. Walking back to the monastery from the Brünn Modern School on Johannesgasse, it is barely a detour to pass by the Rotwang house on Josefsgasse. The maid would have been familiar with the small, smiling figure of Father Mendel.

"Frau Rotwang is in the morning room, Father. Can I take the plant for you?"

"No. No, I will carry it myself, thank you."

The heavy furnishings of a bourgeois house of the nineteenth century, all velvet and plush. Drapes on the tables, heavy brocade curtains, elaborate gas lamps (new marvel) on the walls, and woodwork everywhere — dark, ornate woodwork, giving off a smell of resin and polish and, despite the labors of a small army of maids, dust. Mendel climbs the stairs through puddles of colored light cast down onto the floor from the stained-glass panes above the landing — the Rotwang arms, fanciful and absurd, emblazoned by the morning sun.

"What a *pleasure* to see you, Pater Gregor." That was how she always greeted him, as though his punctual arrival were always a surprise. "Do come and sit. You must be exhausted after a day teaching all those boys." A smile, slightly simpering; a blush. *Rotwang,* red-cheek. She is wearing a dress of some stiff and shiny stuff, undoubtedly the latest thing, undoubtedly the latest color — purple like a priest's vestments for a funeral, one of the new aniline dyes. Against this heavy dress, her neck and face are fragile and pale, like porcelain. Frau Rotwang asks the maid to bring coffee and poppyseed cake (Father Gregor's favorite), and only then does she notice his hand hidden behind his back. A sudden coy glance. "What is it that you are hiding, Pater Gregor? You are hiding something from me . . ."

Of course he is, all the time. He is hiding his devotion; but in its place, with an absurd flourish, like a conjuror in one of the booths in the Klosterplatz producing a rabbit from a hat, he presents a poor surrogate — the potted plant.

The pink of her cheeks spreads. It is almost the color of the flowers on the little shrub. "For me?"

"For you, Frau Rotwang. A fuchsia. I bred it myself. I have taken the liberty . . ."

"The liberty, Pater Gregor?"

"Of naming it Adelaide. The Adelaide fuchsia."

"Oh." A small exhalation of breath. A shock. It is the first time that he has ever hinted at her Christian name, the first indication that he even knows it. The little flowers dance and bob like so many tiny ballerinas as he holds the plant out toward her.

"You are not offended?"

"No, no." Pink, fuchsia pink, suffuses neck and face. "Honored. I am honored." She takes the potted plant and admires it. "It is wonderful. Oh, wonderful." Somehow she contrives to touch his arm while trying at the same time to hold the pot. The pot almost tumbles. She moves forward to save it. He grasps the pot, her wrist, her elbow, and for a moment they have stepped over the invisible barrier that convention draws between them. For a moment confusion threatens to wreak havoc amid the careful formalities of their acquaintance.

"Oh, my goodness. I think I must sit."

He lowers her into a chair and places the potted plant on a side table. There is a blessed interruption as a maid comes in with a tray. Father Gregor feels hot beneath his soutane. The girl is detailed to take the plant to the conservatory, while Frau Rotwang regains composure behind the ornate coffeepot. The balance of things settles into its former equilibrium.

"Now tell me about your children," Frau Rotwang says, pouring. There is the faintest innuendo about her words. Frau Rotwang has no children. Neither, for quite other reasons, does Father Gregor. But both pretend. Father Gregor's children are his plants, particularly his fuchsias, but also his peas, rows and rows of them in the convent garden, twining glaucous fingers around one another and around the pea-sticks, clinging like children to their mother's apron.

"You must come and visit them sometime. I could explain my ideas about them to you . . ."

By way of contrast, Frau Rotwang's children are her dogs, four of them that wriggle around the skirts of Mendel's soutane, and beg for food, and a fifth that goes straight to his mistress and cringes at her feet. "What's the matter with you?" Frau Rotwang asks of it as she lifts it into her arms. The dog laps wetly at her chin, tries to get at a crumb of poppyseed cake that adheres momentarily to the crimson Rotwang lower lip. "Naughty little boy. You are jealous, aren't you?" She gazes over the animal's narrow head at her guest. "Jealous of Pater Gregor."

The dogs are dachshunds, achondroplastic dwarfs. Father Gregor has already asked for their pedigrees . . .

It was in London that I finally broke my enforced celibacy. In my case there is no conundrum, and no inclination to withstand the rigors of temptation; but up to then I had had no more than a long and intense affair with a variety of glossy magazine lovelies who lolled on chaise longues or sat, bold and brave, astride chairs and touched themselves with delicate talons almost as though unaware of someone looking. There were also tawdry videos and occasionally the live equivalent, a slot-machine booth for voyeurs where you could pay rather too much to keep a shutter from falling on the vision of strapped and hirsute flesh on the far side of the glass. But the real thing, that was what I desired.

I did it in the only way within my powers;

don't imagine that it was easy. I took days, weeks, to reach a satisfactory conclusion. You have guessed, of course. Many evenings I drove — oh yes, I drive. I have built-up pedals and an extended gear lever and I park where the hell I please because I've got one of those window stickers. I haven't got *that* kind of pride. My kind of pride is different and far more difficult to handle — many evenings I drove, cruised, in those areas where the assets of the city are displayed to the roving customer's eye. I looked and wondered and let imagination and my fist play their paltry tricks, until one evening, charged up with the impoverished courage of whiskey, I pulled into the pavement alongside a shadowy and expectant figure and wound down the window.

She stepped forward. "I got a place just round the corner, love," she said; and then saw what she was taking on. "Oh, Christ. It'll be extra for you. Sorry, dear, but that's the way it is. Market forces. Extra for special treatment, extra for gross deformities."

"How much?"

"It'd be best if we discuss it at my place. The narks are around and they're being right buggers at the moment. Something about a cabinet minister being shortchanged the other night. D'you mind?" She climbed in beside me. She was lean and brassy, her makeup applied in dense layers of primary color, her legs sheathed in black net. "Bit parky at this time of night, innit? Just carry straight on and turn left at the pub. You should find an empty meter at this time."

Her room was over a Chinese restaurant. The Tu Can. "Only two can play," she said, and shrieked with laughter. She greeted the owner by name as we went in, and muttered "Slit-eyed bastard" after him as I followed her up the stairs. You could smell the cooking and hear plates crashing around in the kitchens below.

"My boo-dwar," she announced, opening the first door.

The room was all pink ruches and fluffy teddy bears and flowery perfume. There was a large mirror at the head of the bed, and another on the wall. A dressing table was flooded with a mess of makeup and tubs of cream and boxes of paper tissue. There was a tube of lubricating jelly, economy size, on the bedside table.

"I don't want the mirrors," I told her.

"No problem." She drew discreet curtains, and the several images of diminutive me and angular, glittering her vanished. "D'you want to get straight down to it? It'll be fifty quid for straight penetration, if that's all right. Twenty quid for a hand-job. I try and avoid too much of the tricky stuff, know what I mean? Can get a bit dangerous at times. Done it before, have you? Well, there's got to be a first time. Oh, and you'll have to use a johnnie, I'm afraid. I used to charge extra for doing it without, but I reckon these days it just isn't worth it . . ." She unbuttoned her blouse, then hesitated and looked at me quizzically. "What you reckon? Everythin' off, or do you fancy the underclothes?" She tossed her brassiere aside to display implausibly pneumatic breasts with carefully rouged nipples. "Like that okay? Come on, dearie, don't be shy. Let me unbutton you." There was a thoughtful pause as her fingers worked. "My, that's not bad," she said.

"It's the only part of me that's unaffected," I told her.

"Let's see what it can do, then." She slid her knickers down — wide-mouthed, loud-mouthed French knickers — and presented herself to my gaze. "What you think of that, then?" She was entirely hairless. A gleaming, nude mons veneris was creased delectably by the pout of naked labia. Of course, it may have been the result of an assiduous use of razor and depilatory cream but, truth to tell, it was probably because she was a victim (happy? resigned? indifferent?) of testicular feminization syndrome (X-linked recessive, mapping to the long arm, Xq11), which condition renders chromosomally normal males (2A + XY) — I quote the literature — "voluptuously female but devoid of axillary and pubic hair."

She was a monster, like me.

I wondered, oh yes, in my desperate palpitating tumescence I wondered whether her mother had shown the developmental asymmetry of breasts, body hair, and vulva that carriers of the recessive condition sometimes manifest, the consequence of Lyonization (delicious, feline term), which turns off one of the X chromosomes at random in each body cell of every normal female, and so allows the feminization syndrome to show itself and not show itself, show itself and not, depending which X chromosome is active in which area. Now you see it, now you don't. Genetic prestidigitation, chromosomal sleight of hand.

"What you think of that, then?" she asked, and I demonstrated my feelings there and then, standing in front of her, while she tutted and commiserated and fumbled around with the Handi Wipes like a housewife with spilt milk. "Wait a few minutes and you can have another go, dear. Don't worry about a thing. I often get 'em like that, you know.

Quite a turn-on, eh?"

She came from Wales. You could hear it in her voice, the faint ring of the valleys still there beneath the glottal stops of the London basin. "You're all right in spite of everything," she assured me as she squatted on the bidet in the corner of the room after it was all over. "Can't be much fun for you, can it? Your parents the same, are they? What are they, circus or something?"

"No, they're not. They're normal."

She nodded, toweling herself between the legs. "Must make it worse. My brother's got a harelip. They say that's the same. Genetic. Come on, get your things on. I've got to get back to my pitch. You'd better leave first, if you don't mind. I don't like to be seen going out with a client." And then, smiling, she added, "You can come again if you like. If you know what I mean."

"I'd like to. If you don't mind." *If you don't mind.* I hated myself for that.

" 'Course not. Here's my card. You can ring in the morning and make an appointment if you like. I prefer doing it that way, in fact. There's an answerphone if I'm not in. Leave your number and I'll call you back."

EVE. FORBIDDEN FRUIT TASTES SWEETEST.

That's what the card said, above her number and beneath a crude line drawing of buttocks and garters. She was brisk and businesslike, selling wares like any other trader; not a tart with a heart, but an honest enough worker. I went to her four or five times and then had a blood test done, just in case. I was frightened, you see. Even with the condom I was frightened. I know how small viruses are.

[Selection]

In 1856 the great work began: seminal, both literally and figuratively. With mathematical rigor unknown at that time outside physics, Gregor Mendel was about to demonstrate the behavior of the fundamental genetic material. He was about to elucidate the dance of genes. But what would you have seen? What does genius at work look like? A stout, obtuse figure in dusty black stumping purposefully up the hill from the monastery every morning on his way to school, and back in the afternoon when lessons are over, calling in for coffee at the Rotwang house near the Capuchin church twice a week. A round, peasant face peering at the world through gold-rimmed spectacles, smiling to himself as though at some secret joke, nodding amiably to passing acquaintances. He is part of the landscape: a mere cleric, a mere teacher leading a sequestered life that is punctuated by the ringing of bells, circumscribed by timetables and calendars, defined by routine. Genius is an elusive quality.

"Good day, Father. How are you?"

"Oh, mustn't grumble, mustn't grumble."

"And the plants?"

"I find they grow on me." A joke he has made a hundred times, apparently without being aware of repetition. He will talk for a minute or two about the weather (a particular interest), about bees, about his pupils, and you will be expected to laugh at jokes that you don't always understand or, if you do, don't find particularly funny. Then: "If you'll excuse me, I really must be going. I have to see about my children."

Children. Sublimation, is that it? One clings to the idea eagerly. Doubtless the Blessed Sigmund Fraud (at that very moment going through his oral and anal phases in not-so-distant Freiburg, now Příbor) would have dismissed it thus. But what does the word explain? Objectively, it was certainly obsession. Mendel took two years merely to prepare the ground and a further eight years to carry out the work. Beginning with thirty-four different varieties of pea, he narrowed it down to twenty-two, and finally settled on seven strains with clearly contrasting characters: angular peas against round peas; yellow cotyledons[1] against green coty-

1. The "seed-leaf" that makes up most of the pea one eats.

ledons; white seed coat and flower against gray-brown seed coat with purple flower; smooth pod against constricted pod; green pod against yellow pod; axillary flowers against terminal flowers; tall stems against dwarf. And while the differing varieties hybridized in the garden behind the monastery, in his mind the logic of algebra hybridized with the facts of life.

$$(A + a)(A + a) = AA + 2Aa + aa$$

That is all it is, you see — the secrets of inheritance speared on the point of a simple binomial expansion. There is all the simplicity of genius. But what is the complexity beneath?

Year One (1856)

A total of 287 artificial crossings were carried out with seventy different plants from the selected pure varieties ($A \times a$).

Year Two (1857)

Hybrids (Aa) from the first-year crossings were planted out and scored. Exact numbers unknown, but there were 511 hybrid plants counted for seed shape and color alone.

These hybrids were left to self-pollinate (which is what they do naturally) and the peas collected, dried, and labeled for the next year.

Year Three (1858)

Four thousand six hundred twelve offspring from the previous year were planted out. They were counted and scored. In this generation the famous three-to-one ratios between dominant types (AA or Aa) and recessive types (aa) appeared. Individual dwarf plants were lifted and potted as soon as recognized, to ensure that they were not shaded by their tall neighbors. (He had a clear idea of the contrast between the inherited and the acquired, you see. He distinguished nature from nurture.) Again, self-pollination was allowed to take place in all plants. In this year Mendel also began to set up *combinations* of two or more characters together on the same plant — the bi- and trifactorial crosses.

Year Four (1859)

In this generation it was shown that all the recessive types from the previous year had produced nothing but recessive offspring, i.e., they were genetically pure. Of dominant types, some (one-third) were now shown to have been genetically pure, while the remainder (two-thirds) again produced dominant and recessive offspring in a three-to-one ratio, showing that they had been carrying the recessive character (i.e., were genetically impure hybrids). This was revealed by selecting one hundred of each of the 1858 dominant types and planting out ten seeds from each plant. This alone yields one thousand plants. In this year there are also the hybrids from the bifactorial and trifactorial crosses that were set up in 1858. Going through his paper, you lose count. From 1859 it becomes impossible to calculate with any accuracy the numbers of plants involved. Fisher[2] suggests over five thousand plants for 1859, and over six thousand for 1860. The greenhouse was working full-time. Row upon row of peas grew in the garden strip behind the monastery. Obsession? Possession? The friar was at once their master and their slave. The work became the focus that drew to itself all the perspective lines of his world, the vanishing point of the whole of his existence. All else — personal inadequacy, nagging spiritual doubts, ailing mother, dead father — disap-

2. Fisher, *Annals of Science* 1, 1936, 115–37.

peared as surely as the demons of night disappear in the plain light of day. The good friar had slipped his moorings and was away on the high seas, leaving ordinary mortals far behind. Land was out of sight below the horizon.

Year Five (1860)

Some monofactorial lines are continued to show that half of the offspring of hybrids breed true, i.e., are genetically exactly as pure as the original stock lines that started the whole work. The second generation from the first bifactorial and trifactorial crossings are also planted out, producing plants with all possible combinations of characters, and showing that a pair of factors controlling one character is inherited entirely separately from a pair of factors controlling another character (what became the so-called "second law"). In that year he also back-crossed double hybrids ($AaBb$) with pure recessives from the stock lines ($aabb$), using both pollen and ovules from the hybrids. In 1861 these back-cross results were sown, and gave a 1:1:1:1 ratio of four different offspring. This was to test his hypothesis, by showing that the double hybrids did indeed produce pollen and ovules of types AB, Ab, aB, and ab in equal proportions, just as he had assumed. In the same year, work was also begun on flowering time in peas, using an early-flowering and a late-flowering variety. Other pedigrees were continued from previous years, and experiments were set up using *Phaseolus,* the broad bean . . .

And so it goes on. Obsession? Given a diverse twist or two by fate — a different interlacing of synapses at some part of the cerebrum, a different twist of the neck at the moment of birth — it might have become the fixation of a psychotic, the hoarder of pornography, the Peeping Tom — or nothing more than the tiresome craze of a stamp collector. Throughout each spring and summer from 1854 to 1871 (by then he had moved on to other species), the man spent hours and hours tending his plants, pollinating, scoring, labeling, harvesting, drying, putting seeds away for the next year, puzzling and pondering, counting and tallying, recording his results in leatherbound books, explaining to anyone who would listen what was going on, feeling his way into one of the greatest secrets of the natural world — that each inherited character is determined by individual, distinct particles carried by the egg and by the pollen. That, for each simple inherited character, every offspring gains one such particle from its father and one from its mother. That the particles remain distinct and identifiable even though contrasting ones might temporarily come together in an individual. That you can follow the movement of these particles down through the generations and that they are passed on to the offspring just as they were gained from the parents. That pure luck determines which of two differing characters is passed on — the choice is chance.

Almost twenty years. Visitors were in the presence of a man inspired — a Beethoven or a Goethe — and all they saw was a dumpy, self-deprecating little friar with a sense of irony, a man who taught in the local high school and had a reputation for being reasonable and fair to his students, a man who smiled vaguely at the world through spectacles whose lenses were clouded with dust and, doubtless, pollen.

You don't display obsession, you see, not true obsession. You learn to hide it. You recognize the expression of indifference or incomprehension that creeps into the eyes of the listener. You learn the art of self-deprecation, the art of crypsis, the art of blending, mouselike, into the background. But beneath your bland and neutral exterior, you create confections of fantasy.

"You seem unhappy, Mrs. Miller."

She looked at me with those disparate eyes. "Please call me Jean. 'Mrs. Miller' seems so impersonal."

"Jean. You seem unhappy. Jean."

Mousy, morose, she perched on a small stool in the pub just around the corner from the Institute, and fiddled disconsolately with a half-pint of lager. I glanced at her legs and imagined, I'm afraid, floral underpants. Apart from those purely hypothetical floral underpants, she was wearing a woolen dress (gray to go with the mouse) and a paisley scarf. Miss Piercey, Miss Mousy. Miss Agouti. The agouti color in mice results from a band of yellow just below the tip of each hair. It is controlled by an autosomal dominant gene. The double recessive form is black-haired.

On her left hand she wore a wedding ring and an engagement ring. "Opal," she said, fiddling with the engagement ring. "Brings bad luck. I told him when we chose it. Opal brings bad luck, I said. He wouldn't listen. Fire opal signifies the fire of my love for you, that's what he said. He said things like that, things that turn a girl's head. I think he just wanted me for one thing, really." I shifted awkwardly on my stool, wondering how many things I wanted her for. Perched like that, I was almost at the same level as her. I could almost imagine leaning across the table (beaten copper) to take her hand and squeeze it comfortingly. "But you don't want to be hearing about my troubles, Doctor Lambert."

"For God's sake, stop calling me Doctor Lambert. If I'm to call you Jean, you must call me Benedict."

"Benedict." She smiled wanly. "Seems an awful long time ago, doesn't it? I'd only just left school, you know that. With just three O Levels. Taken on as a trainee librarian under some scheme or other. You know what I used to dream of?"

Hope and flesh rose in strange concord. "Tell me."

"The chief librarian." Hope dashed, flesh subsided. "He was a lovely man. That's why I left and came to London." Her disparate eyes glistened.

"I don't follow."

"Don't you remember him?"

"I only remember you."

She giggled, and maybe colored a little. "Oh, go on."

"It's true."

"Anyway, he was the chief librarian, and

he was what I dreamed of. Mr. Jacobs, he was. Gordon Jacobs."

Dimly I recalled a ponderous, graying man who had hovered in the background while I eyed the Piercey thighs. He had seemed old; probably he was only in his forties. "And?"

"He was married, with two children."

"Was there anything . . . ?"

"I shouldn't be telling you this . . ." Her fingers were hairless beyond the first joint. Presence or absence of hair on the middle phalanx of the fingers is under autosomal genetic control. My own fingers carry dark wisps of hair like punctuation marks on the mid-phalanx. I watched hers stroke beads of condensation from the glass of lager as she gazed into the past. "It happened once, after closing, by the fiction shelves."

"The fiction shelves?"

She looked up. "Fiction, *F* to *H*. I remember seeing the works of Catherine Gaskin over his shoulder. Do you know Catherine Gaskin?"

"Not personally."

"Oh, she's ever so good."

"What happened? At fiction, *F* to *H*, what happened?"

She blushed and looked away. "What do you think?"

"Right there?"

She nodded. "Right there."

"Standing up?"

A narrowing of the eyes. "Why are you so interested?"

"I'm trying to imagine it."

"*Doctor* Lambert!" She reddened further. "You're ever so cheeky. You're just as cheeky as you ever were as a boy." She took up her glass, almost knocking it over in her confusion.

"Do you mind?"

She took a sip, and laughed with surprise. "Not really. Actually, it's rather fun, confessing." She drained the glass and put it down. Not quite so mousy. "I've never told anyone this, you know? Didn't even tell my mum."

"What happened?"

"With Mr. Jacobs?"

"You didn't still call him Mr. Jacobs, did you? Not while . . ."

"It was the first time —"

"You were a virgin?"

"You really are *awful*. It was the first time that I called him Gordon. Up to then it had always been Mr. Jacobs. But there, at the fiction shelves, I called him Gordon."

"I should hope so. Considering what was going on."

"I thought it sounded rather silly, actually."

"And what happened next?" I had a vision of Mr. Jacobs and Miss Piercey working their way round the whole Dewey Decimal System. "Did you move on to nonfiction?"

She giggled wildly. Perhaps that single glass of lager had gone to her head. "You are dreadful. No, afterwards he got cold feet."

"You felt them?"

"It's a metaphor," she said reprovingly. "Gordon told me that it was all impossible, that I must get an abortion —"

"An *abortion?* You didn't get pregnant?"

"*If* I was pregnant. He would pay, but I must keep it all quiet, that it was all a horrible mistake, that he loved his wife and children, that I should go away, find another job, all that kind of thing. He was in a right panic, I can tell you." She put her hand to her mouth. "Here I am, laughing about it . . ."

"That's what you must do," I told her. "Laugh at it."

"And I gave in to him, you see. That's why I left home. I up and left and came down here, just as he wanted. And then I met Hugo Miller."

"And married him?"

"He married me, more like. Promised me the world and gave me a weekend in Brighton, if you know what I mean." She glanced at her watch. "Oh, Lor, I've got to go or I'll be late. You scientific staff are all right. You can go in and out at all hours, but we honest workers have to keep to the clock." She got up, pushing the table aside and almost upsetting the glasses. "See how clumsy I am? Can't walk straight for thinking. Here, let me pay for my lunch." She began to fumble in her handbag.

"I wouldn't hear of it," I said. "Doctor Lambert's treating you."

She looked at me with shining eyes. "Is he? Oh, how nice. I say, this is strange, isn't it? After all these years."

"Only seven."

"Seven years older, seven years wiser."

"Are you?"

"No."

Images got in the way of coherent thought. I imagined piercing Miss Piercey in the fiction section, she with her back against the Catherine Gaskins, me standing on the top of a library stool with my face pressed against her inadequate bosom; whereas actually we were leaving the pub and walking along the Cromwell Road and people were looking at us in that sideways manner. "That was nice, that was," she said.

"What was? The Catherine Gaskins?"

"You don't stop, do you? The *lunch.*" She

paused, and looked down at me. "I'd expected you to be . . ."

"What?"

"Difficult. I don't know. You know what they say about you?"

"No."

"Difficult. Difficult person, but a first-rate mind. That's what they say. You don't mind my telling you, do you?"

"Not at all."

"That's the ultimate accolade, you see, first-rate mind. But a bit difficult, that's what they say. I'd expected you to be talking about things I don't understand."

"You do yourself an injustice."

"I'm only assistant librarian. I'm not anything."

"You are to me."

We turned in at the entrance of the Institute. "Silly," she said.

Miss Piercey. I haven't explained her eyes, have I? — her asymmetric, quirky, aberrant eyes: the one sky blue and the other sea green. I have described them but not explained them. They are not the stuff of inheritance, of course: they are the consequence of somatic cell mutation, or one of them is, at any rate. I'm sorry to be didactic once more, but you must imagine an

141

early moment in the life of that amorphous cluster of cells that was destined to become the woman herself: the proto-Piercey, the embryonic mouse. No bigger than a pinhead, the little ball of cells bowls along a distant fallopian tube, wafted by the beating of cilia and entirely unperceived by the owner of the tube, who was, for the sake of the record, Mrs. Janet Piercey, *ob.* 15 January 1988. The cells are dividing — 2 . . . 4 . . . 8 . . . 16 . . . 32 . . . 64 — and, by the purest chance, by entire and complete accident — or perhaps by the subtle intervention of some unknown and unperceived chemical mutagen — a single gene on chromosome 19 in one cell of this cluster is copied imperfectly. In the impoverished alphabet of nucleic acids a single letter in a single position is read incorrectly. Previously this gene was unable to achieve its task, which was to cause a thin layer of pigment to be laid down in the middle of the iris. Thus defective, it coded for an iris of cornflower. But now, miscopied — a mere chemical error — it is returned to its original function. The cell in question lies on the left side of the embryo, and all the descendants of that cell now carry one blue-eye gene and one green-eye gene, where the cells on the other side of the cluster carry what they inherited — two blue-eye genes, one the contribution of blue-eyed Mrs. Janet Piercey, the other from blue-eyed Mr. Reginald Piercey. Thus one half of the embryonic Miss Jean Piercey develops green-eyed while the other half continues blue-eyed. Miss Piercey is a mosaic, a melding of cells with different genetic complements. She is, in her own modest manner, a monster.

We have something in common.

Curious how acquaintance merges into friendship. In retrospect it seems to have been a developmental progression, like the turning on of genes during ontogeny: encounter, acquaintance, familiarity, friendship. But is that it? Is there really this logic to it? Or am I merely ascribing purpose to a thing that is nothing more than the chance coming together of two lost souls? They were lost for quite different reasons, but then castaways on an island might not have come from the same shipwreck.

Whatever the dynamics of the thing, quite soon it was the norm for me to wait every Tuesday and Thursday for Miss Piercey to come out of the library at the lunch break — other days were left for the Primers and Codons and Vectors with whom I worked. But twice a week I would wait for her. Mousy and apologetic, nodding earnestly when one of the staff addressed her, looking at the world with those surprising, mismatched eyes, she would smile suddenly when she caught sight of me. I think she felt safe in my company. I think she felt like a child again. Oh, I know the mouthings of amateur psychology make depressing reading. I know Freud is about as interesting as Ealing on a wet Sunday afternoon. But there must be some reason for Miss Piercey and Doctor Lambert befriending each other; conscious or unconscious, there must have been some end in mind. Was it nothing more than the mutual attraction of unfortunates?

The pub was called The Pig and Poke. "I'm the pig," the landlord used to say if anyone asked, "and" — pointing to the barmaid, a middle-aged woman of brassy phenotype and terrifying invective — "she's the poke."

"You wouldn't even touch the edges," she would retort. "It'd be like picking me nose with a matchstick."

The other members of the Institute used to go to the Prince of Wales, so we had the place more or less to ourselves and after a while the landlord (*Mine Host, Eric* — proclaimed on a notice above the bar) began to recognize us. "What you do, then?" he asked. "Work round here, do you?"

"I search for genes," I told him.

He eyed me shrewdly. "I got a mate in Clerkenwell deals in Levi's," he confided. "No mucking, genuine article. You interested?"

Peals of laughter from Miss Piercey. The misunderstanding became a standing joke, a link with the place. "Find any Levi's, then, Professor?" Eric would call from behind his beer taps whenever we came in. "Got any five-oh-ones?"

"Isn't he a scream?" Miss Piercey would say.

It wasn't exclusively the pub, of course. There were lunchtime concerts at the Albert Hall, just the thing for the cultivated office worker or the impoverished and intellectual student. Rather hesitantly I suggested we get tickets for a series on the Slav composers. She was very keen. "I love romantic music," she confessed, as I feared she would; but then, to my surprise, she added, "although I'm happy with the classical period. What I won't stand for" — and those eyes narrowed surprisingly — "is the twentieth century. Well, that's not quite true. I'm okay with Dvořák, but then Dvořák's not really twentieth-century in spirit, is he?"

"I thought middle-European nationalism was very twentieth-century."

Her expression was reproving. I'd found out her real passion. "I mean the musical *form*. Bartók begins to lose me, and people like Janáček — ugh!" She shivered. I'm in the mood for confession: I found her shiver alluring. I made her sit through a performance of the absurdly named *Glagolitic* Mass, and she almost writhed with displeasure in the seat beside me as the chorus writhed with pleasure up and down the scales of the piece. "The whole of my lunch break for that!" she exclaimed. "Great splashes of sound that seem to go nowhere. Have you noticed that every time a melody comes along he deliberately *destroys* it? Did you notice? What's wrong with melodies? Why does the twentieth century hate them so?" But she enjoyed the Janáček piano recital I took her to. Afterwards I bought her a recording that included one of the pieces that was played: *On an Overgrown Path.*

"Most of it is about the death of the composer's daughter," I told her, after she had said how much she loved it. That didn't put her off. I would sometimes go into the librarian's office and find her playing it on her portable tape recorder. Mousy Miss Piercey. There was a little more to her than I had assumed.

So we would lunch together, and occasionally listen to a concert together, and then we would return to the Institute and go our separate ways, she to the stuffy confines of the library, I to the laboratories, the penetralia, the holy of holies, the inner sancta of the twentieth century.

What would Great-great-great-uncle Gregor have made of the labs, I wonder? He had to argue with Abbot Napp for extra space to plant more peas in the garden at the back of the monastery. What would he have made of the corridors and rooms with their humming machinery, their computer terminals, their ultracentrifuges, their slabs of electrophoresis gel, their oligonucleotide synthesizers, their automatic DNA sequencers? What would he make of the fact that we can actually read the messages enshrined in the hereditary particles whose existence he could infer only from watching the way they behave?

"What do you actually do?" Miss Piercey asked. "Aside from the joking with Eric and all that, what do you actually *do*?"

Many things. But one thing in particular. I search for the gene that caused me.

Frau Rotwang's skirts brushed the dew from the grass as she walked beneath the lime trees. A dachshund scampered alongside her and, from time to time, tied its leash around her ankles. When this happy event occurred, Mendel supported her elbow while she skipped on one foot and bent down to disentangle herself. Her ankles — one of them was disclosed for a moment while the leash unwound — seemed impossibly slender. Her dress was buttoned tightly to her neck, where a small froth of white lace bubbled up from underneath. Narrow ankles, narrow waist, slender neck. A mere slip.

Glancing at him with that smile, she asked, "Are lady visitors allowed?"

"Within the gardens, of course they are."

One of the fathers — Anselm, it was — came along the path. He nodded to the couple as he passed. There was a faint hint of disapproval about his expression. "They are so forbidding," she said when he had passed.

"Who are?"

"The monks."

"But I am one."

Briefly she touched his forearm. "Not you, Gregor. The rest."

"Anyway, we are not monks."

"I thought —"

"Friars. Our vocation is amongst the people. And fifty percent of the people . . ."

". . . are ladies."

"Fifty percent are *women*," Mendel corrected her. "I'm not sure that is the same thing. I think rather *fewer* are ladies."

"I'm sure I know nothing about that, Pater Gregor." She laughed, blushing faintly, bringing color to her name. "Now show me your . . . children."

"Over there." He pointed across the lawn, beyond the greenhouse (a building in its own right, this, with brick wings two stories high), toward the wall of the refectory. Peas. He was becoming quite obsessed with them. At first it had been fuchsias, sensible, pretty fuchsias. But now it was only ever peas.

"Lead me to them."

They crossed the grass, ducking under the lower boughs of the limes, caught up in the heavy, cloying scent of the trees, a sensual, female smell at odds with the dusty masculinity of the place. Beneath the refectory windows were the beds, with peas standing in chaotic, anarchic rows, hanging from the pea-sticks like drunks. Rows and rows of peas. "A kitchen garden," she exclaimed.

"An experimental plot. Over there you may see the fourth-generation hybrids from the first series —"

The dachshund lifted one stunted leg and sent a stream of yellow piddle onto the base of one of the plants. Frau Rotwang cried out in horror: "Adolfus! You ill-mannered

149

child!" Almost apologetically, almost as though he were to blame, Mendel muttered something about the exigencies of nature. The dog sniffed at his handiwork.

"But why are there paper bags?" Frau Rotwang asked, as much to distract from the embarrassment as out of any particular interest. The peas — perfectly ordinary garden peas — appeared to have blossomed paper bags. One wondered, one did wonder, whether dear Gregor wasn't a little eccentric. As though in answer to the question, he took one of the uncovered flowers, a deliciously purple and mauve creature just like a butterfly, and opened the petals with his blunt, farmer's hands.

"The bags protect the flowers from pollination by means other than my paintbrush." He withdrew his finger and showed Frau Rotwang a smear of golden pollen. "I, Gregor Mendel, am the one who commands the matings here. No pea may mate without my consent. In nature it is blind chance that determines what crosses take place. Here it is I. I have even grown some of the plants inside the greenhouse to be sure that weevils do not get into the flowers and interfere with my own work. The pea weevil, for example.[3]

3. *Bruchus pisi.*

When I was in Vienna, I presented a paper on the pea weevil to the Vienna Zoological and Botanical Society. It is a determined little fellow, and I cannot trust it not to transfer pollen from one flower to another. I have to be extremely careful, Frau Rotwang, *extremely* careful."

"And did it? Did it pollinate where it shouldn't have?" The word *adultery*, a horrendous, a terrifying, word, seemed to rise up out of the sultry air of their conversation.

"I found that it did not. I am the only pollinator."

"Surely the Almighty has some say in the matter."

"The Almighty works through chance. Chance is his instrument. Thus you" — she looked at him with her cornflower blue eyes — "thus you, Frau Rotwang, have blue eyes through the chance of your mother and your father . . ."

"So do you, Father Gregor."

For a moment they looked into each other's eyes. He felt quite faint. The hot spring day, the heavy perfume of the lime trees, the closeness of the woman with her intense cerulean eyes, all these things contrived to . . .

"Are you all right, Gregor?"

"A little warm. This soutane." But this

soutane was hiding things he could barely admit, even to his confessor. He eased his collar. "So impractical in the sun. Black absorbs heat, did you know that? White reflects, black absorbs. If you come over here, you may see some of the results of my labors. Seed color, for example." He took a branch and held it for her inspection. The flowers at the upper part of the plant nodded and danced like butterflies. "This is a hybrid of the second series. I have just started considering my characters in pairs to discover the relationship of one set of characters with another set. Here you will see that the flowers are carried at the axes of the plant, over there they are at the terminal point. That is another of the characters that I am working with. Another is the seed color." He snapped open a pod to reveal a row of glistening seeds. Six were yellow, two were green.

"Oh." There was something startling about seeing them lying there, couched in cool green, something disturbing and visceral, as though they had been discovered in their most intimate moment.

"Take them."

She hesitated. "I can eat them?"

"Of course."

"I can *eat* your experiment?"

He offered up the cleaved pod. "Please."

She reached toward the seeds. Her fingers were thin and long, her nails as perfectly shaped as almonds. *Mandel,* almond. A single yellow pea was selected, nipped out by those nails, and lifted to her mouth. She had rouged lips, closed like a bud. He watched closely as she took the pea. There was a sudden glimpse of moist tongue.

"Mmmm. Sweet."

"Take another."

"Really?"

"A green one." Somewhere in the background, one of the gardeners was clipping a hedge. The sound was a monotonous rhythm underlying the capricious delights of this presence beside him.

"Green." Another pea vanished. Her mouth worked. The sun seemed unduly hot for the time of year. He wiped his brow. "Another."

She complied. The peas went into her mouth . . . four, five, six, seven, eight. Six yellow, two green. Her jaw moved beneath the silk of her flushed cheek, her *rot Wang.* She laughed and he saw her teeth, as white as seed pearls, flecked with fragments of chewed pea. A ratio of three to one. She had eaten a three-to-one ratio.

"Delicious," she exclaimed.

[Recessive]

Dinner with Jean and Hugo Miller, at 34 Galton Avenue, Ruislip. It was a semidetached house of the kind that was cloned all over suburban England during the 1930s. When eugenics was at its height, when the Eugenics Society was campaigning for selective sterilization, and when Gropius and Le Corbusier and Mies van der Rohe were building concrete boxes all over the continent, this was what they gave the new man and his wife in Britain. "You can't miss it," she'd told me. "It's the only one with the satellite dish painted to blend in with the brick." And there indeed was the dish, painted in careful cryptic coloration and protruding from the wall just above the bay window. Everything else — the immaculately mown front lawn, the herbaceous border with stocks and sweet pea, the discreet gnome fishing in the birdbath, the crazy-paving path, the garage with the Ford Escort standing outside — blended in perfectly with the rest of the street; but not the false brickwork of the satellite dish.

Her husband greeted me at the front door. He was ginger-haired and blue-eyed (both autosomal recessives, chromosomes 4 and 19, respectively), and although the connection between short temper and red hair is entirely spurious, in Hugo Miller's case you felt there was something in it. "You must be Doctor Lambert," he told me, and his tone suggested that I had done something wrong, committed some hideous solecism.

"There's little alternative, is there?" I remarked, and he smiled angrily.

In the narrow hall there was a hatrack without any hats ("the wife's mad about antiques") and a gleaming reproduction of an Edwardian telephone. On the wall was a print of Van Gogh's bedroom at Arles — the room you couldn't get out of because of the uncomfortable, lumpy bed blocking the door — and a framed certificate that proclaimed Hugo Miller a member of the Association of Registered Structural Engineers. There was also a smell, a cloying, cozy smell: the scent of domestic enclosure. "You don't mind if I call you Ben, do you?" he asked as he showed me in. "I feel I know you already, the way the wife's always talking about you. I might have got quite jealous."

Might have.

We went through into the sitting room.

Jean was waiting there with another couple. I forget their names — Coldstream? Downstream? The man was a colleague of Miller's, a systems engineer, whatever that was; while his plump, curvaceous wife was "just a wife," and giggled to prove it. I sat with my feet off the floor and watched the four of them through a potted fuchsia.

"I'm so glad you could come, Benedict," Jean said. She gave an anxious smile, as though trying out the expression for the first time. "Benedict is one of the leading researchers at the lab," she explained. "He discovers genes. He's awfully busy."

Her husband stared at me with pale eyes. "Oh, it's *Benedict*, is it?"

I shrugged. "Ben, Benedict, it doesn't really matter. Not Benjamin, though."

"Benedict," Miller repeated thoughtfully, as he attempted to strangle a bottle. He appeared to resent the fact that he had not been told. "Fine name, Benedict. Shakespearean. A very valiant trencherman, isn't that right? An excellent stomach."

"That's Benedick."

"We saw that wonderful film," Mrs. Downstream added, and blushed. She was trying desperately not to stare, looking rather too much at her husband and at Jean, smiling rather too much when she did summon up the courage to look at me. Perhaps that made her inattentive to my line of vision. I glimpsed a smirk of secret white whenever she shifted her plump legs.

Miller had finally uncorked the bottle. "Try that . . . Benedict." He poured me a glass of wine and watched for my reaction almost as though he had thrown down a gauntlet or something. "It's a little number we found on our last holiday. Comes from a bodega in Aldeanueva. Only one or two people know about it."

While Jean went out to the kitchen, the four of us sipped and nodded and agreed with Miller that, even in the world of wine, discoveries were still possible. That seemed to satisfy him. He liked people to agree with him. There was a tension about him, as though every word he uttered was the opening of an argument. He sat back in his chair and watched me with those pallid eyes. "Jean thinks the world of you, you know that?" I felt he was looking for a slip, some error in my story that would show me up. "Knew you back home, didn't she? She thinks you're the local boy made good. Against all the odds, if you see what I mean."

I did see what he meant. So, presumably, did Mr. and Mrs. Downstream.

"So tell us what you do, if it's not too

difficult for simple souls like us. I get all the gossip from Jean. Oh yes, I know all about the goings-on at your establishment. Olga and her affairs, all that kind of thing. What's your particular angle?"

"On Olga's affairs?"

There was strained laughter. "Your angle on genetics."

I shrugged. "It's a bit boring, really. DNA probes, linkage analysis. We try to locate the actual position of genes on the chromosome." Miller nodded and sucked his teeth and looked as though I was confirming what he already knew. Mrs. Downstream decided that it was all beyond her, she was sure, and she would go and see if Jean needed any help. Miller poured more wine, satisfied now that the men had been left alone. "I've been reading about the human genome project. Downloaded a whole lot of stuff from the Internet. You part of that?"

"Almost everyone is."

"You know what they call it, don't you? They call it HUGO. Human Genome Organization. How about that, eh?" He looked for applause, as though the merit were his. "Anyway, according to what I've read, it seems to me that soon enough we're going to be able to order exactly what kind of children we want. Choosing the color of the eyes, choosing the sex, choosing anything you like. Kids by mail order."

"That's rather a long way off."

"Don't you believe it. Could be the biggest thing since penicillin. I've been on line to some clinic in the States and they're advertising the thing already — test-tube babies, sperm sorting, all sorts of stuff. It's not in the future, it's here and now."

Jean and the Downstream woman came in with the food, and we all settled at the table. There was some bother about where I was to sit — a cushion was offered, that kind of thing. "Please," I told them, "please just let me be. I'm quite all right." But Miller insisted. There was a brittle quality about him, as though the glaze of goodwill might at any moment fracture. Once we were all settled at the table, he nodded toward his wife. "So if you're a geneticist, how do you explain *that*, then?" It might have been some kind of challenge.

"That?"

"That." We looked in vain. Jean blushed, and busied herself with serving vichyssoise. She alone knew what was coming. "The lady wife's eyes," Miller explained, as though stating the obvious. "I've always found it most alluring. But how do you explain it, eh? How does a geneticist explain *that?*"

I saw Jean's blush, and realized that I'd explained the thing to her before, over one of our lunches at The Pig and Poke. We'd laughed about it then. "You remind me of my teddy bear," I'd told her. The memory gave me a tiny stir of pleasure. "Jean is a genetic mosaic. That's what I'd guess."

"A mosaic!" Mrs. Downstream exclaimed. "How very artistic. I think that rather suits Jeanie. She has an artistic touch, what with her antiques and things. We saw mosaics on that trip to Rome, didn't we, Ernest?" They did: polychromatic ones in some church or another, but there were so many of them, the churches that is, that they couldn't remember the name.

"Never mind that," Miller said impatiently. "What's a genetic mosaic?"

I explained. Mosaic, chimera, I explained the classical monsters of the gene world. "You need to know what eye color Jean's parents had . . ."

Miller seemed surprised. "Don't you know? I thought you knew one another as children . . ."

"Blue," Jean said. "Ben never met my parents. They had blue eyes, both of them."

"So one of the blue-eyed genes mutated to green. There's a blue/green gene" — we laughed at the pun — "on chromosome 19,

I think. I'd have to look it up to be sure. It would have just been a chance mutation." I shrugged it off, as you do with mutations. "But very beautiful," I added, and Jean blushed once more to be the object of this attention, to have her genome discussed in such intimate detail, and all the time we were, of course, skirting cautiously around another issue as though edging along the brink of a precipice: my own.

Miller pursed his lips thoughtfully. "Then let me run this one across your bows, Ben," he said. "I heard this chap on the radio the other day, some academic from Northern Ireland. Lynn the name? Richard Lynn? He said that there is a real danger of a decline in the genetic stock of this country. What do you think?" He poured more wine for himself, watching me with an expression that told you that he already knew, that he understood what was going through your mind, and that you were wrong. "Do you agree?"

I shrugged. "What do you mean by 'genetic stock'? And what do you mean by 'decline'?"

Jean sighed. The Downstreams paid careful attention to their plates, as though they already knew something that I didn't. Miller's eyes shifted. "This fellow Lynn said that it was very simple. People in high-grade jobs — us, say — have fewer and fewer children, whereas unskilled workers have more, so the majority of the population in the future is going to come from amongst the unskilled workers. Given that the unskilled are less intelligent than professional people, and given that intelligence is inherited, that means that the overall intelligence of the population is going to decline. QED."

"It's outside my field, I'm afraid."

"No view, then?"

"Oh, a view, yes, of course. But nothing to do with my work. You said I was a geneticist, but my work's got nothing to do with this kind of thing. I've got a view about it, but it's just a view like anybody else's."

"And what about all those Africans that come over here? This Lynn fellow, he says that the best survey done of intelligence amongst Africans shows that they have an average IQ of sixty-nine."

I laughed. "I'd say Professor Lynn was talking nonsense."

"So he's wrong, is he?"

"He's saying exactly the kind of thing that people said at the turn of the century. It was wrong then, and I don't see why it should become right now."

"What do you mean by *wrong*, eh? Morally wrong, is that it?"

"Scientifically wrong. No evidence for it."

"But there are tests. He quoted them."

"With results like that, I'd worry about the test itself more than the people."

"Well, what about genetic disease, then? What about this cystic fibrosis we all hear about? Or anything like that. Now that's your field, isn't it? You can't deny *that*, can you? Diabetes and stuff. Don't we keep all these people alive and allow them to breed, and doesn't that mean that their mutations are kept in the population? Doesn't that Francis Crick fellow say that such people shouldn't be allowed to breed? What about natural selection, eh? Haven't we eliminated natural selection? We keep people alive when in the wild they'd be eliminated because they're weaker, don't we? What does Doctor Benedict think of that?"

"Hugo, please," said Jean. "Let's talk about something a bit easier."

He turned to her. His tone was very patient. "Let me talk, will you, dear?"

She looked at me. It was difficult to read her expression. Apology? Warning? Pity?

"You can't expect me to applaud the law of the jungle, can you?" I asked. "If the law of the jungle held sway, I'd be dead."

Jean closed her eyes. Mrs. Downstream said, "Oh, I'm sure not." Hugo Miller considered my statement. His face was mottled, as though he was attempting to hide a great anger. "Oh, there's nothing wrong with your *living*," he said. "But what about breeding, eh? Should people like you be allowed to breed?"

Embarrassment, adolescent embarrassment. It is an insidious thing because it possesses no status in the hierarchy of emotions. No one wrote poetry about embarrassment. Embarrassment is something you ought to grow out of, like acne; but you don't. I clambered down from my seat like a child dismissed from the table. I ought to have stayed and fought. Benedict Lambert ought to have brought his celebrated, acerbic wit into play. He ought to have destroyed Miller with a few well-aimed shafts. But he didn't. He merely and absurdly felt a fool.

"Please don't fuss," I said to Jean. "Just let me go." But of course she saw me out just the same, apologizing as she opened the door, following me down the crazy-paving to the gate, apologizing all the time. "Hugo doesn't mean harm. It's just his manner. He likes to provoke . . ."

I told her to forget it. I explained that, like freckles or a harelip or a squint, you get inured to it. It was water off a duck's back. And suddenly she gave a little cry, as though of pain, and crouched down as you might for a child, and kissed me on the lips, there on the pavement outside number 34 Galton Avenue, encircled by the embarrassing spotlight of a street lamp. "You're so brave, Ben," she whispered. "You always were. So brave."

I shook my head. "Not brave," I told her. "In order to be brave, you've got to have a choice." Then I clambered into the car and slammed the door.

She stood on the pavement to watch me drive away. She didn't wave, but held out both her hands open, as though in supplication. I noticed the Downstreams peering through the net curtains of the bay window, making of the scene whatever they could. There was no sign of Hugo Miller.

A curious sensation. There is a desire to weep, of course, but you learn early not to give in to that. Lachrymal duct defect may be an inheritable condition, but my dry eyes have nothing to do with any such mutation — they are simply a result of practice. Instead of tears you learn to feel anger, anger directed at a variety of targets: the perpetrator of the offense; humanity in general; the nameless forces that have driven you to this fruitless, impotent emotion; and yourself —

as though somehow you are to blame for your condition. And this anger is combined with a desire for revenge, of course. I'm only human, after all. So, a desire for revenge, a desire to see Hugo Miller beg for forgiveness or mercy or something. And something else, something infinitely more dangerous than any of those emotions: hope. That kiss, you see. Oh, like Dinah's kiss, of course: an accident, a pure piece of mismanagement, a stray shot, aimed at the cheek but wandering off target because of the effort of bending down to my level. Or worse, if not an accident, if actually intended, then perhaps meant as some kind of consolation. Whichever way, not significant. And yet I hoped. You hope against hope, even after thirty and more years, you hope.

I didn't return home that evening. Home was a cheerless, empty basement flat purchased with the money that Uncle Harry left, and furnished with some of those pieces of furniture my father had made for me — diminutive chairs, a low table, reduced wardrobes: a veritable fairytale dwarf's cave it was. But I couldn't face the place that evening, so I drove instead to the laboratories, where the night staff were on duty and one or two colleagues would be at work late. I had an alibi — a culture incubating, or something similar — and I had things I could do, trivial tasks that would bring comfort through distraction. Work is a palliative, you see.

"You all right, Ben?" I was asked.

I was fine. I turned on the computer and logged on to Johns Hopkins to look through some recent papers. I was fine. I read about fragile-X syndrome and about familial colonic polyposis and about mismatch repair. The telephone rang twenty minutes after I'd got there, the direct line to my lab. It was Jean. Her small gray voice fluttered in my ear. "I thought I'd find you there. I rang to apologize."

"You've already done that."

"Actually, I wanted to see if you were all right."

"I'm all right. Just wonderful. How did you know I would be here?"

"I sort of guessed. I sort of knew. I thought maybe that's where you'd go. Am I forgiven?"

"For you, there's nothing to forgive."

"Those bloody people have gone. They went soon after you left. Hardly surprising, I suppose. Hugo has gone to bed."

"And you haven't?"

"I stayed to do the washing up. Hugo's asleep, and I thought I'd give you a call."

The incubators hummed. Someone

opened and closed the doors to the sterile room. All around me was the timeless, chalky light of the labs. Above the shelves of gleaming bottles, the windows were as black as ebony. "Are you ready for bed?"

"I'm just going. Ben, I just rang to say how sorry I was —"

I could imagine her, of course. My imagination in such matters is fine-tuned. I could picture her in the narrow hallway, holding that ridiculous imitation Edwardian telephone receiver to her ear and standing awkwardly, with one foot perched on the other. I could imagine her toes, distorted by a lifetime wearing narrow shoes. I could imagine her hair freshly brushed out. I could see the simple cotton nightdress and the pallid legs. There would be a faint trace of hair on her shin where the razor had not quite done its work. I am an expert on legs. I live at the level of legs. Bereft of their armor of nylon tights, her legs would have an awkward vulnerability.

"I think you'd better finish what you're doing and go home," she said. "Drive carefully."

Oh, poor, sad dwarf, hidden in your cave, your trident hands (fine, roguish, neptunian adjective) working away with method and expertise at solitary delights, your mind nosing into the declivities of bodies both imagined and imaged there on the bedspread in full and iridescent color — "Glorious Gloria is Game for any Guy," so the captain claims, no doubt mendaciously. The imagination works, the fantasies blossom. One tries to keep things pent up for a while, tries to prolong the meager ecstasy, but the inexorable tide is rising. Gloria becomes Olga Codon, becomes the glimpse of Mrs. Downstream's knickers, becomes a distant memory of Dinah, a vivid memory of Eve, becomes Jean . . . Sensation wells up. The surge comes suddenly and anticlimactically, flushing all fantasies away like flotsam from a storm drain, to deposit them, a glutinous liquid, onto the strategically placed towel.

The enemy is self-pity. You guard against self-pity, build bastions of cynicism, dig ditches of irony and sarcasm; but sometimes, just sometimes, the barriers are breached.

Sleep of a kind. The sleep of the damned. To dream of Jean.

[Linkage]

I dream a great deal. What would the Blessed Sigmund Fraud have made of that? I dream of a railway line. Long ago the Blessed Sigmund decreed that railways signify death, so according to him, I dream of death.

My railway line runs from nowhere to nowhere. The empty tracks stretch away into the distance while the train sweeps along, drumming over the rails. Clackety-clack, clackety-clack the wheels go, and the track is everything, the sum total of perception, the only landscape. Sometimes, rarely, there is a disturbance: a signal flashes past, followed by a signal box with a name written on it, a curious and childlike name to go with the childishness of the dream — TATA — and after it comes the sudden relief of a station, the concrete platform rising out of the verge like a wave, the line of forlorn people standing in the rain, a long and bewildering nameboard like an anagram in a crossword, and then there is the open line again, the monotonous thrumming of the wheels, the flashing sleepers, thousands and thousands of them, all without meaning or sense or significance.

The blessed Sigmund is wrong — my dreams are not about death, they are about life: the vacuity of life.

"What do you *do?*" Miss Piercey asks over lunch in The Pig and Poke. You can hear the italics in her speech. "I want to understand what you *do.*"

"At least you're not like your husband. He already seems to know what I do better than I."

She ignores the taunt. "Tell me. Explain."

It is very simple, that is the important fact to grasp. Nuclear physicists, astronomers, chemists — the quintessential scientists, the inheritors of alchemy — have always lived in a world apart, a world bound by the impenetrable barriers of complex equations, of techniques and ideas beyond the feeble grasp of you and me. Not we molecular geneticists. Oh yes, there is a bit of trickery. You need a certain aptitude for puzzles, for riddles, for brain-teasers — but little more. If you have a gift for anagrams or a fluency with crosswords, or if you can worry away at the kind of conundrum you find inside the back cover of a magazine, then you could do it too:

Suzie has a piece of string one yard long. Bill cuts it into five pieces of different length. Then

Jim cuts Bill's fragments into a further six pieces. Suzie now wants to reconstruct her original piece of string. She knows that Bill's cuts were . . .

The molecular geneticists among you will have smiled at the mere mention of the word *fragment*. It has semantic power. But others will have merely shrugged, like Miss Piercey does, "It can't be just a kind of game," she protests.

Oh, but it is. And the techniques are simple, too. About as difficult as haute-cuisine cookery, say: occasionally tricky, but nothing that Miss Piercey couldn't turn her hand to, if need be. Furthermore, in this particular instance the dish and the cook are one and the same thing, which brings a pleasant tartness to the palate.

Meet My Maker, the Mad Molecule

The molecule in question — the celebrated double helix, the acronymic DNA — is by now known to all in one way or another. Even high-court judges need to have some idea of it, even readers of the popular press recognize it, if only as a way of catching out a rapist by analyzing his sperm. When I speak of this, Miss Piercey makes a face which signifies disgust and disapproval.

"But it's there," I assure her, "whether you

like it or not, there in the nuclei of all of your cells."

"The sperm?"

"The DNA. The molecules are there in every cell, carefully folded away like linen in a bottom drawer. Every function of every cell depends on it."

"You mean" — a frown puckers her forehead — "it's there at this moment, wriggling round inside me?" She shifts on her seat, as though things are moving beneath her skirt. And there is that sound as she moves: the faint, intimate whisper of nylon against nylon.

"Every second." I draw a diagram on a paper napkin to explain. I'm afraid it's my didactic manner once more, but it brings results; she leans forward to look. A lock of her hair brushes my face, and her scent envelops me, a faint breath of musk. Are such messages intentional? Does she know what she is doing? As I sketch my diagram, I am constrained to rearrange matters within my trousers. "The molecule has the shape of a twisted ladder," I tell her. "A Jacob's ladder, if you like, but a Jacob's ladder that goes both ways; we may use it to attempt to ascend to the throne of God . . . but we can also use it to descend into the pit. So beware."

"And which way are you planning to go, Dr. Lambert?" Jean asks as she flips the errant lock of hair behind her ear.

The Message

The message of the genes lies along one of the strands of the ladder, and it is written in an alphabet of only four letters — *A*, *C*, *G*, and *T*. That is the alphabet of life. The letters are really chemical groups called bases, and the bases of one strand grasp the bases of the other strand to form the rungs of the ladder. They bond thus: an "A" on one strand always bonds with a "T" on the other; a "C" always bonds with a "G." The result of these rules is that the sequence along one strand is exactly complemented by the sequence along the other. The sequence of letters, say:

GGCATCCTCAGCTACGGGGTGG
GCTTCTTCCTG

is exactly complemented by the equivalent sequence on the other, complementary strand:

CCGTAGGAGTCGATGCCCCACC
CGAAGAAGGAC

I turn the paper napkin for her to look. "Strings of these paired letters go on and on and on into the distance, like the sleepers of a railway. One side is the message, the other the anti-message. Sense and anti-sense, like a looking glass. Just over a thousand of such paired bases makes up an average gene, but the whole molecule of DNA is longer, far, far longer than that." I talk the language of megabases — millions of bases — and Jean looks bewildered: "An average human chromosome," I tell her, "contains a single DNA molecule of eighty million base pairs. That is long, not just in cellular terms but in real terms: It is some *centimeters* long. In each human cell, adding together the forty-six chromosomes, there is a total of about two meters of DNA."

She shakes her head. "But what's it all *mean?* It says 'cat' there." She points with one slender and talon-tipped finger to the scrawl on the napkin. "And 'tag.' It looks like gibberish to me."

"But it's not gibberish to your cells." In the background, Eric roars with laughter over some new joke a customer has just told him. Nearby, the pinball machine shrieks and whistles. And I wonder about Jean's DNA, about her cells, about the very fabric of her body, while she sits there in front of me with her legs artfully crossed so that all I can see above her knees is a triangular tunnel of shadow.

She straightens up to look at me. "So what does this DNA stuff say?"

"It holds the instructions to make you: a phenotypically normal woman, brown-haired, slim, good-looking, nervous, self-deprecating, confused about your husband . . ."

A blush has suffused her cheeks. "All that? Come *on*."

"Or, with one single, hideous spelling mistake in the whole instruction manual, *me*."

She is still. The nervous shifting has gone, the blush has paled. Her eyes, those strange, mismatched eyes determined by some error no bigger than the one within me, glisten. "Oh, Ben," she whispers.

But of course I ignore her little show of emotion, and ignore too the slender hand that reaches across the table to take my stubby one. This is my subject, this is what I do, this is what, for want of a better word, I believe. This is where Ben the scientist takes over from Ben the dwarf. "You must understand that the DNA isn't *carrying* the message: The message is an integral part of the molecule. The message *is* the molecule. And just so, there isn't a fundamental *you* that stands outside all this and watches it from some exalted viewpoint, like a reader looking at a book. It's much stranger than that. You watch it with the machinery that it has created. You understand it — or fail to — with the machinery that it has created. That's the point. The medium really is the message."

"You keep saying it's a message, but if it's a message, how do you read it? What does it *say?*"

I shrug. "It says proteins. That is all, and that is everything. The message decides the proteins your cells can make, and the proteins determine everything else. There are lots of different proteins in your cells because there are lots of different things to do, so there are lots of different genes — maybe one hundred thousand in the entire human genome. We've not yet finished counting, but it won't take long."

"And if the message *means* something," Jean asks, "who wrote it?"

The Genetic Code

It is not a code. A code is created in order to deceive. No one was trying to hide anything, no God was playing games, creating a conundrum, proposing a puzzle, writing a rebus. The so-called genetic code evolved simply to work. It is not a code: it is a *language*, and a disturbingly simple one. Each word in the language consists of just three letters, any three out of the four, *A, C, G,* and *T.* All possible combinations mean something, which means that the language has just sixty-four words. English has twenty-six letters and a vocabulary of some five hundred thousand words, but the language of the genes, which is sufficient to produce systems that can speak all the languages in the world and understand everything that has ever been understood, this genetic language has but sixty-four words. Furthermore, many of the words are exact synonyms of others — there may be sixty-four different words, but together they have a mere twenty-one different meanings.[1]

There is another simplicity in the system. With almost no exceptions,[2] the language of the genes is universal. The same language is used by your own cells as by the virus that is giving you a head cold, or the bacterium that is giving you a sore throat. The genes that make up the oak tree outside your win-

1. Twenty amino acids, and the command STOP.
2. Two trivial differences between nuclear DNA and mitochrondrial DNA.

dow and the fly buzzing against the window pane all speak the same language. All words mean the same thing to all animals and all plants. There has been no Tower of Babel in the history of cellular evolution.

"It seems confusing enough to me," Jean says. And then she looks at me with a curious directness. That is one of the things I find remarkable about her, her childlike directness. "So where do you fit into all this?" she asks. "What exactly does the great Benedict Lambert do?"

What, indeed? Victim and victor, I probe into the most intimate details of the human genome. Where Uncle Gregor Mendel merely discovered the manner in which inherited factors are passed on from father to daughter or mother to son, I finger his factors and pull them gently to pieces, like a little boy pulling the wings and legs from a fly. I mime the action and evoke a delicious shiver from Jean Piercey. "Or a young girl pulling the petals from a flower. He loves me, he loves me not, he loves me, he loves me not."

"And the dwarfs?" Her gaze is steady and direct. She possesses a strange courage.

"Ah, yes, the dwarfs . . ."

I look for meaning among the misprints of life, and so I have become a kind of impresario, a Billy Smart of genetics, a Barnum and Bailey of the genome, an heir to Grand-father Godley and his freak show.

I collect dwarfs.

"What's all this about, then?" one of them asks loudly to the waiting room of the clinic. The room is decked out with potted plants — aspidistra, ficus — and has bright and hopeful pictures on the walls. The man looks around the place suspiciously. He is there with his family. The wife smiles in a motherly kind of way and clips the ear of the child, a blithe and oblivious three-year-old who is trying to tear a copy of *Cosmopolitan* to pieces. They have come from just down the road, from Olympia, where the posters are currently showing raging lions and clowns with red noses and crossed eyes and bowler hats with flowers coming out of the top. Chipperfield's Circus is in town.

"Who is this geezer who wants us?" The father says that. *Geezer.* "Who is this geezer, then?"

A nurse smiles patiently and points out where to fill in the name and date of birth of each member of the family. "Doctor Lambert will then ask you a few questions, if you don't mind. We do appreciate your offering to help like this."

"Help? Help who?" He appeals to me as though to an ally. "Who is this geezer

180

Lambert? Any idea?"

"Doctor Lambert will explain everything," the nurse repeats.

The man looks suspicious. "I don't want anyone trying to *cure* us. Where'd we be then, eh? Out on the streets without a job."

"Don't worry about that," the nurse replies brightly. "There's no cure. Now if you just go with the doctor . . ."

Only then does comprehension dawn. He stares at me. "Oh, *you're* 'im, are you? I fought you was one of us. Blimey, you could knock me down with a feather. In fact that's exactly what they do, most of the time — knock me down with a feather, I mean." He roars with laughter, his face knotting up and the sound rattling the windowpanes of the interview room. He is used to laughing to a large audience, making it clear when things are meant to be funny — which is most of the time, presumably. "You from circus folk, too?" he asks.

"No, I'm not."

The man nods his overlarge head in sympathy. "Just came out of the blue, did you? Luck of the draw, eh? That happens, don't it? I'm Tom Thumb. Well, obviously. You always end up as Tom Thumb. Typecasting. Pleased to meet you." He holds out a stubby hand for me to shake with its twin, my own stubby hand. It is like looking in a mirror, that's the curious thing. Whenever you meet up with another one, it is like looking in a mirror, as though the mutation has overcome all the quirks of inheritable variation and produced a kind of clone. And yet all we share is a jot, a mere tittle, one trivial spelling mistake in the whole instruction book.

I have often wondered what the real Benedict Lambert would have looked like, the one that is trapped within this absurd, circus body, the one without the macrocephaly, the depressed nasal bridge, the pronounced lumbar lordosis, the short, stubby limbs; the one who is, more or less, the height of my father. What would that crypto-Benedict have looked like? My father was six foot one.

"This is the missus, of course," Tom Thumb says. "And this 'ere is the son and heir. Little blighter. He's Joe. Joseph. Not that we're Jewish; just liked the name, that's all." Joe smiles and grabs a fistful of pens from my desk. "There was a sister," the father adds. "But she died."

"Died? When was that?"

"Five years ago. She was only eighteen month old, poor little mite. She was badly hit. It does that sometimes, doesn't it?"

"Yes, it does. Do you have a doctor's report on her, the postmortem document or anything like that?"

"Don't know if we do now. You know what it's like when you're on the road. You don't keep much that isn't vital, and with the poor little mite gone . . ."

Homozygous. She would have been useful. I have four homozygotes, all referred by hospitals, two from the States, all destined to die in the next months. Stunted, twisted, snared by the malign throw of dice, they are particularly *useful*. Informative.

"Other living relatives?"

"I've got a brother."

"Is he . . . affected?"

"Normal."

"And do you think he might help?"

"Dunno. I never see him. To tell the truth, he finds me a bit of an embarrassment." A shrug. "What do you want from him, anyway?" Tom Thumb swells with indignant pride and joins me in a brotherhood of the dispossessed. "Isn't it *us* you're after?"

"Certainly. But we want to build up as complete a pedigree as possible."

"Pedigree, is that it? Like dogs."

I smiled. "A bit like dogs. All we need from each of you is a blood sample. From you, from your brother if he's willing, from anyone else who is related. Your wife's relatives as well."

"Blood samples? She hates the needle, does Deirdre. Don't you, love?"

Deirdre nodded distractedly, easing pens out of her child's fist. "Give the doctor his pens back, there's a good boy."

"Gives her a right twinge, the needle does. What do you want this blood for anyway? Some kind of Dracula, are you?"

"We grow your cells and extract the DNA from them —"

"Oh, I've heard of *that*," Deirdre says. "It's on the telly, isn't it? Fingerprinting. Don't you remember that Inspector Morse? There was this spot of blood and they found the murderer's fingerprints from it. Amazing."

You know pretty soon when you aren't going to get very far. "Something like that," I agreed. "We try to find markers on your chromosomes that we can recognize. That enables us to work out which of your chromosomes your son has inherited —"

"Needles in Joe as well? I'm not sure that I can go along with that."

"It'll be quite painless, I assure you."

"And all the other people you get? Aren't they enough?"

"The more we have, the better. The markers must be informative, you see. We have to find different markers on each of your chromosomes so that we have a way of distinguishing between them."

"Chromosomes?" Tom Thumb's face lights up. He is back on familiar ground. "How do you tell the sex of a chromosome?" he asks.

"I don't know," I answer dutifully. "How *do* you tell the sex of a chromosome?"

Tom Thumb loves it. "Look up its genes!" he cries. "How about that? Look up its genes!"

"That's what we're doing, actually, trying to look up the chromosomes' genes. And once we find the markers, we follow them from parents to children and attempt to find which markers seem to be inherited with the actual condition. If we can find a marker that goes with the condition, that means that the marker and the gene for achondroplasia are likely to be on the same chromosome. It requires a great deal of patience to do the work, but the idea is fairly straightforward. And you can all help."

"What good'll it do us?"

"No good at all, except to know that you will have helped. Maybe in the future there'll be a therapy. Sometime in the future."

Once more that suspicious look. "We don't want any therapy. We'd be out on the streets without a job. What use is a tall dwarf, eh?" He roars with laughter at the idea.

Repeat that conversation as often as you want, with variations for comprehension and native wit, and you have got the first phase, the collection of pedigrees. "I suppose there's some kind of statistical analysis involved, is there?" one woman asked. "Something that will tell you the likelihood of the markers being linked to the achondroplasia gene. I mean, presumably the two things, the marker and the gene, could be inherited together by pure chance . . ."

"Have you studied genetics?"

She shook her head. Bright, intelligent eyes looked out from within her pug face. She was strangely beautiful, as though you could see through a glass darkly, through mere contorted flesh and bone, to the normal woman hidden within. "I'm a solicitor," she explained. "I avoided biology at school, but you try and find out something, don't you? Once you've faced it, you want to understand as much as you can." We were companions in this. She smiled at me with the kind of smile she might have reserved for her husband, as though I were party to an intimacy as great as any she had to offer. For a moment I pictured the two of us writhing together on a bed, clutching each other with stunted limbs. Did such a thought occur to her? She had a normal husband. She had a normal husband, and a normal son and a dwarf daughter, both delivered by Caesarean section. "You should see the looks I get. Sometimes people come up to me in the street and tell me that it shouldn't be allowed. Complete strangers . . ."

Bring on the clowns. Bring on the dwarfs. Let the band start playing.

The Circus

On 29th June, being the feast of Saints Peter and Paul, titular saints of the city, the circus came to Brünn. The whole rigmarole, part fair, part gypsy encampment, a village of caravans and tents and booths, was strewn out on open ground along the banks of the River Schwarzawa, on the far side of the Klosterplatz. It was a fine sight on a bright summer's day, with the smoke billowing and bunting flying and the bands playing and the dark Schreibwald hill rising up behind it all like a vast circus tent. There was a great parade through the town: caravans and clowns, a lumbering elephant and a cage of tigers (two), a team of jugglers and a knot of tumblers, a troop of plumed ponies and a couple of moth-eaten camels with Arab boys on their backs. Dark-skinned strangers were seen in the streets. Shopkeepers kept a closer eye than usual on their stock. Householders made sure to lock their doors.

Mendel went, of course. He could not ignore it. There was the bearded lady; there was a contortionist called The Boneless Wonder; there was a head, a living, blinking, lip-licking human head that appeared to sprout, quite bodiless, from a growing vine; there was a two-headed giant (dried and shriveled and lying in a coffin), and a three-legged boy, and, pickled in a jar like sauerkraut, Siamese twins. He had already been around the hospital, bracing himself for the experience, to take note of some of the deformities that were there. He had already made a pedigree of his own family — the receding hairline, the stoutness, the blue eyes, the myopia. He had already bred mice in the confines of his room in the monastery, and incurred the wrath of Abbot Napp as a result. How could he not turn his attention to the circus?

He went with a party from the monastery, with Pavel Křižkovsky the choirmaster and a group of the choristers and two of the other friars.

There was an atmosphere about the circus encampment. Physically it was an amalgam of crushed grass and coal smoke and the scorched smell of the lamps and a hundred other things that one couldn't put a name to. Metaphorically it was the exotic scent of mystery and alienation, and the sensation that here the measured normality of things was mere illusion, that beneath the certainties lay chaos. There were Frenchmen and Italians, Indians and Chinese, Cossacks and Circassians, a Turkish eunuch and an Arabian belly dancer — or so the poster claimed — and, of course, there were the gypsies, the *cikáni*, their skin dark, their eyes dark, the blood of ancient Egypt running in their veins and through their tongue.

"Indian, I believe," said Franz Bratranek in that didactic manner of his. He modeled himself on Goethe and, like the great man, considered himself a polymath. "Not Egyptian at all. Studies of their language show its relationship with Hindu. The theory is that they migrated from India at some time in the Middle Ages and have been wandering ever since."

"Like the Jews," Mendel suggested.

"*Un*like the Jews," Bratranek corrected reprovingly. "The writings of de Gobineau make the position clear. The gypsies are of Aryan stock, whereas the Jews" — *Zidi*, he called them, although they were speaking German — "are Semitic, and therefore quite alien . . ."

"Jesus was a Jew," Mendel remarked.

The party took its place under the great tent, amid the smell of the crowd and horse dung and straw. The boys of the choir school seethed and simmered. Křižkovsky swatted heads, Mendel fiddled with his glasses, Klacel expanded his width across the wooden bench and, to accompany the first act, in which poodles pranced stiffly around the ring on their hind legs, delivered a lecture on the matter of dog training.

Following the dogs there was a flying trapeze act. The performers were a father and his three sons. Beneath them a woman waved her arms gracefully to emphasize the aerial acrobatics taking place above. The woman wore dangerously short skirts, skirts that barely covered her knees, but fortunately she did not ascend to the summit of the tent. That would have been too much for decency. Bratranek debated whether she might be the mother, whether a woman who had borne three children might yet possess quite so athletic a frame. Mendel polished his glasses vigorously. Next came an interlude with clowns and midgets ("A defect in ontogeny resulting from a humoral imbalance in the family," pronounced Bratranek, as though he were a doctor), and then, while the audience held its breath, a cage was assembled in the midst of the ring.

Tigers.

The word swept through the audience like a rumor of imminent disaster.

Tigers, lions, savagery. A tunnel was being assembled, leading to the outside of the tent, leading out into the darkness of the jungle.

Mendel murmured something to Bratranek, and slipped away.

Families, that was what Mendel thought, more or less. Damn the tigers. *Families.* And he wondered how people could be so blind. Of course it was natural to think about the family of trapeze artists, and thus cloud the issue with matters of training and upbringing and childhood experience and all that kind of thing. It was necessary to separate the effect of inheritance from the effect of nurture. He had taken care to do so with his peas, making sure that the dwarf plants were transplanted where necessary so that they should not be shaded by their tall siblings. Oh yes, the physical dexterity of those trapeze artists must be inherited and, just possibly, that new choirboy's ear for sound —

young Leoš something or other — and certainly the particular construction of the voicebox that gave the potential to sing like a lark. Was that the simile Paul Křižkovsky used? Nightingale, then. But not the fact that he played the organ so, or that he could sing. A fine voice and a fine musician. No, as with the trapeze family, a child's *gifts* were one thing, his *achievements* quite another: his achievements might depend on his gifts, but they had been developed, molded by experience and training, entirely invented, some of them. That was the distinction that Darwin failed to make in his book, to distinguish clearly between nature and nurture . . .

So Father Gregor didn't go out of the tent in the search for the trapeze artists (and anyway, there was the problem of the woman). No, he went in search of the midgets. They were easy enough to find. A diminutive caravan stood on the edge of the encampment with two diminutive horses grazing nearby, of the kind bred for use in the mines. It was obvious.

A gruff voice answered his knock: *"Ja?"*
"Darf ich eintreten?"
"Herein."
German, then. He had guessed Slav of some kind. One expected German blood to

have a certain purity. He climbed the steps and ducked into the doorway, and found himself in a miniature world, the inhabitants small, the furnishings small, the whole interior as though glimpsed through the wrong end of a telescope. He might have been the oddity, crouched in the doorway with his head brushing the ceiling. Three diminutive creatures peered toward him with a curiosity that equaled his own. There was a young woman with a baby in her arms, and an older couple who might have been her parents. Despite differences in age they shared common features with one another, more closely even than the common features that you find within a normal family — large heads and short limbs and the faces of pug dogs. Humoral imbalance, Bratranek had suggested.

"May I . . . ?"

"Come in, come in," the man replied. "Don't stand on ceremony. In fact, don't stand at all. You'll hit your head on the roof." The old couple roared with laughter. The young woman shushed them. "You a priest, are you?" the man asked. "What a surprise. We're not Catholic, you know. Oh no, not Catholic at all. Lutherans, how about that?"

"I've not come to convert you."

He shrugged. "Oh, you can try, you can try. How about converting us to . . ." He glanced at his wife. ". . . giants?" And at the suggestion, the pair of them roared with laughter once more. "Anyway, sit down," the man commanded. "Sit down before you knock a hole in the roof."

So Mendel sat down at their table, while the man opened a bottle of *slivovice* and poured two glasses. "What can I do for you, then?" the dwarf asked.

Mendel considered the options. "I breed plants," he began cautiously.

The dwarf's eyes shone. "Do a bit of breeding myself, I do. Ponies. You saw the ones outside? They bring a good price at Mährisch Ostrau. For the mines, of course. Children like them too. I'd sooner sell them for riding than for the mines, but you've got to make a living. Here, have a fill." He pushed a wooden tobacco jar across the table.

"Thank you. I don't smoke a pipe. Cigars."

"Feel free." The dwarf struck a match and lit his pipe with care and attention. "And what plants do you breed?" he asked through wreaths of smoke.

"Garden peas, fuchsias. Different varieties. I am looking into the matter of inheritance."

"Is that right? A tricky thing, inheritance." He nodded and puffed smoke and nodded again. "Tricky." A sudden roar of applause sounded from the circus tent outside.

"Why tricky?"

The man shrugged and gestured with the stem of his pipe. "Take us."

Mendel shifted on his chair. He leaned forward. "You?"

"Well, take the little one over there." He gestured toward the girl in the corner with her woolen bundle. "Show the pastor, Heike, show the pastor."

The girl Heike tilted the bundle forward to display the same pug face as the rest of them, the same domed forehead, the same flattened nose. Mendel tried to restrain a shudder of revulsion.

"That little blighter's quite normal," the man said.

"Normal?"

"Oh yes. Quite normal. Can't you see? But he did for his mother, God bless her."

"Did for her? You mean . . ."

"Dead. Three months ago in Vienna. Heike's not the mother."

"And the father?"

"My son-in-law. You'd have seen him in the act. He's the one that hides inside the bucket. He's like us and yet his son is normal."

"What happens to the child, then?"

"Oh, we'll have him adopted. We can't have him growing up here, can we? It wouldn't be right. And he wouldn't be much use in the act, would he? I mean, who'd come to see the largest dwarf in the world?" He roared with laughter, and as though his joke had been heard inside the big top, there was another burst of applause outside.

Mendel stood up and banged his head on the roof. "See what I mean?" the man said. "It wouldn't be natural, would it?"

"I must go. They'll be wondering where I've been."

"Suit yourself."

"May I come back? Tomorrow, maybe? I'll bring you some of my plants. Fuchsias."

" 'Course," the man replied. "Not that I can do much with plants, moving about as we do. That's why it's ponies. But they'll look nice enough in here."

The next day he got their names and their ancestry, the whole tribe of them:

Johann, the grandfather, known as Big Johann. His wife, Magda. Their children, Johann (known as Little Johann), Willi,

Heike, and Birgit (the dead one). All dwarfs. And Johann and Magda told him something of their own ancestry too. All dwarfs, except Magda's maternal grandfather. "That's what I was told," Magda said. "That's what they always told me." And there was something else: "When you get one of us having children with one of you, then it's all right," the man explained. "But when two of us have children, sometimes it goes wrong."

"Goes wrong?"

"Not an ordinary baby. One like us, but more so. Smaller." He held out his own hands, small, stubby things, to demonstrate. "Little runts, they are. Never last more than a few months. My wife gave birth to one such twenty years ago."

Of course none of this is certain, he wrote in his notes, *being merely a small sample. One needs many examples to confirm the mathematical proofs, the records of whole families; but it is at least indicative. Big Johann tells me that it is a well-known fact in their world that a dwarf mother never gives birth to one of these severe dwarfs by a normal man.*

A HUMAN PEDIGREE

Demonstrating the Inheritance of Dwarfism

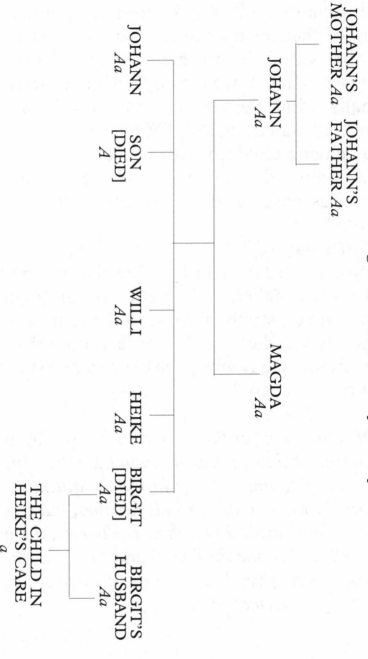

He handed the diagram to Bratranek. "There. I have added my own supposition of their inherited characters, but otherwise that is just as I was told it. It fits my ideas perfectly. Unlike garden peas, in mankind it would seem that the character of reduced growth dominates over the normal. I would consider delivering a talk on the matter to the Society, but I fear it would anger the Abbot. What do you think?"

Bratranek peered at the diagram. His expression was stern. He pursed his lips and pulled at his chin and frowned in the same way that he frowned at idle and foolish students. Mendel watched anxiously. "What do you think? Magda's mother is unknown, as you may see — Magda was abandoned as a child outside the caravan of circus folk, so they told me. Anyway, assuming both Magda and Big Johann to be hybrids, and assuming my theories to be correct, they would expect to give rise to normal children in a ratio of three dwarfs to each normal, and the fact that Magda did not produce a normally heighted child is no more than the workings of pure chance. Further, it would seem that any dwarf of the non-hybrid kind is of the nature A, that is, pure — although unable to breed and thereby demonstrate such purity of type because of early death. What do you think?"

"What do I think?" Bratranek gestured helplessly. "They are mere monsters, deformities, things against the perfection of nature. And where does it come from, this character? I mean, normal people do not make dwarfs."

"Ah, that's a question!" Mendel leaned over the thin man's shoulder and pointed to the figures. "Look at Birgit's husband. As far as I could ascertain, he came from parents who were both normal. So in a sense these people *are* normal. They differ only in this one thing, and that difference could happen to anyone. Exactly how it arises I do not know, but there is no doubt that it does happen. I guess it to be something occasional and spontaneous, a change in the inherited characters owing to some error — a sport. A normal character transmogrifies into an abnormal one, and despite not having inherited diverse characters from his parents, the new carrier becomes a kind of hybrid. Contrary to Darwin's assertion — the poor man is far off the track with his ideas of hybridization — this kind of transmogrification I would assume to be exceedingly rare."

"What has Darwin to do with it? These are aberrations —"

"My dear Bratranek, this is every bit as important as Darwin's theory, I can assure you. And in contrast to his, this idea is precise, almost mathematical. It calls other matters into question. Are we just children of chance? Are we merely products of mathematical probabilities, little different from the tossing of dice?"

Bratranek snorted. "That is mere foolery. If that were so, how could such a perfect thing as a human body ever be produced? If it were mere chance, then all of us would be monsters!"

"And there's this: Should I have warned the family that within their makeup lies this character for normality, which for them is anything but welcome? Magda herself was lucky. Her daughter Heike, as yet unrealized as a woman and a mother, carries the factor hidden within her body. It may be that a tortured childbearing lies ahead of this poor creature who appears so alien to us, but who differs in nothing more than a single inherited character."

In the lab the refrigerators hum, the ultra-centrifuges whine, the suction evaporator whirs. Patricia Primer, now revealed as plain Pat Storey, her gestures still awakening Benedict the goat, crouches over a rack of tubes and injects liquid from a micropipette. She flips the used pipette tip into a bin, snaps on a replacement, sniffs up another sample. Mere microliters. She glances round and smiles, the precise movements of her hand barely pausing. Her smile has the same effect on me as her gestures. What would she think, I wonder and have often wondered, if she knew about Eve? What would she think if she knew how I lust after her? Would she be surprised? Shocked? Flattered? Disgusted? Perhaps all those things.

"There's a box arrived by courier. I put it over there."

"Box?"

"From the States. Maybe it's those cultures we're waiting for."

"Why didn't you open it?"

"Not in the habit of opening other people's mail. It might be love letters. Or dirty magazines."

"Packed in dry ice?"

"Hot stuff." Back to the work.

Ochre Codon (Olga Conlon, you will be pleased to learn, but known to many as Olga Condom) emerges from the sterile room with a medical flat in which a pale yellow culture liquid slops. She is large and loose, having been through at least two of the other postdocs and one of the project leaders in the last year. I have wondered, of course. Benedict the goat has watched her plump knees and wondered about her plumper thighs. She sweeps past toward the incubators, drawing after her a particular scent, as sweet and corrupt as a blown rose. Vincent Vector, Eric Venables in real life (tried with Olga and apparently failed; she is free but not easy), crosses her path, moving from PCR thermal cycler to electrophoresis gel, carefully stepping each time over an expanded polystyrene box that lies almost in the center of the lab floor. Green lights on his PCR machine plot the rise of temperature — 76, 77, 78, 79 — and record the number of cycles, while the tubes inside, clutched by a heating block, proliferate DNA fragments on the rocket trajectory of an exponential curve — 2, 4, 8, 16, 32, 64, 128 . . . After thirty-two cycles you have 1,073,741,824 identical copies of the original molecule. It seems like getting something for nothing.

"I'm doing that family from Edinburgh," he says.

"The one with the homozygote?"

"That's right."

Benedict the goat, Benedict the propositus, humps the box up onto a bench and clambers onto a stool to open it. "Just like Christmas," he says.

"Hanukkah," says Olga over her shoulder.

The sender-label on my Hanukkah present says THE REDUCED HUMAN STATURE FOUNDATION, CHICAGO. As I remove the lid, the ghostly breath of dry ice rises to greet me. Couched within the mist, packed among steaming slabs of dry ice, are thirty plastic tubes, each red-capped, each labeled, each with a small plug of white matter in the tip. The plugs are made of frozen white blood cells cultured from five families with achondroplasia. The pedigrees, carefully cross-referenced to the tubes, have already been downloaded over the Internet.

"When can we . . . ?"

"Oh, crumbs," says Pat helplessly. "I can't possibly deal with them for a week at least. We'll have to store them."

"Get one of the graduate students to do them."

"Probably bugger them up."

It is a mundane world, a world of inconsequential chat while you follow a protocol that has been followed a hundred times before and can be followed now without thinking. Like cooking, very like cooking. A protocol, with its echoes of diplomacy, of law, of etiquette, is actually a recipe. You are constructing a sauce béarnaise. As with cooking, the uninitiated get it wrong and the sauce béarnaise curdles. Mere repetition is necessary to get it right, like Mendel with his cross-pollinations, hundreds and hundreds of cross-pollinations with a ninety-nine-percent success rate ("a very few [errors] . . . among more than ten thousand"[3]). You or I would get it right about once in every ten attempts, until we had repeated it dozens of times, until it had become routine . . .

"How's the library lady?" Olga asks. As she passes by, she ruffles my hair. Whether this is something I love or hate, I have never decided.

"She's fine."

"You seem . . . quite close."

"She's an old friend. From home."

The conversation dies away as she pulls on latex gloves (two pairs) and positions a Perspex screen between her and her rack of tubes and begins to make up a radioactive probe. Someone — is it Pat? — begins to hum a tune. In the silence everyone works.

It is a game of patience, this search. A game of watch and wait, of dealing the cards and reading the messages traced out in the cryptic bands of radioactive DNA probes. You deal and deal again. The patients queue up in the clinic, a whole circus assembly of

3. Mendel, *Versuche über Pflanzen-Hybriden*, 1868.

the dwarfed and stunted, to fill in forms and surrender blood samples. White blood cells are spun like a merry-go-round, and lysed[4] and digested and amplified,[5] and the little samples of DNA, translucent like semen, glistening like seed, are sorted and tagged and identified. The secret of life in a speck of jelly. Once upon a time the mystery was enshrined in the tabernacle on the altar, in a sliver of wafer. Now it lies, stripped open for mankind to read, in a polyacrimide denaturing gel.

Great-great-great-uncle Gregor would have understood.

Finding the Gene

You extract the DNA from cells. Then you use specific enzymes (called *restriction enzymes*) to chop the whole lot up into manageable pieces. These enzymes cut at specific, known places in the DNA message. I have a catalog at hand that lists ninety-three such enzymes; we have fifty different ones stored in the fridge. I am not talking about

4. SDS lysis, proteinase K digestion, phenol/chloroform extraction, ethanol precipation, and Tris-EDTA resuspension.
5. PCR using 1 U *Taq* polymerase and 30 cycles of denaturation, annealing, and elongation.

the frontiers of science here. Nowadays these things are commercially available. Using the enzyme of your choice, you carry out a digest, and then, from the whole mess, from the tens of thousands of different genes present in the gelatinous blob of DNA, you try to pick out the one that interests you.

Analogies, metaphors, similes. Searching for a needle in a haystack, that's the obvious one. There are 3.3×10^9 base pairs in the human genome. Thirty-three billion letters. Do you need a yardstick? Does your brain seize up when people start talking about the number of centimeters from here to the moon and the total length of all the blood vessels in the human body, that kind of thing? Well, I have a copy of the Bible on my bookshelf — it must be a copy that Jean left behind, because, let me assure you, I'd never have bought it — and I have done a rapid estimation of the number of letters in that edition. Fifty letters a line, fifty-five lines a page, 1,668 pages. Number of letters? Four and a half million, more or less. It includes the Apocrypha. So the human genome, the sum total of all the human genetic material, is some thousand times as big as the entire Bible. Only a fraction of those letters actually code for genes, but still, finding a single gene is difficult enough. Like searching the Bible for a single sentence.

Or how about this one: searching for a murderer among the whole population of a city?

Ah! You are closer now, aren't you? You can immediately play the flatfooted policeman and think of some kind of strategy. You know that this person exists, you know what he has done (a serial killer, perhaps), but you don't know where he lives. You can think of ways you might start, can't you? How about a door-to-door search, starting at Abbess Close and running through the A-to-Z to end up at Zoffany Street? Takes forever. You want to narrow down the search, increase your chances of getting it right, look only in those parts of the city where he might appear . . .

Just as the city is divided up into districts, so the human genome is divided into chromosomes. The first step is to identify the chromosome on which your gene lies. So we find families with achondroplasia and pick through their DNA. Like policemen looking for possible associates of the unknown man, we are looking for specific, known genetic markers and hoping to find one that tends to be inherited with the crime. The genetic markers are known as Restriction Fragment Length Polymorphisms (RFLPs), but they are referred to, always referred to as *riflips*. It sounds like something a jazz drummer might play: "Give me a riflip, man."

You follow the riflips with radioactive DNA probes. At first it is purely a matter of luck. There are RFLPs known throughout the whole human genome, in every district of the city. It is pure chance whether or not you choose to follow one that is actually linked to the gene that interests you. It may take a few weeks, it may take years. You just keep guessing and keep trying. Like any police investigation, the work is repetitive and painstaking. Like any police work it has its share of luck, good and bad.

Once you have found a linked marker, you find out which chromosome the marker came from. And once you know that, you know in which area of the city the suspect lives. You find other, closer, more intimate associates. And finally you can find the street.

It has taken us one year, almost exactly, to get our first linked marker. It is named, prosaically, D4S412, and it lies on chromosome 4. Precisely, the marker lies in the short arm of the chromosome. We need markers on either side of the gene, we need markers nearer the gene. We can begin walking the chromosome toward our goal. We are closing in, focusing on my own existence. Soon we will have identified the street, and then finally the house number, so that one quiet afternoon when there is no one around, when the children are all at school and the housewives are out at the shops, we can walk up the path to the ordinary front door and ring the bell.

[Dominant]

One day Jean didn't appear at work. I happened to go into the library for something, and she wasn't there behind the desk.

"Where's Miss Piercey?" I asked the head librarian.

"Who's Miss Piercey?"

"Miller. Mrs. Miller."

The man shrugged. "Phoned to say she was ill."

I imagined an alluring fever, the cheeks flushed and the bedclothes awry. But later in the morning there was a call put through to the lab. "It's me," said a voice. "Jean. Can we meet?"

"Meet? Where are you? Aren't you at home?"

"Not really." Not really? How could you not really be at home? The words made me angry. She did make me angry at times, with her willing stupidity, her calculated determination not to understand, not to think for herself, not to realize that she too had a brain. How, in God's name, could you *not really* be at home? "I'll explain when I see you," she said.

"Where?"

"The pub?"

"But why didn't you —"

"Just meet me there at the usual time. And make sure there's no one with you." There was a murmur of determination there, just a faint gleam of iron. "Just be there."

At The Pig and Poke I took my drink and a slice of quiche and retreated to what, over the weeks, had become our corner. "The missus left you, has she?" Eric called across as he pulled a pint of bitter. "Hey, how about this one? This'll grab you. How do you tell the sex of a chromosome?"

"Look up its genes."

His face fell. "You've heard it already." Then he brightened up as another regular entered. The joke was repeated, with roars of laughter to signal the punch line and gestures of acknowledgment in my direction. "Jeans and genes, you got it? That's what the professor there does, looks up the sex of genes, isn't that right, Prof?" he shouted.

I agreed that it was, more or less. A group of Belgian tourists came in to provide a blessed distraction. I turned back to my drink and the disconsolate slice of quiche; and Jean was sitting beside me on the bench.

There was an insubstantial quality to her apparition, as though she had not come in by normal means but had slipped, ghostlike, through the walls. She held her head in profile, tilted slightly forward as though she were examining very intently something that lay on the floor in front of her. The mouse-white skin across her cheekbone was reddened and swollen; her upper lip was puffed up, bringing a sudden and unfamiliar irruption to the modest curves of her mouth. "He hit me," she said quietly. "I don't know what to do. I don't know where to go. I need help, Benedict." I'd never realized that weeping could be such a silent thing. As I sat there helplessly, I wondered about the physiological basis for it, that soundless and incessant seepage of liquid from two tiny ducts in the eyelids. It seemed bizarre. I fumbled for things to say, but they fell to pieces in my hands and I was left only with useless fragments.

"I don't want to stay here," she said. "Where can we go?"

"I can't go anywhere. I've got a lecture straight after." Then inspiration struck. I searched around in my pocket and found the key to my flat. "Here, take this. Take a taxi. Have you got some money?"

She had some money.

I told her the address. "You can rest at the flat for as long as you like. I'll join you after the lecture. You're welcome to use the place . . ."

The tears had become tears of gratitude. How could I tell that? How can tears change their identity? She took the key without saying anything. I must admit to a certain tremor of anxiety. I didn't want her poking around within the doors of 28A Pearson Street, within the confines of my cave, and coming across my carefully tended collection of unusual photography and videotapes. Was Winsome Wanda, I wondered desperately, still lying with her legs splayed artlessly across my bedside table? But one must take risks in life. "I'll be back at about five," I told Jean. "You just make yourself comfortable till then." Which implied, somehow, that after that I was going to make her uncomfortable. She got up from the stool and turned away from the bar and went out through the door.

"Was that Jean, then?" Eric called. "She seemed all in a rush, didn't she?"

"Got an appointment." I turned back to my quiche, no longer feeling very hungry, wondering a whole lot of things. Miss Piercey was no longer mousy; but at what cost?

Doctor Benedict Lambert lectures at Imperial College on the latest developments in linkage analysis and homeobox genes. He lectures to a packed house, for the diminutive Doctor Lambert, the vertically challenged Doctor Lambert, the deformed and pitiable Doctor Lambert, has, ironically, a growing reputation. There is standing room only. The aisles are packed. People peer in through the glass panels in the doors and see that there is no more space. But don't imagine for one moment that they have come to hear about the *HOX7* gene and Wolf-Hirschhorn syndrome. I mean, who would be interested in such a thing? No, they have come to see the performer. Oh yes, I can offer them some good slides of fruit flies with antennae growing out of their heads and mice with stunted legs, but the monster they have come to see is there on the lecture stage, disappearing behind the lecture bench on occasion, cracking jokes about reduced stature in albino mice and showing slides to prove it, waving his magic wand at projection images of a homeodomain protein and how it might bind to the chromosomal DNA during the regulation of gene expression. The spotlight is on the midget; the hanging gardens roar and clap.

It is little better than the circus.

Hanging gardens? A literary allusion, gentle reader. Aldous Huxley again. A poem.

And all the time, there is just one thing in my mind, so much so that I muddle up the *HoxA3* gene in mice (complex head and neck deformities) with the *HoxA7* gene (ear and palate deformities), but no one notices — as I pontificate, all I think of is the eponymously named Miss Jean Piercey waiting in my shadowy basement flat. Slightly bruised, she lies, sleeping the sleep of the persecuted, on my bed. The bed is full size; I have a small chair and a lowered desk, but I sleep in the luxurious acres of a normal bed. Lest she awaken, I open the door (lowered handles) with care, and gaze unnoticed on her sleeping form. Her mousy hair is strewn across the pillow. Her mouth is half open and her breath (sour, tainted with fear) rasps gently between bruised lips. One hand cups her cheek, the other lies abandoned on the sheet. Miss Piercey. Snow Gray lying beneath the breathless gaze of her single, admiring dwarf. She has cast aside her dress and is wearing only a slip. Her legs are spread apart, almost as though she is caught in mid-stride running some desperate race, and her slip is caught up in all this silent rush so that the silken skin of one pale thigh gleams in the pallid afternoon light that filters down into the basement from the upper air. If I incline my head I can peer up into the scented shadows beneath the slip and glimpse pink flowers gathered there, a bouquet of sweet pea lain on a white cotton ground.

"Oh Christ, it's you!"

A curious ejaculation, given the circumstances. Fright? Disappointment? Relief? Who can tell? "I must have been flat out," she says, sitting up, arranging her skirts so that silken thighs are no longer exposed, but only the twin oysters of her patellae. Had she noticed the thoughtful and reverent inclination of my head, bowed as though before some idol? "God, how embarrassing."

Is it? "I'll make some tea," I suggest hurriedly. "You want some tea? Then you can tell me all about it."

But first? First, trapped by the exigencies of human physiology, I must repair to the bathroom and unzip my trousers and see again in my breathless memory those sheer thighs, that small cluster of flowers. "I'll do the tea," she calls through the door. I mumble some kind of reply. Nacreous, traitorous fluid lies in glutinous strings across the bidet. "If I can find the things," she adds.

I emerge into a calmer, more relaxed

world. There is time to hurry into the bedroom and consign *Playmate* and *Stud* to the bottom of a heap that also contains copies of *Science* and *Trends in Genetics* and offprints of my latest paper. In the kitchen Miss Piercey is apologizing, fussing over the teapot and a packet of plain chocolate digestive biscuits that she has found among the cornflakes and the pasta. "Do you have a special mug?" she is asking as she bends down to open a cupboard that for me lies at the correct height. "How did the lecture go? Gosh, you must be so nervous facing all those people and they all know so much, don't they? Aren't you afraid of being caught out?"

Nothing like as afraid of being caught out with you. A naturalist with a butterfly, the specimen settled on his hand, its wings opening and closing as though contemplating flight: a moth, a miller, flexing its wings and inducing a tornado in a distant, foreign land.

"Sit down and relax," I command her. "Just relax."

She does as she is bidden, suddenly and without argument. "I'll be fine after a nice cuppa," she assures me. "Just fine. And then I'll be out of your hair. I don't want to give you any trouble. It's awfully good of you to do this for me, but . . ."

"Where will you go?"

"To my aunt back home, I suppose. I can't go back, not to him."

"What happened?"

She shakes her head.

"Tell me about it," I suggest.

She shrugs. "It's not as easy as all that. Not that I don't want to. I mean, I need to get it off my chest to someone, but it's not that easy to explain."

"But he hit you. That's fairly straightforward, isn't it?"

"He does hit me, sometimes. Slaps. This was maybe worse than usual, I don't know. But he does." Another shrug. The gesture is important in Jean Piercey's life. It signifies all those things you can't do anything about, and they are legion. I shrug often enough, I suppose. But I prefer a bleak and humorless smile.

"Why don't you go to the police?"

"He'd go mad."

"He seems to go mad enough as it is. What's his reason?"

"Reason?" Another shrug. She stares into her mug of tea, as though maybe there's a reason in there. "Hates me, I suppose. Just fed up with me."

"How long have you been married?"

"Six years."

"And no children?"

"Hugo says it's my fault."

"And then he hits you?"

She didn't answer directly. "Silly thing is, he's no bigger than me. You've met him. He's no bigger than me."

E. B. Ford, Fellow of All Souls and Honorary Fellow of Wadham College, sometime Emeritus Professor of Ecological Genetics at Oxford University, known as Henry to generations of undergraduates:

". . . the XYY type tends to be ill-adjusted, being aggressive in a way which often leads to crimes of violence, so that such people find their way into prisons. Here we have an instance of the widely established fact that intelligence and psychology are under genetic control."[1]

Here we have an instance of the widely established fact that experts are frequently stupid and prejudiced and usually have their heads stuffed firmly up their arses. By the time the good Henry wrote those words it had been established in the United States (Pyeritz et al., 1977) that a *maximum* of one percent of XYY males may spend part of their lives in mental-penal institutions.

That leaves a *minimum* of ninety-nine per-

1. *Understanding Genetics*, Faber 1979, p. 42.

cent who won't.

I wonder what the percentage is of Emeritus Professors of Ecological Genetics who ought to spend part of their lives in mental institutions? Does All Souls count?

I feel obliged to report that in the course of my own research, I, Benedict Lambert of the Royal Institute for Genetics, have discovered an inherited factor that is a *certain* causative agent in criminal behavior. It is particularly closely correlated with criminal behavior of a violent nature. There is no doubt about this. The figures are incontrovertible. I am talking about 99.9 percent confidence limits. Perhaps my name should be given to this factor, in the way that discoverers so often become eponymous. Think of Down and his syndrome; think of Huntington and his chorea. Perhaps this one ought to be the Benny factor. I suppose I'd be accused of flippancy.

Ninety-five percent of the total British prison population possess the Benny factor; the proportion goes up to ninety-seven percent when you consider violent crime. With sex crime the correlation between the Benny factor and the crime is virtually total, complete, one hundred percent. Thus, to follow the argument of the good E. B. Ford and others to the logical conclusion, all we have to do is identify people who possess this factor (a trivial task, let me assure you; anyone with a modicum of intelligence can be trained to do it) and isolate them from the rest of the population. Perhaps we could get them to wear some kind of distinguishing mark on their clothes; possibly we could introduce some kind of preventive detention, camps where carriers may be kept under careful supervision. Clearly there would be unfortunate ramifications of such a policy, but the advantages to society will far outweigh the disadvantages, for with this genetic marker identified and crime banished from the streets, who will care that these people will be shunned by all decent citizens, discriminated against in the workplace, refused insurance or mortgages? Who will worry that their credit rating will be zero, that people will stare at them in the street and children will throw stones? The world will be a safer place without them.

Later, when the general population is used to the situation, we might even consider a . . . final solution.

You've guessed, haven't you? The Benny factor is the Y chromosome. Not the possession of an *extra* Y chromosome, but the possession of just *one*. It is the simple fact of being male. Whenever the biological determinists, the eugenicists, the E. B. Fords of this world, start mouthing their rubbish, remember that: lock up all the males and violence will disappear from the streets.

"You're staying here," I told Jean.

"I can't."

"Of course you can."

"What'll people say?" She wept silently, her face patchy and ugly. "What'll they say?"

"For God's sake, what do you think they'll say? They won't imagine there's anything between us, will they? For Christ's sake, they won't imagine *that!*"

The tears dried. She looked at me with a strange sadness. "You shouldn't say that kind of thing."

I laughed. "My dear Mrs. Miller, I've been saying that kind of thing all my life. I don't aim to stop now. I offer you some kind of refuge from your foul husband — incidentally, I thought he was quite revolting —"

"He's not really like that —"

"Oh, for God's sake! I offer you refuge, and it is entirely your own affair whether you accept my offer or not. But don't try to get me to pretend I'm not what I am. Or that he isn't what he is, come to that."

"But you must —"

I held up my hand, my small, pudgy hand

that probes into the intimate secrets of the human genome. "I'm not going to argue about anything. You just stay safely with me for as long as you like."

She did feel safe, of course, for she knew that what I said was true: there was no danger. No danger from me, I mean. So she stayed for supper and we chatted a bit afterwards, and then she went to sleep in my bed and I went into the sitting room and made some kind of bed on the sofa; and when she was fast asleep I crept softly back into my room to look at her.

She was in no danger. I merely coveted the sight of her crushed face on my pillow, the mousy hair sprayed carelessly across the cotton. As I stood there looking at her she stirred gently, entirely oblivious of my presence. I am in the mood for confession. While she slept I cautiously extracted her underwear from the neatly folded pile of clothes on the chair — pants, brassiere, tights, the whole delicious, fragrant bundle — and tiptoed out to the sanctuary of the bathroom. I sorted through my trophies in an agony of tumescence and expectation. The bra was 34A. The knickers bore the name of the patron saint of Judeo-Christian commerce, *Saint Michael,* and were decorated with pink and red and yellow blooms. Sweet pea? At the gusset there was a faint mark like a brush-stroke of pollen — a delicate suggestion of nether, perhaps equally bruised, lips. I pressed the scrap of cotton to my face and drew in her sharp, sour, sweet, secret scent and knew things about Miss Piercey that I had only imagined . . .

Coming into the tiny kitchen the next morning she had a rueful smile on her rather less bruised lips. "You washed my underthings."

"I thought you'd want them clean."

"You shouldn't have."

"A labor of love."

She smiled the kind of smile that warns you not to be silly. Perhaps she knew. I had never granted her much in the way of understanding, but perhaps she understood. "I don't normally do this, you know," she observed as she sipped her breakfast coffee.

"Do what?"

"Stay the night with other men." She even giggled.

That morning we went to work together, going up the steps of the Institute together, calling a "Good morning" to the receptionist together, and climbing the grandiose stairs side by side to the first floor. She had to go slowly to let me keep up with her. The librarian looked askance as she went in.

"I'm sorry I wasn't able to get in yesterday, Mr. Blackwall," she said. "I wasn't well."

The man sniffed disapprovingly. "There's been a phone call for you. Your husband. Wants you to call him as soon as you get in."

I watched her expression. I saw fear. I know fear well. I've grown used to it. Fear for me is a matter of existence. I walk among giants and I know fear. I stood, abject with terror, in the bike shed at school and watched bare and grimy knees advance on me, and I knew fear. I probe with small, plump fingers among the molecules of inheritance and I know fear. The mere act of existence for me is an act of fear. I feel fear merely by being; but none of this is the fear that I saw in Jean's expression as she went into the library office to phone Hugo Miller.

"Go back if you think you must," I told her over a flabby meat pie in The Pig and Poke. Her husband had wept on the other end of the phone, wept and pleaded for her to come back, begged for forgiveness, swore devotion, all the usual things. He needed her more than he needed anything else in the world.

She thought about it hard. She wasn't stupid, Jean Piercey wasn't. Wasn't, isn't. She is just one of those people who have been educated to be stupid, that's all. Failed the eleven-plus. Cannon fodder. Someone's got to stamp the cards, someone's got to sweep the streets and empty the bins, someone's got to lick the stamps and check that the forms are filled in properly. Someone's got to say "yes, sir; no, sir." Someone has got to have narrow horizons.

"The second time you leave, it won't come as such a shock," I warned. "You don't want to lose the advantage."

I didn't want to lose the prize.

"I can't stay. I haven't got any things."

"Go and get them. When does he finish work? Go and get them. Now."

She giggled. The word *giggle* has a bad press. Children giggle, schoolgirls giggle, giggling is what you do round the back of the bike sheds when they take their dicks out to show you. Jean Piercey's giggle bubbled with something else — genuine amusement, the rich, dark, unexpected amusement of anarchy. "That'd teach the bastard, wouldn't it?" she said.

Bastard? Not mousy Miss Piercey at all.

So I drove her out to Ruislip. We left the Institute at three o'clock and I drove her out to Galton Avenue and I waited in the car on the other side of the road outside number

35, while she crept up to her own front door like a housebreaker. She took only a few minutes inside, and then she was out again and hurrying down the drive with a small suitcase in her hand.

"Did you see the curtains?" she asked breathlessly as we drove away. "Did you see?"

"Which curtains?"

"Next door, of course. Twitching. This is net-curtain country. They see everything, they know everything. They've got me labeled now. Tart. Going off with . . ." I noted the pause. ". . . a strange man. Just you see."

"What'll he do when he finds out?"

"Stew in his own juice."

We went out to dinner that evening at a little place in the Old Brompton Road. To celebrate the escape from Colditz. That's what she called it. "Isn't that where they locked everyone up? I saw it on the telly ages ago." She insisted on *truite aux almandes* as the only thing she could recognize on the menu. I offered to translate the rest, but she appeared happy with the choice. "Hugo always says French food is a load of pretentious nonsense. Normally we eat Indian. Or Chinese. Do you like Chinese?"

I agreed that I did like Chinese. "Chinky

nosh," she said with relish. "We used to have one every Friday, Hugo and me. It used to be fun." She raised flakes of white meat to her mouth. "We never had trout."

Trout Hatcheries

In trout hatcheries you don't want males. Males are inconvenient. Quite apart from the fact that they don't produce babies, they mature earlier than females and once mature they show aggressive tendencies, particularly at high population densities. In a normal trout population (50:50 male and female), half the population is therefore a potential danger to the other half. So why not do away with the males?

But you need males to breed, I hear you cry. Your tone is a little desperate, I must admit, because I suspect that you realize that, with all the sperm a male trout produces (or a male human, come to that), you don't need very many; but you do need one or two.

A short, and I hope unnecessary, biology lesson:

Male trout, just as male humans, are XY; that is, in every body cell there is one X and one Y chromosome. It is that fact which makes them male (and, as in humans, gives them criminal tendencies). Females, on the other hand, are XX. This means that the sperm cells from each male may *either* carry an X *or* a Y chromosome; whereas all the eggs from a female will carry an X. When a Y chromosome sperm cell fertilizes an egg, the result is an XY baby — a male. When an X sperm does the job you get an XX female. So, just as with humans, fifty percent of trout are male and fifty percent are female. And your next generation has fifty percent nonproducers, fifty percent that are nothing more than bags of sperm, fifty percent with criminal tendencies.

It's that damned Y chromosome again.

So this, in trout hatcheries at least, is how it's done:

You rear some female trout (XX, of course), but you dose them with male sex hormone. This turns them into males of a kind. They produce sperm, for example. But genetically they remain XX, and so every sperm cell produced carries an X chromosome. Using these "males" as a source of sperm, every fertilization will be by an X sperm with an X egg. Every baby trout that these "males" father (if you'll forgive the expression) will turn out a female.

"I think that's disgusting," Miss Piercey said, but it didn't stop her eating the fish. I ordered a bottle of white Burgundy, and then another. She ate and drank with abandon, and her laughter sounded loud in the land. We drank a toast to freedom and the death of bullies. "I always thought Burgundy was red," Jean said, eyeing her fifth or sixth glass with suspicion. "I've got a burgundy coat at home. That's red."

"There's red and there's white. Mix them together and you get rosé."

She looked at me slyly. "They don't do it like that. I read it in a magazine . . ."

"Oh, but they do. Pure red crossed with pure white makes rosé, like with sweet pea. Incomplete dominance, like with sweet pea."

"Sweet pea sounds rude . . ."

"Diabetes mellitus. Autosomal control with low penetrance."

She giggled over the dissected corpse of her trout. "What on earth are you on about? You don't half talk, you know. I don't understand half of what you say sometimes, truly I don't. What's penetrance, if I might ask? That sounds rude as well."

"Penetrance is as pure as the driven snow. Mere genetic jargon."

"You know, Hugo never really talks to me. Maybe that's the problem. Wonder what he'd think if he knew where I was now. When people talk, at least you know what they're thinking, don't you?"

"Do you? Do you know what I'm thinking?"

She stopped, and considered me, head on one side, looking at me directly, not with that sideways and evasive glance that so many people have. "You're thinking I'm a silly chatterbox, like as not."

"I'm not thinking that at all," I said, quite truthfully.

"What did you used to think all those years ago in the library back home, I wonder?" She had a strange and distant smile. The question didn't seem to be directed at me, so I didn't offer an answer; but I could see that she knew, more or less. She wasn't stupid. I think I've said that before.

Our absurd, trivial chatter meandered on, and by the end of the meal Jean was gently pissed, slightly unsteady on her feet but putting a brave and earnest face on things. "I've had too much. Got no head for it at all. My father was TT, did I tell you that? No drink in the house. Ooh, what a disgrace I am."

We found our way back to the flat and let ourselves in with conspiratorial whispers. "What the hell would Hugo think if he saw me now?" she wondered aloud. "Staying with a strange man, I mean. What'd he think?" She was skipping on one foot and trying to take her shoes off at the same time.

"What d'you think he'd think?" She spluttered with laughter at her muddled words. "What d'you think he'd think I'd think?" — and lurched into the doorjamb. To save herself from falling, she balanced with one hand on the top of my head. It was the first time she had touched me. The second shoe finally came off, and she flipped it into the bedroom. I followed her stockinged feet (big toe sadly distorted by narrow shoes) into the bedroom. "What'd he think, Benedict? What's Benedict think?"

I offered no answer. I'm not sure I was capable. I was stone cold sober, but more intoxicated by far than ever she was. I watched her undress. "What are you looking at?" she demanded, but she didn't stop. Jacket, shirt, skirt, tights, all of them came off. They lay in a puddle on the floor. "What are you looking at, young man?" Her skin was very white, as though it had never seen the light of day. Slightly unhealthy. Almost albino. Her breasts seemed paltry in their flimsy cups of nylon. There was a soft fold of flesh over the top of her pants, an unevenness in the flesh of her thighs. She had a large mole about two inches across on the inside of her right thigh — a somatic cell mutation with the ever-present possibility of transformation into malignant melanoma. I hadn't pictured that. Much of the rest, yes — the prominent navel, the faintly mottled skin, the scribble of hair in the crease of her groin; but not that melanic blemish. "I'm not taking any more off with you standing there, you know." Her hips were wide and rather clumsy. She put her hands on them. "I'm not, you know."

"I thought you might want me to wash your things."

"Oh, you did, did you?" Her tone was faintly belligerent, alcohol doing its work. Miss Piercey far from mousy. Pissed as a newt, in fact. She considered my suggestion through clouded mind, and me through ill-focused eyes. "That's what you want, is it?"

I shrugged. It wasn't, but it'd do.

"Turn around," she said, finally. "And no peeping."

I did as I was commanded. There was a confused movement behind me, and I turned to see a flash of white flesh and a heaving of the bedclothes and Miss Piercey lying as sleek as a corpse beneath the sheet and eyeing me over the top. The garments in question lay on the floor in front of me. "Night, night," she said; and giggled.

[Penetrance]

Next morning she was contrite. She stood at the door to the kitchen looking pale and slightly ill. And curiously young, like a child caught out. "I feel awfully embarrassed."

"There's no need."

"I must have been disgusting."

"Lovely. Funny."

"Drunk. There's nothing funny about drunk. My father used to be really cross when he saw a comedian acting drunk. Perverting the young, he used to say. I think I ought to go."

"Don't. Please don't."

It was framing it as a request that did it. She was so used to being told what to do, but I *asked* her to stay, and the tone was one of pleading. It was surprising coming from me, I suppose. She came into the kitchen and sat down. It was all a bit absurd: me on my own chair at the low table; she perched awkwardly on a stool above me. "You *want* me to stay," she said. She wasn't looking for confirmation. It was a statement of fact, edged with amazement.

"Of course I do."

That lunchtime it was Janáček's *Sinfonietta for Orchestra* at the Albert Hall, with a brass section like the band of the Grenadier Guards. In 1864, at the age of ten, Leoš Janáček joined the choir school at the monastery of the Augustinians in Brno, where he studied under the choirmaster Pavel Křižkovsky. Thus said the program notes.

Like Mendel, Janáček was from northern Moravia. They would have shared the accent. Like Mendel, Janáček was fascinated by the countryside and by wildlife. He must have walked around the monastery garden with the friar; he must have seen the mice in their cages and the bees in the hives on the slope behind the chapter house; he must have played with the pet vixen, an orphaned animal that had been rescued as a cub by a friend of Mendel's; he must have heard the fat friar's stories about animals, and lectures condemning catapults. Mundane things, the matters of childhood that etch themselves more deeply into the memory than any adult experience.

Genetics is of scant interest to musicians, and music of rare concern to geneticists (although tone deafness [dysmelodia] and perfect pitch are probably autosomal dominant traits with imperfect penetrance[1]); so biographies of Mendel never mention Janáček and biographies of the composer of *The Cunning Little Vixen* never mention Mendel. Such is the narrow way we perceive the past. When, at the age of nineteen, Janáček was appointed to the position of choirmaster in place of Father Pavel Křižkovsky, it was Abbot Gregor Mendel who appointed him.

"Parp, parp, parp. I *hate* this kind of thing," Jean complained delightedly. "And it just makes my headache worse." She laughed at the clash of brass, and the people beside us stared, both at her laughter and her diminutive companion. She leaned toward me and giggled. "Solemn bastards," she breathed into my ear in startling tones. I wondered whether the effects of the night before had quite worn off. And then, "I wonder what Hugo would think."

"Forget Hugo." But she couldn't. Of course she couldn't. The concert came to the end, and the exiguous audience spilled out into the winter sunlight, and she was still thinking of Hugo.

"Did you love him?" I asked.

"Love him? The question doesn't mean very

1. Kalmus and Fry, *Annuals of Human Genetics* 43, 1980; Profita and Bidder, *American Journal of Medical Genetics* 29, 1988.

much, does it? I was used to him. 'Used to' gets as strong as 'love,' you know that? Like you love your parents, I suppose. You're used to them. It's not belittling. It just *is*."

"And you felt this way about Hugo? Even though he beat you up?"

"Felt, feel. Still do, I suppose. He can be . . ." She paused. We turned into the Cromwell Road.

"Can be . . . ?"

"Very loving," she said.

We checked through the gate and climbed the steps of the Institute. She stopped in front of the doors. "Oh, Christ," she said. It wasn't the kind of language Miss Piercey normally used. But then quite a lot about Miss Piercey was different now.

"What is it?"

"It?" She could see through the lights in the door. In my own diminutive world all I could see was polished oak. She glanced down at me. "It's him." Taking a deep breath, she pushed the door open. "It's him," she repeated.

Hugo Miller was standing in the hallway beneath the bust of Karl Pearson, looking like someone who has been directed to the wrong crematorium. There was an unsteadiness about him, as though he were balancing on the edge of a cliff or the blade of a knife or something. "Where have you been?" he demanded when he saw who it was coming in through the door. "Where the hell have you been?"

I was ignored. I occupy a level of existence in which young children move. At parties, the Christmas party at the Institute for example, I inhabit a world of legs and knees and crotches, and unless I can maneuver the conversation over to the side of the room where there might be a sofa or something, I have to jump up and down and wave my arms about to get noticed.

"Hugo," she said.

I pushed past her and stood between the two of them. Piggy in the middle. But Hugo Miller looked over me, overlooked me, didn't even allow me to swim into the lower reaches of his consciousness. "How dare you run out on me like that?" he shouted above my head. He sounded incredulous. So too did the receptionist, the redoubtable Miss Conway, who, it was rumored, had been at the Institute ever since the days of Bateson and Pearson. "In Christ's name, where the devil have you been?"

"Your theology's slipping," I warned him.

He turned on me, turned *down* to me. "You shut up, you little twerp. It's probably your fault."

"Please don't make a scene, Hugo," she said quietly. She had the subdued voice of a loser.

"Scene? I'll give you scene. You just come here." He took her by the arm. There was a momentary scuffle over my head. Hugo grabbed one of Jean's arms, I grabbed the other. We pulled. From the outside, from Miss Conway's viewpoint for example, it would have seemed absurd, like something from one of Fellini's films: a dwarf and a full-grown man pulling at either side of a thin and rather bewildered woman. "Do you want to go with him?" I cried to her. "Do you want to?"

He barged me out of the way. "Get off, you bastard!" But I held on, and so he dragged Jean toward the door with me hanging on the other side like a terrier. "Let go, Benedict," Jean cried, "or he'll hurt you."

Or he'll hurt you.

"Let go, Benedict," she cried once more.

Did I release my grip, or did she merely slip out of my grasp? I thought about it long afterwards. Whatever happened, Miller pulled her away from me and pushed her out through the door. Then he glanced back at me standing helpless in the middle of the checkerboard floor of the hallway, and his face contracted in a spasm of loathing. "It's none of your fucking business, do you understand? You're nothing but . . ." He paused, as though searching through his vocabulary for the right word. Then he found it, got it spot on, hit the target: "Nothing but a nasty little mutant."

"Well!" exclaimed Miss Conway.

"Well what?" I asked.

"Well, I never."

I retreated to the laboratory. Emotional? Agitated? Those are the feelings of normal people. I am a little mutant.

"Is everything all right, Ben?" Olga asked. "You look a bit upset."

"Not me."

She was busy proliferating the DNA of a suspected rapist for the scientific department of the Metropolitan Police. The polymerase chain reaction (PCR) enables the most minimal sample of DNA (in this case from a smear of dried semen from the victim's underwear) to be amplified until there is enough of it to carry out comparative tests and so identify the owner. PCR is the photocopier of the world of genetics, quick and easy and taken for granted. You place the sample of DNA that you want to copy in a test tube and heat it up. At 94°C the double-stranded molecule surrenders to the heat: it melts, opening up into two single strands, laying open its molecular message. Then the mixture is cooled to about 70°C, and as it cools a DNA polymerase enzyme assembles new strands on each half of the original molecule, new images of the exposed message, casts from the mold. The sample (double the DNA now) is heated up again. Once again the double molecules open up, casts separating from molds. Cool again, and new complementary strands are assembled once more, the genetic message reproduced exactly, new cast from mold, new mold from cast. Heat again, and the DNA opens once more; cool, and it is replicated . . .

The process goes on, the number of molecules of DNA doubling for each cycle: 2, 4, 8, 16, 32, 64, 128, 256, 512 . . . You see nothing. It takes place in a miniature test tube in an automatic heating block. Photocopying the messages of life.

What would Great-great-great-uncle Gregor have made of that? He who inferred the existence of heredity particles only by counting numbers, by reckoning ratios, he who fumbled with language — *merkmal, anlage* — to try to give these unknown, unimagined, unimaginable entities semantic substance, how would he have come to terms with the modern reality — that now you can make unlimited copies of a gene at will?

"I wonder what he was like," Olga said thoughtfully.

"Who?"

She leaned over the bench, her lower lip bitten in delicate concentration as she pipetted into a tiny plastic test tube. "Our rapist."

"A man."

A pause, and then a quizzical glance across at me. "All men?"

"Not all."

You must picture Doctor Benedict Lambert in white gown and face mask and latex gloves. To work with such tiny amounts of DNA, you must work in conditions of the utmost sterility lest a stray bacterium get in on the act and eat up the carefully preserved sample. DNA is a most nutritious substance, providing sugar and organic nitrogen in abundance, plus essential phosphorus. Quite a treat. There is also the danger that DNA from cells of your own skin may contaminate the sample; if you're careless, you might end up amplifying your own DNA instead of the rapist's. It would be like the witness to a crime identifying one of the innocent men standing in the identification line instead of the suspect.

Olga crossed the lab to the PCR machine and keyed in her requirements — temperatures, time, number of cycles — then popped the tube into one of the hollows on the heating block. She was humming one of her mindless tunes.

"Did you have lunch with Miss Library?"

"Mrs. Miller."

"You know who I mean. She's quite pretty. In a mousy sort of way. Where do you go? Not that dreadful Pig and Poke?"

"I like the place."

Another of those glances. Take it or leave it, answer as you please. "You fancy her?"

"I'm fond of her."

"Oh yeah? *Fond* are you? I've heard of fond. I expect old erection here" — she pointed to the tube of DNA — "was *fond* of his victim. *Fond* is a prude's word, Ben. You *fancy* her. That's what you say. You fancy Miss Library something painful. And who knows?" She grinned, gap-toothed, like the Wife of Bath. "Maybe she fancies you."

Once the amplification has taken place, you digest the DNA with enzymes and separate the fragments by gel electrophoresis. Then the fragments are denatured into single strands using half-molar sodium hydroxide, and transferred to a nitrocellulose filter by Southern blotting. The filter is then washed with a radioactive probe to identify specific DNA repeat sequences. They go by the name of VNTRs — Variable Number Tandem Repeats. The pattern of these sequences is then photographed. The resulting picture looks rather like the bar code on a packet of fish fingers in a supermarket. The pattern is unique to each individual, that's the point. Your sperm is your undoing.

I wondered, I still wonder, would Hugo Miller's DNA contain within itself, somewhere within the intricate sequence of its bases, the seeds of his own violence? Monoamine oxidase A deficiency or something of that nature — a plain *reason* for his behavior instead of the cryptic complexities of upbringing and environment?

The phone rang at the flat when I got back that evening: a woman's voice with more than a hint of anger in it, and more than a hint of Scots. "Is that Doctor Lambert?"

It was.

"Ruislip police here. There's a Mrs. Miller with us at the station. She's been hurt."

"Hit?"

"I didn't say that, sir."

"I didn't say you did. I asked a question."

There was a pause on the other end of the line and a small hiss of electronic anger from the speaker. "Mrs. Miller gave your name, Doctor Lambert. I think it'd be better if you were to come round to the station, sir."

They were startled to see me, of course. The whole world is startled to see me. It overlooks me as though it were expecting a normal trunk to appear in the space over my head, like the Cheshire Cat's body materializing behind its grin; and then, when that doesn't happen, it looks down at me in something like surprise, something like revulsion, something like the expression of someone looking into the deep freeze and seeing a human head there at the bottom among the frozen peas and the fish fingers. "Are you by any chance a medical doctor, sir?" The Scots accent was even more marked in the flesh — a considerable amount of flesh, in fact. Positively obese. And angry with it.

"I'm a genetic one."

She frowned, as though I might have been making a joke and this was not the time for jokes. Or being sarcastic. But this *was* the time for sarcasm. "Is Mrs. Miller a patient of yours, sir?"

"She's a friend, a colleague. Is she hurt?"

"The doctor's seen her," she said. "There's nothing too bad."

I followed the policewoman's large blue backside down a corridor. I was at just about the same level. Blue serge and black lisle stockings. Legs like Indian clubs. For a moment I wondered how the woman would appear, shorn of the uniform of officialdom, stark naked and wobbling as she moved. Little more alluring than me, I guessed. Then she opened the door onto an interview room and I forgot all about that, because there was Jean sitting at a table, clutching a mug of tea in her hands. She had a cut and swollen lip and a black eye. One cheek was puffed up, and there was a plaster over her left eyebrow.

"I didn't know if you'd come," she said quietly. And she apologized, actually apologized as though she were to blame — as though she had been brought in for drunken driving or something. "I'm sorry, Benedict. I'm awfully sorry. They wanted me to go into hospital for observation, but I said no. I just gave them your name. I know it was silly, but that's what I did. The thing is, when you've been married for a few years you don't have many people to turn to, do you?"

The policewoman looked at me doubtfully. "Mrs. Miller's had a nasty experience. She'll need a bit of peace and quiet."

"What happened?" I asked. I wanted to put my arm around her, of course, to bring her that fragile thing that we call comfort. But of course I couldn't reach.

"We were called by the neighbors," the policewoman said, but I hadn't really asked her.

"And Hugo? What about Hugo?"

Again it was the policewoman who answered. "Mr. Miller is in custody at the moment. But unless Mrs. Miller brings charges, there's nothing much we can do."

Jean looked at me with those absurd eyes. "I don't want that. That'd be awful, wouldn't it?"

"Not as awful as what happened."

She sipped her tea and shook her head. "Awful," she repeated.

And that was how she came to stay. An angel of mercy, I was. Cherub. A cherub of mercy. An ugly, aged cherub of mercy, bereft of wings. She still had some of her things at my place, and we bought others, going round the shops almost like a husband and wife, laughing at the looks we got. We were, in a way, happy. In my shadowy basement flat I think she felt free for the first time in years, because of course I imposed no restraint on her. I couldn't dare to. She settled into the flat and she seemed quite unconcerned about the incongruity of things. "Snow White and her single dwarf," I said once, and she grew really angry. A delightful sight, Miss Piercey angry, as angry as when I remember her catching someone sneaking out of the library back home with a stolen book tucked away in a carrier bag. "Benedict Lambert, don't you dare say things like that! We are what we are inside, not what we look like."

She sounded like my mother. She had a childlike sense of optimism, and the mere fact of my existence couldn't cure her of it. She was convinced that "things would work out." We were therefore a ménage of opposites: hopeful against hopeless, cheerful against acerbic, tall against dwarf.

She didn't bring charges of assault or battery or any of the other things the police suggested against her husband, but the courts did put some kind of restraining order on him anyway. "Restraining order" sounds like a muzzle, but it didn't stop his phoning her at work and abusing her. "Got a man, have you?" he would ask her. "Nothing but a fucking tart."

She tried to reason with him, but it was pointless. Hugo Miller appeared to be partway round the bend and straining to discover what was beyond the corner. "You're not supposed to be telephoning me, Hugo. And apart from everything else, it's bloody inconvenient interrupting me at work." I don't know whether she got the expletive from me. It wasn't the kind of word she used normally, but then times weren't normal, were they? Times were bloody abnormal, in fact.

"I'll have to get somewhere of my own," Jean told me. "I'll have to get out of your hair."

"You'll do nothing of the sort."

"You want me here? You're always snapping at me, always telling me what's wrong and what's right."

I explained that that was just my manner, that when you've been in my business for long enough, the didactic manner becomes normal, that I was nothing more than a bore and should be told to shut up if necessary.

"You mean you want me?" She laughed. "Want me here, I mean?"

"Of course I do."

"But I've kicked you out of your bed and everything. You can't forever go sleeping on the sofa. It's not right."

"It's all right by me for the moment."

"Until?"

"Until you invite me in with you."

A pregnant silence, if you'll forgive the expression.

"Is it true what they say, then?" Eric asked one lunchtime.

"What do they say, Eric?"

He drew a pint of bitter and sniffed, as though considering the matter. "That you two are shacked up together."

"It's not what you think at all," Jean said indignantly.

"Who says that?" I demanded. Among other things I felt a stir of pride. Quite unjustified pride of course, but then all too often pride operates without justification.

"People," Eric replied carelessly.

"People should mind their own business."

He nodded, as though at one of the eternal verities. "They never do, though, do they? Anyway, good luck to you, I say."

Jean eyed me curiously over the steak-and-kidney pie. "Cheeky devil."

"Me or him?"

She pursed her lips in that way she had. Her two eyes, the green and the blue, considered me in their own, asymmetric manner. "Both of you," she said.

I'm looking for a moment, of course. *The* moment. Was it then in the pub, when Eric brought the subject up, thrust it, so to speak, into her consciousness? Or was it the morning when she suddenly and without apparent reason smiled and reached across and touched my cheek as we sat at the breakfast table? Or when we ate at that French restaurant and talked of trout? Or later, when we went to a piano recital and heard some unknown Czech pianist play *On an Overgrown Path* with such intensity that Jean actually wept, there in the recital room among the suppressed coughs and the faint air of tedium? Or was it one Saturday afternoon when there was a Toulouse-Lautrec exhibition at the Tate Gallery and a party of schoolgirls stared after us as we moved from *The Moulin Rouge* to *Jane Avril* and one of the girls whispered in a voice that echoed from the ceiling, "Look, Miss, it's *'im.*" Jean laughed. It was a bitter, ironic laugh. She was learning. As the wretched schoolteacher hurried her children into the next room, Jean looked at me and laughed. Was that the moment? Materially, no. Materially it required other things, a concatenation of events. But, beneath the plain material cause of things, was it then, as she looked at me and laughed?

After the exhibition we walked out into the afternoon and strolled along the embankment. The tide was out. Gulls cried in the wind. The heavy slick of the river slid past like bile. A small steamer was battering its way downstream toward Chelsea while on the mud flats a pair of herons picked fastidiously over the debris. Across the river, the bulk of Battersea Power Station lay like a vast, inverted dining table. Jean glanced down at me. "Can I tell you something, Benedict?" she asked, and her tone was portentous, the sound I dreaded, the sound of doctors about to deliver judgment. *I'm afraid there's nothing whatever we can do . . .*

"Please don't."

"You're so brave," she told me. "I mean, I've got problems, but compared with yours they're nothing. And you never mention things. Never. You can even laugh."

Things.

"It's not being brave," I assured her with the famous Benedict carelessness. "To be brave you've got to have a choice. You've got to have the option to be a coward. When you're like me there's no choice."

She looked at me with those eyes, and I read a muddle of pain and pity there. "If you weren't like you are . . ."

"It'd be another world."

She stared into the wind. Those eyes, those matchless eyes, were glistening with tears. But the wind might well have done that. It was cold and raw, coming from the Essex marshes. "It'd be easier," she said. "That's all. Easier."

We got back that afternoon in a shared mood. Sentimentality, perhaps. Sentiment, certainly. The two float dangerously near each other, like related bacteria in a culture, infecting each other with plasmids, passing the genes for mawkishness and insincerity, love and lust, back and forth. And laughter helped. And alcohol. All these things.

"What do you want to do?" she asked as she cleared away the supper dishes. We had drunk more of a very ordinary *vin ordinaire* than was good for us, and had laughed immoderately over *el cheapo* and *chateau plonc*.

"That's up to you."

Miss Piercey was a different woman. No longer a mouse. A rat, a laboratory rat, white and sleek and with a mind of her own. We looked at each other through some kind of haze of alcohol and pity, and, in tones clouded with embarrassment, she told me that she wouldn't mind. It was just . . . It wasn't easy . . . It'd be difficult . . . if I saw what she meant . . . "There, I've said it," she ended up, having said nothing. She began to wash the dishes brusquely, as though angry about something.

"You'll break the plates," I warned her, but she took no notice. We drank coffee without talking, and then she put the cups in the sink and announced that she was going to bed.

I'm looking for *the* moment; but perhaps

it doesn't exist. Perhaps that is just the way our minds work, thinking that a significant event must have a cause. Perhaps it is no more than chance, the terrifying machinations of chaos. I sat there and listened to her moving about the flat, going to the bathroom, flushing the lavatory, splashing around in the basin or the bidet. Doors banged shut. A kind of silence fell. What had been said? What, if anything, had been agreed? The arrangement with Eve had been so much simpler.

I tiptoed along the corridor to her door and tapped softly, in case she might hear.

"Who is it?" she called, in case it might be someone else.

"Can I come in?"

"Wait a mo' . . ."

I could hear sounds beyond the wooden panel. Then: "Turn off the light."

I did as I was asked, and opened the door into a blanket of darkness. The air was scented with her perfume, the smell vivid in the dark — slightly florid, slightly overstated, entirely dangerous. "Over here," she said softly, as though I might not know the layout of my own room. I closed the door behind me and crossed the room to the bed, putting out my hand and finding the cool touch of the sheet; and then hot, soft flesh. She stirred in the shadows. I touched silken skin, an edge of bone, a declivity that ended in a deft thicket of hair. She made a sound that was difficult to interpret, a small, voiced exhalation that might have been distress.

"Are you all right?" I asked. My eyes had begun to accommodate to the dark. The exiguous light that seeped through the curtains from the light shaft now gave vague substance to the room, to the bedside table and the chair and the ghostly body laid out like a corpse in front of me. The ghost's voice came back to me after what seemed like a long pause. "We shouldn't," she whispered.

My fingers moved. "Why not?"

She sighed, having no particular answer. "What do you want to do?"

I was shaking. With fear, with excitement, with impure joy, I don't know. I have no wish to classify and delimit my feelings. All I know is, I was shaking as I knelt before her like a supplicant at an altar (because it was the easiest way, in fact) while she presented herself like one of my mice, making small, mouselike sounds, a faint whimpering, a mewing, a desperate *cri du chat.* My once-trembling fingers had found sudden and surprising dexterity.

"Oh God," she whispered, although surely God had nothing to do with it. "Oh God, oh God, oh God."

I leaned forward and tasted her, and she had a strange and bittersweet flavor that I had never imagined nor could ever describe: taste mingled with touch, a mysterious combination. Unsteadily I got to my feet and poised behind her, the mattress wobbling beneath me, her buttocks clutched for capricious support. "Be careful," she whispered in the darkness, rather absurdly. "Oh God, be careful." I leaned forward against her. "You're so big," she said. "So big."

That night my semen coursed in glutinous coils into the core of Miss Jean Piercey: tiny bullets of potency, as potent as any other man's, wriggling and shivering their way out of the acid world of the vagina, hoovered up by the nuzzling trunk of her cervix, sucked, pulled, wafted up through the darkness of her womb toward the distant tubes.

We slept apart. I didn't want her to wake and find me beside her.

She looked drawn in the dawn, as though she hadn't slept properly. "What do we do now?" she asked, fiddling disconsolately with a teapot and kettle. A scene of domestic bliss. Giant Honey Pops for breakfast.

"Continue as before, more or less," I suggested.

"And what if I get pregnant?"

The sound of water pouring. An exhalation of steam. Otherwise, silence. In the midst of that silence did she, I wonder, compute the odds? Was she even aware that they existed?

"If *what?*"

She stirred the brew. "Pregnant," she repeated.

"How in God's name . . . ?"

"What's it got to do with God? You always say you don't believe in him."

But God had much to do with it. The Egyptian god Bes was an achondroplastic dwarf. He was the god of entertainment, the god who frightens away the demons; but he was also the god who protects pregnant women. "But aren't you on the pill or something?"

"I told you to be careful. But I didn't want to stop you. In case you misunderstood." Speaking thus to the sink and the pot of steaming tea and the frosted window beyond whose panes was a decorative light shaft full of drainpipes and electrical conduits. "I thought you'd think I didn't want you," she said softly. "There can't be much chance, can there?"

"You sound like a schoolgirl."

"Do I? Do you know how schoolgirls are?"

I ignored the taunt. "The chance of me, my dear, the chance of *me* happening was one in fifteen thousand. And here I am. Chances are things that have a habit of happening. So when was your last period? And why the hell aren't you on the pill, any-way?"

She looked up suddenly, her mismatched eyes bright with anger. "I didn't need to be, did I? I didn't need to be on the pill, because Hugo Miller couldn't make babies, could he? I thought I'd told you that. All his sperm is . . ." She searched for the word, and found it sure enough. "Deformed. Two tails, three heads, I don't know what." She sniffed. "Anyway, my last period was about a fortnight ago."

I buttered my toast with care.

[Mismatch]

God.

You were wondering when I was going to get around to him, weren't you? After all, Mendel was a priest, a friar who had dedicated his life to the service of the Almighty. He must have celebrated mass every day, either alone in one of the side chapels of the convent church, or before a congregation up at the ornate high altar, the fanciful, florid, and fantastic Silver Altar, with a thirteenth-century icon of the Madonna and Child buried in its center. He was ordained in 1847 and was thirty-six years a priest. That makes thirteen thousand masses, more or less. Thirteen thousand recitations of *Credo in unum Deum, Patrem omnipotentem, factorem coeli et terrae* — I believe in one God, Father Almighty, maker of heaven and earth. It has a quaint, old-world ring. The question is, did he?

Jean went to church. This startled me, I'll admit. It was the very first Sunday after I had picked her off the streets, so to speak, before we had any kind of real intimacy (although Benedict the diminutive goat was speculating, of course, speculating all the time on the possible and the impossible). "I'm just going out for a bit," she told me while clearing away the breakfast things. She seemed almost furtive, as though she had a secret to hide.

"Going where? It's Sunday."

"Precisely."

The church she had found (she had spied out the land in advance) was a redbrick confection designed during the last century by William Butterfield. Saint Mary Magdalen. In its neo-Gothic extravagance it might have been a branch of the Royal Institute for Genetics; but of course it also looked the twin (dizygotic, not identical) of the convent church of the Assumption of the Virgin Mary at the Augustinian Monastery in Brno. In fact you could put those two buildings side by side and an untrained eye would be hard put to distinguish between them for style and date: both slate-roofed; both dark brick (the one red and black, the other dusty mauve); both grimed by traffic fumes; both pinnacled and buttressed; both witnesses to arcane rites and superstitions and redolent of incense. There is a difference in date, of course. The Augustinians' church in Brno was consecrated in the fourteenth century, whereas a plaque beside the main door of Saint Mary Magdalen is

to commemorate the laying of
the Foundation Stone
on 28th May 1856
by Doctor Edward Bouverie Pusey
On behalf of the Ecclesiological Society

You'll notice the date: the height of the Tractarian movement in England, when Pusey was expounding the doctrine of the Real Presence, and Newman was going over to Rome; exactly the same time that Father Gregor, Roman by birth and upbringing, was watering his first-generation peas and about to discover a real presence deep inside them, the factors for tall and dwarf, for pure white and dark, corrupt purple.

"Do you believe, then?" I asked her.

"Of course I do." There was a note of defiance about her reply, as though she expected an argument. It transpired that she also used to sing in the church choir in Ruislip. "They'll miss me. I used to take the soprano solos, me and another girl."

"She'll do them all, then."

"Dawn, she's called. Her voice wasn't as good as mine. Isn't. Isn't as good."

And Father Gregor, what exactly did he believe? Some of his letters are extant. Iltis quotes from them in the biography. There are letters to his nephew Alois Schindler, to his parents and his brother-in-law, to one of his fellow friars, and of course there are the ten he wrote to Nägeli. In none of them is there a mention of God. Not a mention, not even a conventional piety.

My Dear Parents . . .
Your grateful son, Gregor.

Nothing else. When he tells them of the attempt on the Emperor's life in Vienna (1853), Franz Joseph's escape is merely "lucky." Not "by the grace of God"; just "lucky." The failed assassin is "executed on the 26th of last month," but no mercy of God is invoked. Mendel was delighted to learn that everyone was well at home and that his younger sister was happy in her married life. He sent his love. He didn't send his blessing. He merely sent "good wishes for the Easter holidays"; and signed himself their "grateful son, Gregor."

It is hard to demonstrate a negative, but at the very least all this epistolary evidence points to a priest who had managed a remarkable separation of faith from daily life.

At a time when Charles Darwin, who once planned on taking holy orders, is struggling with the religious implications of his scientific work, Gregor Mendel is apparently ignoring them entirely. For example, in 1870, when a tornado struck the city of Brünn, he wrote a long account of the phenomenon for the Society for Natural Science (they may not have appreciated the work on inheritance in garden peas, but at least they'd be able to understand this):

Although the spectacle is a most imposing one from a distance, a tornado is extremely disagreeable and dangerous for all those who come into close contact with it . . . it is only to a lucky chance that I owe my having got off with nothing more than a fright.

Not the hand of God, you'll note. Lucky chance. After a meticulous, objective, exact description of the storm (*our tornado was an exception to the law which meteorology has recently established for the rotating of storms in the northern hemisphere, according to which the rotation is always counter-clockwise . . . all the objects that were hurled in through the eastern windows of my quarters came from the SSE, SE, and ESE . . . but according to the law of circular storms the missiles ought to have come from the NNE, NE, and ENE . . .*), he goes on to give an account of some local women, in town for the grape harvest, and their views of the phenomenon:

> *. . . they came to the conclusion that Old Nick had broken loose, and they took refuge in a neighboring watchman's hut. But the Evil One sought them out in this retreat, for a moment later the roof was torn from above their heads, and they had much ado to save themselves from being carried away with it . . . my informant was greatly concerned lest he should scatter the burning brands he was obviously carrying with him over the town . . .*

Old Nick. No hand of the Almighty, no God moving in a mysterious way (the cause of tornadoes is still uncertain, and Mendel's own explanation is impressive in its attempt to link objective observation to physical theory), no merciful God letting the good people of the town off with nothing more than damage to buildings. In fact, no God at all. Just a joke about the superstitions of peasant women.

I have a theory about that storm. In a letter dated September 1870, Mendel is still reporting optimistically on how his work is going; but a mere fortnight later the storm struck. In his report to the Society for Natural Science, Mendel doesn't even mention it, but that storm destroyed the magnificent greenhouse in the monastery garden, the greenhouse that he had used for more than a decade for much of his experimental work. I think the destruction of the greenhouse, coming as it did on top of the scientific world's indifference to his discoveries, broke his heart. It wasn't God, of course; it was nothing more than the same lady whom Mendel understood so well, who was, is, so much a part of his theory of inheritance — random, destructive, but also occasionally creative Lady Luck.

And Benedict Lambert? What is his relationship with the Prime Mover?

"Don't you believe, Ben?" Jean asked me sorrowfully. She asked it more than once, as though in the meantime I might have changed my mind, or seen the error of my ways, or suffered my own road to Damascus. "Don't you believe in *anything?*"

"I believe you're sitting there. I believe in you."

"But that's obvious."

"That's why I believe it. A merciful, personal God is far less obvious, which is why

I don't believe it. You must admit" — I held my hands out, as though to display myself just in case she hadn't noticed — "it's a bit difficult to believe that a loving God could do this to me."

Her eyes filled with tears. "Oh, Ben," she said. "Poor, poor Ben."

But, of course, there is more to it than merely being a victim of one of nature's practical jokes. There is also my work. You see, in my work I have called God's bluff — I have looked behind the scenery. From the auditorium the whole set looks very impressive. There is a reasonable three-dimensional effect, a sense of perspective, an adequate illusion of depth. You can even believe it well enough when you are actually on stage and trying to remember your lines, trying to come in on cue, trying not to upstage one actor or steal the scene from another. But I have peered behind the scenery . . . and there's nothing there. Just the darkness and a few bits of scaffolding. Nothing else. Not even the back wall of the theater.

Give me a platform and I can move the earth. Archimedes, of course — everyone knows that. But he was talking more than just a bit of elementary physics. He knew that he hadn't a snowball's chance in hell of moving the earth. He too had seen behind the scenery.

Give me the nucleotides and I can make Man in my own image.

How did Jean reconcile her faith with the fact that she was living in sin? That is a question I failed to answer. So too did she, I guess. It weighed on her, that's certain. Those few weeks together were eaten into by guilt. Exactly how is difficult to explain. At the time I didn't want to inquire too much, didn't even want to talk about it, in case, as with so many phenomena in science, the mere act of observation changes what you are observing. Best leave it alone and see what happens.

And then again, does it matter? Seen from another perspective, those weeks appear strangely ephemeral, an evanescent coming together of persons to make a transgenic creature that doesn't survive long, a chimera.

The practicalities of the relationship? You want to know, of course. How did we do this, how did we arrange that? How did we . . . ?

What do you want — photographs?

I didn't move into the bedroom with her. I suppose I wanted to spare her the fright of seeing me as I was; and as she never suggested that I should, I guess that she was happy to be spared. So it was in all-forgiving and all-absorbing darkness that we actually coupled. Sometimes it was funny — no, at first it was always funny — and sometimes it was ecstatic. Often we laughed; sometimes we wept; and occasionally, just occasionally, I had the sensation that I was almost freed from my bonds. Whoever, whatever, tied the knots of this tortured and twisted body of mine, for those few weeks Jean's agile fingers began to loosen them. Sometimes I felt that her perfect body was almost consuming my own, the beautiful engulfing the ugly, the good swallowing up the evil; but on other occasions I sensed that I was fouling her.

You may have detected a change of tone in that passage. Benedict Lambert has lost his sharp, sour cynicism. Well, yes — for a while. But I'll bring it back, don't worry. Modern stories don't have happy endings. For the moment, though, leave me with that: connubial bliss, domestic contentment, spiritual communion; and strange looks from the neighbors. At the corner shop I think they presumed we were brother and sister. At the Institute we began to keep strictly apart, indeed we actually stopped our bi-weekly lunches; and like any new wife she complained that she saw less of me than she used to before it all happened.

"You're always coming back late."

"Do you want to see more of me?" I asked.

She looked at me thoughtfully, her mismatched eyes seeing more than I ever used to give them credit for. "What do you want me to say, Ben? Of course I do."

"Is that the truth?"

"Of course it's the truth."

"The whole truth?"

"Is this a court of law?"

"What are you hiding, then?"

"Oh, for God's sake, Ben, I'm hiding nothing." She laughed. One of those bad-tempered, dismissive laughs. But I did wonder what her motives were for all this. I wondered it then, in my ignorance; I wonder it now, in my wisdom.

"I don't understand what you see in me," I told her, and her reply was subtly tangential to the question:

"It's precisely what I see *in* you that matters."

The trouble was, I had no experience, nothing beyond that awful abortive friendship with the girl called Dinah. I had no yardstick against which to measure things, no test of fidelity, no assay of affection. In the laboratory I understood the context in which my molecules, my fragments of DNA, my pet proteins, operated; living with Jean I was adrift. Often I found her distracted and miserable — "What's wrong?" "Nothing." "Is it my fault?" "No" — and I had no means of judging whether the problem was trivial or terminal. Sometimes she would laugh at something — a silly, edgy laugh — and I didn't know whether it was laughter at my expense, or our expense, or just at herself.

So what did I bring to her? Isn't love an exchange, a give and take? What was my own contribution to this *ménage à une et demi*, apart from sarcasm and impatience and an ego the size of my own overgrown head? Well, there is one part of my body that is entirely unaffected by my condition, I can assure you. I have already told you that. Once the barriers were down, once we had slipped past them and reached the territory of shared delights, Jean Piercey clung to that particular part with all the desperation of a shipwreck victim clinging to the wreckage.

I warned you that cynicism would return.

Then she began to tell lies. Truth is, after all, only relative, and even DNA, that most innocent of molecules, lies. For example, the dinucleotide sequence CG is a mutational hot spot[1] — the cytosines (C) of such pairs tend to be methylated, and a methylated cytosine may be deaminated into thymine (T). Thus the message no longer reads CG but TG, and when the molecule replicates, the mistake will be repeated: the other strand in the ladder will no longer have GC but AC. A mutation. The lie will have been repeated, and like any lie it may be repeated often enough to be mistaken for the truth.

The result is me.

Jean's lies were similarly trivial in their essence — hushed conversations on the phone, terminated abruptly when I came in ("Oh, no one that matters. A friend, that's all"), unexplained absences from the library, that kind of thing. Nothing that mattered or was even significant except to a mind such as mine. I knew that she had been in touch with Hugo, but this was not that. I am trained to spot the lie, to pick out the mismatch, to see the mutation. This was something other. Eventually I confronted her, sat her down in the armchair in the sitting room, with subdued afternoon light coming down the light shaft from the exiguous garden, and quizzed

1. Duncan and Miller (1980), "Mutagenic deamination of cytosine residues in DNA," *Nature* 287, 560–61.

her. She looked away from me.

"What's going on, Jean?" I repeated. "You're hiding something from me. What is it? Look at me, for Christ's sake." I remember that her tape of *On an Overgrown Path* was playing, the piece entitled "The Barn Owl Has Not Flown Away!" with its strange arpeggios and measured, hymnlike melody.

She looked at me. One blue eye, one green. The sky and the earth. "I'm pregnant," she said.

[Transformation]

Doctor Benedict Lambert and Miss Jean Piercey discuss the future. The future is a mere jot buried somewhere within the endometrium of her uterus, a thing no larger than a grain of wheat but infinitely more alive. They discuss the chances, which are, precisely, fifty-fifty, one to one, one half, point five. It's the same thing, however you wish to look at it. I chose my words with care: "There's a fifty-percent chance of it being" — pausing, loathing the word, finding no other — "normal. At present, prenatal diagnosis by ultrasound is uncertain. Anyway, it isn't possible at all until after the twenty-fifth week, which is rather late. So it's the toss of a coin . . ."

"Then we've got to stop it."

"Of course. If that's what you want. I can hardly plead on the part of the child."

Her eyes, her matchless eyes, blistered with tears. "You're not being fair."

"Tossing a die isn't very fair. It just happens."

Abruptly she changed tone, like changing

gear in a car. From muddled pleading she endeavored to become businesslike. "But we're responsible. And the situation that we're in. I mean, I'm still married. And we're not. So how could we possibly . . . ?"

I held up my hand. "There's no argument. I agree."

"But you've got to see things from my point of view. From *his* point of view —"

"His? That's a toss of a coin as well. Same odds."

She snapped at me. "His, hers, you know what I mean."

"I do. I've agreed. There's nothing more to discuss."

"It'd be a terrible problem for the child, Ben," she said. "Our situation —"

"Me, that's what you mean. Me. The child might be like me." That brought a moment's silence.

"That's being unfair."

"Of course I'm being unfair. Unfair is the only weapon I have."

She looked down at me. Miss Jean Piercey looked down at me just as I had, for so long, looked down on her. "All right, Ben," she said. "If you want to force me to say it, I will: the child might be like you. And I wouldn't want that."

I am inured to hurt. You build bastions

around you, Maginot lines of defenses, iron curtains of barbed wire and razor wire, minefields and free-fire zones. Watchtowers stand guard and searchlights play over the whole area with a chalky, bleak whiteness, throwing everything into harsh relief. There are no gates. And Jean Piercey had walked through, past the guards, over the tripwires, ducking beneath the coils of wire and skipping round the fencing and lying down before me with that magical, impossible thing: a normal body. Oh, how I loved her body! I'll avoid the question of soul and stick with matters of the flesh, things I can measure, things I can understand. How I loved the trivial imperfections of her body, the rough skin of her knees, the tiny tributaries of broken veins on her legs, the variegations of color on her hands, the faint brushstrokes of hair on her arms, the embarrassed flush of a blackhead on her chin, the mole on her thigh, the looseness of her breasts, the unevenness of flesh around her nipples, the strange, hypnotic fragrance of beast and angel, of mire and myrrh, that hung about her. And this body wanted to destroy my child, which might be me, a second Benedict, another squat and crumpled creature, betrayed by mutation and the courtly dance of chromosomes.

Well, of course. What would you have done?

The technicalities were easy: Certificate A of the 1967 Act (*not to be destroyed within three years of the date of operation*) to be completed by two medical doctors —

We hereby certify that we are of the opinion, formed in good faith, that — (ring clause number four) — *there is a substantial risk that if the child were born it would suffer from such physical or mental abnormalities as to be seriously handicapped.*

— and a booking made at a convenient clinic. They were very caring people at the clinic, full of gentle explanations couched in reassuring terms. One of the counselors took me into her office. It was a homely place with positive pictures on the wall: Van Gogh's sunflowers, a Bonnard of a half-naked girl washing herself at a zinc tub, a Monet of a boating party on the Seine. Did those ethereal girls in silk chiffon get pregnant, I wondered? It seemed unlikely. The fat-bottomed girl at the tub was quite another thing: she probably already was, and by someone else's husband.

"Are you a friend of Jean's?" the counselor

asked. Her phenotype was difficult to ascertain: hair dyed pale silver, eyebrows meticulously plucked, irises glinting behind tinted contact lenses, skin burnished by UV light, body strapped and girded and padded.

"I'm the father. Not of Jean Piercey," I added with a smile. "Of her child."

Barely a flicker across the featureless *maquillage*. "I see."

"I'm sure you do. That makes it pretty incontrovertible, doesn't it? The argument for abortion, I mean. No adequate prenatal test. Fifty-fifty chance of ending up like me. Who'd bet a lifetime on the toss of a coin?"

She gave an abstract smile, abstract in the sense that it signified neither amusement nor sympathy, nor anything else that might normally be subsumed under the signifier *smile*. "Termination," she corrected me. "Not abortion. And once the medical decisions have been made, the reasons are not our concern."

"I'm sure not. But I expect they'd have agreed if there was a one-percent chance of a cleft palate, so who can complain?"

"Jean is the one we need to care for now," she said.

"Of course. We're hardly caring for the child, are we?"

"The conceptus," she said. "A child is

quite another thing."

"It certainly is. Do you know what my job is?"

"Is that of any importance, sir? We came here to talk about Jean. But if you only wish to talk about yourself . . ."

"I'm a geneticist," I said. "I work on DNA probes to try to identify genetic disorders. So far I've failed to find one that will enable my own condition to be identified, and as a result of that failure I'm conniving at the destruction of my own child."

Her tone never wavered. "Would you like to speak to another of our counselors, sir? We have Mr. Morgan available at the moment."

"I'm talking to you."

That glacial smile. She looked over my head as though searching for a more interesting interlocutor at a cocktail party. "I'm about to be busy," she said.

"Go," I told her. "Please be busy somewhere else."

I went in search of Jean. She was already installed in her room, her few possessions laid out on her bed — washing things, nightdress, a change of underwear. She stared out the window at the backyard of the building. The Post Office Tower loomed over the roofs, like a totem, like a phallus: not exactly

279

the kind of thing one wanted in the landscape just there. "I'll be all right," she said. "There's no need to wait. I'll see you afterwards."

We had already decided about afterwards. Afterwards she would go home to her aunt for a week. She needed to get away and sort herself out. What hold did I have over her? She'd get in touch once she had sorted things out. She was sorry. Terribly, terribly sorry. Being sorry was habitual with her.

So I left her in the clinic, and so in due course they came and took her away to the operating theater and anesthetized her and laid her on a slab. Her legs, those vulnerable, childlike legs, were splayed out and draped in sheets while a surgeon probed with instruments of stainless steel. And then the small thing within her, a thing mere millimeters long but already quite a good likeness of a human being, a thing of dubious genetic makeup that would have had problems making its way in the world whichever way the coin came down, was sucked into the void.

Mendel's work came to the attention of the world only in 1900, sixteen years after his death. By 1905 the *Gesellschaft für Rassenhygiene* (the Society for Racial Hygiene) was founded in Germany, followed by the

Eugenics Education Society in Britain (1907),[1] and the American Eugenics Society in the United States (1923). In the face of a genetic deterioration that they saw everywhere about them, these organizations pushed long and hard for the adoption of legislation that would preserve the genetic fitness of the population. "How long are we Americans to be so careful for the pedigree of our pigs and chicken and cattle — and then leave the ancestry of our children to chance or to blind sentiment?"[2] they asked.

The leading exponent of British eugenics was Sir Ronald Fisher; the prime mover in the United States was the Yale economist Irving Fisher; the first director of the Kaiser Wilhelm Institute for Anthropology, Human Genetics and Eugenics in Germany was Eugen Fischer.

You'd better be careful if your name is Fisher.

Things change, people change, the mutability of circumstance is what impresses. Two days after the operation I collected Jean from the clinic and found her changed.

1. Renamed "Eugenics Society" in 1926.
2. Placard at an exhibition of the American Eugenics Society, quoted in Kevles, *In the Name of Eugenics*, 1985.

Where before she had always stumbled into any silence with ill-considered words, now there was a willingness to leave a silence alone. "Yes, I'm all right," was all she said. "No, there's no pain. They told me there might be some bleeding, like with a period. That's all."

Miss Piercey, in her gray wool dress, clutching her little suitcase, clipping down the steps and across the pavement to the car, experiencing no pain.

I took her to the station as she had asked, and saw her onto the Nottingham train. Her aunt would meet her at the other end. Everything would be all right. I needn't worry.

I rang her often over the next few days, and heard evasion on the other end of the line. "Not yet," became her stock phrase. And silence was another stratagem, an unaccustomed silence so that I found myself asking whether she was still there. "Of course I'm still here." But I didn't see what was inevitable about it. "When are you coming back? I want to see you, Jean. Don't you understand that?" It was difficult for me to put it into words. I had been trained in the skills of evasion and concealment as much as in the techniques of DNA analysis. If you are as vulnerable as I am, you acquire reticence with your mother's milk: "I miss you."

"Please, Ben, please." But "please" was never formulated into a request. It never became "please do this" or "please do that." It was no more than a plea for suspension, for indecision, for keeping things the way they weren't and never had been. Perhaps it was the tide of hormones that had swept through her, I don't know. Hormones make changes: they are the molecules through which the mind exerts its effects on the cells and vice versa, chemicals that latch on to proteins embedded in the cells' membranes and, by so doing, switch on functions as yet unobserved and unimagined. Thus the androgynous child becomes man or woman; thus the adolescent becomes boisterous and belligerent; thus the mother becomes maternal or the bereaved becomes despondent; thus the mouse turns rat.

When she finally came up to London it was on a day-return ticket, almost as though she had come for negotiation. We went for lunch to The Pig and Poke, and it was as though we were meeting on neutral ground. Eric was strangely silent behind the bar. "Nice to see you back," he said, and phrased it as though it might be a question if she cared to answer it. But she just smiled and said thank you and took a slice of quiche — "your favorite, isn't it, love?"

— and sat down with me.

"I don't know, Benedict," she said when finally we began to talk. "I just don't know. I feel . . . different." She fiddled idly with her food, avoiding my eyes. "You won't tell Hugo, will you? About what we did." I hope you noticed the past tense there, gentle reader. I noticed; oh yes, I did. This is a verbatim record, I assure you. I was sensitive to the slightest nuance, the faintest hint, the mere breath of betrayal. I had a tape recorder in my brain. "I've spent a lot of time thinking about us," she said.

"So have I."

She gave a little, gray, distracted smile. "I'm sure."

"And what conclusion have you come to?"

Silence. Choosing her words took time, time to sort the original from the dross, the insight from the platitudes. She selected the platitudes with unerring accuracy. "It was strange. Strange," she repeated. "Strange and wonderful . . ."

"But?"

"But not right." She looked to me for agreement.

"It seemed all right to me —"

"I wasn't myself, you see —"

"Perhaps you were yourself for the first time in your life —"

"And I did things I shouldn't have done. We," she corrected herself, "*we* did things we shouldn't have done."

"Shouldn't have? Who's making the rules, for God's sake?"

She looked away, across the bar, toward the electronic pinball machine with its flashing lights and its starships and its intergalactic spacewomen with pointed breasts and swaths of blond hair and atomic laser guns. Mousy Miss Piercey, on the survival side of an abortion, of an extramarital affair, of life itself. "I don't know," she said. "But there *are* rules. There *must* be rules."

"Oh, come on, Jean," I retorted. "For God's sake, grow up."

She looked back at me with that thoughtful smile. "Isn't it curious that the less people believe in God the more they invoke him?"

"Where did you read that? *The Reader's Digest?*"

She fiddled with her food. Her hands were beautiful. Have I said that before? Her hands were truly beautiful, slender and silken and articulate. "I've been in touch with Hugo," she said eventually. "I've spoken to him. He rang me up — I don't know how he knew I was at my auntie's, but he did. He was very upset."

"Aren't we all? It makes me really happy

to find that he's no different from the human race."

"You're being sarcastic as usual. He was tearful."

"Tearful? Don't make me laugh."

"And he wants me back. Not on his terms. On mine."

One of the customers strolled over and began to play the pinball machine. It buzzed and shrieked and flashed, as though it didn't believe what she said either. *Tilt!* it shrieked.

"And what might your terms be?"

She ignored my question. "That poor little mite," she said, thinking suddenly and erratically of the child that never was.

"Might have been," I retorted.

"Don't try to be clever, Benedict."

"The poor little mite is dead, Jean. You can't have second thoughts now."

She stared at me in surprise, as though the idea had not occurred to her before. "It was a kind of murder, wasn't it? Expedient murder." I'd never heard her use language like that. It was almost more shocking than if she'd said "fuck." She was right, of course. There's no way around it. Murder.

In 1924 the U.S. Congress passed the Immigration Act, designed to limit immigration from eastern and southern Europe on eugenic grounds. By 1935 twenty-nine states had sterilization laws on their statute books. In 1933 the Sterilization Law had been passed in Germany and a system of Genetic Health Courts (*Erbgesundheitsgerichte*) had been set up. The science spawned its own vocabulary. There were *Erbämter* (genetic officers) who sifted through *Erbkartei* (genetic files) in *Erbklinik* (genetic clinics) for traces of *Erbkrankheit* (genetic disease). None of this had anything to do with being Jewish — in Germany just as in the United States it was the feebleminded, the schizophrenic, the epileptics, the alcoholics, and those with serious bodily malformations who went under the surgeon's knife. The curious thing is this: abortion wasn't much advocated in either country. It was practiced only under certain, limited circumstances. Even by the eugenicists it was, you see, considered immoral.

Jean went back to her aunt after that. She'd resigned from the Institute and claimed she was doing some kind of temporary job at the local library, helping with the cataloging or something. She had slipped from my grasp.

But had she ever been within it? I doubted it then, and I doubt it now. A fragile specimen, a moth settling for a moment, flexing its wings gently and capriciously, then fluttering stiffly away. I pursue my metaphors with all the enthusiasm of a collector: a noctuid moth, gray and mottled — a miller. But I couldn't have trapped her in my short and clumsy fingers.

Some days later, Hugo Miller called on me. I was at the flat, putting the final touches to my latest paper, working through a summary of the linkage analysis, watching the figures glistening on the computer screen and seeing there the culmination of a life's work — is that putting it a bit strongly? I don't think so — when the phone rang. "Can I come and see you, Ben? I know you don't want to see me and all that, but I need to. Really. Would you mind?"

"Who's that?" Of course I knew who it was. I wondered how he'd got my number.

"It's Hugo. Jean's husband. Would you mind?"

Would I? I anticipated his arrival with detached curiosity, his actual presence with indifference. He settled into one of the armchairs — "nice little place you've got here, convenient" — and it was clear from the way he spoke that he had no idea what had happened between us, in this very place, in the room next door with the light turned out so that she shouldn't see. Presumably it was something he would not have believed even if he had been told it outright. I have the perfect alibi, don't I?

"I want her back," he said.

"Well, I haven't got her."

He seemed amused at the idea. He chuckled a bit and showed his teeth to me as though I might be an orthodontist. "I know you've been a good friend to her. I know you've been on her side in all this — no, I don't blame you, not at all, Ben. Don't blame you for one minute. You've done things according to your lights and I know I was a bit of a bastard . . . but I want her back."

There was something about him, a certain drabness, a tawdriness that suggested someone on the way down. He needed a shave, and with Hugo Miller it just didn't look like designer stubble, it looked like rusty iron filings smeared across his chin. "I'm having trouble at work, you know. It's the situation . . ." He waved a hand vaguely, as though to illustrate ineffable problems. "You see, it all comes down to the fact that we can't have babies, that's what it is. I went to some kind of counselor, can you imagine? She wanted Jean to come too, and she did . . ."

"Who did what?"

"Jean came."

"Jean went with you to a marriage guidance counselor? She never told me." A slip, that. He gave me a sharp look, a glimmer of his old self staring out through those tired and defeated eyes.

"Why should she? Anyway, she did. This counselor woman asked lots of questions and we had to fill out questionnaires — separately. They made us agree that we'd tell the whole truth and they put us in separate rooms so we couldn't discuss things, I guess. It was like one of those television game shows. You know the one? The one about how good a partner you are. Myself, I can't imagine how anyone could go on one of those things and have all your secrets broadcast to the whole bloody country. Anyway, we filled in these forms and afterwards we discussed what we had written, and it was quite a shock, I can tell you."

"Shock?"

He was silent, staring morosely at the beer I'd given him. I clambered up onto the other chair and sat opposite him and waited.

"Total honesty, that's what the woman said."

"And were you?"

"It wasn't me, it was her."

"She wasn't honest?"

"Too honest, if anything."

"How can you be more honest than total?"

He ignored that particular issue. "There was this question about . . ." He paused, as though trying to work out a difficult move in some board game or other. His tongue slid across his lips. His mind skipped erratically. "I'm sorry about that scene at the Institute that day, Ben," he said. "I don't know what got into me. I'm . . . sometimes I don't know myself, really."

"The shock," I reminded him.

He laughed humorlessly. "Yes, the shock. One of the questions in this bloody quiz was 'Have you had any affairs?' Outside the marriage, it meant. Not before."

"And?"

"She had. She said that she had." He looked at me with appealing eyes, hoping to be told it was all nonsense. "You know her, Ben. Has she been having an affair with someone? Eh? You must know. Didn't she stay with you for a while after we had our bust-up? I heard that from someone, don't know who. You must know if she had another man."

"No," I said.

"You mean she didn't, or you don't know? Christ alive, it's bloody serious, this. I never

291

thought she had it in her. She said she'd had another man, and . . ."

"And?"

"And she'd got pregnant."

Oh, the astringent kiss of irony. I watched him sitting there in my armchair, where Jean had crossed her languid legs, and I toyed with all the possibilities. Of course I did. Revenge, revelation, confession, all those things crossed my mind. And questions of loyalty. And questions of that most unfashionable of emotions, love.

"Pregnant," he repeated. "She said she'd even had an abortion." And Hugo Miller began to weep, there in my diminutive sitting room, crouched in my armchair like a child, weeping like an adolescent. "I'd do anything to get her back, Ben, anything at all."

[Nonsense]

A bitter February evening in the city, gaslit and muffled by snow. Footsteps sounding along Johannesgasse; huddled figures stamping their feet on the pavement outside the doorway of the Modern School; clouds of breath rising up through the cones of light as greetings are called. A carriage disgorges someone who has come from out of town. Someone else hopes that the janitor has remembered to leave the heating on. In the entrance hall there is a doffing of coats and hats. At a desk the secretary of the society, von Niessl, ticks names off a list and directs members toward the assembly hall.

Forty-five people in the audience. On the podium a table draped with a heavy, tasseled cloth. A white linen sheet is hung on one wall, and in the middle of the room stands a large, gleaming magic lantern with cooling vents in its side and a brass chimney to disperse the fumes from the lamp. One of the committee members fiddles with this gadgetry. "Lantern slides," people whisper excitedly while von Niessl calls the meeting to order:

"Gentlemen" — he hesitates and nods at two of the audience — "*ladies* and gentlemen, this is a moment we have long been waiting for." Von Niessl beams down on the man seated beside him. The members of the society nod and smile. Stout, balding, broad-faced Father Gregor acknowledges the recognition with a nervous gesture of both hands, as though warding off applause. "Who here does not know of Pater Gregor's countless offspring?" von Niessl asks. The members chuckle knowingly. "Who has not had cause to visit the gardens of the Königinkloster and see them for himself?" Catching Frau Rotwang's eye, von Niessl adds gallantly, "Or *her*self." And Frau Rotwang blushes prettily while Father Gregor coughs. "Who does not know that this illustrious society is honored by the membership of a man who has carried out hybridizations of great importance for the future of agriculture and natural history? So now, after many years, we have the privilege to hear of this work from the man himself."

Mendel clears his throat again as he rises to his feet. There is scattered applause, but he waves it to silence. His manner is apologetic, self-deprecating. "I'm not used to my pupils applauding my lessons, or my congregations applauding my homilies," he says, and the audience laughs. Frau Rotwang's eyes shine with admiration. "Furthermore, the distinguished members of the society do not yet know what I have in store for them. Maybe by the end of my talk they will not wish to applaud."

More laughter. Shaking of heads this time, assertions that everyone will find it all *most* instructive. The laughter subsides and people settle themselves, men rubbing their hands and stroking their whiskers and looking altogether serious, Professor Makowsky opening a notebook and holding his pen poised over the page.

Mendel glances at his own closely written notes. "I have entitled my address 'Experiments in Plant Hybridization, with Particular Reference to *Pisum sativum,* the Garden Pea.' Although I deal with the pea, I would like to preface my work with the remark that this work was inspired by artificial fertilizations undertaken in ornamental plants carried out in order to produce new color varieties, particularly members of the genus *Fuchsia* . . ."

Von Niessl nods and writes. Frau Rotwang smiles happily. The lecture is under way, one of the most momentous scientific events of the nineteenth or indeed any century.

And what did he talk of?

He talked of numbers and ratios, of chance and probability, of characters — *Merkmale* — and segregation. He showed that for a given inherited character — "let us consider, for example, the characters of tall and dwarf in these plants" — each offspring receives two constant characters, the dominating one *A* from the tall parent and the recessive one *a* from the dwarf parent. If each parent is a hybrid *Aa,* then each is capable of contributing either *A* or *a* to its offspring. When these factors come together in the offspring, "it is entirely a matter of chance which of the two kinds of pollen combines with each single germinal cell. However, according to the laws of probability, in an average of many cases it will always happen that every pollen from *A* and *a* will unite equally often with every germinal cell for *A* and *a*. If you will bear with me" — smiling around the audience — "I can best show this with a diagram."

There is a disturbance while the lamp is lit and the gaslights turned down in the room. People mutter in the shadows. A diagram appears suddenly on the linen sheet, vast, blurred, and upside-down. Muttered apologies come from the figure at the magic lantern while things are put to rights, while the slide is inverted and brought into sharp focus. For the first time the arcane laws of genetics are presented to the world. Mendel's own diminutive figure is silhouetted against the picture as though dwarfed by his discovery. "In fertilization, you may see that one of the two pollen cells A will meet with a germinal cell A, the other with a germinal cell a; and equally, one pollen cell a will become associated with a germinal cell A, the other with a.

Pollen cells	A	A	a	a
Germinal cells	A	A	a	a

Individuals formed				
therefrom		A	$2Aa$	a

"The result of fertilization can be visualized by writing the designations for associated germinal and pollen cells in the form of fractions, pollen cells above the line, germinal cells below. In this case one obtains — slide, please —"

$$\frac{A}{A} \qquad \frac{A}{a} \qquad \frac{a}{A} \qquad \frac{a}{a}$$

There are mutterings in the darkness. Do they signify discontent? He casts sharp shadows across the wall and into the future, this small stout friar with the obtuse manner and the abstruse jokes. This is a moment like few others in the history of science and his audience is laboring along in his wake.

"What I show here represents the *average* course of self-fertilization of hybrids when two differing characters are associated in them. In individual flowers and individual plants, however, the ratio in which the members of the series are formed may be subject to not-insignificant variations. Next slide, please. Here you may see the series for hybrids in which two kinds of differing characters are associated. In fertilization every pollen cell unites, on average, equally often with each form of germinal cell; thus each of the four pollen cells AB unites once with each of the germinal forms $AB, Ab, aB, ab:$"

$$\frac{AB}{AB} \quad \frac{AB}{Ab} \quad \frac{AB}{aB} \quad \frac{AB}{ab} \quad \frac{Ab}{AB} \quad \frac{Ab}{Ab} \quad \frac{Ab}{aB} \quad \frac{Ab}{ab}$$

$$\frac{aB}{AB} \quad \frac{aB}{Ab} \quad \frac{aB}{aB} \quad \frac{aB}{ab} \quad \frac{ab}{AB} \quad \frac{ab}{Ab} \quad \frac{ab}{aB} \quad \frac{ab}{ab}$$

Can you wonder that a great silence fell in the room, the silence of incomprehension, of indifference, of boredom? Can you wonder that the applause at the end was thin and the congratulations lukewarm? There were polite questions and a little discussion. But as the members of the Brünn Society for Natural Science dispersed into the cold night, there was a vague sense of embarrassment, a feeling that they had been called out in the cold evening on a fool's errand. They had come to see about plants and hybrids; they had got mathematics.

"But this is not even hybridization," someone was heard to remark, a man who had read Darwin and considered himself as well up in the understanding of such things as anyone in the society. "Hybridization is the crossing of separate species. This is nothing more than crossing different varieties." He pronounced the word *varieties* with contempt, as though he had said *gypsy* or *Jew*. "What is the point of worrying about whether you have green or yellow seeds? What matters is whether species themselves are mutable or whether they are distinct . . ."

"And what does *mathematics* have to do with biology?" complained another. "In the whole of Gärtner's work, or Darwin's work, come to that, there isn't a single mathematical formula . . ."

Wise nods, stern agreement. Not anger,

but disappointment and frustration, coupled with a sense of resentment at a wasted evening.

"It was fascinating, Gregor," Frau Rotwang assured Mendel. She was waiting in the entrance hall as the audience left. She used his Christian name alone. She was solicitous and concerned.

"Do you think they saw it all?" He polished his spectacles and then carefully fitted them on his face. "Do you think it was too much for them?"

"It was fine." She laid a consoling hand on his arm. She hadn't understood a word.

And what have I achieved with my dwarfs? I can hear you asking the question. Never mind the personal crises. What has Doctor Benedict Lambert of the Royal Institute for Genetics, remote ancestor of this Gregor Mendel, what has *he* discovered?

The audience waits, shuffling papers, coughing and muttering. Those noises, minimal enough, fade away into an expectant hush as the side door opens and Benedict Lambert steps onto the stage. All eyes watch the diminutive figure as he lays out his papers and his overhead projector transparencies. He glances up at the tiers of expectant faces almost in surprise, almost as though he had come in here for some other purpose and had not expected this crowd.

"Good morning," he says conversationally. Then he slips his watch from his wrist and lays it carefully on the lecture bench (a complete affectation this: there are wall clocks sited conspicuously around the theater) before looking back at the audience. The director is there, of course, seated front center: James Histone, CBE (when, oh when, will it be *Sir* James?). Like a portrayal of the Almighty in a medieval fresco he is surrounded by an aureole of lesser beings — the project directors, the postdocs, the graduate students, and finally, mere peasants on the outer edges, the undergraduates. And somehow Miss Jean Piercey is there, over on the left-hand side, five rows back. Her phenotype has changed. She looks different; but her mere appearance still brings a jolt to Benedict Lambert's equanimity. She smiles.

He takes a deep, calming breath, and begins:

"The most common form of dwarfism in humans is achondroplasia. This condition, characterized by disproportionate short stature, proximal shortening of the extremities, macrocephaly, midface hypoplasia, bowing of the lower limbs, and exaggerated lumbar lordosis, is inherited as an autosomal dominant character with 100-percent penetrance. Therefore there are no carriers of the condition. To possess one such gene is to own the deformity."

There is a great silence.

"To possess two ACH genes, one inherited from each dwarf parent, to be homozygous for the condition, is to die in infancy. As a consequence of this, more than 90 percent of cases are sporadic — that is, they are the result of chance mutation. Increased paternal age at the time of conception appears to be a significant factor, suggesting that mutations of paternal origin are involved. Furthermore, with an incidence of approximately one per fifteen thousand live births it is one of the more common *de novo* Mendelian disorders, which in itself provides sufficient reason for attempting to identify its cause."

A pause; an ironical smile; just a touch of bitterness: "The more astute among you may be able to work out another motive."

The director laughs. Thus sanctioned from the center, amusement spreads toward the periphery of the theater like ripples in a pond from a thrown stone. The celebrated Benedict Lambert has done it again: he has laughed to scorn the very gene that has wreaked havoc with his own body. Captain

Ahab, perhaps? We have both been mutilated, certainly. But Ahab pursued a vast beast, a phenotypic complex of muscle and bone and blubber and nerve, while I pursue a mere molecule, a fragment of a molecule, a sequence of chemical bases that the human eye will never see. Yet both of us pursue our obsessions with a measure of hatred and a measure of love. Even Jean smiles, although her smile has more than a touch of irony to it.

"Over the last few years I and my team" — a nod here in the right direction — "have collected a number of pedigrees associated with this condition, and we believe that we have finally localized and identified the gene."

A rush of excitement throughout the theater, although they knew it already. That, after all, is why they are here. All this has something of the drama of a well-known play: you know the plot well enough, but at the climactic moment, there is still the thrill of catharsis. Lady Macbeth still terrifies; Uncle Vanya still evokes empathy; the Master Builder still climbs his tower to frighten the watchers below. I point to a chromosome map, striped like a barber's pole, flung up onto the screen behind me: "Multipoint linkage analysis gives us a location for the achon-

303

droplasia gene in the short arm of chromosome 4, distal to the gene for Huntington's disease. The ACH location is close to the locus of the *IDUA* gene, and indeed initially *IDUA* was considered a candidate gene for the condition. However, *IUDA* mutations are known already to cause a number of symptoms that do not resemble ACH in any way . . ."

There is silence, anticipation. The surface of the ocean stirs and heaves. Will the great white whale emerge and be revealed in all its power?

". . . and at least four other genes in the same area presented themselves as alternatives. One of these was the gene for fibroblast-growth-factor receptor 3. The fact that this gene is expressed in cartilage-forming cells in the mouse made it seem likely to be the one we sought. Subsequent sequencing of this gene has confirmed this suspicion . . ."

We have read the texts. Like latter-day Bible scholars, like exegetes, we have read the words of the scroll of life. I give you a message from this enigmatic, molecular world:

5′ . . . GGC ATC CTC AGC TAC GGG GTG GGC TTC TTC CTG . . . 3′

and this, the cry of the beast:

5′ . . . GGC ATC CTC AGC TAC AGG GTG GGC TTC TTC CTG . . . 3′

That is it.[1] Can you spot the difference? In all the thousands of letters that make up the message, just one change spells disaster. G to A, a simple transition at nucleotide 1138 of the *FGFR3* gene. Guanine becomes adenine. It is a trivial thing in the infinite and infinitesimal machinations of the human genome. It is an error in a single base pair, an error in the transcription of a single letter. There are 3.3×10^9 base pairs in the human genome. So, one mistake in thirty-three billion letters and we (B. Lambert et al.) have focused in on that single letter error. It seems like textual analysis gone mad. But you may rest assured that there is nothing trivial about this error, this one-in-thirty-three-billion chance (how Great-great-great-uncle Gregor would have loved that!). No, this footling mistake means that during the synthesis of a particular protein an amino acid called arginine is slipped into one position that ought

1. The sequencing was carried out by the dideoxy chain termination method (Sanger et al., 1977) using the Pharmacia ALF automated sequencing system.

to be occupied by a different amino acid called glycine. To be precise, this occurs in the transmembrane domain of the protein, the part of the molecule that fits through the cell membrane. The protein is fibroblast-growth-factor receptor 3.

The result is me.

I would like to make a comment on that word *domain,* in the manner of a Bible scholar offering a gloss. *Domain* is, of course, cognate with *demesne,* the land immediately adjacent to a manor house and retained by the owner for his or her own use. It is also a district, a region; the territory or sphere *of.* A further glance through the *New SOED* (1993 edition) gives other, specialist uses: a physics one (*in ferromagnetic material, a region in which all the atoms or ions are orientated in the same direction*), two mathematical ones (*a set with two binary operations defined by postulates stronger than those for a ring but weaker than those for a field* and *the set of values that the independent variable of a function can take*), and a logical one (*the class of all terms bearing a given relation to a given term*); nowhere does it give this particular biochemical one. I almost wrote a definition myself and posted it off to the editor-in-chief at the Clarendon Press — *a more or less functionally distinct region within the tertiary structure of a protein*

— and then I thought better of it. I will stick with the felicitous nature of the original definition in the *OED*: ". . . a heritable property, ʟME."

I might have entitled my story *The Lost Domain*. It has the same sense of remoteness, of abstracted innocence, as Alain-Fournier's strange masterpiece. But now the domain that was lost is found. Ahab has spotted the whale. Now what?

The audience stirs with admiration, and with the thrill of malice, of — Uncle Gregor would have known the word — *Schadenfreude*. Each and every member thinks: There, but for the grace of God, go I.

I look up at the hanging gardens of academics and aspiring academics, and each looks back at me: close on a thousand eyes. "Of course, treatment of this condition is out of the question." I change the transparency on the overhead projector and the message is writ large across the screen of the lecture theater. "But there is this:"

5′ . . . GGC ATC CTC AG<u>C TAC A</u>*GG GTG GGC TTC TTC CTG . . . 3′

"This is the mutant section of the gene. I have marked the mutated base with an asterisk. The double underline indicates a restriction site for the endonuclease enzyme *SfcI*. This restriction site is not present in the unmutated sequence. This leads us to a very simple method for identifying the mutation."

I pause while they argue it through in their minds, the ones who are in the trade getting there and whispering to their neighbors to show they have worked it out; the others, those who are just here for the sensation, the bizarre theater, waiting patiently for me to produce the solution like a conjurer returning the torn five-pound note whole and undamaged after showing it to everyone in shreds.

"We have designed PCR primers that will amplify this section. The section includes the entire transmembrane domain and includes the mutation site. It is one hundred sixty-four base pairs long. As I said, in the normal form it does not present a restriction site for *SfcI*. The mutant form, because of the restriction site created by the transition[2] from G to A, will be digested by *SfcI* into two fragments, respectively fifty-five and one hundred nine base pairs long. Such fragments may easily be resolved by electrophoresis in polyacrimide gels, and may be readily

2. Transition: a purine-to-purine or pyrimidine-to-pyrimidine point mutation. Purine to pyrimidine or vice versa is a transversion.

distinguished from the full hundred-and-sixty-four base section. We have shown that all three segments are present in heterozygotes, only the full-length one is present in unaffected controls, and in the three homozygous patients tested so far, only the two fragments are present. Thus we have a straightforward prenatal test."

The applause rings around the theater. The act is over. Ahab has harpooned the whale.

Or merely spotted it?

Ah, there's the rub. We've found the mistake, we've identified the error, but how does that become me? How does the single spelling mistake end up as a total distortion of the whole meaning of the book? Developmental genetics is, in some way, a question of pattern-making. It is also a matter of complexity and of sensitivity to initial conditions, the sure signature of that modish department of mathematics, chaos theory. For, after all, the most noticeable aspect of genetics to the man or woman in the street is not what proteins you can or cannot make, nor even whether you have dark or light skin, or brown or fair hair — the most noticeable aspect of genetics is family resemblance. "Doesn't he look like his mother?" they say. "Hasn't she got her father's nose?" "Isn't he the spitting image of his grandfather?" You hear it up and down the High Street. They lean over the prams and they wiggle their fingers around and they make their little genetic judgments. Mother used to assure everyone with an air of desperation that I possessed Great-uncle Harry's BIG TOE.

All this is fine, but unfortunately there is no gene for the shape of your nose, or the cast of your brow or the shape of your toe. Genes only work through proteins. It is one gene: one protein; not one gene: one big toe, or one gene: one Grandfather Reginald's face. Each gene carries the message for a particular sequence of amino acids, which in turn makes a protein, and a particular protein may do a number of things, but one thing it does not do, ever, is make a particular shape. Proteins are enzymes (can you metabolize galactose? can you make the pigment melanin?) or they are signalers (grow faster, become a woman, become a man, become a homicidal maniac) or they are workers (contractors, transporters). They are not Father's nose or Mother's chin; or Great-uncle Harry's big toe.

Yet in some sense father's nose exists; and mother's chin; and, possibly, Uncle Harry's big toe. In some way the proteins do conspire together to make patterns, and the patterns are the things that you recognize, and if you change some of the crucial proteins (but not others) the pattern changes. I've said it before, haven't I? — I don't resemble my mother or my father or my sister. I had that sense of dispossession from the very start. With the dubious exception of my big toe (*pace*, dear Mother), I don't look like anyone from my family: but I do look like every other achondroplastic in the world. All because of a single-letter spelling mistake in thirty-three billion.

If you want a real research project, if your ambition is to pick up a Nobel Prize or two, if you want to become Lord Histone, O.M., C.H. (forget the bloody knighthood), if you want to be remembered by posterity as Uncle Gregor Mendel is remembered, then

FIND OUT *HOW*.

After the lecture I received the plaudits. A whole congeries of the interested and the fascinated gathered round, almost suffocating me in their enthusiasm to touch. And on the edge, Miss Jean Piercey. I finally encountered her in the corridor outside.

"Hello, Benedict." She was too shy to bend and plant a kiss on my cheek, but bold enough at least to stay and talk, to make a suggestion, to issue an invitation to lunch. I detached myself from the grasp of others and we went off together, not to the usual pub but to a wine bar somewhere in the King's Road, all wooden wine racks and chalked notices announcing the latest bargains; somewhere with no associations.

"Well done, Benedict," she said as we watched each other over (a manner of speaking: of necessity we watched each other *through*) glasses of Pouilly Fuissé.

"What did you think of it?"

"I didn't really understand a thing," she admitted. "Except that you've found your gene."

Did the irony strike her, the none-too-subtle pun on her name? A month or two earlier and I'd have said not; but now I wasn't so sure. "Found one, lost one," I said, and she gave a wry smile. She'd had her hair cut short and she wore more pronounced makeup than before, just a dash of lipstick, but a darker, redder hue. The changes gave her a strange new slant. Phenocopy. In humans, artificial modifications of the phenotype appear to bring with them changes in the person — nature following in the steps of nurture. You are what you want to be. The changes made her look younger and yet wiser. Wisdom has never been the prerogative of the old. No longer a mouse; a vixen, perhaps. In her sharp little jacket (cut tight, cut deep) Miss Jean Piercey shone amid the vinous shadows of the wine bar, and the waiter who brought our plate of tapas glanced surreptitiously down her front to see what mammary delights might lie there couched in black lace. I felt myself stiffen, not in protective outrage but in plain, animal tumescence.

"I'm becoming quite the flavor of the month," I told her when the man had taken his lascivious eyes to another table. "Some Mendel organization wants me to go to a conference in Brno, can you imagine? The Mendel Symposium, or something. They've got wind of the Harry Wise connection."

"And you'll go?"

"Oh, sure, I'll go. When fame and a free bed calls, I'll go anywhere. I'll tell them that Granddad Gottlieb used *his* Mendel connection to run a freak show, and I'm doing just the same. That'll stir them up."

She smiled wryly (new expression) and fiddled with the stem of her glass. "You shouldn't say that kind of thing."

"Just try and stop me."

There was a pause. "You know I'm back with Hugo?" She tried to introduce it as a casual aside, as she might have commented on the wine. "On a trial basis, of course. No commitments, no recriminations . . ."

"No beatings?"

She colored a little. "No beatings. He's stopped drinking. Drinking had quite a lot to do with it . . ."

"So you're happy?"

She shrugged. "I don't want you to think . . ." But words still failed her. The real words usually did. Platitudes were still her forte. "I don't want you to think that you weren't" — a hasty correction — "*aren't* very important to me, Ben. But . . ."

But. The word has featured large in my life. My own butt is disproportionately big. Maybe that's it. What was the lie my mother always gave me? "It's not what you're like on the outside, it's what you're like inside that counts." I didn't believe it then and I don't believe it now. The phenotype wins through, you see. In medieval times the good were always beautiful, the bad ugly. It's little different now. Nowadays the ugly are unforgivable, that's all. "But it wouldn't have worked, is that what you want to say?"

She shrugged. "It couldn't have, could it? We'd have been under such pressure all the time."

I agreed with her. It was perhaps that agreement that broke down her little array of defenses. Her eyes, those disturbing, mismatched jewels, glistened. "My bloody mascara will run," she said, applying the edge of a tiny lace handkerchief to her lower lids. "I was determined to be tough about this, and look what you've made me do."

"Me?"

She smiled bravely through tears. "Not you. Luck, circumstance, heaven knows what. You always said it was just the toss of a dice."

"Die," I corrected her. "Dice is plural."

"Pedant."

"You know your foul husband doesn't suspect who it was? He knows you were having an affair, but he has no idea it was me."

That, as they say, threw her. "How do you know that?"

"He came around to ask my advice, that's how. Good old Ben. A shoulder to cry on, if you can get down that far. And no danger, no *danger* at all. He came and asked whether I knew who it was and whether I could help him get you back and all manner of stuff. 'You're a good friend, Ben. You'll help us, won't you?' That kind of thing."

Her face almost crumpled. It looked like a paper mask about to collapse in the rain. "Please don't, Benedict," she pleaded.

"I won't. I'll be well behaved and decent.

I'll listen while you tell me *your* problems, and my problems can just go hang." Not surprisingly, that brought a certain tension, a little measure of silence. We chewed our tapas. Miss Piercey's mouth worked delicately on the fragile, moist things, as once it had worked . . . no. No, I must not pursue that line of fantasy, not yet, at any rate.

"So you know we've been going to a counselor, me and Hugo?" she said when the emotional climate had cooled a little. "Did he tell you that?"

I pleaded ignorance. "Town councilor?"

"Ha, ha. Marriage counselor. They don't call them that anymore. Partnership counselor or something. It's been quite an experience." She looked up brightly, her tears dried. "You know one of the things she said?"

"Get a dog?"

"Have a child. She said I need a child. Can you need something like that? It sounds awfully selfish. Anyway, she said that Hugo being unable to was part of the reason for everything. If you see what I mean."

"Adoption?"

"She suggested that I get pregnant." A silence in our own segment of the wine bar. Raucous laughter from a group of men in dark suits, escapers from some plate-glass aquarium. Jean fiddling with her tapas as though it just hadn't been said. "She said that to me, on my own. She said that the" — Jean hesitated with the word, searching for euphemisms — "termination —"

"Abortion."

"Abortion was part of the problem, but another part is his own feelings of inadequacy. So we ought to have a baby."

"But he's sterile."

"I know that, but he thinks there's some kind of chance, however small. IVF, you know the kind of thing. He thinks something could happen . . ." And then she stopped fiddling, either with the tapas or with words, and looked me dead in the eye. "But I *know* I can get pregnant, don't I?"

"Of course you do."

And then she delivered her quiet and devastating blow: "I want a child by you, Benedict Lambert," she said quietly. "I want your child."

The whims of women. Like racial stereotypes, you desperately deny their existence, and yet there they are. One cannot deny them. Like the violence of men, the whims of women exist. Jean Piercey, thirty-seven years old, almost flawless, almost beautiful, wanted my child . . . having just disposed of one up the orifice of a surgical vacuum cleaner. She wanted my child. Clutching my hand across the table, as though engaged in a bout of comradely arm-wrestling, she spelled it out: "I don't want a stranger's, Benedict. Hugo's is no good, and I couldn't bear to have a stranger's sperm inside me. It'd be . . . like a kind of rape. You tell me that your" — she masticated the word thoughtfully — "*problem* is nothing more than a single spelling mistake or something. You said it in the lecture, didn't you? All that AGA stuff. And at the end, didn't you say something about a prenatal test?"

Something.

"Well, couldn't the two of us make a normal baby? It's the first clever idea I've had, Ben. In my whole life. Can't the two of us make a normal baby? Can't you do it for me artificially? Isn't it possible?"

The idea stirred me. I visualized further couplings, additional planned writhings on my disordered bed, the Piercey body — newly adept, revitalized by pain — once more splayed open to receive the one part of me that is the normal size. How long could I prolong such delightful labors? But I was honest with her: "But you'd have to risk another termination — terminations, plural — if we were unlucky. The toss of a die, you see. Half the fertilizations would be . . . just like me."

"That's not quite what I meant. Couldn't we do" — she looked embarrassed, glanced over her shoulder as though to see if anyone was listening — "do one of those test-tube-baby things? And couldn't you choose the right embryos? Can't you do that sort of thing these days? Couldn't you take a single cell from an embryo and test it?"

Oh, it was clever all right. No fool, Miss Piercey. A cunning little vixen.

No fool Benedict Lambert, either. He pondered. He eyed the woman across the table. He considered both his and hers. It was, of course, all within the bounds of possibility.

"It might be arranged. I could get you into the Hewison Clinic. They'd set up *in vitro* fertilization, and we'd do a biopsy of early embryos. But . . ."

"But?"

"They've done something similar with X-linked disorders, I believe. It'd have to go before the ethics committee, unless . . ."

"But we could *do* it? It is possible?"

I looked at her. Loving, loathing? The two contrary emotions seemed very close at that moment. "There'd be a price to pay," I said.

She almost looked for her purse. "Surely

319

that's something we could manage, Hugo and I. I'm sure I could persuade him into giving a sperm sample." She clenched her fists as though in anticipation. "Ben, all this came to me while you were being mobbed by those people at the end of the lecture. I've thought it up and it's the first really clever idea I've had, and you could help me do it. I could persuade him to give a sperm sample and then we could substitute yours . . . and you could identify the right embryos. There wouldn't be any problem with money —"

"That's not the price I meant. Not a monetary one."

She hesitated. "What, then?" Did understanding dawn a moment before I made it explicit? Did she realize? It seems reasonable, doesn't it? More than reasonable: logical. Isn't that how babies are made?

"You can't really deny me, can you?" I pointed out, not unreasonably. "Not after all that's happened."

There was a silence.

"How could you, Ben?" Her tone was of disappointment, mainly disappointment. Perhaps there was also a note of betrayal, perhaps even a touch of outrage. But mainly disappointment. "In God's name, how could you?"

"God's back, then, is he?"

"It'd spoil everything." There was an edge of desperation about her voice now. "It would spoil a special memory, Ben."

"I don't want a memory," I replied. "I want the real thing. This is the one occasion in the whole of my life. Don't you understand that? The one time I've ever been able to love anyone."

Her eyes glistened in the subdued light of the wine bar. There were candles on the table. They glimmered in the sheen of tears. "Oh, Ben," she said reproachfully. "Oh, poor, poor Benedict."

My paper on the localization and identification of the ACH gene was published in *Nature*. The same month, to the chagrin of James Histone, CBE, I was nominated for the Mendel Medal at Villanova University. I received faxes and E-mails from all over, from the States, from France, from Germany. As always with such things, a dozen research groups leaped artfully onto the bandwagon. As always, people contacted me for pointers, for guidelines, for advice, for samples from my cell lines, for places on my team. And one Doctor Gravenstein mailed me from Cornell with a proposal for a conference. She was secretary of the Mendelian Association of America. You could hear her broad, edgy, transatlantic vowels behind the silly electronic scribble that came over the screen: *I heard about you, back last summer at Cold Spring Harbor. They were talking about this little guy hunting for his own ACH gene. They should name it after you, shouldn't they? The Benny factor? Hey, that's funny . . . Look, is this story true about you being a relative of Gregor Mendel himself? Why don't you participate in the Mendel Symposium that we're putting together, Ben? What do you say to a week in Moravia in return for a lecture on your current work?*

A few days later I got another message: *We'd really like you to give the keynote address, Ben. Molecular genetics right there on the podium, for Christ's sake.*

[Recombination]

"Now watch."

"What?" The slender figure — tight waist, bustle, an absurd little hat with a pheasant feather in it — leaned over the microscope and peered into the eyepiece. She presented one cheek, as soft as a petal, as flushed as a fuchsia, to his gaze. "What do I watch?"

"Watch. You need patience. Things happen slowly in the world of plants. Patience, patience."

A disk of bright white, like a sun seen through mist; a pond, a pond in slanting sunlight, shining bright white; and, floating in the disk, spheres that might have been plants floating in the pond, might have been planets hanging in front of the sun.

"They are . . . ?"

"The grains. Pollen. From the peas."

Frau Rotwang looked up impatiently. "Nothing."

"You must watch. It takes twenty minutes, half an hour, something like that. Just wait and watch."

"Twenty minutes!"

"Shh."

Silence in the close atmosphere of the greenhouse. One of her dachshunds lying on the brick floor, panting in the heat. The priest watching, the woman watching, the atmosphere, thick with the exhalations of fuchsia and snapdragon, of sweet pea and columbine, barely stirring. A strange, opalescent light lay all around them, bathing them like amniotic fluid. In the background a gardener was potting some plants, but his presence did not intrude on their curious intimacy around the gleaming brass microscope.

And there, suddenly (you couldn't see it happen but suddenly it was just there), one of the grains had a protuberance, a pale and translucent finger growing from it. "Yes!" she cried.

He bent his head close to hers, catching the drift of perfume from her, a different sensation altogether from the scent of greenery growing around them in the greenhouse. "That's right. Watch."

He pulled his head back and let her place a single, cerulean eye to the eyepiece once more. Wisps of hair escaped the confines of hat and pins and touched his face delicately as he withdrew. He wondered whether blond touched with the faintest hint of copper was the work of some factor hidden within the cells of her fragile, fragrant body.

She was watching still, unaware of his examination of her. "There are more of them now. Oh, how extraordinary, Gregor! How can this be? Aren't plants static things that grow only? Can I see them *move?* Are they growing before my eyes?"

"Barely, but yes, it *is* possible to see them."

"Oh, how wonderful. They are like . . ." and she paused, embarrassed: for it was suddenly clear exactly what they were like, those rootlike growths that extended themselves from the surface of the pollen grains, those snakelike protuberances. She didn't pursue the simile, but instead asked a question softly, as though fearful of the reply. "And what do they do?"

"What you are seeing happens at the pistil of the flower. Of course the pollen comes from the male part. It lands on the stigma, and these tubes grow down to the ovules."

She was silent. He could see the blush spreading on the cheek that was presented to him, the right cheek suffused with pink. Rotwang.

"Now, if I might be allowed . . ."

"Of course." She straightened, suddenly hot, suddenly uncomfortable, and watched while he fiddled with the mirror beneath the microscope and adjusted the focus somehow. His fingers, for all that they were thick and coarse (peasant fingers from a peasant background — he boasted of it), were remarkably articulate and nimble. She'd noticed that before.

"Now look again at the very tip of the thing . . ."

The tip. She looked again. It glistened. "Oh. It seems . . . an intrusion just to watch." A snout, a snake, a . . . the word *penis* alighted for a moment in the forefront of her mind, and then mercifully blew away.

"Look right at the tip," he said. "Just *inside* the tip, can you see? A small body . . ."

She could. A faint, opalescent, oval thing barely distinguished from the tube itself that carried it. "I can, yes, I can see it."

"That, I believe, is . . . the male cell."

"Oh, my goodness."

"It is that which carries the factors. I feel sure they are somehow inside that oval body carried in the very tip of the pollen tube. Can you understand that? They are something material, something chemical . . ."

She looked up at him, trying to cling to the substance of what he said, trying not to think of her husband, trying not to think of shame and pain. "But in what way are they there? You cannot have all the characters of a plant in there."

He nodded. "Somehow you can. You must have. That is what my work tells me. One set of factors in the ovule and one set in the pollen. And I believe they are packaged in that cell that you see. Oh, I don't know how, exactly. I don't understand what their chemical substance is. But they are there. And the same is true for animals."

"And us?"

"We are animals."

"Gregor!" She felt faintly shocked, and covered her confusion by looking again, but she must have jogged the microscope, for the view had gone just as surely as if shutters had been drawn down. Within the eyepiece there was only black.

"It's finished, Gregor," she said, and then, as he hurried to adjust the instrument once more, she added, quite flatly, in a matter-of-fact manner, as though it meant nothing at all, "We are leaving."

His fingers paused in their neat and accurate movements, then continued in their work. "Just wait a moment and I'll have it right. You must have moved the mirror."

"Brünn, Gregor. We are leaving Brünn."

He stopped, straightened up. She looked around distractedly, searching for her parasol. The dog jumped up, wagging its tail, eager to be off. "Why?"

"Why what?"

"Why are you going?"

"Oh." She shrugged vaguely. "I'm expected at home. By lunchtime."

"No, Brünn: why are you leaving Brünn? For how long?"

She blushed, picked up her parasol, almost tripped over the dog. "Forever. There are business reasons, of course, but Herr Rotwang also feels the political situation is too . . . uncertain. Oh, I don't understand these things. This trouble with the Prussians in Denmark. Holstein, is that it? He feels it may come to war, and Vienna will be safer. Can it really come to war over a quarrel in a faraway place of which we know nothing?"

The priest shrugged. He rarely discussed politics. He had views, of course — even, in his youth, strong ones. But involvement was a thing he shunned. They argued politics in the convent, Klacel and the others, but he tried not to get too involved. Involvement tainted you. He looked at Frau Rotwang. So admirable, so modest a lady. "We'll keep the country house, of course," she was saying. "But I am afraid we won't often be here in Brünn. The town house is up for sale."

"It'll be different," he said. "Without you,

I mean." The inadequacies of language; but then what else was there? There were only words. No other language applied. And words could be both a barrier and a revelation. Look what had happened, or hadn't happened, to the paper on the garden pea. He began to put the microscope away. "I will miss our talks."

She put out her hand and touched his arm. "I don't *want* to go, Gregor," she said, and he turned back to her and there was a moment, mere seconds in time, in which, somehow, they held hands, clumsily, he holding the back of hers — very slender, gloved in lace — and she half turning her hand so that her fingers held his. The dog whined. In the background the gardener inverted a pot, knocked it sharply, and removed a plant entire. In that moment Frau Rotwang leaned forward and kissed the friar on the cheek. Then she had called the dog and was walking over the brick floor between the plants toward the door, toward the bright, fresh day. She paused and bent to put the dog on its leash, then put up her parasol (bright pink with ribboned edges) and went out. He stood watching her through the misty panes as she went down the path toward the gate that gave onto the Klosterplatz where her carriage waited.

Miss Jean Piercey, Mrs. Jean Miller, down-soft, angora-soft, scented gently with jasmine and orange blossom, tasting of sweet pea, and sweat, and pee, a delicate and rancid melding of flavors that drove Benedict Lambert to paroxysms of tumescence: Miss Piercey, lying on my bed again, lying in the light of day seeping through the curtains into my underground lair, lying with her smile, telling the truth with her closed and averted eyes.

"Oh, Ben," she whispered, "be careful."

Of course. We couldn't risk anything. We had to be careful, if one can be careful with such a thing. So she lay there passively, being careful, while I ordered her this way and that, lapping at the secret smile of her vulva, nuzzling like a truffle-hound at the downy excrescence of her femoral mole, biting, gently, the silk of her inguina and the mouse-gray of her perineum, turning her and holding open the globes of her buttocks, Miller-like, to kiss the slate-gray bud at the very quick of her. She stirred and moaned, like an animal in distress. Tight muscles unclenched like a fist to allow the entry of the tip of my tumescent tongue. I balanced behind her on the bed and poised myself against her. "Ben!" she cried from somewhere distant and indistinct. "Oh, Ben. Ben, not that. Please not that."

But it was that. While she buried her face in the pillow and made muffled mouse-sounds of pain, it *was* that. A sudden explosion into the void. And quite safe.

Does it shock you? The genial and courageous Benedict Lambert suddenly become the dastard, the pervert? But what do you expect? What would you do if you had a life sentence and one miserable hour of freedom? Wouldn't you be tempted to break a few of the rules?

Afterwards it was soft tears and gentle recriminations and apologies. I couldn't help myself, I pleaded. You must understand. To possess you as no other ever has or ever will. Very poetic. To take a virginity from you that will never belong to anyone else. Surely you must understand. And she claimed that she did, more or less, although it didn't seem right, that's all. Not natural.

But what is natural? Nature is what nature does. Am I natural? Is superovulation followed by transvaginal ultrasound-guided oocyte retrieval natural? Is *in vitro* fertilization and the growth of multiple embryos in culture, is all that natural? Two months later, in a lab in the Hewison Clinic for Human Fertility, I watched shivering spermatozoa clustering around eggs, *my* spermatozoa clustering around *her* eggs. Consummation beneath the microscope. Is that natural? They shone in the circle of light like dancers beneath the spotlight, a whole corps de ballet flickering and jostling round the prima ballerina. Jean's contribution had come after the heavy, coaxing hand of hormones, followed by aspiration of secondary oocytes direct from the ovaries. My contribution had come after the heavy coaxing of my own hand and a careful contemplation of Suzanne, a voluminous girl with a tendency to examine her labia minora in front of the camera.

Is that natural?

Nature is what nature does.

Was Great-great-great-uncle Gregor's artificial pollination natural?

"I really don't like it, Ben." Doctor Anthony Lupron is a friend and colleague of mine. We have published jointly. We have drunk together, and on one occasion — his winning of fifty pounds on the football pools — got drunk together. I have stayed with the Lupron family in their cottage in Devon. I know his wife and children well. But Doctor Lupron did need persuading.

"What's the problem? You've spoken to Jean. You know the situation. You've seen his sperm count. What's the problem?"

332

"Not informing the partner, that's the problem."

I laughed. "But why should you worry about that? I mean, even if her husband were normally fertile, what would there be to stop her getting pregnant by whomever she chooses and never telling? You know as well as I do that it happens all the time."

He knew as well as I did that DNA screening for familial genetic defects (fragile X, cystic fibrosis, etc.) has quite incidentally revealed that, all unbeknownst to the legal father, something like ten percent of the children of happily married couples have in fact been fathered by . . . a different male.

"I suppose so."

"And you know that she has already been pregnant once. By me."

He grinned. "You old devil, Ben."

"And you know that the only alternative to what we suggest would be sperm donation, and Miller has already refused to contemplate that. And . . ."

The argument, you see, was incontrovertible.

I bumped into Jean and Hugo in the waiting room of the clinic after they had harvested the eggs. Hugo looked relieved at the sight of a familiar face; Jean blushed and looked away. We exchanged a few companionable words: It's wonderful what they can do these days, isn't it? What do you think the chances are? Doctor Lupron said we'll know in two days. No, it didn't hurt — they put me almost to sleep.

And then I left them to contemplate their parental future.

Which leads to the other question: What about Hugo Miller's semen, yielded with autocaresses similar to my own, in a room just down the corridor from the place where Suzanne and I took part in our ephemeral and one-sided relationship? What about that vital fluid, surrendered with much blushing to a severely smiling nurse?

Glutinous, pearl gray, and entirely devoid of motile spermatozoa, Hugo Miller's semen was flushed down the sink.

The fertilized eggs divide. There is a curious asymmetry about their progress: 2, 3, 4, 6, 10. You let them go that far, to the ten-cell stage. It is all natural enough. But is the magnified eye that gazes down at them natural? Is the light that floods them with photons for the brief examination? And the micromanipulators, elaborate little constructions of girderwork mounted on the microscope,

Meccano creations of levers and handles and gears such as some manic child might have dreamed up, handled with such elegant skill (I watched down the auxiliary eyepiece) by Miss Allele MacMaster, graduate research student from Saint Andrews; are those particular tools natural? Is this why *Australopithecus* fumbled with the first fragment of flint? Allele's delicate little Pictish hand twists and turns, and in the bleak field of the microscope the glass needle, as brilliant and sharp as a lance, skewers an embryo's zona pellucida to inject a drop of acid Tyrode's solution. There is a moment's fumbling and jostling beneath the spotlight. The lance withdraws. A second probe is pushed through the hole and a single embryonic cell is snatched from the jaws of differentiation and development and spat into a separate tube.

PCR amplification of a gene from a single cell is possible. It is not easy, but it is possible.[1] I did the work myself. Among all the other tubes, among the cultures and the clutter, it was easy enough to have a few things of my own, labeled with my own cryptic codes. To avoid contamination from stray

1. Handyside et al. *Lancet* i: 347–49 (1989); Coutelle et al. *British Medical Journal* 299: 22–24 (1989).

DNA, I used new equipment with disassembled and sterilized micropipettes, and I set the tubes up in the sterile room. It is therapeutic work. You lose yourself in the method, in the regimented sequence of events, in the order and the organization. You forget about lost lovers. You forget about ethics. You forget that you are picking at the genetic material of your own potential children. The method is the message.

Once the right length of DNA has been amplified (60 cycles of PCR using nested primers to guarantee purity), it is the simplest matter in the world to perform a restriction digest[2] and find out whether there is that rogue misspelling, that *fuck* for *luck,* that AGG for GGG deep in the heart of the *FGFR3* gene. The enzyme digests . . . or doesn't digest; and then the sample of digested — or undigested — DNA is loaded onto a gel and a gentle electric potential eases the fragments along, jostling and straining. Digested fragments travel farther, because smaller, than undigested pieces. The DNA is stained with ethidium bromide so that the fragments may be viewed directly under ultraviolet light to find out how far they have gone, and whether there are the

2. Restriction enzyme *SfcI.*

telltale digested fragments that mean:

MUTATION

and therefore:

DWARF

or not. A 164-base-pair fragment means normal. Jean would have given that to all the eggs. If the sample for a particular embryo contains only fragments of that size, then her 164-bp contribution has been matched by an identical one of mine, and the embryo is unaffected. If, beside her 164-bp fragment, the lane also shows a 109- and a 55-bp fragment, then that embryo has received the mutation from me.

It was evening when I finally pulled on a rubber glove and picked the slab of gel out of its mold. It shivered in my hand like something on the edge of life, a cloudy gray submarine growth, a jellyfish. I retreated to the dark room. It took no more than a few moments to put on a protective mask, to clamber onto a stool, to lay the gel on the viewer, to snap on the UV light, and bring the slab of jelly to life. Deep inside glowed bands of ghostly mauve.

"What's that?" Eric asked, barging in for something or other.

"Oh, nothing special."

He put on goggles and peered over my shoulder. "Isn't that one of ours?"

"Just checking something."

He barged out again. The slab of jelly looked like any other of the hundreds of gels we had run. It *could* have been any one of them; but it was mine.

Besides the controls there were eight lanes. Eight lanes, eight embryos:

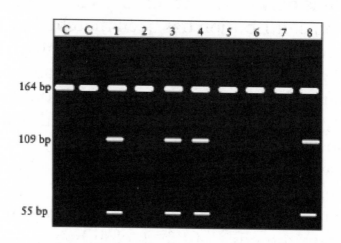

You don't have to be an expert to read it, do you? It was one of Uncle Gregor's ratios. Embryos 2, 5, 6, and 7 were unaffected; 1, 3, 4, and 8 were carrying the mutation. Fifty-fifty. One to one. One half. Chance, pure chance out of such a small sample as eight, had conspired to make it exact. Four of those fragile clusters of jelly, four of those proto-Benedicts or proto-Jeans, had received the extra restriction site from their erstwhile father. They were carrying the achondroplasia gene and would become, without a shadow of doubt, like me. The other four were clear. And I could decide.

The Rotwang family went to Vienna, as so many families had done in the past and would do in the coming years, fleeing political unrest. For the moment Vienna was far enough, but within seventy years you would have to travel to another continent altogether to be quite safe, and the people you would be fleeing from were those who had turned genetics into a creed.

That torrid summer, Mendel forgot Frau Rotwang. Memory is a labile thing. Whatever he had thought of her, he forgot her. At least he expunged her from the surface of his memory, from that part that wrestled with the intricate dance of genes. That torrid summer an attack of the pea weevil, *Bruchus pisi,* decimated his crop and he was constrained to abandon the plants that had been his children for almost a decade. He sniffed and shrugged and turned to the other species. Stubborn, bespectacled, introverted, he wandered among the beans and the four-o'clock, the campanula and the snapdragons, his scissors snipping away at anthers, his camel-hair brush slipping, penislike, between the petals and dusting pollen from one flower to another. He collected the seeds, labeled them, and stored them; and the next season planted them out once more and waited. Yet again seeds swelled and sprouted, lines and lines of them — radicles nosing down into the soil, plumules ascending into the air, cotyledons opening to the sun like a pair of grasping hands. Rows and rows of fragile seedlings watched over by the friar, counted, reckoned, balanced — stock, maize, four-o'clock . . .

His ideas held, more or less (although he complained often enough to anyone who would listen about the difficulty of finding suitable plants, and the lack of time, and the lack of notice that anyone took): if you take two different varieties and cross them artificially, the offspring resemble one of the parents. (It was not always so: in four-o'clock, *Mirabilis jalapa,* for example, the hybrids were often intermediate between the two parents for flower color; but that didn't upset him. Dominance was not always complete.) Then, if you self-pollinate the hybrids, the next generation gives you a ratio of three-to-one for any particular character pair; or, if the dominance was not complete as in *Mirabilis,* one-to-two-to-one. He had seen the same thing happen in mice. It meant that his simple mathematical model held true:

inheritance was governed by particles, one contributed by each parent, no mingling of blood. There was nothing mysterious about it, nothing vague or mystical, no nameless fluids or influences, no hand of God. Just the plain facts of probability, a handing out of beads to children, like a gift from each parent, one bead from each parent for each inherited character.

Of course there were complications — pod color in *Phaseolus* (bean), for example. In this case he crossed dwarf bean, which has white flowers, with scarlet runner, which has scarlet flowers. The almost infertile hybrids had a variety of flower colors, ranging from scarlet to pale violet, and white flowers appeared only rarely (one in every thirty-one). Nevertheless, other characters (height, for example) obeyed the same rules as in his original peas, and even the flower color could probably be explained if, instead of the color arising from just one inherited factor, it was actually the result of two or more factors working additively.[3] This would also explain the range of different colors obtained. More-

3. *Versuche über Pflanzen-Hybriden*, 1866. What would now be called polygenic inheritance: a brilliant further insight into genetic theory. This idea would quite escape the so-called rediscoverers of his work at the start of the twentieth century.

over, in the case of stocks (*Matthiola*) he obtained precisely similar results to the pea . . .

But who would listen?

He even set up fertilizations under the microscope, using single pollen grains, in order to demonstrate that his assumption of one pollen grain to one ovule was true.[4] But who cared?

He demonstrated more of his hybrids to the Society for Natural Science, but species hybrids this time, things the members could understand, mules of the plant world, mongrels, bastards, mulattoes, half-castes, complex mixtures showing a blending of various characters that the audience could relate to, but that were essentially uncountable and therefore of no real scientific interest. They did not want the mathematics of chance and probability or a deduction about the existence of inheritable, discrete factors. They did not, assuredly they did not, want to stare the future in the eye. "Science is physics; or it is stamp collecting," Ernest Rutherford said. Stamp collecting was what interested the Brünn Society for Natural Science. They wanted to see bizarre crosses and

4. Letters to Nägeli, July 1870 and September 1870.

strange monsters, neither one thing nor the other, neither fish nor fowl. It was the educated class's version of going to the freak shows in the Klosterplatz. It almost came as a surprise when von Niessl (doubt that *von*) asked him to prepare his lecture on the pea in the form of a paper for inclusion in the Proceedings of the Society for the year 1865.

For publication Mendel went back to his original data. He tells us that in one of his letters. He went back to the original data and worked long hours going over the counts and tallies, checking them through, recalculating ratios, finding nothing out of place; then even longer hours copying it in his meticulous copperplate hand.

That torrid summer, like the thunderstorms that built up in the afternoon sky, the political crisis broke. Who now recalls the Schleswig-Holstein question, or remembers that there was a Seven Weeks' War between Prussia and Austria? But that torrid summer, following the triumph or disaster (it depends on your point of view) at the battle of Königgrätz, the Austrian army was routed and Brünn was occupied by Prussian troops. They came as a surprise, a storm out of a calm summer day, preceded by nothing more than a vague sense of unease and a few fantastic rumors. At one moment there was the ordinary life of the city, and then, suddenly, Prussian soldiers were parading in the Grosse Platz with their *pickelhauben* and their new breech-loading rifles. Their band played in the Augarten. They performed elaborate maneuvers in the parks beside the Schramm-Ring and the Kaiser-Ring. The King of Prussia visited the city just as Napoleon had before the battle of Austerlitz (who could have doubted that everyone saw the parallel); and a troop of cavalry was billeted on the monastery.

The invaders brought with them famine and cholera. The hospital just up the hill from the monastery filled to overflowing. The bells of the Augustinian church tolled almost continually for the dead (until the authorities forbade the practice because it was damaging to the citizens' morale). And all that torrid, pestilential summer, Mendel wrote and revised and rewrote.

The paper on hybridization in the garden pea was published in the *Proceedings of the Brünn Society for the Study of Natural Science.* It was sent to 120 other societies and organizations around Europe. Copies went to the Universities of Vienna and Berlin, to the Royal Society and the Linnaean Society of

London, to the Royal Horticultural Society at Kew, to Uppsala and Paris and Rome and St. Petersburg. No one read it. This was one of the three most significant and famous papers in the whole history of biology,[5] and no one took any notice. He also had forty offprints made of the paper, but we know of the fate of only five of them. To whom the others were sent, we just don't know. One imagines Darwin, one imagines Haeckel, one imagines Huxley, one imagines Purkyně. But we don't know.

By the time of publication, the Prussians had gone and the city of Brünn appeared peaceful again. More than that, it appeared unchanged. Once again the Lord Lieutenant had taken up his position in the city. Once more the Estates were meeting in the Landhaus. The Empire, that shambolic collection of German, Magyar, Slav, Italian, and Jew, had been left untouched. Its borders were entire. Once more the military bands played in the Augarten — Strauss they played,

---

5. There is no competition. The other two are the Darwin-Wallace paper on evolution by means of natural selection, delivered to the Linnaean Society (1858); and the Crick-Watson letter to *Nature* on a suggested structure of DNA (*Nature*, 1953). There are no papers greater than these; on these hang all the law and the prophets.

Strauss, Strauss, Strauss — for all the world as though the Imperial Army had not just been defeated in war.

It is one of the dangers of the historical perspective to mistake the momentous for the mundane. Nothing much had changed except that the balance of Middle Europe had been reset. Nothing much had changed except that the German people had stumbled incoherently — they could hardly be accused of efficiency in the matter — a further step toward the apocalypse. Nothing much had changed except that an unknown friar, shortly to be elected abbot, had discovered the mechanics of inheritance and had, all unbeknownst to himself, created a new science that was to be taken up by the *Gesellschaft für Rassenhygiene* (the Society for Racial Hygiene) in 1905 and the Nazi Party two decades later. It was a science that would ultimately lead to the ovens of Auschwitz.

[Antibody]

Mendel cheated. Oh yes, that's the story. Useful, isn't it? The Stalinists, in their desperation to demonstrate that Mendelism was a fraud, nothing more than a capitalist-fascist plot, used this calumny to support their point of view: Mendel cheated, genetics is a lie, Lysenko is right, the environment is everything, man can be molded by his circumstances, the revolution will create a true socialist environment, and man will fit perfectly into the earthly paradise like a hand into a glove. And thus the great experiment of Communism finds justification for its view and millions have to die before everyone (well, the majority at least) tumbles to the fact that the evidence is now stacked against the hypothesis of an earthly paradise and the great experiment can be brought to a close.

Mendel cheated.

But it was not some Soviet toady laboring away in a genetics laboratory somewhere in Omsk or Tomsk who caught the great man out; it was Sir Ronald Fisher. I particularly like the use of the title — it makes the accusation so much more authoritative. *Sir* Ronald Aylmer Fisher (1890–1962), graduate in mathematics at Cambridge University, sometime professor of eugenics at London University.

Eugenics? Does your mind stall? Do you feel shivers down your spine? Does the flesh on the back of your neck crawl? Oh yes — there was a professor of eugenics at London University. Fisher occupied the Galton Chair of Eugenics, founded by Charles Darwin's cousin and first held by a brilliant racist called Karl Pearson (he of the chi-square test and the Pearson correlation coefficient, biologists and statisticians please note). There was a chair of eugenics at Cambridge as well, but the university had the decency to change the name of their department to plain *genetics* in 1943 when Fisher moved there; by that time, presumably, the stench from continental Europe was becoming unbearable. In London the senses cannot have been so acute: the title of the Galton Chair was not changed to plain "Genetics" until 1961.

So, Mendel cheated. The problem is, you see, his results were too good.

EXAMPLE:
F_1 generation total: 1,064 pea plants; of which 787 tall and 277 dwarf.

348

Theoretical ratio 3:1. Actual ratio 2.84:1.

It is rather close, isn't it? But that is not quite the point. You could toss a coin one hundred times and find that it came up heads forty-eight times and tails fifty-two times, and no one would be too surprised. But if you claimed that every time you repeated the experiment it came up similarly close to 50:50, people might start getting suspicious. The tall:dwarf values I have just quoted are almost the *worst* that Father Gregor found. His other experimental ratios are all as close or closer to the ideal 3:1.

2.96:1 3.01:1 2.95:1 3.15:1 2.82:1 3.14:1

There they are, the actual values. The problem with Mendel's work is that time after time, repetition after repetition, his results were simply too close to the expected ratios. Expected by whom? By Mendel, of course. It was Sir Ronald Fisher who showed that the probability that Mendel could come consistently so close to his expected ratios by pure chance was so small as to be negligible. Considering Mendel's 3:1 ratios alone, the probability of his having got greater deviations from the expected ratios than he actually found is .95. In laymen's terms, Mendel had a ninety-five-percent chance of getting *worse* results than he did. Put backwards, he had only a five-percent chance of getting as perfect a set of results as he did. Ergo, Mendel cheated. Putting all his known results together, the probability of his having got greater deviations from the expected ratios than he actually found is .99993. That means that he had a 99.993-percent chance of getting *worse* results than he did. Put backwards, he had only a .007-percent chance of getting as perfect a set of results as he did, which is no chance at all.

So, he cheated. Mendel spent a decade of his life on his breeding experiments on the garden pea, further tested the validity of his theories on *Antirrhinum, Matthiola, Fuchsia, Campanula,* and a further eighteen species, and, thanks to the idiot Nägeli, *wasted* God knows how much time on trying to repeat the work on *Hieracium* — and all the time he cheated.

The trouble is, he was right.

The ninth edition of the *Encyclopaedia Britannica* was published with an article on "Hybridisation" by G. J. Romanes. Romanes was one of the most devoted disciples of Charles Darwin, and had consulted the great man at length during the preparation of the article. Darwin recommended that he read W. O.

Focke's book *Die Pflanzenmischlinge*, and, moreover, he actually lent Romanes his own copy. This book, published in 1881, outlined Mendel's work on *Pisum, Phaseolus,* and *Hieracium,* and also mentioned him in the historical section, which Darwin particularly recommended Romanes to read. Romanes duly researched and wrote the article, and the name G. Mendel duly appeared in the bibliography. Darwin's copy of *Die Pflanzenmischlinge* was duly returned, the pages for the work on the *Papilionaceae* still uncut, as they remain today; which is doubly curious as one of those pages (110) also mentions Darwin's own work with garden peas. Indeed, the references to Mendel and to Darwin are immediately adjacent to each other, the two names separated by "(*loc. cit.*)" and a period.

Who was it who said, "You will find it a very good practice always to verify your references"? Darwin didn't check his references, and neither did Romanes. They cheated. And Darwin needed Mendel. Oh yes, indeed, Darwin *needed* Mendel. As far as he had any clear ideas about a matter that was of prime importance to his theory of evolution by natural selection, Darwin believed in the blending theory of inheritance. That is, he held that offspring tend to be a *blend* of their parents' characteristics.

The trouble is, he was wrong.

By logical extension of this blending theory, a species should show less and less variation over a number of generations. Any artist knows that if you take the whole spectrum of colored paints and solemnly mix them together in pairs, finally and inevitably you will end up with muddy brown. And any naturalist knows that this is not what happens with plants and animals. Like anyone else with eyes, Darwin looked around him and, rather than muddy brown, found a bewildering, dazzling range of variation within each species. He saw, to use the technical term, polymorphisms. So to account for this undeniable variety he further postulated a high degree of spontaneous variation — what we would now call mutation.

The trouble is, he was wrong again. A high mutation rate implies an instability in the genetic material, which in turn would mean that you couldn't guarantee what you inherited from your parents. In such a case, natural selection simply wouldn't occur because the genes selected in one generation wouldn't necessarily be passed on to the next. By the time they got there, they would probably have mutated.

No, what Darwin *needed* was Mendel. And

he recommended a book that referred to Mendel's work (a total of fourteen separate citations), and Romanes even quoted Mendel in his bibliography, and neither of them verified the references.

In fact Mendel had already seen this difficulty of the blending theory in the *Origin of Species* and come to Darwin's rescue — in his *Pisum* paper he points out that if you cross parents differing in seven pairs of characters and then you allow the hybrid offspring to self-fertilize, in the second generation you will have 2,187 different genetic constitutions. He even generalized the rule, in one of his most brilliant insights: if n designates the number of characteristic differences in two parental plants, then 3^n is the number of genetically different individuals produced in the second generation after self-fertilization. Assuming that all the character pairs show complete dominance, then 2^n is the number of different combinations of phenotypes that would occur. Thus, in the case of his seven pairs of characters, you would obtain 128 different phenotypic combinations. That's where the variety that Darwin needed so desperately comes from, from a reshuffling and recombination of Father Gregor's factors; and the full explanation is there in his original paper. And no one noticed.

Later, in response to criticism of this very weakness, Darwin moved toward a belief in the inheritance of acquired characteristics. In *The Variation of Animals and Plants Under Domestication* (1868 — note the date; it was just two years after Mendel's paper was published) he envisaged body cells shedding hereditary particles, called gemmules or pangenes, into the blood. These entirely fictitious things, these fabrications, were visualized by him as models of the cells from which they come. They subsequently assemble to form the sex cells and thereby get passed on to the next generation. But because they originate from body cells they may therefore be affected by whatever has happened to the parent cells. Thus the effects of the environment on the body cells will end up being inherited.

That's Darwin.

The trouble is, he was wrong again. He also seemed unaware that this particular theory completely contradicted the blending theory. Of course, it is never difficult for human beings to hold two contradictory beliefs at the same time. Look how many believe in a merciful and loving God, despite all the evidence to the contrary. Oh no, contradictory beliefs are by no means *impossible;* but they're not very scientific.

At exactly the same time as Mendel was working so brilliantly, so doggedly, with such piercing insight into the matter of inheritance, August Weismann of the University of Freiburg im Breisgau performed an experiment of mind-boggling stupidity to disprove the theory of the inheritance of acquired characters. This experiment involved chopping off the tails of mice. Weismann bred mice through five generations, more than nine hundred of the wretched animals, laboriously chopping off all their tails.

And by the fifth generation? Mice with tails.

I wonder whether his colleagues tried to hush the whole thing up. Or maybe he himself tried to keep it quiet, working late into the evening when no one else was around and keeping the cages and cages of tailless mice behind locked doors. Chop, chop, chop. Disposal would have been a problem. What did the cleaning lady imagine the good professor was up to? Or did he wrap the tails in newspaper and slip them into some rubbish bin on the way home? Chop, chop, chop. Did Weismann imagine he was contributing to the sacred body of man's knowledge? Chop, chop, chop. Five generations. At least the iniquity of the fathers is only visited upon the children unto the third and fourth generation. There is something quintessentially Teutonic about Weismann's insistence on going one further than God. He showed this talent in other directions, becoming the first honorary chairman of the Society for Racial Hygiene.

Mendel kept mice. I've told you that. I'll bet he didn't do anything so idiotic as cut their tails off.

I keep mice. We have thousands of them in the animal room at the laboratories, tiny, mewing creatures with pink noses and twitching whiskers. Some of them are monstrously deformed.

Let us listen to E. B. Ford, sometime Emeritus Professor of Ecological Genetics at Oxford University and friend of that enthusiastic eugenicist Leonard Darwin:

The total number of plant and animal species now described lies between 1,100,000 and 1,200,000. It would have been far less in Mendel's day, but still very large. Yet he based his views upon a single species: the edible pea, Pisum sativum. *It is true that he corroborated them to a slight extent by work on, unfortunately, a related plant: the bean,* Phaseolus. *He also pub-*

lished the results of his experimental crosses with the hawkweeds, Hieracium *... Thus Mendel's conclusions, though probably developed from a consideration of living organisms in general, were really only established from his monumental study on peas. Are the principles apparently derived from experiments upon a single species really applicable to over a million others, exhibiting all the diversity of animal as well as of plant life? It seems questionable indeed. Oddly enough, it would not have done so had Mendel merely used one other, chosen with discrimination ...*

Antirrhinum, Aquilegia, Calceolaria, Campanula, Carex, Cheiranthus, Cirsium, Dianthus, Ficaria, Fuchsia, Geum, Hieracium, Ipomoea, Linaria, Lychnis, Malus, Matthiola, Mirabilis, Phaseolus, Pirus, Potentilla, Prunus, Tropaeolum, Verbascum, Veronica, Viola, Zea.

Oddly enough, Mendel tried as best he could. It was just that everyone else was too stupid to understand what he had done. One wonders how E.B. himself would have measured up ...

Cyril Burt cheated, of course. We all know that now (or almost all of us, but there are already some revisionists around). The curious thing is, we should have known it all along. We should have looked into his figures, poked around in them, looked up his references (tricky, that one, because a good number of them simply didn't exist), generally picked at the fabric of his work to see whether it would come apart at the seams. By *we* I mean *they*, of course — the people who took it all at face value and actually encouraged its use in education: in the eleven-plus examination. Pigeonholing at eleven years old. The children of the middle class go to the grammar schools; the children of the working class go to the secondary moderns.

What Cyril Burt set out to show was that intelligence is inherited, or such a large portion of it as makes no difference. He did it by testing people's intelligence. He tested people at random, he tested members of families unto the third and fourth generation, he tested identical twins. And he came to the conclusion that intelligence is about as inherited as, say, shortsightedness.

Burt used an array of tests and then labored long and hard at the mathematical analysis of his results. He also used straightforward personal observation, a curious method that appears to go something like this: you chat with someone; you are an expert in such matters; off the top of your head you decide what his IQ score is; you are right. He did all this and, following in the footsteps of Spearman, who had come to the conclusion that intelligence is a unitary *thing*, which he called *g*, and whatever you've got you've got, and we can't do much about it, Burt decided that if you can identify a person's intelligence at an appropriate age (eleven was the earliest age possible for reliable identification), then you can decide what education such a person needs and deserves. There's nothing crueler than raising false hopes in a child, is there? No more attempt to train a dwarf as a basketball player than give an average man an academic education.

Now, I don't want to kick a man when he's down (actually I do — given my particular disadvantage, it's the only way I get the opportunity), nor do I wish to speak ill of the dead, although if the libel laws don't allow you to speak ill of them when they are alive, then I don't see that you're left with much alternative. But the blunt fact is, Cyril Burt was a fraud. He invented data to fit his prejudices and he even invented coworkers to fit his data. He was a lifelong scandal, and all in the name of genetics. But I did all right by him. I passed the eleven-plus. So, probably, did you, if your parents couldn't afford a private school and you're anything near my age and are reading this book.

Consider this little gem: shortly after the death of Alfred Binet in 1911, one of his admirers, Henry Goddard, administered the Binet test (adapted for English-language use) on behalf of the U.S. Public Health Service to immigrants at Ellis Island. He used two women to administer the tests, because women are gentler and more sympathetic. In 1913, working with Hungarians, Italians, Russians, and Jews, these two ladies discovered that 80 percent of these immigrants were feebleminded, the percentage differing little from group to group. Eighty percent.

Anton Mendel was exactly the kind of person who might have emigrated to the United States. I wonder how he would have fared in such a test? I wonder how his small, frightened, confused son Johann would have fared?

As a result of Goddard's pioneering work, people of reduced intelligence were denied entry to the U.S.A. Furthermore, quotas were established that effectively excluded those nation groups that he had demonstrated to have such high levels of feeblemindedness — the southern and eastern Europeans, the Slavs . . . and the Jews.

Richard Lynn, of the University of Ulster at Coleraine, is on record as using a survey of black African intelligence to calculate the average black African IQ. The figure he comes up with is 69. Murray and Herrenstein, in their book *The Bell Curve*, were more modest. They took the median of eleven different studies and came up with the figure 75. Therefore, on average, black Africans are at the moment about as feebleminded as southern Europeans and Slavs and Jews were at the start of this century. Isn't it amazing what can happen in three generations?

You do understand, of course, that organic evolution, the changing of gene frequencies to any significant degree, is simply impossible in so short a time. So the sudden discovery of normal, "white" intelligence in the descendants of Slav and Jewish and Italian immigrants to the United States has nothing to do with race, nothing to do with genes and evolution, nothing to do, in fact, with any useful *thing* called intelligence. Genes code for protein. They don't do anything else, and there simply isn't any protein with a domain marked "intelligence." I have no idea what there is, but I can assure you there isn't that. Any change there may have been in the performance of Jews and Slavs in intelligence tests is — must be — entirely a result of environmental and social changes. The same thing is happening to American blacks and will happen, presumably, to Africans . . . unless people like Lynn and Burt and Goddard get to work on them.

A test of my own. First you must read each of the following quotations:

1. "The effect of all racial crossing is therefore in brief always the following:
   a. Lowering of the level of the higher race.
   b. Physical and intellectual regression and hence the beginning of a slowly but surely progressing sickness."
2. "If both parents are feebleminded, all the children will be feebleminded. It is obvious that such matings should not be allowed. It is perfectly clear that no feebleminded person should ever be allowed to marry or to become a parent. It is obvious that if this is to be carried out, the intelligent part of society must enforce it."
3. "Taken on the average, and regarding both sexes, this alien Jewish population is somewhat inferior physically and mentally to the native population. We know and admit that some of the chil-

dren of these alien Jews from the academic standpoint have done brilliantly; whether they have the staying power of the native race is another question. No breeder of cattle, however, would purchase an entire herd because he anticipated finding one or two fine specimens included in it."

Now here's the task, and it is a difficult one: you have to identify which quotation comes from the writings of Henry Goddard; which comes from the pen of Karl Pearson; and which is from Adolf Hitler. Don't cheat.[1]

Trofim Denisovich Lysenko was born in 1898. He cheated, of course. We all know that now, but the curious thing is, we knew it at the time (we over here on the other side, that is), whereas the ideas of Goddard and Pearson and Burt were all accepted, more or less, and the ideas of Jensen and Murray and Lynn and Herrenstein are still at least considered. Because, unlike Pearson or Goddard or Burt or the others, Lysenko was on

1. ANSWER: They are, in order, Hitler (*Mein Kampf*, 1924); Goddard (*Feeble-mindedness: its causes and consequences*, 1914), and Pearson (with Moul, *Annals of Eugenics*, 1925).

the wrong side. He was a Soviet communist.

In the 1930s, Trofim Denisovich and his henchmen set about trying to prove that inheritance doesn't actually exist in any coherent, Mendelian form. The environment is everything. It is the environment that induces changes in the organism and these changes subsequently become inheritable. This theory, with its echoes of Darwin's pangenesis, fitted admirably into the creed of communism, where all men are malleable and, given the perfect socialist environment, will grow into perfect socialist beings. In fact Lysenko treated his experimental plants in much the way that Stalin treated the peoples of the Soviet Empire. He transplanted them, he froze them, he generally oppressed them and mistreated them.

By 1940 Lysenko was director of the Institute of Genetics of the USSR Academy of Sciences. At the meeting of the Lenin All-Union Academy of Agricultural Sciences of 1939 he had made a personal attack on the leading Soviet geneticist, Vavilov, and in 1940 Vavilov was arrested. He was exiled to Siberia and died in the care of the Gulag in 1943 — all for studying Mendelian genetics. What, one wonders, would Father Gregor have made of that?

Lysenko finally put his seal on the study of genetics in the Soviet Union at the 1948 meeting of the Lenin All-Union Academy. The remaining Mendelian geneticists recanted, and the teaching of Mendel's work was banned throughout the Soviet Union and beyond into the countries of the Soviet Bloc. The ban continued until 1965, which, by the purest coincidence, was the one-hundredth anniversary of the delivery of Father Gregor's paper to the Brünn Society for Natural Science. Although Trofim Denisovich was then stripped of his political powers, he was not stripped of anything else. He retained rank, honors, and academic posts, and continued into ripe and august retirement, finally dying in 1976.

In the inner room of the Mendel Museum there is the portrait of Mendel in his abbot's costume, looking grim and bilious — the so-called Great Prelate Portrait. There is also a typewritten list on a table:

Arrested and Shot Scientists	Dead in Prison
N.M. Tulaikov, 1937	N. I. Vavilov, 1940–1943
N.K. Belayev, 1937	G. D. Karpechenko, 1941–1942
I. I. Agol, 1938	L. I. Govorov, 1940–1942
V. N. Stepkov, 1937	A. B. Alexandrov, 1938–?
N. P. Gorbunov, 1937	G. A. Levitsky, 1940–?
A. I. Geister, 1937	. . . and many others
R. I. David, 1937	
G. A. Nadson, 1938	
S. G. Levit, 1939	
G. K. Meister, 1939	
G. K. Muralov, 1939	

Committed Suicide	Held in Prison and in Exile
D. A. Sabinin, 1951	S. S. Chetverikov, 1929–1934
	A. A. Sapegin, 1933–1935
	V. P. Efroimson, 1932–1935; 1948–1955
	D. D. Romashov, 1939–1954
	N. V. Timofeev-Ressovsky, 1945–1955
	. . . and others

Biologists don't actually expect to be on the firing line, but given the nature of what they do, I suppose it's inevitable. Look what happened to the chemists and the physicists.

Here's another question: Benedict Lambert is sitting in his laboratory playing God. He has eight embryos in eight little tubes. Four of the embryos are proto-Benedicts, proto-dwarfs; the other four are, for want of a better word, normal. How should he choose?

Of course we all know that God has opted for the easy way out. He has decided on chance as the way to select one combination of genes from another. If you want to shun euphemisms, then God allows pure luck to decide whether a mutant child or a normal child shall be born. But Benedict Lambert has the possibility of beating God's proxy and overturning the tables of chance. He can choose. Wasn't choice what betrayed Adam and Eve? They chose to eat of the fruit of the tree of knowledge of good and evil, and once they had done that, they knew that they were naked, and they chose to try to hide it. That was how God found them out. It was the last remnants of their innocence that let them down. If they'd been streetwise, they'd have brazened it out. They'd have kept to their nakedness and pretended not to notice — they would have deceived God. Presumably we'd all be a lot better off now if they had.

So to Benedict Lambert. What did he choose? That's your test. Eight green bottles sitting on the wall; eight plastic tubes sitting in the refrigerator. What to do with them? Which of them accidentally fell?

I know you don't really need this; you're already up there with me, aren't you? You're already confronting nature from the awesome viewpoint of God. Nevertheless, allow me to spell it out. Here are your options. You may:

1. select two of the four normal embryos and send them over to the clinic for implantation within the willing, warm, wet, waiting uterus of Mrs. Jean Miller née Piercey, or
2. select the four achondroplastics, the four stunted little beings, the four chidren of Ben, and send them over instead, and curse the whole bloody world and all its machinations and injustices, or
3. refuse to usurp the powers of God and choose instead to become as help-

less as He . . . by choosing one normal embryo and one achondroplastic and leaving the result to blind and careless chance.

Which?

[Insertion]

Jean Piercey lying supine on a table, with her knees drawn up and the coralline folds of her vulva displayed to view. I am afraid I can only imagine it. It was Anthony Lupron, gowned and masked and accompanied by two acolyte nurses, who performed the embryo transfer, not I. It was he who inserted the speculum and aspirated mucus from the tight little bud of her cervix. It was he who glanced up over her crest of hair and asked whether everything was okay, whether she felt relaxed and comfortable, whether the Janáček playing gently in the background — *Piano Cycle: On an Overgrown Path* — was loud enough. It was he who loaded the embryos and slid the catheter tube gently, gently into her vagina and up through the cervical canal into her womb. She winced slightly. "Patience," he murmured. "Almost done." Delicately the catheter spat. A soft, aspirant sound. Ah.

"There."

Slowly, slowly they lowered her legs. The gentle strains of Janáček soothed her. A nurse stroked her brow while the bed was tilted back to raise her hips above the level of her head. "Now just you relax," they said.

So it was Anthony Lupron who committed the ultimate deflowering of Jean Piercey. I was merely in the waiting room with her husband.

A scented cave, a dwarf's cavern dripping with stalactites and running with hidden rivulets and concealing somewhere deep within its declivities sparkling treasure — glittering jeweled eggs, something from the workshop of a cosmic Fabergé, something fabulous and priceless, something lost to human knowledge. It lies there convoluted and burgeoning, folding itself into fantastic shapes, coiling and infolding, metamorphosing and changing. A sea-change, into something rich and strange. Those are eyes that were mere pearls. Coral is become bone . . .

There are still moments in the manipulation of man or molecule when you are powerless. You splice a gene into a bacterium, transfer it to a culture medium . . . and you wait. You transfect a mouse embryo with human DNA and watch, breathless, to see what happens. You spit two glistening embryos through a catheter tube into a receptive womb . . . and wait, listening. Human chorionic gonadotrophin, a 25-kilodalton glycoprotein hormone, is the first cry a budding infant makes, a tiny molecular cry for recognition amid the roaring and screaming of the mother's blood. You sample at day fourteen, listening for that cry, sniffing with antibodies for that infinitesimal scent. Like a dragon, you can smell treasure.

I was fumbling around the kitchen, preparing breakfast, when the phone rang. Caught between toaster and coffee machine, caught between ferment and fear, I lifted the receiver with caution.

"Is that you, Ben?" But it was not the distant tones of Jean, or the detached tones of Anthony Lupron with the result, positive or negative, of the HCG test. It was my sister, Beatrice. "I hoped I'd catch you before you left for work," she said. "I'm reading the *Daily Mail*. You're in it."

"I'm in it?" My first sensation was one of panic. Visions of gnomic treasure evaporated. I pictured only the mundane facts, those little tubes in the deep freeze, each with its tiny plug of frozen matter at the bottom. I thought of my careful circumvention of the ethics committee, my assiduous manipulation of phials of sperm to substitute mine for his, to commit adultery by sleight of hand. Had Miss Allele MacMaster got wind of something irregular and blown the story to the newspapers? Or had Jean herself, nursing who knew what seed, been overwhelmed by a fit of conscience?

"Ben? Are you still there?"

"What does it say?"

Beatrice hesitated. My family has always hesitated when confronted by me. They have always had to think carefully about how to dress up the most mundane thought, sugar the most innocuous pill. She hesitated, and in the pause I wrote my own headlines: GENETICIST CHOOSES HIS EMBRYOS; SPERM SWITCH IN FUTURISTIC ADULTERY; BRAVE NEW DWARF. The possibilities were legion. A thoughtful leader in the *Times* would discuss the ethical implications of embryo selection in terms both circumspect and self-righteous. The *Mail* would rave about the end of civilization. Members of the Warnock Committee would beat their public breasts. And I, cringing dwarf, would be torn limb from limb by the hounds of public opinion. I already could hear them baying in the distance. "What does it say, for God's sake?"

"It says 'Dwarf Biologist Discovers Himself.' "

"Read it."

"All of it?"

"Just the start."

Beatrice cleared her throat. The sound came down the line like a little flutter of embarrassment. "Apparently it's all about that lecture you gave. 'Super geneticist Ben Lambert has finished his search of a lifetime. Genetic engineering techniques and years of patience have finally led him to discover the gene that has ruled his own existence, for Ben, thirty-eight and a researcher at one of the world's leading genetics laboratories, is' " — another hesitation — " 'a dwarf. Little in body but big in spirit, he . . .' " Her voice trailed off. "It sort of goes on like that for a column and a half."

I breathed relief. I felt like a murderer pulled up for a speeding offense. When I passed the newsstand that morning, the man held up the *Sun* for me to see. "This you, Ben?" he asked. "Must be you, I guess. Not many of you around, are there?" Somehow, by one of those quirks that govern such things, the story had filtered down out of the scientific journals and flooded all at once into the various tributaries, ditches and sewers alike, of the popular press. There on an inside page in the *Sun*, opposite Pouting, Protuberant Pamela, was Brave Benedict. The news vendor looked at me with renewed curiosity, as though fame were something just as interesting as deformity. "Seems you done yourself a bit of good. What's it all about, then?"

"Genes and chromosomes."

"I've heard of them. You know what the male chromosome said to the female genes?"

"No, but I'm about to."

"There're no flies on you, darling. It's on page fifteen. There's a whole bunch of genetics jokes. There's a competition for the best one."

"Try *me*," I suggested.

In the street, passersby seemed to stare with new curiosity. DWARF GOES WHERE NO MAN HAS GONE BEFORE, said one newspaper; LITTLE GUY, BIG DISCOVERY, said another. "You the bloke in the paper this morning?" someone asked on the bus. "You 'im? Bloody marvelous, I say." At the laboratories the phone never seemed to stop ringing. The receptionist fielded a lot of the calls. She told the callers I wasn't available for interviews or photographs, wasn't available to do a show at the London Palladium or Chipperfield's Circus, wasn't prepared to pose with three naked models for an advertisement for color film. But one call she did pass on to me. Jean's voice, distant and anxious, sounded in my ear. "I saw you in the paper."

"So did everyone else. How are things?"

"They're okay." *Okay* is a relative term. I

waited for her to continue. "I'm in the clinic," she said quietly. "I've just had the result of the test."

"And?"

A small electronic whisper. "There's a baby. Ben, I'm pregnant."

It is difficult to reconstruct an emotion. At times it is difficult even to admit to one. I have practiced long and hard at denying entry to such twin imposters as triumph and disaster, or love and hate, but sometimes the barriers are breached. So I admit that standing there in the laboratory office with the telephone receiver in my hand and the desk before me strewn with the rough notes of my speech to the forthcoming Mendel Symposium, I felt a sharp lance of anguish for the child's future, muddled with a sensation of triumph.

There was a rush of static silence in the receiver. I had almost forgotten Jean. "Are you there?" she said. "Benedict?"

"Yes."

"Ben, I'm frightened. Will it be all right? The baby, I mean. Will it be all right?"

"I'm sure it will. It'll be just like its mother."

Another silence. The problem with the telephone is that silence is all you've got as an alternative to speech. "I wish," she said quietly. "I wish it could be like its father."

"That can be arranged."

"You know what I mean. Stop trying to trip me up."

"You're tripping me up," I replied tartly. "Have you told your husband?"

She ignored my question. When she spoke, there was a hint of anxiety in her tone. Even down a few miles of wire I could sense the shiver of doubt. "It *will* be all right, won't it, Ben?" The voice trailed off into the faint whispering of the ether. "Ben . . . ?" And I could picture that mouse-gray head filled with doubt, that soft and stubborn face bewildered by the gambler's sense of the shifting nature of things, the capricious machinations of the world of wagering. "Ben, you did do it right, didn't you?"

"Do you mean have I dumped you in it? Do you mean have I played the kind of practical joke on you that life played on me? That's what you're asking, isn't it? Did I close my eyes and pick one out at random? God knows, that's what God did with me."

She made a sound, like the cry of a mammal in pain. "Ben," she cried. "Ben . . . please . . ."

And suddenly fulfillment was transformed into anger. Anger at the docile stupidity of her, at the pleading, whining kindness of her, at her naïveté. "Well, you'll have to wait and see, won't you?" I said to her. Then I put the phone down.

Unforgivable? Have I forfeited all sympathy? But you must understand I have never looked for your sympathy. Even if at times I have gained it, I can assure you I have never sought it out. Sympathy is an unctuous, slimy emotion. It is tainted with *Schadenfreude,* rank with contempt, fetid with the implication that I, the target, am somehow less than you, the sympathizer. I don't want your sympathy. I have never asked for it. Never so much as once have I played the poor, sad dwarf, smiling through his tears.

Another call that was put through to me that morning was from the BBC. One Jake Toogood. "You must be just about sick of people calling at the moment," he said, and I agreed with him heartily. "But I was wondering whether we might meet up to discuss the possibility of our doing a documentary about you. Not just the scientific thing, but the personal interest as well. How does that sound?"

"I really don't think —"

"Just a chat, to see how the land lies. Don't throw me out without hearing me out, there's a good fellow."

Jean standing at the mouth of my cave. Jean pallid about the mouth, the iron railings standing over her head like a crown of virtue. Jean railing at me with accusation and censure. Jean clambering up onto the moral high ground while descending the steps that lead down to the door, a different Jean from the shrinking gray moth of the past. "How could you *do* this, Ben?" She spoke in italics, almost as though speaking to an idiot child that has crapped on the carpet. "How could you *do* this to me?" She was dressed all in black, as though she had come to mourn something.

"You'd better come in."

"Are you trying to get revenge or something? Is that it?"

"No, it's not it."

"Because you've succeeded. Oh yes, you've succeeded." Her accent slipped when she was angry, the ugly vowels of the Midlands breaking through the varnish that she had acquired since moving to London. "You've had your revenge. You've *had* it."

I ushered her in through the front door, watching the way she moved, eyeing her from the angle of Ben, examining the sleek and subtle motion of her legs, the delicate flexing of them as she sat at one of the up-

379

right chairs (designed for normal people, this one). "Stop looking at me like that." She turned away from my gaze, her hand going distractedly to her hair as though she felt something was out of place. Her eyes, those mismatched eyes, stared round my cave with a vagrant cast in them. "You've changed the curtains."

"I've changed my life."

"Don't try that." She looked back at me and shook her head. "For God's sake, don't try to play on my sympathy, Ben."

"Because you haven't any?"

"I haven't any *left,*" she snapped. "You've used it up, don't you see that? You've exhausted it." She held out helpless hands. "You must tell me, Ben. You can't just leave me like this . . . If you don't, I'll get rid of it again —"

"It's not it."

She stared at me as though she had only just noticed me crouching there. "What's not it? What the hell do you mean? You're always playing with words. You're always playing with people, for God's sake. As though it was some kind of game."

"It?"

"Oh, shut up."

There was a moment's truce. She tried once more: "What's not *it?*"

"The baby's not it."

"What do you mean?" She touched her belly. Oh, how well I knew it, that pale, sleek presence beneath the folds of her dress, that fold of silken skin, umbilicus bulging slightly, abdomen declining gently toward a shadowy valley. How well I had known its fragrant pastures, its hidden pubescent delights. "What do you mean?" she repeated.

"It's not *it*. It's a boy."

A stillness. She sat there in my dwarf's cavern, a giantess among the normal men, gravid with a boy. "You *know?*"

"Of course I know. It's a he. He'll have blond hair from your mother — isn't that right? — and a widow's peak from my father. His skin will be pale and freckled like your own, and his eyes will be brown like mine. His nose will be aquiline like my father's, but he will not have my father's cleft chin. He will be, like my mother, left-handed. This, incidentally, is a disadvantage, left-handed people having a lower life expectancy than right; but I don't think you want to worry about that too much. Above all, above every other little quirk and curiosity that he possesses, he will grow straight and sleek and will eventually reach five feet eleven inches. He will be . . . *normal*."

Jean watched me carefully. It was an expression that was quite new to her. But then she was changed in so many ways. "You can't know all that. You can't." Her expression metamorphosed. Her eyes hardened. Her lips tightened, turning white at the corners. There was a pallor about her neck. "You can't know all that," she repeated, and her voice was louder now, as though there were some force behind it, driving the sound out through her teeth. "It's another of your bloody, superior jokes. You can't know about everything, you and your bloody genes, you *can't* know everything! You can't play God!"

By now she was shouting. It was positive feedback, anger making her angrier still, like the cascading effect of enzymes, the second stimulating the first to stimulate the second, a dangerous and unstable cycle of hate and loathing and loathing and hate, until she was standing over me like a harpy, with her fists clenched and her face contorted. "YOU CAN'T PLAY WITH ME LIKE THIS!" she screamed. "YOU'RE NOT GOD!"

And then she hit me.

That, I suppose, broke the cycle. After the storm comes that sullen calm, and a thin drizzle of tears. She sat down in her chair and covered her face with her hands. "I'm sorry, Ben. Oh God, I'm sorry."

I picked myself up, touching the side of my head where the skin smarted. She made to rise, but I held up my hand as though to ward her off. "I'm all right," I said. "Don't worry about me. I'm quite all right. And I *do* know he's a boy. I do know he's a boy and I do know he'll be tall. I didn't play God, Jean. Unlike God, I chose . . . with something approaching love."

She smiled bitterly. Miss Jean Piercey smiled through tears and misery at her dwarf. "Love of whom, Ben?" she asked. "Yourself?"

"Of course we want the labs and all that. I mean, it'll be great to have you going over some of the simpler techniques, demonstrating the gene machine, that kind of thing — can you *really* make your own genes? — but . . ."

"No, you can't, yet. But what?"

"But we're also after the personal thing . . ."

Jake Toogood was heavy and loose, with an ill-fitting fawn jacket and a crumpled navy shirt with the name Armani embroidered discreetly on the pocket flap. He had a cleft chin (autosomal dominant) and a fringe of blond hair (autosomal recessive) hanging in a long curtain around the edge of a bald cranium (sex-limited autosomal dominant). His accent was Cockney hybridized with transatlantic. He turned his nose up at the quiche and ordered wine rather than beer and asked me whether I really wouldn't rather be somewhere other than The Pig and Poke. I told him that I was quite happy with the place, that it was my local, that I felt at home there, that at least it wasn't a pretentious little wine bar run by someone called Damien; and Toogood suddenly found qualities in the place that he hadn't seen before.

"Great, Ben," he decided, "just great. It's just the kind of thing we're after — the personal interest. Friends, family, how you cope with life. Getting up in the morning, getting to work, doing the shopping, getting a beer in the pub, all that kind of thing. As well as the genetics. Incidentally, Ben, are your parents — ?"

"There's just my mother."

"Is she . . . ?"

"Is she what?"

He looked awkward. *"Normal."*

"She's normal."

"And your old man?"

"Also normal." I looked him straight in the eye. "I'm a mutant."

He barely winced. "That's great, Ben.

Great. Might your mum . . . ?"

"I haven't even said whether *I* will yet. I'm not a bloody circus act —"

"Circus? Christ, no, Ben. Grant me a little more taste than that. This is BBC 2, for God's sake — bread as well as circuses, that's the idea. A bit of everyday life, a bit of real science. I want to show that people like you are . . . just like people like me. Only smaller. Know what I mean? I saw that 'Science Scene' program you did. All very well and good, but the guys doing science documentaries are rather the breathless schoolboy type, aren't they? You know — 'Wow, how many megabytes is it? Can you fly to the moon with it?' That kind of thing. No, I see this film as Benedict the man, struggling with life like anyone else struggles with life, only . . ."

"Only?"

"Only more so. Your voice-over explaining how you cope, what drives you, what you believe or don't believe, you know the kind of thing? I want it to be your story, from your viewpoint. Literally, as well." He crouched down, just to make it clear. "Lots of low camera angles. The world according to Ben." He cut at the air with the blade of his hand.

"What's that guy doing?" Eric called from

the bar. "Giving you grief, is he?"

"He's from television."

Eric nodded as though that explained all. "How's Jean, by the way? Haven't seen her for ages."

At Eric's words, Toogood's eyebrows rose. He tensed visibly, like a pointer sensing game. "Who's Jean?"

"A friend."

The fact of a friend, a female friend, lay there between us. Toogood swallowed, wiped his mouth with a paper napkin, and leaned toward me. Behind him the pinball machine uttered a shriek of joy and rang up thousands and thousands of points. "Not a girlfriend, is she?" he asked in a whisper. "These days we can handle almost anything we like on TV. What I mean is, do you have a girl, Ben?" He smiled a gap-toothed smile that had excited Olga when we'd looked around the laboratories. "Or a boy, for Christ's sake, if that's what suits you. It doesn't matter one way or the other. But what does a guy like you do for sex?"

"A Scientist of Our Time" went on the air a few months later. You will have seen the thoughtful documentary. You will have watched the world according to Ben, a world of low camera angles, of upward slants, of obstacles provided by the things of everyday life — chairs, laboratory benches, public lavatories, buses, and, of course, people. Perhaps you asked yourself why. Why did Benedict Lambert ever walk the streets of London against the background of his own caustic commentary on the passing tide of humanity, their genetic quirks, their mutations, and their variations? What was his motive?

". . . all these people on the King's Road, staring at me in horror and pity, are no less victims of their genes than I. It is just that my condition is more apparent and is considered a defect . . ." pause for a woman with a dachshund to pass by ". . . except in the case of this breed of dog . . ."

Whyever did he discuss matters of race and gender, of beauty and ugliness, of behavior and comportment?

". . . instances of clearly inherited behavior are few. There is monoamine oxidase A deficiency, which leads to aggression and violence; there may be a form of male homosexuality, with its gene located on the long arm of the X chromosome; there are few others yet. But I'm afraid they will come . . ."

Whyever did he bare his barrel chest to the world?

". . . you learn to live with the physical problems. It is the emotional wounds that never heal . . ."

Why did he waddle, like a circus act, across the television screens of the nation? Why did he climb, like a clumsy chimp, up the rungs of a great helical DNA ladder constructed in the television laboratories out of plastic and metal, to perch on the key to his lifelong search, an adenine:thymine base pair? Why did he squat there like the great god Bes on his throne and observe the camera, the audience, the whole bloody world through a three-dimensional puzzle of plastic atoms to ask *why?* — why should a man be at the mercy of a molecular maze such as this? "A reasonable estimate is that on average every one of us carries about four harmful recessive mutations. Sometimes, if you are unlucky like me, you carry a dominant one . . ."

Why?

Of course the question is false. Scientifically, I mean. Philosophically as well, in all probability. We are what we are; there isn't anything else. But still you find yourself asking, don't you?

WHY?

[Suppression]

On New Year's Eve, 1866, Mendel sat down and wrote to Karl Wilhelm von Nägeli, enclosing a copy of the paper. Nägeli was Professor of Botany at the University of Munich. An appropriate man to turn to, you might think. In his own work Nägeli had mapped the cellular nature of plants and identified the zones of cell division in shoots and roots. In his writings he had already touched on the question of inheritance. He had been one of the first to make a distinction between inherited and acquired characteristics — between nature and nurture — and in the manner of scientists throughout the ages had attempted to clarify the vagueness of his ideas by coining terms.

Oh, the deception of naming, the seductiveness of language! Give an idea a name and it suddenly appears to take on a concrete existence, *beauty* becoming a yardstick against which we can measure our loathing or our admiration, *truth* becoming a testament enabling us to lie, *love* rearing its ugly snake's head and handing you the fruit of the tree of knowledge. Oh, the reification of abstracts! Think of *Kultur* and you want to reach for your gun. Think of *Lebensraum* and *Volk,* and the storm-troopers begin to march. Think of *Rassenhygiene* and the ovens begin to smoke. Nägeli's own particular coining was not exactly sonorous, but still very Germanic — *idioplasm:* the material of inheritance. He saw the idioplasm as being built up out of corpuscular hereditary factors, but until this moment had nothing in the way of empirical evidence to support the idea. Now this vague and fanciful concept was about to have substance given to it.

> *Highly Esteemed Sir,*
> *The acknowledged preeminence that your noble self enjoys in the detection and classification of wild-growing plant hybrids makes it my agreeable duty to submit for your kind consideration the description of some experiments in artificial fertilization.*

I suppose it was the manner of the day, but one does wish Mendel hadn't cringed quite so much. If I could have acted as secretary, things would have been rather more terse and to the point. Perhaps:

Dear Nägeli,
I enclose a copy of my recent paper on hybridization in Pisum *which I feel you ought to read. If you don't grasp its importance, for goodness' sake pass it on to someone who might . . .*

But that, I'm afraid, is wishful thinking. The answer from Nägeli came two months later. It reeks of condescension:

Honored colleague,
It seems to me that the experiments with Pisum, *far from being finished, are only beginning . . .*

Only beginning! Eight years, and somewhere around thirty-three thousand plants! Only beginning! I feel rage mounting like a substance in my throat. It is something that I need to hawk up and spit out, foul and pungent, into the eye of this bearded fraud. He might have gained eternal fame by recognition of the enthusiastic, naive friar from Brünn; he might have gained applause instead of opprobrium, immortality instead of the dusty death of a minor entry in the encyclopedia. But Professor Karl Wilhelm von Nägeli cannot see beyond his own nose. We are forced to witness Mendel bowing down before this second-rater:

> *In the projected experiments . . . I shall be entering a field in which your honor possesses the most extensive knowledge, knowledge that can only be gained through many years of zealous study . . .*

Extensive knowledge, indeed. Mendel had suggested that he might repeat the garden pea work with *Hieracium,* hawkweed. This ugly beast was Nägeli's favorite experimental plant, but it is an absurd plant for artificial crossing. It is a member of the Compositae family, along with the daisy and the dandelion, which means that it has flowers composed of minute individual florets no more than a millimeter in diameter. Artificial pollination has to be carried out using a lens. But there is worse, far worse than this. The plain fact is that the hawkweed genus usually sets seed and produces offspring without fertilization. It is, in the florid world of botanical language, *parthenogenetic.*

I particularly like that term. *Parthenos* is, of course, a maiden or virgin. Mary the mother of Jesus was one such, and according to dogma she produced her son by the process of parthenogenesis, which means, quite simply, virgin birth. Mendel would have believed this dogma, or if he had doubts he would have suppressed them, but let that point go. The term *parthenogenetic* applies to hawkweed no less than to the Virgin Mary: hawkweed makes babies without sex. Hawkweed is quite useless for genetics.

One wants to weep. One wants to be able to call across the gulf of one hundred and thirty years, across the Communist dictatorship and the Greater Germany of the Nazis, across the smoking ruins of two world wars; one wants to shout out a warning across the implacable barrier of time. But he is deaf to all entreaty, the stout, stubborn friar with the puzzled expression and eyesight growing ever weaker as he struggles with minute flowers with even more minute sexual parts, as he attempts the impossible, to make the damn hawkweed *breed*.

Yet there is this, toward the end of his eighth letter to Nägeli, written in July 1870:

Of the experiments of previous years, those dealing with Matthiola annua *and* glabra [stock], Zea [maize], *and* Mirabilis [four-o'clock] *were concluded last year. Their hybrids behave exactly like those of* Pisum. *Darwin's statements concerning hybrids of the genera mentioned in* The Variations of Animals and Plants under

Domestication . . . *need to be corrected in many respects.*

That passing mention is momentous. It is confirmation, if confirmation were ever needed, that Mendel repeated the *Pisum* work on other, unrelated species and got the very same results. It also drags Darwin into the equation. Mendel is shouting his findings to Nägeli, and still the idiot takes no notice. The correspondence dribbles on for a few years, but the work is beyond all recovery now. Mendel has lost his way. He is fiddling around with unsuitable material and ill-defined characteristics and corresponding sporadically with a botanist who hasn't understood his findings at all. He is at sea again, but wandering vaguely without map or compass and with no hope of finding land.

The last extant letter to Nägeli comes after a gap of a full three years:

Highly esteemed Sir and Friend,
Despite my best intentions I was unable to keep my promise given last spring. The Hieracia *have bloomed and faded here once again without my having been able to pay them more than a few fleeting visits. It is a real grief to me that I have to neglect*

*my plants and my bees so completely. Since
I have a little spare time at present, and
since I do not know whether I shall have
any next spring, I am sending you today
some material from my last experiments in
1870 and 1871 . . .*

It is rare that a man is genuinely ahead of
his time. Even the greatest discoveries in science are made in their appropriate time.
Crick and Watson proposed a structure for
DNA when Franklin and Wilkins were just
focusing in on the thing themselves (Crick
and Watson more or less filched the vital
information from the other two), and just
when the whole world of biology was waiting for it. Darwin was mulling over natural
selection, going round and round in circles
in fact, just at the time that Wallace was
thinking the same thoughts, just at the time
men like Huxley were ready to take up the
flag and turn the defense of natural selection into some kind of crusade. Few are
ahead of their time . . . but Gregor Mendel
was. He was so far ahead (and this is the
litmus test) that even when he spelled it
out and people read the argument (for example Nägeli, for example Focke) they still
couldn't grasp the importance. They could
see what he had done, they could understand

exactly what he had found (they would have to have been defective not to, so clear and concise is Mendel's writing), and yet they could not perceive the significance. When finally his time did come, three men (de Vries, Correns, von Tschermak) stumbled over the great paper all in the same year, all quite independently of one another, all having repeated, more or less, the experimental work. The world of scientific thought had finally caught up with the fat friar.

"My time will come," he was reputed to have said. It came sure enough, but by the time it came Father Gregor, Great-great-great-uncle Gregor, was dead.

Life after Jean? It was a fragile thing. I constructed new habits out of the fragments of a past that I had almost forgotten. I'm not looking for sympathy, just stating facts. That has been my training. I found solace in my work, of course.

At the Royal Institute for Genetics the defective FGFR3 *gene has already been cloned in* E. coli *bacteria; we have already persuaded the bacterium to express the protein in culture. There is now the theoretical possibility of finding a way to inactivate the mutant gene. In vitro experiments are proceeding using cultured skin fi-*

broblast cells from . . . the author.[1]

I nurtured my cultures and I counted the months and I thought of her. I peered down the microscope and watched my own cells floating like galaxies in the black void, gleaming bright in their amniotic world (choose your metaphor), absorbing amino acids from the medium and constructing from them the rogue protein that had betrayed me; and I thought of her. I found a different kind of solace in the arms of one of Eve's many sisters — Dawn, shall we say? — a creature equally as pneumatic as her crepuscular sibling, but blessed with two X chromosomes and a consequent flock of pubic hair. But I thought of Jean. Of course.

When it came, her phone call was unforeseen and unexpected. I had forgotten the peculiar softness of her voice, the weakness of her vowel sounds, the apparent passivity. They were qualities that had annoyed me once. "Ben? Is that you?"

"What do you want? I'm rather busy at the moment."

"Ben, can you come see us? Would you, Ben? Hugo would like that."

"And you wouldn't?"

1. See "Progress in the study of Achondroplasia," *Trends in Genetics* 11, May 1995.

"Ben, please. It might be a bit suspicious if you don't."

"It's part of an alibi, is it?"

"Don't be like that."

"What should I be like? What in God's name *should* I be like?" For a few moments I felt the obverse of love but I obeyed her summons, accepted her invitation, however you like to put it. I went. Of course I went. Revisiting the scene of the crime, if you like.

Hugo Miller's tone was of feigned surprise when he opened the door of number 34 Galton Avenue. His pale eyes stared in amazement. "Good Lord, it's Ben!" he cried, as though my arrival were entirely unexpected. "Good to see you. Come on in, come on in. You know the way, don't you?" Oh yes, I knew the way, but still he showed me. He exuded bonhomie, he exuded paternal pride, he exuded domestic smugness. "Good of you to come. Must be miles out of your usual way. Saw you on the telly the other day. Quite a thing, eh? Good of you to drop round."

Like a proud parent entering a nursery, he showed me through into the living room. And there was Jean, standing by the coal-effect electric fire — Jean in a pink denim maternity dress, Jean blushing like a child and smiling at me and holding her swollen abdomen as though otherwise it might hit the floor.

"Hello, Ben," she said. "It's been a long time."

I stood in awe before her. I stood silently before the metamorphosis that blind, molecular instinct had wrought. I marveled at the transformation. Two strings of DNA — hers and mine, united in mysterious conspiracy — had done this to her. Distorted and out of proportion, yet she was beautiful. That was the absurd thing. Beautiful. I wanted to tell her of her beauty. I wanted to make her understand. I wanted to go down on my knees in front of her. Does that sound mad? I wanted to cling to her knees and tell her of her beauty and beg her to return to me. I wanted to shout out to the red-haired, freckled fool who fussed around her that the child was mine, that I had slavered over her body, that I had belabored her with that one part of my own body that is not stunted, that it was I who had impregnated her with my own, potent seed. But instead I just stood there and smiled at her with my carefully designed smile; the smile I use on the whole world.

Did I want to feel the nipper move, Hugo wondered.

She eased herself down into a chair. "I'm sure Ben doesn't want . . ."

"How do you know what he wants? Go on, let him feel."

She shrugged and placed her hand on the mound in her lap. "Just there."

"Go on, have a feel," insisted her husband.

Reluctantly I advanced on her. She took my squat hand in her slender one and pressed it to her swollen abdomen, just above the knot of the umbilicus. I could smell the familiar scent of her. I glanced up, and our eyes met over the mound of her belly. Was there a momentary glimpse of complicity there, or were those mismatched eyes mere globes of jelly and gristle? If you focus on the outside of a body, on the outer integument, on the skin and hair, on the strange, glassy eyes in their sleek orbits and the curiously molluscan ears, if you concentrate on all that and realize that it is mere machinery, nothing more than a confection of sinew and cartilage and bone, driven by muscle and wired and controlled by an overambitious neural network, then you can begin to dismiss the person underneath. But that's the difficult bit, because the mask is so convincing.

"Have you got it?" Hugo demanded.

There was a lump. "There's a lump," I said.

"That's a knee, I expect. The little beggar's upside down, isn't it?"

And then the lump moved, a deep, glutinous stirring beneath the surface, like something swimming in treacle. Abruptly I straightened up and backed away.

Jean smiled. "He always moves around at this time of day —"

"*He,* dear?"

Jean reddened, fumbling for an escape. Sweat glistened on her forehead. "I *fancy* it's a he. It's my dream. I want to call him Adam. *If* he's a he."

Hugo was watching her solicitously, as though searching for symptoms of something or other. "Are you all right, dear? Hot flush, is it?"

"I'm quite all right, dear."

"Of course they can tell us the sex," he explained, "but we didn't want to know, did we? Of course we didn't. Well, you've got to let nature take its course, haven't you? Those people at the clinic were marvelous, but medicine's done enough to help us, and now it's over to Mother Nature, isn't it, darling?"

"I suppose so." She changed the subject, and the moment of anxiety was over. "How's the work going? I've been really starved of news. Is Miss Conway still at the Institute? And what about the dangerous Olga?"

But I really couldn't take much of Jean's brittle chatter or her husband explaining to me the latest advances in *in vitro* fertilization and intracytoplasmic sperm injection. I had a cup of tea and left them to their marital contentment as soon as I decently could. "You know what Jean and I would like?" Miller said as he showed me to the door. "We owe you quite a bit, really, putting us onto the fertility people, that Doctor Lupron and everything. You know what we'd like, Ben?"

Jean was hovering anxiously in the background. She must have known what was coming, must have been powerless to prevent it. "What would you like?"

"We'd like you to be the nipper's godfather," Miller said.

We've got a slot free on the third day, and I was thinking, Gravenstein mailed me. *How about giving a lecture on eugenics? Now that'd be something.*

I'm not a historian, I wrote back.

Eugenics now, she replied. *The new eugenics.* In vitro *fertilization, population screening, embryo selection, gene therapy, that kind of thing. You guys are right into that, aren't you? I've got someone here at Cornell who could do it all right, but you'd be something else, Ben.*

402

So, in addition to the keynote speech, THE NEW EUGENICS, a lecture by DOCTOR BENEDICT LAMBERT, appeared on the on-line program for the Mendel Symposium, accessible through the web site of Cornell[2] and the Masaryk University, Brno.[3] I spent time in the library, with Galton and Davenport and Pearson. I learned about the Society for Racial Hygiene, and eugenic sterilization programs in Germany and the United States. I read the words of Francis Crick and Hermann Muller, Nobel laureates the pair of them, and Eysenck and Herrnstein and Jensen, professors the three of them. *That's great, Ben,* Gravenstein assured me when I sent her my lecture outlines. *Now, when you get to Brno I'll be there to meet you at the airport and take you to the hotel. Morgan McClintock, our chairperson, will be there too. He's looking forward to meeting you . . .*

So to Moravia. So to the forgotten city of Brno. While my child grew in Jean's womb.

And life after the garden pea? Life after the disappearance of his paper into the oblivion of one hundred twenty academic libraries?

2. http://www.cornell.edu
3. http://www.fi.muni.cz/masaryk

Life after the disappearance into the void of the forty copies? Life after Nägeli?

They elected him abbot in 1868.

This shall not prevent me, he wrote to Nägeli, *from continuing the hybridization experiments of which I have become so fond; I even hope to be able to devote more time and attention to them once I have become familiar with my new position.*

It was, of course, an illusion. Although he gave up his teaching, as abbot, he found less and less time to devote to the experimental garden.

Despite my best intentions I was unable to keep my promise given last spring. The Hieracia *have withered again without my having been able to give them more than a few hurried visits . . .*[4]

That was it, really. The excitement and optimism of youth gave way to the dullness of middle age. His scientific interests degenerated into mere stamp collecting — beekeeping and meteorology — while his innate stubbornness found an outlet in a bitter

4. Final letter to Nägeli, 18 November 1873.

and pointless dispute with the fiscal authorities over tax demands on the convent. A stream of letters to the taxman issued from his pen. He argued, he debated, he looked for loopholes, he looked for escape clauses; he never gave ground.

He retreated within his carapace. *My time will come,* he said. He took his temperature readings and his rainfall readings, he grafted fruit trees and cultivated flowers, he smoked, he coughed and wheezed, he heard the pounding of his heart in his ears, he felt the gross oedemic swellings of his legs, and he never let anyone but his two nephews past the barricades of isolation. They were medical students, the sons of Theresia, being supported at the medical school in Vienna by their uncle. Thus was Theresia's generosity as a little girl paid back.

"They want to put me away," he told them.

You may imagine their condescending smiles at Uncle Gregor's suspicions. "Who, Uncle? Who wants to put you away?"

"The brothers. They want to get me declared insane and sent to a lunatic asylum. They want to pay their damned tax and get on with living their tiny little lives. You know that the bishop has set them to spy on me? You know that? They all want me to surrender. But I won't. Oh no. Look, let me show you this . . ." And another of the letters would be produced, the page closely inscribed in his careful copperplate hand, full of the twists and turns, the repetitions and reiterations of a mind obsessed.

But a spark still glowed among the ashes of genius. There is the *Notizblatt*, a fragment discovered in the library of the monastery long after Mendel's death. It is a page of jottings written in his careful copperplate hand on the back of the draft of a letter dealing with monastery business of 1875:

V_1	=37	~~$V1+gV1$~~	~~=112~~	~~White V=93~~	
g	=37	V_1W+gW	=300	UViolet 250–50	
gV_1	=75	W	=150	White 166+16	
V_1W	=150	gV_1	=75	lBlue 65–10	
gW	=150g		=37	dBlue 27–10	
W	=150V		=37	Viol 93+56	

It goes on down the page. He is still playing around with numbers and ratios, trying to fit experimental results with expected values, trying to nose out further applications of the laws he had discovered. There is the odd correction, the occasional scribble, but as you read it you can feel him thinking, as palpably as if he were sitting there before you at his wide desk in the prelate's quarters, with his glasses propped up on his high forehead and his face set with concentration. It is like watching the dying of a brain, the last firings of the last neurons, the last breath of life.

[Expression]

The simultaneity of events. A bright afternoon in *Mitteleuropa,* with the sun slanting
on the fields and forests of Moravia and glittering on the concrete and glass of Brno's
suburbs as a coach brings travelers back from
the north; a dull day of drizzle in the offshore
western island, with rain glistening on the
tarmac and running in shimmering rivulets
down the windows of the Hewison Fertility
Clinic. The two worlds coincide, come together contingently if not spatially, as the
phone rings in the reception of the hotel in
Brno at the exact moment that passengers
troop in from the car park outside.

A distant, almost apologetic voice: "Ben?
It's me."

What does one say? What does one say
that has not been said already so many times
that the words have lost their savor? Thus it
is merely, and bathetically, hello.

"The pains have begun. The doctor
warned me that it'll still be quite a long time
. . . Anyway, I just thought I'd let you know."

Then the receiver is returned to its cradle

and the worlds separate again like fragments flung apart by a silent and irremediable explosion: the coach passengers are queuing for the lift to take them up to their rooms (only one lift is working, and that can manage only three people at a time); and Jean is replacing the receiver, closing her eyes, breathing deeply and steadily as she has been taught.

Her husband was with her for some of the evening. "Get some sleep," she told him. "Nothing's going to happen for hours." He went home with a display of reluctance. She had a disturbed night, drifting in and out of sleep, jerked to wakefulness by spasms of pain, allowed to doze back to unconsciousness until the next assault. Occasionally a nurse looked in to see how things were going, smiling in that crisp and distracted manner nurses have.

"All ready for the battle, Ben?" Gravenstein asked as we sat down to breakfast next morning. She surveyed the food with dismay. "Christ, how do these Czechs keep *any* control over their weight?"

It was another day of sun in central Europe. The dining room was dissected by shafts of light. They cut across the groups at breakfast, spotlighted their shifting alliances and friendships, highlighted their promiscuity of mind and body. "You see that guy from Stanford, and the woman from Manchester?" Gravenstein said confidentially. "Well, they came down in the elevator at *exactly the same time.* How about that? That is the *third day* running that it's happened. And I know for a *fact* that she has a husband and two children back home." The woman was blushing at something the Stanford man had said, blushing and looking round as though to spot eavesdroppers. Gravenstein caught her eye and smiled conspiratorially across the room at her.

After breakfast I made a call to London. An anonymous voice told me that she was sure all was going well, but no, I couldn't speak with Mrs. Miller. Mrs. Miller was in labor.

It was drizzling and gray when Hugo arrived at the clinic that morning. An anemic half-light flooded the city with vague and unsubstantiated promises of better things to come. Jean lay there in the labor room looking old and drawn, her face slick with sweat. She lay in a plain white gown, with a fetal cardiac monitor attached to her swollen belly. A nurse turned a knob on the machine so that Hugo could hear the strange rippling sound of the baby's heart, like horses galloping toward the scene of some unknown battle far in the electronic distance.

"There it is," said the nurse proudly, as though the child had something to do with her. "What a tough little thing."

"You look exhausted," Hugo said to his wife, and Jean smiled at him and achieved that trick women have, to comfort the expectant father when it is the mother herself who should be comforted. "I'll be all right," she told him, as though she had a say in the matter. "A bit tired, but I'll be all right."

Coincidence. The simultaneity of events. Jean lies on a bed in the Hewison Fertility Clinic while I mount the podium of a lecture theater at the Masaryk University of Brno, watched by the worthies of the university, by the officials of the Mendelian Association of America, by representatives of Hewison Pharmaceuticals, by members of the Mendel Symposium. Jean brings comfort, while I trade in discomfort:

"One hundred thirty years ago, in a school building not far from here, a quiet, introverted, stubborn friar gave a lecture on the breeding of peas. With that lecture he lit a fuse, a fuse that burned unnoticed for thirty-

411

five years until the very opening of this century, when the bomb exploded. The explosion is going on still. It engulfed me from the moment of my conception . . ."

There is a spasm of pain and guilt on the faces in the audience.

"Perhaps it will engulf us all eventually."

Silence. The heartbeats gallop onward, careering toward delivery.

"You may plot the course of this explosion as a cosmologist might plot the evolution of a supernova: it began with prejudice and it blossomed with legislation." There is a slide flung up on the screen, a list of salient events and dates. "It began in the early years of the century with the foundation of such organizations as the Society for Racial Hygiene in Germany and the Eugenics Education Society in Britain. It reached an important marker in 1933 with the Eugenic Sterilization Law in Germany, and high tide in 1939, by which time almost four hundred thousand German men and women had undergone eugenic sterilization."

The pain mounts, swelling inside her, racking that slender, white body as though determined to assert its mastery. She breathes in small gusts of trichloroethylene and the pain recedes. A nurse times the intervals between spasms as an interrogator might time the length of torture, turning subjective experience into a measured science, waiting for the confession, waiting for the moment when the body yields up only what is expected — the truth. "There's a good girl," she says comfortingly. "Won't be long now, dear."

Dilation of the cervix is complete by 9:15 A.M. The coincidence is exact. I deliver my lecture; Jean delivers my child. Times are corrected for difference in time zone. I have thought of everything — at precisely 10:15 European Time I glance at my watch and move from the past to the present:

"The old eugenics died with the Third Reich, but make no mistake, the new eugenics is with us. It isn't in the future, it is here and now. There are modern eugenicists here in this lecture theater at this very moment." People shift uncomfortably in their chairs and glance around surreptitiously to see if they can spot one another. Is there some kind of password, a subtle sign of recognition? The chairman looks anxious. "Each year in the United States alone some thirty thousand babies are conceived by anonymous sperm donation. At the very least the donated sperm is certified to come from genetically healthy donors. At the worst it comes from William Shockley."

And the nervous silence fractures into laughter. They laugh with relief, their mouths open like fish gasping for water; while I, poor dwarf, stand before them and wonder about my child. "Or if not from a Nobel Prize winner for physics, perhaps from the father of them all, Hermann Muller, the man who first conceived — if you will forgive the expression — of a sperm bank." More laughter. Good old Ben.

"We all know Muller, don't we? He's one of ours: a geneticist, the man who demonstrated the link between ionizing radiation and mutation, the man who worked on the mutational effects of the Hiroshima bomb. Nobel Prize in 1946. Hermann Muller gave his sperm to the Repository for Germinal Choice on the condition that it must not be used for twenty-five years after his death. That brings it to maturity just about now."

They laugh at my circus act, but what I tell them is only the truth.

"In the first edition of his book on eugenics, Muller, like the good old-fashioned socialist he was, favored the breeding of children who embodied the characteristics of Lenin and Marx. Things had changed by the second edition. By the second edition, Muller was back in the States after his sojourn in Russia. By the second edition, Lenin had been dropped in favor of Descartes; and Marx had lost out . . . to Lincoln."

They are rolling in the aisles. Ben Lambert is a regular guy, they think. Tears are running down the chairman's face.

"But it isn't a joke." They don't want to believe me. There is nothing funnier than Nobel Prize winners making idiots of themselves. It is the most marvelous joke, surely. "Today respectable medical clinics are offering sperm sorting to enable parents to choose the sex of their children."

The laughter stumbles, like a dwarf on a doorstep. Surely Ben the clown, Ben the circus act, Ben the regular guy who is so brave and so goddamn *funny*, is not going to fall down on this one . . .

"The clinics call this service 'family balancing.' A recent opinion poll in the States suggested that, if given the choice, sixty-seven percent of couples would choose to have a male child. One wonders where the balance is in that." The remaining laughter is a paltry, anxious thing. The clown has fallen, and it isn't for laughs. He's not waving his arms around like a fool while the hanging gardens roar and sway with mirth. This is no pratfall.

"Then there is the other matter, the question of genetic disorder. Forget gene therapy.

Gene therapy is way in the future. I talk of today. Today the same clinics offer screening for genetic disease and genetic diagnosis of pre-implantation embryos. Who can blame them? The demand is there, isn't it? Which of you would want a child with anencephaly, or Tay-Sachs disease, or" — the art of the well-tempered pause, timed to the nearest nanosecond — "achondroplasia?"

Silence. I can play them as one would play a fish, a foolish flapping trout, gasping and thrashing and not knowing which way to turn.

"Now you can choose your embryos and implant only the healthy ones and thus avoid the unpleasantness and waste of having to abort fetuses that you don't want. Thus you improve the genetic stock without even mentioning the idea . . ."

In the delivery room, Jean lies with her legs up in some kind of harness. Her vulva gapes, a maw of coral red, rimmed with matted hair — a dwarf's cave from which a dwarf is struggling to emerge. Oxytocin, a nine-amino-acid polypeptide coded for by a gene on chromosome 20, lashes at the muscles of her uterus. The acolytes of obstetrics crowd around. Gowned and masked, Hugo Miller hides in the background and barely watches.

Jean breathes deeply and the nurse beside her whispers encouragement and a brown and wrinkled thing presses at the entrance of the cave . . .

"That is today. Today you can already screen for a thousand or so disorders. But what of the future?" What indeed? Of course they already know about the future, most of them. The future is there in the test tubes back in the lab, in the gels and the genomic libraries. The future is a strange beast in the final throes of birth. "In the future — the near future — you will be able to choose other qualities in the embryo: the child's eye color, hair color, skin color, and height. Height is one of the most significant, because of all our prejudices it is the most ingrained and the most insidious. We *love* height." I stand there before them, deformed and diminished. They writhe in their seats, as though I have them skewered.

"Hitler," I tell them in case they hadn't already guessed, "Hitler would have loved it . . ."

"There we go." The head emerges, flips over the threshold of the cave, discovers features — a brow, eyes clenched tight, a nose. Fluid flows from the old, wrinkled mouth.

The face turns toward its right, almost conversationally, as though it has been called to look at something, the mole on the inside of her right thigh, perhaps. A thin cry escapes into the oppressive air of the delivery room. "Luverly," a voice says. Hugo Miller faints.

"At least the old eugenics was governed by some kind of theory, however dreadful it may have been. The new eugenics, *our* eugenics, is governed only by the laws of the marketplace. You get what you can pay for."

In the lecture theater there is only silence — the silence of complicity.

"Are we really such intellectual dwarfs" — ah, they shiver at that one — "as to imagine that the laws of supply and demand can be elevated to the level of a philosophy? Because that is what we have done. We have within our grasp the future of mankind, and as things are going the future will be chosen according to the same criteria as people now choose silicone breast implants and liposuction and hair transplants. It will be eugenics by consumer choice, the eugenics of the marketplace. All masquerading as freedom."

The baby shoulders its way out, the obstetrician's cupped hands supporting it, feeling around its neck for the umbilical cord.

"There we are, dear. Bear down, bear down. There we are . . ." There is a momentary air of relief in the delivery room, a fleeting sensation of triumph. Then a sudden disturbance — "Oxygen," a voice calls. "Oxygen!"

These things happen simultaneously: the baby is lifted up with its umbilical cord hanging from it like a gray gut; an oxygen mask is clamped onto Jean's face; Hugo Miller is hurried out of the room. The baby is a boy, but no one remarks on the fact.

I flew back that afternoon. "It was wonderful to have you share your ideas with us," Gravenstein said as she left me at the airport. "A real privilege."

The plane was half-empty, the cabin staff uninterested in the passengers, more concerned with some kind of dispute that was going on among them, an argument over shifts and hours. They slung shrink-wrapped trays of food down as one might toss feed in front of penned animals. Through the windows, in the raging, sterile world on the surface of the wing, the sun dazzled like an explosion, like the great flash that had swept across the Nullarbor Plain almost forty years before. We crossed the new greater Germany and the Low Countries, and began the slide down from a bright universe of light, down through layers of cloud into a twilit world where car headlights glimmered in the rain and streams of tourists returning from Ibiza shivered as they waited for their luggage.

I phoned from the airport. "I'm sorry, sir," a sterile voice told me. "We cannot divulge information about patients over the phone."

"But I'm a close friend, for God's sake!"

"I'm very sorry, sir."

The telephone at 34 Galton Avenue went unanswered. I retreated to my cave and lay there, wounded. Not until next morning did my telephone ring: it was Hugo Miller on the other end.

Overweight, oedemic, short of breath, Mendel knew his fate. He had discussed it with his nephews, medical students the pair of them. He had heard his heart pounding in his ears as he lay in bed. He had struggled for breath while lying down, and felt the breathlessness drain away as he sat up. The diagnosis was not difficult even in those days: his heart was failing and the fluid was backing up in his tissues, swelling in his legs and blocking the efforts of his kidneys and his lungs.

He had a woman from the town and a nun to look after him. They bandaged his legs and feet and helped him from bed to sofa.

They changed his dressings and they brought his food and they dealt with his bedpan when he couldn't shuffle to the bathroom. He rarely complained. He faced his last illness with a stubborn stoicism, the same stubbornness that had driven him to plant his damned peas and count them, thousands of them, year after year; the same stubbornness that had caused him to battle with the taxman to the bitter end; the same stoicism that had caused him to utter the words *Meine Zeit wird schon kommen* — my time will come — when the whole world ignored his work.

On December 20, 1883, he wrote this to Josef Liznar, one of his former pupils, now professor of meteorology at Prague:

You are now entering upon the years of most active work, whereas I must be said to be in the opposite condition. Today I have found it necessary to ask to be completely excused further meteorological observations, for since last May I have been suffering from heart trouble, which is now so severe that I can no longer take the readings of the meteorological instruments without assistance.

Since we are not likely to meet again in this world, let me take this opportunity of wishing you farewell, and of invoking upon

your head all the blessings of the meteoro-
logical deities.
    Best wishes to yourself and your wife,
        Gregor Mendel

You see? There at the end, that wry joke — no invocation of the God of the Christians; just the meteorological deities.

He died seventeen days later.

[Hybrid]

Miller met me outside the Hewison Clinic. A grayness had come into his face. It had chased away the bright red anger that used to lie just below the surface, and left him devoid of any kind of energy. He fingered things distractedly — the lapels of his jacket, the newspaper beneath his arm, the bouquet of flowers that he held awkwardly against his chest — as though he had been struck blind and was searching for some vital message of explanation. "Good of you to come, Ben," he muttered as I approached. "Good of you to come."

He merely shrugged when I asked about her. "They don't seem to know anything, that's the problem. An embolism, they say. Amniotic fluid or something. They say they've done tests, they say all sorts of things. But beneath it all, they just don't know."

Together we went through the automatic doors into the foyer of the clinic. Subdued lighting and air-conditioning gave a constant atmosphere to the place irrespective of whether it was day or night, cloudy or fine, sweltering August or dank February outside. A fountain was playing quietly in one corner. An original Klee from the private collection of John Hewison hung on the wall, adding strange, embryonic shapes to the amniotic quality of the place. From inside her glass tank the receptionist nodded recognition when Miller approached. "Of course," she said when he gave his name. "Of course." She told us the room number and bestowed on us a smile of encouragement.

A notice board advertised:

GENETIC SCREENING
MOLECULAR BIOLOGY
ENDOCRINOLOGY   OBSTETRICS
MATERNITY

Miller rearranged the bouquet of flowers in his arms like an inexperienced father holding a baby for the first time and looked down. "Okay, Ben?" I nodded. There was an absurd camaraderie between us, an artificial thing constructed of embarrassment and dread, and a shared incomprehension. Together we set off in the direction of *Maternity*.

What was I expecting? You're wondering, aren't you? What was on Doctor Benedict Lambert's mind as he walked through the corridors of the Hewison Clinic beside the cytologically cuckolded Hugo Miller? No one thing, of course. No single, succinct idea occupied the Lambert brain. The remarkable thing about the human mind is that it can hold so much at once, such simultaneous complexities of thought, such bewildering coils of sensation. So: triumph, curiosity, horror, anticipation, plain fear, I felt all those at least. Perhaps a few more. A multiple hybrid of emotion, a monster spawned by the malign hand of chance.

MATERNITY

There was a plain corridor, hushed and humming. Each door bore a mother's name. One or two boasted a florid ribbon of blue or pink. There was a thin wail of infant on the comatose air.

MRS. JEAN MILLER was down at the far end, behind a notice that warned NO VISITORS PLEASE.

A doctor, as crisp and white as cauliflower, came out as we were about to knock. Her expression was brisk and optimistic as she greeted Hugo. She barely registered surprise at the sight of me at his side. She would have delivered monsters, easing them out of the distended vulva with practiced hands, glancing knowingly at the obstetrician as she did so: dwarfs, spina bifida, anencephalics, mongols, clubfeet, harelips, conjoined twins, the whole gamut of mutation and mistake. She was hardened in matters of teratology.

"This is the baby's godfather," Hugo explained. "Ben Lambert." The doctor seemed to find that quite reasonable, the kind of surrogate status you might expect from one such as me. "She's quite comfortable," she said, holding the door open for us to enter.

How, I wondered, how could the doctor *tell?* Jean lay motionless on a bed in the center of the room, like a corpse on a catafalque. Gleaming machinery obtruded pipes and wires into her inert, mouse-gray form. Beyond her was a window that looked out onto the neo-Gothic buttresses of the Royal Institute for Genetics. At the foot of her bed was a cot from which came the faint, penetrating noise of neonatal presence.

The doctor gave a bright, hopeless smile. "She has the *will* to get better, that's the thing." But it was plain that will didn't come into it. Jean was not willing anything. She was lying still beneath a sheet, with wires coming from her head and her chest, with a tube draining from her nose, with an intravenous drip inserted into her arm, with all the intrusive apparatus of modern medicine keeping her just this side of the divide. Oscilloscopes traced the flashing lines of heart-beat and brainwave.

"Where shall I put the flowers?" Miller asked. There were vases of gladioli and chrysanthemums ranged around the catafalque. A nurse moved among the blooms like an acolyte performing some obscure religious rite. One expected candles burning.

"Give them to me," the nurse said. "Aren't they lovely? I'll get another vase." Were they lovely? They were hybrids, polyploids, monsters in their own right — waxy, florid, and deformed.

I went to the bedside. From where I stood, Jean's profile appeared etched against the window — the gentle dome of her forehead, the crest of her brow breaking into the second, suave wave of her nose that itself was poised delicately to break across the purse of her lips. Oh, I had watched that profile, seen it laugh, seen it sip, eat, speak, cry, and, in the forgiving shadows, kiss. Oh, I had seen it all! "Jean?" I called softly. "Jean?" But Jean didn't answer. It wasn't clear whether she was even there any longer.

"And the baby?" Miller was stooping over the cot, peering down at whatever lay there.

"Oh, he's lovely," the nurse said. "He's truly wonderful, Mr. Miller."

I leaned toward Jean — was it Jean? It

seemed to be Jean in the way that a sculpture seems the person it portrays, seems even to breathe as you watch it, seems on the verge of speech — and I touched my lips against one smooth, gray cheek. Was it Jean? There was the soft presence of down, the faint pubescence that I knew so well. Would a kiss from the frog prince bring the sleeping beauty back to life? But Jean stayed still, her chest rising and falling gently beneath the sheets, her breath wafting in and out through her nostrils like the faint breath of a mouse.

I turned away from the bed. A tenuous wailing came from the cot at the foot of the bed, and the nurse moved Miller aside. "It's time for little Adam's feed, isn't it?" She reached down and lifted the baby out, our baby, and held it up for the proud father to see. I saw a knotted, flushed face, a crest of dark hair, tiny molluscan ears, vague eyes, miniature limbs clawing at the air. What Miller saw I have no idea.

"Isn't he a fine little one?" the nurse asked. "Does he look like his mummy or his daddy?"

The baby turned its head, looking, or seeming to look, around the room. Probably it was searching for its source of food. "There," the nurse exclaimed, "Adam's looking at you, Mr. Miller."

"They can't focus when they're newborn," he retorted. "He can't see a thing."

"But he *looks* as though he's looking."

"May I hold him?" I asked.

I saw the nurse glance at Hugo for approval. "Doctor Lambert's the godfather," he said, as though the status of godfather conferred some kind of right by proxy. Smiling, the nurse bent down toward me, and for a moment the scrap of flesh writhed in my arms. I felt what? I must confess that I felt something remarkable. But what, exactly? Well, I felt like my father. Is that absurd? Perhaps. Bathetic, certainly. Sergeant Eric Lambert, Royal Engineers; Mr. Lambert, ineffectual teacher of physics; Eric, inadequate father and passer-on of genes, the man who had never looked me straight in the eye. I felt like him. There was nothing cerebral or contrived about the feeling; it was vivid, even visceral — genetic perhaps, if there is something mystical in the machinations of the genome. I felt like my father. More than that, more than mere illusion, pathetic fallacy, whatever you wish to call it, for a moment I *was* my father. I was the man I had always longed to be. I was tall.

"Little mouse," I told my son; and he did look like a mouse pup, one of those pink and naked things that we rear in the laboratory.

I left shortly after that. There wasn't much to stay for, really. Doctors appeared, with the exclusive air of the priesthood about them. They showed a faint impatience with Hugo's presence and no desire to have me around. One of them, the consultant, began to tell the others about the case, pontificating like a barrister before a docile jury.

"She'll wake up," a nurse assured me as I went out. "I know she will. It's just a matter of time. We keep talking to her, keep giving her baby Adam to cuddle, and she'll wake up. The human brain is a wonderful thing."

Don't worry. I'm not going to lose my grip on things. Benedict Lambert is not going to embarrass you. He is going to remain calm and remote from the muddy universe of the emotions. He is going to describe the facts, the remote horrors of modern medicine, the infusions of radioactive tracers, the brain scans, the electroencephalograms, the intravenous drips, the tubes and the needles; and he is going to remain remote from it all. The doctors talked of amniotic fluid embolism, of lesions in Jean's brain, damage in the hippocampus, the pasture where the mind grazes among scents and smells; and meanwhile Jean lay inert and unresponsive, a mere construct of metabolizing cells, her DNA being transcribed into RNA, the RNA being translated into protein, the proteins working in their intricate and ineffable manner, and nothing happening. Nothing that was Jean.

Hugo came to see me at my flat a few days later. He didn't warn me of his visit. There was just a shadow coming down the steps outside the front window and a ring on the bell, and there he was when I opened the front door, a grim, stolid figure like an undertaker's mute looming over the open grave. My heart lurched — no dwarf organ, but a full-sized thing pulsing just below my sternum, making my chest throb with the effort. "She's all right, isn't she?" I cried.

"Jean?"

"Of course."

He nodded, as though agreeing to the obvious. "Well, she's just the same. They call it stable, but that doesn't really mean anything, does it? The dead are stable, aren't they? The fact is, they don't know what they're doing. Look, can I come in for a moment? I was just passing by and I thought . . ."

I stood aside for him. Of course he couldn't have just been "passing by." You couldn't have just passed by my flat on the way to anywhere. He had come with intention and deliberation. I settled him down, made him a cup of coffee, that kind of thing. "You're a friend, Ben," he said, as though seeking assurance of the fact. "I need your help."

"So tell me."

"They're talking about it being permanent. The damage to her brain, I mean. Even if she does wake up, she's not going to be the same . . ." He perched on the edge of a chair, like a man sitting on the edge of a cliff and trying to summon up the courage to jump.

"You've got to keep hoping . . ." I said, but the sentence trailed away lamely. Have you got to keep hoping? It has always seemed a dubious proposition to me. Anyway, Hugo Miller ignored my exhortation.

"That's not what I came to see you about," he said. He glanced around almost furtively, as though there might be a dozen listeners hiding in the corners of my sitting room. Then he leaned forward confidingly. "I don't know how to put this, Ben. Perhaps I shouldn't be talking about it at all, seeing the state Jean is in, but I've thought about it a lot recently . . ."

"Thought about what?"

"The baby."

"What about the baby? The baby is fine. It's Jean who's not well."

"That's not the point . . ." He picked at his fingernails and bit his lip and glanced around again. Then, finding no eavesdroppers, he breathed in sharply, looked directly at me, and said, "You see, the baby's not mine."

I laughed. Oh, a merry little laugh. "Not yours? How can that be?"

He seemed emboldened by confession. "I've done my homework, Ben. I know about all this Mendel stuff. And I know that I've got blue eyes and Jean's got blue eyes — well, one of them's green, but you explained about that, didn't you? — and the baby's got brown eyes. That's just not possible. Is it?"

"Oh, but —"

"It's unusual for a baby that young to have brown eyes, isn't it? But it has. And they can't have come from me."

"These things are never certain . . ."

He looked straight into my brown eyes, and his own blue ones were perplexed, as though they were looking at something obvious but difficult to see — like one of those optical illusions where, once you know the trick, you can resolve a drawing of an old man's face into a picture of a mother and child. "She's been unfaithful to me in the past, I know she has. She confessed it. And now I think she got together with that doctor and used someone else's sperm. And they didn't tell me. That mine was no good, I mean, not even for that *in vitro* business. That's where you come in."

I looked around for a means of escape. "Me?"

"You can tell me. It's my right to know, for God's sake! You can clear the whole thing up. All I want is one of those DNA tests done — fingerprints or whatever it is you fellows call them . . ."

"A DNA test?"

"On the baby and on me. Ben, you must help me. I want you to find out if the baby really is mine . . ."

"And if it's not?"

"I don't want it. If it's not mine, then I don't want it."

There is a story. It comes from Holland. It has something of the status of an urban myth, yet all the elegant simplicity of truth. A Dutch woman undergoing *in vitro* fertilization treatment joyously became pregnant. It duly transpired that she was carrying twins, and of course both Mummy and Daddy were delighted. The wonders of science and all that. Together they watched the little creatures on the ultrasound screen, heard the twin hearts, thrilled to the twin movements. And when the babies were duly born (one hopes — oh, how one hopes! — that the father was present at the happy event), one of the emergent babies was white-skinned and blond-haired and blue-eyed, just like Mummy and Daddy . . . while the other was black. It transpired that during the *in vitro* fertilization process, there had been contamination with sperm from a previous hopeful father . . .

Science as practical joke. Maybe that's all we're worth. Slapstick comedy. The conjuring trick gone hilariously wrong, the conjurer triumphantly pulling from the hat not a docile white pigeon but a black and raucous crow.

I looked at Hugo Miller sitting there in front of me, replete with bigotry. "You don't need any tests," I told him. "You don't need any tests because I can tell you the answer here and now. The child is nothing to do with you, Hugo. Nothing whatsoever." I savored the moment, relished the expression on his face, the stupid O of surprise. "*I* am the father. Ridiculous Ben Lambert is the father. Adam is ours — Jean's and mine. Nothing to do with you at all. Do you understand that? He is nothing to do with you.

I was her lover and you were too damned prejudiced to realize it."

There was a long pause. Outside sounds came down to us — an ambulance siren wailing in despair, a motorbike blaring past, footsteps clip-clopping along the pavement. Someone shouted at someone else: "Fuck *off*, will yer?"

"I see," said Hugo, quite softly. He rose from my chair. There was even an ironic smile somewhere up there among the freckles and the taut nerves. "I see." He stood on his solemn dignity in front of me and (a strange, old-fashioned gesture) half-bowed to me as though to the dwarf king on his throne. "I suppose it's only what I guessed," he said. "Deep down."

There is an absurdity about the cuckold, isn't there? Always was, always will be. Cuckold Syndrome. The ten percent of all happy and oblivious and, above all, faithful husbands who are not, in fact, the fathers of their sons and daughters. Something both absurd and touching. There is even a trite little evolutionary argument to explain their existence, that women choose them as husbands for reliability and protection, while seeking out some strapping, youthful genes to unite with their own and thus make genetically fit babies: the mother bird inviting the cuckoo to come into her warm little nest.

Hugo nodded, as though confirming his suspicions, then turned, stiffly and solemnly, and walked to the door. I watched him go out and climb up the steps from my cave, up to the street of normal height. I confess to a feeling of mild elation. Not triumph, nothing excessive — but the plain feeling that I had won. Benedict had achieved his child and passed his precious genes on to the next generation. Adam the man was in some new sense mine; and Jean, comatose or not, would become mine too. I would contact my sister to come and help me out (a nice, practical part of the fantasy, that). And I would visit Jean in hospital and talk at her, watch her; even, necrophilically, when the nurse's gaze was elsewhere, slip my hand beneath the sheets to touch her. Oh yes, in my elation I imagined that.

[Deletion]

A January day in middle Europe. The sky possesses that hard, enamel quality that it has when drained of moisture. Trees stand outlined against the blue like carefully dissected lungs: tracheae, bronchi, bronchioles branching into a myriad of sharply etched tips. No leaf. There is snow on the roof of the Gothic church, snow piled against the walls and against the buttresses, hard, compacted snow that has lain for weeks. The cold is profound.

In the church, before the great silver altar, beneath the geometric decorations across the vault, the choir sings *Requiem aeternam dona eis, Domine.* The setting is by Křižkovský and the choir is conducted by a small, bouncy little fellow who was once at the choir school. He wears an embryo mustache across his upper lip. In his black frock coat he has something of the air of a circus ringmaster. He is Leoš Janáček.

Et lux perpetua luceat eis . . . The choir tails away into chill silence and the coffin is gathered up from the catafalque and shuffled toward the door. A crowd waits in the square outside. The people are solemn and morose, hunched in black. Clouds of breath rise from their mouths as the coffin is carried from the church and loaded into the hearse. A miter rests on top of the coffin, with an episcopal crook laid diagonally across.

The silence is broken by the snorting of the horses, by the creaking of their harness and the iron drumming of wheels on the cobbles as, at a solemn pace, the cortège makes its way into the Klosterplatz. Black plumes nod and shake in the cold air. A bell tolls from the church tower. Columns of steam rise from the horses' nostrils. The stalls in the Klosterplatz are all closed. The booth with the bearded lady, the tent with the freak show, the shooting range, the stalls where they sell tawdry trinkets, and the beer shop where the old men drink — all are closed. The people of the town line the streets in silence as the procession passes along the Büger-Gasse toward the river.

Tears? Not many. The bishop himself has celebrated the requiem mass, but his homily was about duty and devotion to one's vocation, not about love. The Lord Lieutenant of Moravia is there, but his thoughts hang on whether the tax disputes of the last decade will now be laid to rest with the deceased, and whether the new abbot will be a more amenable man than his predecessor. The dead man's nephews offer masks of resignation to the world — they are medical students and must demonstrate control in the face of death. The Protestant pastor and the Jewish rabbi show ritual solemnity; the professors and teachers and members of the various learned societies of the city display the blank expressions of duty and incomprehension; the businessmen and shopkeepers are mainly curious. There are also pupils and former pupils and the common people, Czech and German alike. Some have memories of him as a younger man: it is that image they mourn. And an old lady, the widow of Herr Rotwang of Vienna, follows the hearse in a black carriage. She has memories, sunlit, curious memories of peas and fuchsias, of beans and hawkweed, of conversations never understood and emotion never expressed.

The wheels of the carriage drum on the bridge like the rattling of a salute. The procession passes out of the city and enters the cemetery through the north gate. It halts for the pallbearers to hump the coffin onto their shoulders. They shuffle it down the gravel path to where an open grave lies ready. The mourners edge nervously around the pit while the Prior of the Augustinian Monastery sprinkles the coffin with water.

"Anima ejus, et animae omnium fidelium de-functorum, per misericordiam Dei requiescat in pace."

The bearers struggle with ropes, and the coffin edges its way into the ground.

After the ceremony the mourners disperse hurriedly, almost guiltily, almost as though getting away from the scene of some disgrace. No one, no single person in the whole crowd, understands the importance of the man who has just been buried.

The next day, with the help of one of the brothers, the prior goes through the dead man's possessions. They find little of interest beyond the bound books. The books will go into the monastery library. The other stuff, papers mainly, all covered in that immaculate copperplate hand, appear worthless. They glance through some of the sheets, scan without understanding the pages and pages of charts and diagrams and symbols. Numbers — hundreds, thousands — beetle across the pages. Letters point arrows at other letters. Lists and columns and sums run from top to bottom like the accounts of a shop or a business, swarming like insects from one page to the next. The prior shakes his head at the absurdity of it all, at the amount of energy that the man expended at

. . . what? Mere vanity?

The sad thing about death is the absurdity and the self-delusion it reveals.

Later that morning the man's servant takes all the rubbish out into the garden behind the monastery and piles it onto a bonfire. The paper is dry. It catches quickly. The flame is ghostly in the bright air. The smoke is a more substantial thing, billowing up toward the sky, drifting up over the fruit trees that he tended, up over his beehives, over the bushes, over the roofs of the church toward the Spielberg Hill.

[Chain Termination]

The Hewison Fertility Clinic's proud portals gleam with plate glass and travertine, like the face of an airport terminal building delivering passengers into the twenty-first century. Hugo Miller goes up the steps and the doors whisper open to admit him to the future. Watch him; many people did. The receptionist — Asian, as sleek as caramel and toffee — even smiled a warm and sympathetic welcome. Watch him: dusty red hair (RHC gene on chromosome 4), blue eyes (chromosome 19), lobeless ears, mean stature, dull mind, bad temper. What else? Anything from the Benedict Lambert catalog of the absurd and the bizarre? Jumping Frenchman of Maine Syndrome, perhaps? Benign Sexual Headache? Photic Sneeze Reflex? Piebald Trait? Whistling Face Syndrome. Misshapen Toe. Thick Lips and Oral Mucosa. Stub Thumb. Smiling Dimples. Shawl Scrotum. Rocker-bottom Foot. Round-headed Spermatozoa. Inverted Nipples. Any of those? Watch him progress through the halls of the clinic: a melange of traits and tendencies, of transcription and translation, of modifiers and moderators, of neurons and synapses; all adding up to what? What will he do? What stirs that mind?

> *Tell me, where is fancy bred.*
> *Or in the heart or in the head?*

Oh, indeed, tell me. If you know the answer. Curious that the most profound of the Bard's questions should be embroidered into silly little song. But where does fancy lie? Is it nurture or nature? Solemnly, with determination and intent, Hugo Miller walks past fountain and potted palm, past Paul Klee, through the aqueous, amniotic world toward the domain of

MATERNITY

And meanwhile, what do I do? I wait. Benedict the brave waits trembling with excitement amid the soft and sensuous beds of molecular biology, amid the machines that whisper truths about the human condition for which the Bard could only write ditties. Benedict waits for he knows not what, and while he is waiting he picks delicately through the human genome like God picking through the mind of a soul in purgatory.

"Terrible about your library lady, isn't it?" Olga says as, with her arms embracing a Perspex shield, she prepares a radioactive probe. "Have you been to see her, Ben?"

My reply is vague; but my thoughts are focused. In my thoughts I am, as always, the protagonist: Hugo Miller will deny his interest in the child and I will step in to stop the adoption order, claiming right of custody. A DNA analysis will establish my paternity. Adam will be mine; and in a sense, even lying comatose in her hospital bed, even kept alive by intravenous drip, Jean will be mine. I will have won.

Something like that.

A hushed and somnolent corridor. MRS. JEAN MILLER. NO VISITORS PLEASE.

Jean lies softly on her bed, dreaming of the future. The baby sleeps, with nothing to dream of. At the opening of the door a nurse looks around from a trolley of bottles and sees Hugo Miller standing in the doorway brandishing a tape recorder. "I thought perhaps some of her favorite music . . . Doctor Lupron suggested . . ."

The nurse smiles compliance. "Why not?"

"It's one of those Eastern European composers. She often used to listen to it." He sets the machine down on the table near

Jean's head, and plugs it in. Quite soon a disembodied piano begins to play, a painful, nostalgic sound filtering into the still air of the room; the nurse pauses from her work to listen for a moment. "That's lovely," she says. "I don't go much for the classics myself, but I do like a good tune." Then she goes back to her work with the brisk and practiced manner of an undertaker laying out a corpse, fiddling with machinery, changing the bottle on the drip, twitching at the sheet that lies over Jean's body, glancing at the sleeping baby. Then she pauses with her hand on the door handle. "Lovely music, isn't it? Sad, though. Who did you say it was?" But she doesn't listen to the answer. "I won't be gone long," she says. "There's the bell if you need anything."

Oh no, he doesn't need anything. When she has gone he crosses the room and turns the latch on the door. Later they will ask about that latch. Why should there be such a thing on a hospital door? they will ask. And that will lead on to other queries. Was it all premeditated? Was it all planned? They will argue about it for days. Had the idea lain there in the back of his mind like a fish sliding beneath the still waters, a shark within the submarine tanks of the clinic? Had he thought it all out? What motive will they decide on? What will be the reason, the cause, the etiology? How will they explain it all away?

> *Tell me, where is fancy bred.*
> *Or in the heart or in the head?*
> *It is engender'd in the eyes,*
> *With gazing fed; and fancy dies*
> *In the cradle where it lies.*

At ten o'clock I went into my office and phoned the clinic. I remember the time largely because I had been watching the hands on a wall clock in the lab, largely because I didn't know what to do, and was wondering when to do it. So at ten o'clock I phoned the clinic.

The glossy tones of the retail trade answered, "Hewison Fertility. Can I help you?" But when the receptionist heard who was calling, the tone changed from cheerful optimism. By now they all knew the stunted, the remarkable Benedict Lambert. By now they all understood that congenital disaster was going to stalk the hushed corridors of the clinic for as long as the Miller case remained unresolved. There was a brief burst of soothing music in my ear, and then another, more senior voice was there assuring me that Mrs. Miller was still quite comfortable. No, there wasn't any change in her condition, but she was quite comfortable. The new voice used that word *stable.* "In fact, Mr. Miller has just this minute gone to see her. Would you like me to put you through to her room?"

And it was only then that some kind of dim understanding broke through, perhaps like the first glimmer of doubt that crept into the mind of the obstetrician when she held me, proto-Benedict, bloodied and bowed, aloft between my mother's splayed legs. "It's a lovely little boy." But doubt stirring deep down there among the cheerful optimism of birth — that those limbs were altogether too short, that head too swollen, the bridge of the nose too depressed — the merest, deepest flicker of disquiet, the faint concern that all was not right. "Yes," I said to the woman on the telephone. "Yes, please put me through. Quickly . . ."

He stood at the bedside, doubtless aware of the press of time, the urgency of the moment. The telephone burbled softly, but of course he didn't answer it. Maybe it spurred him to act. He turned to the baby's cot and peered down at the dark head, at the clasped eyes and the single, clenched fist, while the piano played *On an Overgrown Path* with a sudden arpeggio, then a thoughtful melody, then the arpeggio repeated once more — the cry of the barn owl, for the barn owl has not flown away; although it soon will. Hugo Miller set to work. From Mendel to the future: the tenuous chain of descent, the passage of DNA down the generations, was soon broken.

I suppose that at that moment I was struggling out into the forecourt of the Institute. It was pouring with rain. Watch: a dwarf, panicking through puddles.

About the Author

A graduate in zoology from Oxford University, Simon Mawer teaches biology in an English school in Rome, where he lives with his wife and two children. He is the author of four previous books, including *Chimera*, which won the McKitterick Prize for first novel.

The employees of Thorndike Press hope you have enjoyed this Large Print book. All our Large Print titles are designed for easy reading, and all our books are made to last. Other Thorndike Press Large Print books are available at your library, through selected bookstores, or directly from us.

For information about titles, please call:

(800) 257-5157

To share your comments, please write:

Publisher
Thorndike Press
P.O. Box 159
Thorndike, Maine 04986